BURNING MAD!

Longarm had little choice but to kick the door all the way open and blaze away as the startled jasper near the stove with that ten-gauge tried in vain to swing its muzzle up in time. For nobody with a pistol and a lick of sense tried to take a man with a ten-gauge alive in a close-quarters fight. So Longarm nailed him twice in the chest to sit him uncomfortably on the hot stove . . . Then he just fell forward off his hot seat, too dead to notice his pants were on fire . . .

DON'T MISS THESE
ALL-ACTION WESTERN SERIES
FROM THE BERKLEY PUBLISHING GROUP

THE GUNSMITH by J. R. Roberts
>Clint Adams was a legend among lawmen, outlaws, and ladies. They called him . . . the Gunsmith.

LONGARM by Tabor Evans
>The popular long-running series about U.S. Deputy Marshal Long—his life, his loves, his fight for justice.

LONE STAR by Wesley Ellis
>The blazing adventures of Jessica Starbuck and the martial arts master, Ki. Over eight million copies in print.

SLOCUM by Jake Logan
>Today's longest-running action Western. John Slocum rides a deadly trail of hot blood and cold steel.

TABOR EVANS

LONGARM

ON THE
SANTEE KILLING GROUNDS

JOVE BOOKS, NEW YORK

LONGARM ON THE SANTEE KILLING GROUNDS

A Jove Book / published by arrangement with
the author

PRINTING HISTORY
Jove edition / August 1994

All rights reserved.
Copyright © 1994 by Jove Publications, Inc.
This book may not be reproduced in whole
or in part, by mimeograph or any other means,
without permission. For information address:
The Berkley Publishing Group,
200 Madison Avenue,
New York, New York 10016.

ISBN: 0-515-11459-6

A JOVE BOOK®
Jove Books are published by The Berkley Publishing Group,
200 Madison Avenue, New York, New York 10016.
JOVE and the "J" design are trademarks
belonging to Jove Publications, Inc.

PRINTED IN THE UNITED STATES OF AMERICA

10 9 8 7 6 5 4 3 2 1

ON THE
SANTEE KILLING GROUNDS

Chapter 1

Just as surely as there'd never been a bronco that couldn't be rode, or a rider that couldn't be throwed, there were some gals a man was only wasting flowers, books, and candy on. So that was why Deputy U.S. Marshal Custis Long was alone in bed when a horse-drawn fire engine thundered past the open window of his furnished room in the wee small hours.

Longarm, as he was better known to friend and foe, struck a match to consult the dollar alarm clock on his bed table while assuring himself the comings and goings of the Denver Fire Department were no business of a federal peace officer. Then he cussed them good when he saw it was almost four A.M. So that damned rooster down the alley wasn't just complaining about the noise.

Longarm punched his pillow thicker in the middle, and lay his head back down to see if he could catch a few more winks before it was time to cuss that alarm clock. It sure seemed to be ticking a whole lot louder than it needed to just to move its hands. And that damned fire seemed to be close, and even worse, upwind.

It sure was odd how almost identical smells could be mouth-watering or gut-wrenching, depending on whether one smelled bacon sizzling over a log fire or humanity going up in smoke along with a frame building. Some gal down the way seemed upset as hell about that as well, judging by all that screaming. So Longarm sat up to swing his bare feet to

1

the threadbare rug as he wiped at his sleep-gummed eyes and muttered, "Sounds as if they could use a hand with that crowd, and it's almost time to go to work in any case."

This was not the whole truth. Longarm wasn't supposed to report in until well after dawn, and he'd seldom arrived on time without a damned good reason in the six or eight years he'd been riding for the Justice Department under Marshal Billy Vail of the Denver District Court.

A few minutes later he had his federal badge pinned to a lapel of his tobacco tweed suit as he legged it along the cinder path toward the ruddy false dawn of that fire. As a rule, he tended to keep his badge, like his vest-pocket derringer, out of the light until such time as he might need to show them to somebody. But he knew there'd be local lawmen moving in on that same fire, and some few members of the Denver P.D. might not know him. So this was just not the time to let strangers wonder why a tall drink of water with a determined stride and a .44-40 riding cross-draw under an opened frock coat was bearing down on them so suddenly.

But as Longarm approached the surprisingly large mob gazing up at that pillar of fire against the sky to the west, he heard a familiar voice call his name. So he broke stride in his low-heeled cavalry boots, spotted Sergeant Nolan of the Denver P.D., and elbowed on over to join him, saying, "Morning. I know this is none of my own beeswax, Sarge. But ain't that Widow Dugan's rooming house, and how come they seem to be pouring coal oil instead of water on the fire?"

The shorter and stockier Nolan grimaced and said, "You're right about the old gal who ran the place. They think she's still inside. Along with at least half a dozen others. Only one who got out was the Mex serving gal. As you can plainly see, they ain't figured out what they're pouring all that water on across the way. A fireman I was just talking to said he suspects the serving gal poured a heap of something that floats on water inside, before she struck a match and tossed it as she was skipping out to give the alarm!"

They both heard that same shrill female scream from somewhere closer to the puffing steam engine. Nolan confirmed all that noise was indeed coming out of a skinny

2

young Mexican gal. "The fire marshal wants her to see the bodies when they bring 'em out. She keeps hollering she's innocent, as you just now heard. But lots of firebugs break down after they see what a mess they've wrought."

Longarm told himself he'd only legged it over here to help them with the crowd. He almost meant it when he told Nolan he'd go see if they needed help around the engine, small boys and smoke-shied fire horses being such an uncertain mixture. But as he worked his way through to the fire engine, stepping over the canvas hoses on the trampled muddy ground, he saw Nolan's copper badges had things so under control he had to argue some to get himself and his own badge through to the group gathered round the tall diamond-stacked steam engine. It was pumping water from nearby Cherry Creek through the air at that raging inferno of stubborn ruins, causing growing mud puddles.

Someone had cuffed the gal by one wrist to a brass fitting of the engine's big red chassis. She was young, but not all that skinny as soon as a man looked closer. Most men would have. Her frilly Mexican blouse was down off one tawny shoulder, and her pretty left tit was all the way out in the ruby light as well. She was bawling too hard to tell whether she was really pretty or not. Longarm glanced down to see she had her Mexican *zapatos* neatly laced around her trim ankles as well. But most damning of all, her flouncy print fandango skirts had been firmly cinched around her trim waist with a red sateen sash. So Longarm had no call to question the fire marshal's suspicions about a gal smelling smoke, waking up, and tear-assing out to sound the alarm in attire suitable for a church fiesta.

As Longarm joined the group, the fire marshal in command cast an uncertain eye on his federal badge, tried to shrug it off, and then just had to ask how come Uncle Sam seemed so interested in private property burning on the unfashionable southwest side of Cherry Creek.

Longarm smiled sheepishly and said, "I can't afford the fancier rent on the other side, so I room just a couple of streets over. I answer to Custis Long, riding for Marshal Billy Vail, who gets to sleep up on Capitol Hill with the other swells."

3

The fire marshal smiled knowingly and said, "We know all about you, Longarm." He proved it by never mentioning that other pal of Longarm's up on Capitol Hill, one far prettier than his boss. The back-fence gossip had that pretty young widow woman sore at Longarm because of some new gal in town.

Pointing his chin at the handcuffed Mexican maid, the fire marshal said, "She keeps pretending not to understand us when we ask her what she poured all over the wood inside that had been already varnished. I understand you savvy Spanish, Longarm?"

Longarm shrugged and replied, "Enough to find my way to the railroad station or buy me a tamale instead of a straw hat, I reckon."

He moved closer to the weeping gal, ticked the brim of his dark brown Stetson to her, and introduced himself in Spanish by his formal name and title. But the young suspect stared up at him owl-eyed and gasped hopefully, "Are you not the *muy simpatico* lawman my own people call El Brazo Largo?"

So since he saw her English was at least as good as his Spanish, Longarm replied in English. "Aw, mush. How are you called? And before you go batting your pretty eyes and fibbing to me, I want you to study harder on why it makes no sense for a young lady to be up and about in her party duds at four A.M. on a workday morning."

The girl murmured, "I am called Rosalinda Lopez y Madero, and now that I have had the time to think about it, I see there is no use in my pretending I have not been wicked."

The fire marshal had naturally been listening. He brightened and said, "Lord love you, Longarm, I was told you can get greasers and Injuns to talk, but how did you just *do* that?"

Longarm answered dryly, "For openers, I find it helps if you don't call Mex folk greasers. After that, we still ain't let the lady have her say."

The fire marshal snorted, "Shoot, didn't you just now hear her admit she'd been wicked? And wasn't she the very one who turned in the alarm on the far side of the creek? And dressed the way you see her now?"

Longarm turned back to the girl and quietly asked, "What might you be dressed for, Rosalinda?"

4

She stared down at his belt buckle or lower, either blushing a heap or lit up a deeper shade of red from the fire across the way, as she quietly confessed, "I was supposed to be in bed, in my attic room, because as you just said, the coming dawn will be that of a workday and my *patrona* had a lot of work in mind for me. *Pero* there was this *baile en el barrio,* a how-you-say neighborhood dance? So I slipped down the back stairs for to be a willful child, as my *patrona* puts it whenever I wish for to have a little fun."

The fire marshal demanded, "Is that why you set fire to the place you worked at? To get out of working so hard for a stricter boss lady than you could abide?"

Before the terrified girl could answer, the fire marshal called out, "Whatever you're doing, keep it up, Jacobs! I could swear you have the Injun sign on that stubborn cuss now!"

One of the slicker-clad and gum-booted figures outlined by the flames called back, "I can't say whether we floated that oil out the back way or whether its just burned its fool self away. You're right about it being stubborn. Never fought so much fire sprouting out of one frame house in all my days with the department!"

The fire marshal, as well as most of those others, moved closer to the smaller but still dangerous fire, leaving Longarm the chance to question the girl more calmly as well as thoroughly. He'd been lied to by experts, some of them even prettier, so he knew he could be fooled. But her story began to hold more water as he made her repeat it more than once, trying in vain to poke holes in it before he smiled down at her and conceded, "If you're fibbing you're mighty good at it. I admire anyone smart enough to tell a simple tale and stick to it. You say you were coming down the street from that forbidden party a quarter mile away, saw the place already afire, and just ran to get help. I hope you can see how easy it will be for *la policía* to check your story with others who might have been at that same party. While we're at it, how come you told them before the fire woke you up in bed?"

She muttered something about being ashamed of herself for sneaking out to go dancing.

He said, "There's a swell poem you should've read about

the tangled webs we weave whilst trying to deceive. But Mister Robert Burns never wrote in Spanish, and in any case I've noticed heaps of Anglo folks make that same mistake. You should have seen right off how tough it would be for a lady to get dressed up in the attic of a burning building and then make her way downstairs safe and sound while everyone else got trapped inside!"

She stared hopelessly down at her handcuffed wrist as she sighed and said, "I knew I should have told the truth as soon as they said I was lying, *pero,* as you say, we tangle ourselves up with everyone yelling and the air filled with the reek of burning flesh. Now that you know the true story you will tell them for to let me go, no?"

It was a good question. Longarm told her to stay put while he asked some others. Then he headed across the puddles and hoses to see what else might be going on, having to work his eyes harder in the trickier light. For by now the fire had about burned itself out, leaving little more than two brick chimneys and some blackened and smoking timbers standing. So it was by the weaker glow of a nearby street lamp that he was able to fathom the grim task the slicker-clad firemen were performing now. The wet cotton sheeting over the contorted forms they were lining up in the muddy front yard told a man just about what was going on. Longarm wasn't sure he wanted any more details. By the time that frying bacon smell was gone, a body had been literally burnt to a crisp.

The fire marshal and Sergeant Nolan were consulting as they stood in a puddle at the foot of one sheet-covered litter. As Longarm joined them the fire marshal pointed down at what seemed like a sheet-covered pretzel and growled, "That's what's left of Widow Dugan. Remind me I don't aim to get cremated like no Hindu when I go!"

Longarm shrugged as he swept his eyes over the other contorted forms, observing, "Oh, I dunno. A dead body can get mighty disgusting no matter what you do with it before it turns back to dust, like it says it's supposed to in the Good Book. A corpse ain't disgusting quite as long if you leave it in the damned fire instead of wetting it down and hauling it out this soon. They don't twist up that way if they're already

6

dead when the flames get to 'em and . . . Now that sure is a peculiar thing to study on, third litter from the end."

The fire marshal and Sergeant Nolan had been to events as grim as this one in the past. But the fire marshal nodded knowingly and said, "Already considered that one. Widow Dugan didn't offer hired rooms to many drifting drunks in her day. If you'd like to be charitable, it's possible he was overcome by smoke in his sober sleep and never woke up like the others."

Longarm cocked a thoughtful brow and demanded, "Let's talk some about them others. I make it half a dozen, and that hired gal back to your engine says that sounds about right. All but the one twisted up like unborn babies, the way folks wind up when they've been burned alive while feeling it considerably."

Nolan swore at Mexicans in general. The fire marshal swallowed hard and said, "Goddammit, we know what the poor old gal and her roomers went through. Until just recent, the front door had been padlocked on the outside. We're saving the lock and latch we salvaged for the Mex gal's trial, and it's a crying shame the only way she'll get to die under our sissy constitution won't pay her back a tooth for a tooth for what she put these poor folks through! We found all but that peaceful-looking one piled up in the vestibule, all tangled as they hammered in vain to get out and just curled up and died, like you said, whilst the flames licked at their flesh and laughed at their screams."

Longarm moved over by the oddly dignified remains as he asked where *they'd* been found. The fire marshal called out to a nearby member of his department, who called back they'd found that one atop some bedsprings in the stairwell. "He must have been sort of welded to the springs and followed 'em on down when the second story collapsed."

Longarm hunkered down, took a deep breath, and lifted the wet cotton from the figure's head. It was even worse than he'd been set for. He'd expected little more than a blackened skull. The glass eye glaring up at him from one ash-filled eye socket took him by surprise, and together with that one gold tooth somehow made the half-cremated man seem uglier,

7

perhaps because they lent distinctive features to what would have otherwise been a featureless charred skull.

Looming over Longarm for his own first look at this particular victim, Sergeant Nolan proved he rated his stripes when he took a few thoughtful moments and declared, "Faith. I know many a man with one gold tooth up front like that, and there's more than one poor drifter with a glass eye. But would you like to strike a match a bit closer to that handsome face?"

Longarm did it, but he didn't like it much. The heat or perhaps the collapse of the ruins had cracked the glass eye staring wildly up from the charcoal remains, but you could see it was almost jade green.

Nolan nodded. "If it walks like a duck and quacks like a duck, it must be Brick Flanders in the charred flesh. Sure, they'd told us he'd been seen around Denver last month, and Widow Dugan has taken in disreputable roomers before!"

Longarm shook out the waterproof Mexican match and moved the damp sheeting further out of the way as he muttered, "Let's hold our fire till we see if this one's wearing that famous ring."

As Longarm thumbnailed another light further down the charred corpse Nolan confided to the fire marshal, "They say Brick boasted of having taken a family seal ring from a Union officer at Chambersburg. Himself having ridden as a Confederate irregular before he went entirely bad and all and all."

The fire marshal naturally asked who in thunder they could be jawing about. So Nolan explained, "The green-eyed and red bearded cuss was wanted for everything but singing 'The Yellow Rose of Texas.' So how might we be coming with that signet ring, Longarm?"

The federal deputy got rid of that second match as he rose to his full imposing height and replied, "He lost his famous beard in the fire, and it didn't do his cock and balls a lick of good either. But that distinctive ring on one claw, together with the gold tooth and green glass eye, makes me strongly suspect this burnt bastard has to be Brick Flanders or somebody a whole lot like him."

He pointed at the girl still cuffed to the fire engine across the way as he continued. "Pending further evidence to the contrary, gents, I suggest you let Miss Lopez go, with one handsome apology, before she takes it in her head to sue the city, county, and entire state for calling her a suspicious greaser."

The fire marshal protested, "She *is* a suspicious greaser, and the only suspect we have for setting this mighty suspicious fire!"

Longarm insisted, "I can promise you it wasn't a poor but honest hired gal, without even checking her simple alibi. Rosalinda Lopez may have her faults, but she wasn't wanted by the law until just a few minutes ago. So why would she want to murder a wanted outlaw and set fire to the place she lived and worked in as a cover for no crime at all? Brick Flanders was wanted seriously, dead or alive, by four states and the Pinkertons. The federal government wanted a few words with him about a post office robbery as well."

Nolan nodded thoughtfully. "I see what you mean. No matter what she did to him or how she phrased it, she'd have had no sensible reason for refusing to accept the hearty congratulations and handsome bounty money that would have gone with his demise in any way, shape, or form!"

The fire marshal tried, "Maybe she ain't all that sensible, and a firebug in the hand is worth two in the bush! This mysterious glass-eyed cuss wasn't the only one done to a turn in them flames after a mighty determined arsonist poured something like Greek Fire around inside, padlocked the doors on the outside, and . . . Let me see. I reckon a lit candle, burning down to some tinder in a corner, would have given her time to traipse all the way over to that Mex dance before anyone noticed, don't you?"

Longarm shook his head and said, "Nope. If they back her about the time she'd have arrived and the time the party busted up after three A.M., your notion just gets too risky. Without jumping to half as many conclusions, I'm betting on the coroner's team telling us this one cadaver was good and dead before the fire started. But the other victims appear to have been awakened by the flames, not too drunk, drugged, or even sleepy to have piled up on the wrong side of that padlocked door. I'd only be guessing about how much money old Brick here had left from that payroll robbery up near Fort Collins. But they rode off with heaps of hundred-dollar treasury notes, and last I heard, only a few of 'em had been cashed."

The fire marshal pointed wearily at the still-glowing embers of the Dugan house. "You can kiss any paper money anyone had in there good-bye then."

Longarm frowned. "I hadn't finished. I vote we turn a mighty upset as well as innocent gal loose. What do you gents need, a diagram on the blackboard? A wanted outlaw, last seen packing a tidy fortune in handy treasury notes, is killed by a person or any number of persons unknown, who then help themselves to his money and set fire to his rooming house to confound us, as they have, on the way off to parts unknown."

Nolan stared soberly at what remained of the front doorjamb, a few yards away, as he made the sign of the cross and marveled out loud, "Jesus, Mary, and Joseph, what sort of a nasty devil would burn other innocent souls alive just to make sure this one body here might pass as another victim?"

To which Longarm could only reply, "I'd say you described such a killer or killers about right, Sarge."

Chapter 2

Any lawman worth his salt knew something about tracking down outlaws through dusty file cabinets and desk clutter. But Longarm felt he read sign better in the field, and nobody ordered him to delve deeper into the mysterious fire, once the local law had declared it a serious violation of the Denver Municipal Code and the county coroner had confirmed that the glass-eyed cuss had a .36-caliber bullet in his well-baked brain. For everyone agreed with Longarm's notion that some false-hearted pal had killed an outlaw on the dodge for his money and lit out after that clumsy but downright vicious attempt to cover up.

The same logic Longarm had used to clear Rosalinda Lopez seemed to indicate the killer or killers of an outlaw wanted dead or alive had to be a wanted outlaw or wanted outlaws as well. Grim autopsies of the other bodies hauled from the burnt-out rooming house established the old widow woman, along with a neighborhood loafer she either slept with now and again or hired on and off, had died in the fire with four roomers Rosalinda could name, whether they'd been using their real names or not. One of them, old Brick Flanders, had told everyone to call him Calvert Tyger, which had been not only a mite dramatic, but the name of another owlhoot rider entirely last heard of during his funeral oration down Durango way. The other three roomers with any call to have been upstairs in the wee small hours when the fire was set had all died with

11

Widow Dugan and her lover cum hired hand. Meaning the one hired gal who'd survived had never seen the killer or killers. A good two dozen witnesses, some of them Anglo and none known to be murderous arsonists, verified where the Mexican gal had been both before and after anyone could have set fire to the place she worked and lived in. Longarm had felt it only right to put the homeless gal up until she found herself another place to stay and, as it turned out, another job, which she did in twelve hours or so. Young gals who seemed willing to work that hard for little more than their room and board were sort of tough to come by since the Great Depression of the '70s had commenced to fade from recent memory.

So Longarm was working on another chore entirely a few mornings later, and hardly remembering Rosalinda Lopez, when he found his way across Colfax Avenue suddenly blocked by a one-horse shay pulling out of the morning traffic to stop with one wheel rim threatening his balls if he stepped off the granite curb. He took a step back, and would have said something mighty impolite if he hadn't noticed, just in time, who'd been driving that fool shay.

The young widow of a rich old mining magnate could have shown up in a coach and four with a posse of flunkies. But Longarm had noticed she seemed a tad shy about being seen with him by broad day on the public streets of Denver. A week ago she'd allowed she'd as soon never see him anywhere at all, and this morning he saw she'd draped a heavier veil than usual from the brim of her black velvet hat. So he just ticked his own hat brim to her and waited to see if she meant to pull a gun on him or just drive on.

She did neither. She sighed and said, "Come closer, you silly. I don't want to shout at you in the middle of town at this hour!"

Longarm moved closer and rested one booted foot between the rungs of the curbside wheel as he mildly inquired what she wanted to say to him discreetly.

The widow woman with the light brown hair smiled timidly through her veil. "I'm not going to say I'm sorry. It's your very own fault you have such a dreadful reputation, and I still think I was right about you and that Chinese waitress that time.

But, well, I guess I bought some malicious gossip about you and that librarian they said you'd walked home after closing hours."

Longarm shrugged and said, "I did walk the lady home. Her quarters weren't all that far from the library, but it was getting dark and she allowed she was new in Denver. Did your back-fence biddies tell you I walked her home more than once?"

The widow woman nodded soberly and replied, "That's not all they told me you and that henna-rinsed hussy had been up to. And you heard me tell you never to darken my door again."

Longarm shrugged and asked, not unkindly, whether anyone had seen him lurking about her brownstone mansion up on Capitol Hill.

She replied with a strangled sob, "No, and it's starting to hurt around bedtime! So all right, I was wrong about where you spent last Thursday night. My biddies, as you so rightly called them just now, told me you'd been seen taking that librarian home after work, and not coming out of her place again until at least as long as a certain gathering down that same block lasted."

Longarm nodded and answered easily, "We noticed all them old hens sipping tea on that front veranda in the cool shades of the gloaming. We've established I walked that librarian home from her new job more than once. Are you asking whether she likes to get on top like some folks I know?"

The young widow he knew well indeed seemed flustered. "Custis! Don't talk that way in broad daylight! I know you didn't spend the night with her, as I was told. I read all about it in the *Rocky Mountain News*!"

Longarm laughed incredulously and replied, "The time I left a library gal alone and chaste as ever was in the newspapers? Well, I never. I've told them reporters to quit making up tall tales about me lest they get me killed the way they did poor Jim Hickok. Where did it say I'd made a play for that new gal in town?"

The gal he'd been going to town with longer laughed despite it all and declared, "You big oaf! I meant that front-page story

13

about you investigating the mysterious deaths by fire in your own neighborhood. I mean, if you were helping them put out the fire at four A.M., you could hardly have been where those ever-so-helpful friends of mine told me you were, could you?"

To which Longarm could only modestly reply, "I was asleep in my very own bedding when the fire engines woke me up and I done what I had to. Where did your own pals tell you I was spending my lonesome night?"

She sighed. "They were just jealous of another poor widow woman's good fortune, I suppose. Am I forgiven, Custis?"

He chuckled fondly and said, "Sure. You forgave me for that gal who slings hash at the Golden Dragon, didn't you?"

She started to say something meaner, sighed again, and told him she'd be expecting him that evening for a late supper, after things got sort of quiet up along Sherman Street. Then she snapped her buggy whip coyly, and drove on before he could tell her he wasn't certain he'd be free for the evening.

He figured he would be, unless he got lucky. But it seemed sort of reckless to commit oneself to a late supper before knowing who one might or might not meet at noon for dinner.

He went on to serve the federal warrant his superiors at the Federal Building had wanted him to. There was only a little cussing and no real physical danger involved in hauling a rich mining man into federal court on a claim filed under false pretense. But a man had to think ahead if he didn't aim to be saddled with even less interesting chores, and so, seeing the morning was well worn down by the time he'd caught up with that mining man in his private club, Longarm ambled over to a drinking establishment open to the public. It was handy to his office and famous for the swell free lunches they served with moderately priced drinks.

Like many more respectable saloons in towns even smaller than Denver, the Denver Parthenon had side entrances and private rooms toward the back for more discriminating gents and all womankind. So Longarm wasn't too surprised to be told by a swamper, as he was stuffing his face with beer and pickled pig's knuckles at the main bar, that some lady wanted to see him in one of their private chambers. That was what they called the cubbyholes stuffed with small tables and firmly padded benches.

Hanging on to his beer schooner, but swallowing all the free lunch in his mouth, Longarm followed the swamper back towards the crappers, tipped a whole dime once he'd been shown the right door, and went on in to find himself staring down in some confusion at the severely uniformed Miss Morgana Floyd, head matron of the orphan asylum out Arvada way. As if to prove that Mother Nature tended to share her favors fairly, the somethat younger petite brunette, who'd also told Longarm not to darken *her* door, was built way smaller across the hips than the Capitol Hill widow woman, and Longarm recalled her breastworks as a tad perkier, if smaller. Though if push came to shove, that widow woman had a prettier face to admire, especially while she was doing all the work on top. But little Morgana was a kissable head-turner in her own right.

Longarm didn't try to kiss her as he straddled a bentwood chair across the table from her. He saw she'd already ordered herself a glass of cider with a straw. He still asked if she'd eaten yet, but the petite brunette shook her head. "I have to get back to the dry-goods store and my buckboard. I only took advantage of this run into town to see if I could catch you here alone for a change."

Longarm sipped some beer suds without answering. Everyone who knew where he worked had a pretty good notion where he lunched a good part of the time. Morgana sighed and said, "I'm sorry. That was catty of me. But darn it, Custis, a friend I trusted did say you were still seeing that widow lady up·on Capitol Hill!"

Longarm resisted the impulse to reach for a smoke as he replied, "If your spies were jawing about a certain widow woman who never done 'em no harm, I ain't been up to her place for quite some time, as a matter of fact."

This was true, as far as it went, and women seemed able to tell when a man was really fibbing. So Morgana nodded and said, "I should have known those other girls were jealous of me. What gave their vicious plot away was the way they overdid the tall tales they told about you. I mean, what would even someone like you be doing with a librarian west of Curtis Street and a wealthy Capitol Hill widow at the same time?"

Longarm couldn't resist answering, "I dunno. Sounds like *fun*!"

The frisky brunette with her own notions of fun laughed easily and said, "I'll bet you would, if you had the chance. But then I read in the *Post* how you'd been involved in that rooming house with some Mexican lovely, as your friend Reporter Crawford described her. So I naturally had to wonder how you could have been sparking all those other girls if you were over there in your own neighborhood at four in the morning. You should have seen them trying to squirm out of that when I confronted them with the morning papers!"

Longarm shrugged and said, "I only met Rosalinda Lopez over by that fire. They had no call to say I found her all that lovely as I was questioning her while she was handcuffed to a blamed fire engine!"

Morgana smiled, and reached across the table for his free hand. "I read how you'd cleared her as a suspect in that nasty arson-murder case, darling. Then, as I just said, certain so-called friends went too far. One of them told me you'd checked into the Wazee Hotel with that pretty *señorita*. I confess I believed her at first, recalling the time you took *me* there, to save us a long wet ride on that rainy evening, you said."

Longarm was starting to grow weary of the game and said so, as gently as he could manage. "Look here, Miss Morgana, whether I was in the Wazee Hotel with you or any gal willing to go there with me is no beeswax of a lady who told me better than ten days ago not to darken her door again. But for the sake of another lady I have no call to leave open to gossip, I checked Rosalinda Lopez into a hotel I could get a good rate from because the poor little gal had been burnt out and had no place else to go. If your pals had been watching closer, they could have told you I never even went up to her new quarters with her. You're commencing to steam me some with this toad squat about a kid I've never even swapped spit with!"

Morgana, who'd exchanged more than that with Longarm,

16

squeezed his big paw harder and assured him she'd already figured that much out for herself. "I know you'll think it was awful of me, Custis. But when I found out where that Rosalinda Lopez was working, I made it my business to make friends with her by sort of bumping into her a few times at the market down the street. Once we got to talking, it was easy enough to—"

"You're right, I don't like it," Longarm said. "Did you get her to tell you how I'd had her name tattooed on my chest, along with two lovebirds and a floral wreath around the whole shebang?"

Morgana stared soberly across the table. "She seems to think you're some sort of saint she calls a brass lark or something as outlandish, dear. She told me how you talked them out of arresting her and staked her to a fresh start, with no strings attached, and she confided she might have let you have a little, if you'd behaved like anything but a perfect gentleman to a frightened but not too inexperienced young girl."

Longarm smiled thinly and sighed. "Why do we always find out at least ten minutes after the steamboat leaves us standing on the dock like the fools we are? What are you suggesting I do now, go hang around that same market till she comes by for some fresher provisions?"

Morgana said firmly, "Don't you dare. You're taking me to that Sunday-Go-to-Meeting-on-the-Green over in Eastern Park this weekend."

Then she squeezed harder as she coyly purred, "We'll get fresh later, after you've melted my resolve with plenty of spiked punch and potato salad, the way you did that last time. I'll slip into the same summer-weight frock, and we'll spread our own blanket in that same grove of weeping willows a little apart from the picnic grounds, and then, as the sun goes down, who knows what I might let you do to me in the cool shades of evening?"

He couldn't think of anything they hadn't wound up trying already. But a good place to take one pretty gal was as good a place to take another pretty gal, and he knew that if they'd told this gal from way out to the west of town about another Sunday-Go in Eastern Park, a gal who lived in East Denver was twice as likely to have heard about it, and made plans of her own involving willow trees in the cool shades of evening.

So all Longarm could say to this other gal was that he'd sure be proud to take her out yonder if he possibly could. For he had almost three full days to figure out why it would be impossible.

Chapter 3

After he got back to the office after lunch, Longarm asked Henry, the pasty-faced clerk who played the typewriter and kept the files, whether they had any field work pending, say, over in the Indian Nation or at least a day's ride from the Denver city limits. But Henry said their boss, Marshal Vail, had said nothing about field work on his way to a meeting with Judge Dickerson down the hall.

Henry added that meanwhile Longarm was due to relieve old Deputy Weaver, riding herd on a government witness at a nearby hotel. So Longarm dug a folder on the late Brick Flanders out of the file to give himself some reading on the job and maybe, with any luck, a weekend that would otherwise be awkward down in the southwest corner of the state.

The train robber's doxy who'd agreed to turn state's evidence had been installed in a first-class suite of a second-rate hotel facing Tremont, near the Overland Terminal. Tom Weaver didn't seem too sorry to have Longarm take his place, despite the witness for the prosecution being a junoesque natural blonde who said she'd answer to Honey whenever they got tired of calling her Miss Elvira. She behaved well enough as they were introduced. But as soon as Weaver left, the buxom bawd unpinned her honey-colored hair and commenced to unbutton her calico bodice with a remark about the weather that sounded sort of dirty. She spoke a bit plainer about his stuffy-looking pants as she threw her bare self down on the sofa in the suite's parlor. "I'm glad now your fellow deputy was a sissy. For you're so much younger as well as tall and handsome. So tell me something, handsome, are you tall in every way?"

Longarm hung up his hat and coat, since she was right about the afternoon heat in downtown Denver, but helped himself to a chair on the far side of the room, closer to the door, and reached for one of his three-for-a-nickel cheroots as he chuckled fondly and told her, "It ain't going to work, Miss Elvira. I know what them other ladies told you about compromising the arresting officer. I do wish outlaws would quit trying to practice law on the fly, but you see, in this case neither Weaver nor me had anything to do with arresting you and your former lover. So even if you tempted us into greenhorn horny behavior on duty, you or your lawyer couldn't use it in court for all that much. It's established you eloped with the Keller gang from a house of ill repute, and you'd never get the jury to buy one of your mere guards forcing a confession out of you at dick-point."

The big naked blonde sat up, her firm ivory tits at an even more tempting angle as she brazenly laughed. "Couldn't you just point your dick at a lonely gal as a favor, damn it? I don't need to be advised of my constitutional rights again. I need me a good stiff dicking. For I haven't been screwed since your posse tracked us down near Trapper's Rock a good two weeks ago, and I'd have never been working in that Grand Junction whorehouse to begin with if I hadn't been born with a romantic streak."

Longarm resisted the impulse to ask if she meant that streak of pink almost parting the blond fuzz and staring boldly across the room at him from behind her carelessly bared thighs. He lit the cheroot instead, shook out the waterproof Mexican match, and suggested they'd both feel cooler if she'd like to stretch out on the bedstead in the next room in her birthday suit. When she coyly asked if he'd like to come along and stretch out with her, Longarm smiled wistfully and confessed, "I got a romantic streak of my own that's never going to forgive me for this afternoon, Miss Elvira. But as tempting as your pretty face and handsome form might be, I still have to look at my

20

own face in the mirror whenever I shave, and I like it better when I still see a professional lawman staring back at me."

She rose to her full height in nothing but her high-button shoes, and Longarm's crotch tingled about as much as they both would have expected because, two-faced whore or not, all that perfectly shaped naked flesh would have tempted a more saintly cuss. Then she slithered in his direction and purred, "How would you like just a quick come, with me sort of sitting in your lap?"

Longarm knew how much he'd like it. So he got to his own feet before she could straddle his weak nature and replied firmly, "How would you like me to handcuff you to a bedpost in the other room, Miss Elvira? My orders are to protect you from anyone who might not want you to testify in court, whilst making sure you'll be in court to testify. I ain't getting paid to take no shit off a prick-tease, and whilst we prefer to keep you material witnesses comfortable as well as safe, there's nothing in the department rules preventing us from holding you across town in our Federal House of Detention, locked up with nobody to sass but a tough old matron who's seen and heard it all."

The big blonde stopped crowding him, although he could smell her warm body odors. Damn it, she'd just had a bath and taken a vinegar douche down yonder. As he tried not to inhale, the mighty warm-natured witness sighed and said, "You must not like girls. Are you one of those boy-buggers they whisper about, Deputy Long?"

Longarm sighed. "I don't bugger nobody on duty. But if it's any comfort to you, I'd likely be tempted even more if I was stuck with sleeping alone later tonight. But I ain't, praise that other gal's romantic streak, so why don't you go have a lie-down, if you feel more comfortable bare-ass, whilst I catch up on some reading from my office files?"

She called him a son of a bitch, went back to the same sofa, and flopped down to start playing with her fool twat right in front of him, complaining that no true gentleman would let a poor weak woman be abused that way. It got even harder, and so did his old organ-grinder, once she commenced to moan and groan about wanting it in her as she was coming all alone.

By this time Longarm had taken the file from a side pocket of his frock coat, and even managed to read the first few pages without understanding a full paragraph. It seemed the one called Calvert Tyger had been the leader of the five-man gang who'd pulled that big payroll robbery. All the while old Elvira was sobbing, "Jesus, don't let me waste this passion on my fucking fingers!"

The late Brick Flanders had been second in command. Another outlaw had answered to Chief, and was thought to be of Indian blood. The others were more casually described, and might have been saddle tramps picked up for the occasion to hold the horses, act as lookouts, and such. At that point Elvira gasped, "My God, I really came and now I feel even hotter for some reason!"

Longarm knew her reason. Everyone imagined sex was even better than it really felt when they could only feel it with their frantic paws. He went back to the file. One of those purloined treasury notes had been cashed in Durango just before Calvert Tyger had died in yet another rooming house fire, and that seemed sort of suspicious as soon as you read the same line over. It was easy to read the same line over, then over some more, with a naked lady jerking herself off in the same room with him.

Longarm sighed and said, "I wish you'd do that in the bedroom, Miss Elvira. This other case I'm reading about is serious."

She left her hand in place between her naked thighs as she told him she was serious too. But he went on reading, so she tried it another way, demurely observing, "I'll bet that lady you're meeting later has to be the bee's knees in bed. Is she pretty? Does she let you shove it up her ass for a change now and then?"

Longarm read on about how the three known ringleaders, Tyger, Flanders, and the mysterious Chief, had all deserted General Pope's column during that Santee rising back around '63. But that wasn't what Uncle Sam wanted them on. Sibley's Sixth Minnesota had already broken the back of Little Crow's ill-advised attempt to turn the clock back by the time Pope finished organizing his bigger force of limited-service Union vets and paroled Confederate prisoners. Some said Pope had mopped up after Sibley so thoroughly because of the piss-poor showing he'd made at Bull Run.

"Does she suck it hard for you when you get tired?" the material witness demanded as Longarm read on about the two Galvanized Yankees, or rebs released from Fort Sandusky to fight the Sioux, who had lit out in the company of an Indian scout and three officers' throughbreds in the summer of '64. They'd headed West with the war still raging in the East, then lost out on the general postwar amnesty by stealing yet more army mounts and hitting both a post office and a federal payroll shipment between spates of more local rampaging.

"I'm wild and wanton and I'm not ashamed to say so!" yelled the buxom blonde as she threw herself naked on the rug near his feet, bracing her heels to either side of his own so she could thrust up and down at him with her raging crotch as Longarm mildly observed, "So were the three young rascals I'm trying to read about in this folder, till more recently leastways. A lot of water has flowed under the bridge since we were all young and foolish enough to think them banners and bugle calls were really going to make this world a better place. It says here the ones we know best as Tyger and Flanders took to pulling better-planned jobs for a lot more money at a time, with the times spread ever wider apart."

She sobbed, "I can't spread my thighs any wider. You're either made of iron or they cut off your balls in that war you're so fond of bragging about!"

He sighed. "I never did much in the war worth bragging about. I feel sort of foolish now about some of the chances I took as a fool kid. I wonder if Tyger and Flanders were starting to wise up at the last. Nothing here to indicate whatever happened to Chief or lesser members of their gang."

She rolled over on her hands and knees to wiggle her bare and shapely rump at him. "Nobody takes it brown as good as me. If you're not man enough to stick your dick up my ass, I'd be proud to show you how I can puff on a smoke if you'd like to stick the end of that cheroot in me."

He chuckled and replied, "Lord love you, I pay more for

these here cheroots than I can afford on my salary, Miss Elvira."

He had to look away as he softly added, "This afternoon I seem out to earn every penny Uncle Sam pays me!" For while her winking rosebud rectum was only interesting, the bawdy bitch had a downright pretty pussy, and she must have known how rare that was, judging by the way she was winking that at him as well, in alternate contractions of her obviously well-trained love muscles.

He lowered his eyes back to the file in his lap, but it was tough to make much sense as he sat there reading with a raging erection while Elvira begged him to let her take care of it for him.

Then somebody knocked on the door and the big blonde was running into the bedroom, snatching up her summer frock as she tore past the arm of that sofa. So Longarm rose to answer the knock on the hall door as she slammed the door behind him.

It turned out to be Smiley and Dutch from his own outfit. Deputy Smiley never smiled. Smiley was the family name of the otherwise morose breed. Nobody could pronounce the High Dutch name that went with Smiley's shorter, more cheerful-looking, but deadly sidekick. So everyone called him Dutch, and he didn't seem upset about that. Longarm knew Marshal Vail always sent them out as a team to get the work of one well-balanced deputy out of them. Smiley was a good tracker who tended to walk into traps with his eyes on the trail, while Dutch, who could have doubtless shot his way out of the Alamo back in '36, seemed to need the guidance of an older and less ferocious pard to keep him from gunning the wrong folks.

Longarm allowed he was a mite surprised to see them so soon in his own tour of guard duty. Smiley said, "The boss has something else for you to do back at the Federal Building. He said you're not to stop off at the Parthenon on your way back."

Longarm said, "I won't. Did old Billy say what he wanted me for?"

Smiley shook his head. "Nope. He gets pissed when you

question his orders. He just told us to take over for you here and send you back to him on the double. Is there anything me and Dutch ought to know about this witness gal we're supposed to be riding herd on?"

Longarm started to say she was just a whore with unusually wild ways. Then he frowned thoughtfully and said, "I'll tell you better in a minute. After I present you to the lady."

It wasn't that easy. Longarm had to knock more than once before the big buxom blonde came out, fully dressed with her hair piled more primly atop her head, and demurely howdied Smiley and Dutch in turn. She sat back on that sofa and behaved as if butter wouldn't have melted in her mouth as Longarm explained the change in plans.

Then Longarm grabbed his hat and coat and signaled Smiley to step out in the hall with him as he was putting them on. He warned the hatchet-faced breed, "Something's up. She was just now offering me all three ways for free. Yet now she's gone all ladylike, or at least like a whore who ain't about to give nothing away just to be friendly."

Smiley shrugged and grumbled, "It's no secret you're more of a ladies' man than me, or even Dutch."

Longarm modestly but sensibly insisted, "I ain't *that* pretty. I just told you she's on record as a trail-town whore, and I repeat she was offering to take me on a heap for nothing. Meaning she had something in mind. You know why I don't expect her to make you two gents the same kind offer?"

"You don't have to rub it in." Smiley said.

"It ain't that the two of you are too ugly for a trail-town whore. It's because there's *two* of you!"

Smiley looked doubtful and remarked, "Oh, I dunno. They say Silver Heels used to take on a dozen or more men a night, and Silver Heels was more refined than your average whore."

Longarm nodded. "She ain't reluctant to take on the two of you because it would be undignified. She likely feels it would be a waste of frigid effort because there's no way to get the drop on two separate gunfighters screwing one gal in turn."

Smiley scowled and demanded, "Who in thunder do you suspect of having that sort of sneaky stunt in mind, pard?"

25

Longarm shrugged. "She never told me. But try her this way. Say she made that deal with the prosecution just to get her own sassy ass out of the sling. Say that now that she's had time to calm down and size up the situation, she's decided she'd as soon not bother with appearing in court against her pals. So say she and some other pals we never caught are planning for her to leave the prosecution one less witness?"

Smiley thought. "Make as much sense for them to just kill her. Where in these United States could a striking blonde like that one duck a serious federal warrant?"

"After dying her striking hair? How would you like me to list 'em, alphabetic or numerical? For all we know they *plan* on killing her, albeit I'm sure they only suggested a train trip of a hundred miles or more."

He left his frock coat open as he consulted his pocket watch. "I'd best get going. You boys are in charge of her now. But if it was still me on duty here, I'd be keeping my eyes peeled for some slickery."

Smiley stepped back inside. Longarm headed for the same stairs he'd come up only a short spell back. Then he reconsidered and ambled back to the rear stairwell, more for practice than anything else. He'd checked into this particular hotel before, although later in the evening and in more of a hurry, lest the gal cool off while he signed them in. So he'd never taken the time to explore all the ways in or out, and a man just never could be sure there might not be some future time when an alternate escape route might save him from another guest smoking in bed or an irate husband prowling the halls in the dark.

He didn't find the back stairs all that astounding as he followed them down to the ground floor. Once there, he found himself in the service hallway leading from an alley entrance to the lobby out the other way. He tried the alley door. He saw anyone could leave at any time, but had to knock if he aimed to enter. He shrugged and headed for the lobby to leave the more dignified way. As a paid-up manhunter Longarm was hardly aware of his actions as he paused in the shadows of the archway out to the lobby to determine just who else might be on the premises at the moment.

26

He saw that aside from the clerk there were three gents lolling in the lobby. Two of them were seedy older men who looked as if they were just waiting around for the rest of their lives to unravel. The third man was far younger and seemed as proddy as a schoolmarm on her wedding night.

The squirming cuss in that far corner chair was wearing high-heeled riding boots, a telescoped black Stetson, and a shoulder holster along with his seersucker summer suit. There was no federal law against squirming in one's chair, or even packing a concealed weapon. But Longarm still got out his badge and pinned it to his lapel as he considered how he wanted to approach a total stranger whose only known crime was the way he made the hairs on the back of a lawman's neck tingle.

That shoulder rig would give the squirt in the seersucker suit a pretty good edge in a contest against a cross-draw man. But nobody outside of Ned Buntline Western novels got paid to indulge in quick-drawing contests, with the loser never getting the chance for a rematch. So Longarm drew his .44-40 in the shadows of the archway, and held it pointed politely at the floor. It was handier than any holstered side arm in any sort of rig. But before Longarm could step out into the lobby, a fourth man came into view at the bottom of the front stairwell. This one was dressed more like an undertaker who punched cows on occasion, and Longarm crawfished deeper into the shadows when he saw the one who'd just been upstairs was headed to join the one in that far corner. The one in black wore his own gun cross-draw under his coattails. Meaning that, like Longarm, he'd taken time to study on the various conditions and positions in which a man might be called upon to get his damned gun out quickly.

Longarm already had his gun out. He reached under his own coat for the handcuffs clipped to the back of his gun rig as he tried to read lips at that range. The way they moved their hands told as much as Longarm needed to know. Knowing he could be wrong, he took a deep breath, stepped out in the light, and threw down on the two of them as he crossed the lobby, announcing in a firm, friendly voice that he'd sure hate to gun the first dumb bastard who failed to raise both hands empty and just hold 'em that way for now.

His words were not taken lightly. The one in black groaned at his rising pal in seersucker, "Aw, hell, you told me Longarm had been relieved, you asshole!"

Longarm said, "He told you true. I reckon I could tell you what you just heard upstairs with your ear to the door and me not as helpless with my pants down as you all planned. But why go into all that bullshit here when it's just as easy to cuff the two of you together and run you over to the Federal Building to tell it to the judge?"

Chapter 4

There was bullshit to spare as Longarm's two suspects got to test their own versions, in separate rooms, on various suspicious lawyers and lawmen interested in the case. It was Longarm who suggested, out in the hall, that the prosecution might explain the facts of life to Miss Elvira Carson, the beautiful dumb blonde. The prosecutor snorted, "Don't teach your granny to knit socks, Longarm. It's obvious the friends of the lover she agreed to testify against never recruited that professional gunslick to ride off in any golden sunset with her. They flimflammed her with some bull about getting her out of town once she tricked her guard into taking off his gunbelt behind closed doors. But what'll you bet they'd have gunned the both of you on the spot if she'd been able to seduce you?"

Longarm sighed. "She tried to seduce Tom Weaver first. I just talked to him down to the crapper. Tom confessed he was as tempted as the rest of us. But lucky for us all, he's happily wed to a frisky younger gal, even if he hadn't been an old pro. I just now gave Tom a mild cussing for not warning me about her in fuller detail."

The government lawyer chuckled. "Deputy Weaver no doubt had you down as an old pro too. It's just as well they took enough rope for us to hang the whole bunch, with or without that whore's reluctant help. Wait till you've questioned a hired gun who finds his fool self involved in a train robbery only the assholes who hired him took part in!"

Longarm smiled thinly and resisted the impulse to show off with a remark about federal jurisdiction. A government lawyer doubtless knew they could let a killer who hadn't killed anybody off, if he wanted to be helpful as all get-out.

Leaving the rest of the mess to those who seemed to want it, Longarm ambled down the hall to his own office to see why they'd sent for him a good two hours before.

As he entered the reception area young Henry looked up from his typewriter with a knowing grin. "You sure do like to live dangerously. Marshal Vail was just out here asking about you, all red in the face with steam shooting out his ears."

Longarm explained he'd been detained, and headed back for Billy Vail's office. But Henry said, "He's not there. He went out after cussing you a lot, like I said."

Longarm shrugged and headed on back in any case, lest he and old Billy wind up tear-assing through various doors in search of one another, the way the actors did in that comical French farce at the Apollo Hall.

It seemed smarter to just go on in and enjoy a sit-down smoke as he waited for old Billy to get back from wherever he'd gone.

Longarm knew it was rude, but he still swept his eyes over the clutter atop the marshal's desk in hopes of guessing what all the fuss was about. There were wanted flyers and yellow telegrams all over the green blotter. A familiar letterhead told Longarm they'd gotten another letter from Reverend John Dyer, that snowshoeing itinerant missionary who'd have been proclaimed a saint by this time if the Methodists went in for that notion. For it took more simple goodness than most could manage to spend more than one's own yearly salary on savage cowboys and drunken Indians. And how many mortal fathers had ever forgiven a saddle tramp for murdering his only son, Judge Elias Dyer, saying he knew the killer had only been the weak-willed tool of crooked Colorado politicians?

Longarm hadn't been raised rude enough to read the mail of a gent who wasn't in trouble with the law. So he sat down and lit up, casting a thoughtful eye at the banjo clock on one oak-paneled wall. He could see Billy Vail was due back any minute, if only to close up for the day. He wondered what in thunder might old Reverend Dyer have to say in that confounded upside-down handwritten letter?

Longarm had heard the saintly old missionary had come out to the Rockies after the war from the Great Lakes country, where he'd been first a mining man and then a preacher to the already Christian Chippewa, as most white folks called the Ojibwa. So the kindly old preacher's tips on Indian matters tended to be more accurate than some the government liked better. Dyer had fought hard to save the west-slope hunting grounds of the Ute, and both the B.I.A. and U.S. Army could have saved themselves some scalps if they'd paid more attention to Dyer's warnings about misunderstandings before the Meeker Massacre and the Milk River Ambush.

Dyer's earlier Indian followers, the Ojibwa back around Lake Superior, had been sworn enemies of the Santee and their kin. French folks had shortened and adopted the Ojibwa words for a son-of-bitching enemy. So later English-speaking settlers had felt no call to change the spelling from "Sioux." The Santee branch of the far-flung folks who preferred to call themselves Nakota, Dakota, or Lakota as one moved east to west, could be swell pals or vicious enemies, as the spirits moved them. Old Dyer, as well as Tyger, Flanders, and their mysterious pal called Chief, would have all been back yonder in Santee Country around the same time, whether preaching to Indians or swapping Confederate Gray for Union Blue to get out of a prisoner-of-war camp and strike a blow for the white race in general.

Longarm still managed not to read Billy Vail's mail before the older, shorter, and far stockier marshal grumped in on his restless stubby legs, smoking a shorter, stockier, and more pungent cigar, grabbed his own seat on the official side of the desk with his back to the window, and growled, "I heard. You made us look good and so I can't say I'm downright cross with you. But I swear I'm sometimes sure that if I asked you for a light you'd set the building afire! I sent you to guard that material witness for the prosecutor, not solve his case for him, and who told you to run off with the files on that more serious

31

payroll robbery? I needed 'em to read more'n you needed 'em to wipe your ass with, damn it!"

Longarm smiled sheepishly. "Sorry, Boss. I didn't know you were working that case, and I was reading too. I'll buy that toasted cadaver hauled out of the Dugan rooming house as the real Brick Flanders, if you'll let me run over to Durango with a federal writ allowing me to open the so-called grave of the late Calvert Tyger."

Vail shook his bullet head. "I got a better place for you to head. But next week will do. My old woman told me all about that Sunday-Go in Eastern Park. For she's on the same entertainment committee as a certain young widow woman you've asked me not to mention by name."

"I don't mind missing that shindig as long as it's in the line of duty," Longarm said.

Vail chuckled. "What's in the line of duty, the Sunday-Go or a mighty long train ride back to southwest Minnesota?"

Longarm blinked. "That's far enough to get me out of a hair-pulling contest, I reckon. But whatever for? I told when I got back from that last wild-goose chase to Rice County that neither Frank nor Jesse had been anywhere near Northfield since that big bank robbery and shootout back in the autumn of '76, and this more recent as well as more profitable robbery is hot! I mean that literally. For I somehow doubt all that paper money burned away in not one but two roominghouse fires."

He looked about in vain for an ashtray on his side of the desk, flicked ashes from his cheroot on the rug, and observed, "They say it's good for carpet mites. I'll believe the real leader of that gang died from smoking in bed after I see who's buried in his grave. It don't add up, Billy. Five or more outlaws light out with a government payroll, most of it in high-denomination treasury notes with their serial numbers on file. Then the only two gang members we know by name go up in smoke, bang, bang, and we know for a fact that last fire was deliberate!"

Vail sighed. "I wish you children wouldn't interrupt your elders. I don't want you wasting time over Durango way because it ain't as important who got buried, or even how he died, not only yonder but many a day ago. You track where the trail's still warm, old son, and one of those very treasury notes you mentioned turned up more recently at the Granger's Savings and Loans in New Ulm, not Northfield, Minnesota."

Vail leaned back in his seat and picked up Reverend Dyer's letter to wave at Longarm as he continued. "I don't think Frank or Jesse cashed it either. Even if New Ulm wasn't closer to the Dakota line, the dumb son of a bitch who paid for his seed corn and a mess of hardware with a hundred-dollar treasury note has his local name and address on file with that merchant who broke such a whopping wonder of paper money for him. You can't bite a hundred-dollar note to test it, you know. So it's a wise notion to write down who came in with it, and he did."

Longarm nodded soberly. "I had to break a twenty-dollar silver certificate in a Chinese restaurant one time. It sure got noisy, and it was just as well I was packing my badge and identification."

Vail said, "It was a bank teller who spotted the serial number and told his superior, who naturally made some noise at the merchant who'd deposited it, until said merchant got out his books and could produce the homesteader and homestead claim number of the jasper I want you to move in on in your own discreet way. Both the townsmen who spotted the note and the sheriff's department of Brown County have been slicker than usual, contacting us instead of blundering in, thanks to that cautiously worded flyer we'd listed all of them serial numbers on. The homesteader who spent that stolen treasury note filed his claim under the name of Israel or Izzie Bedford. Claims to be a New Englander who rode with General Pope against Little Crow's Santee."

Longarm grimaced. "I caught him in a lie already. Long Trader Sibley, as the Indians called him, had already whipped the Santee good with his Minnesota Volunteers by the time Pope arrived with his limited-service regulars and paroled prisoners to mop up."

Vail shrugged. "Be that as it may, this letter from a preacher who was there at the time confirms there was indeed a New England shavetail called Israel Bedford mopping up Indians in the dubious company of Galvanized Yankee noncoms called Calvert Tyger and Brick Flanders. Dyer can't say who the one called Chief might have been, if he was with them at the time or not. He says he still remembers Tyger because of the unusual name, and Brick Flanders came to mind as soon as he read my questions about red beards and glass eyes."

Longarm asked, "How come he remembers Lieutenant Bedford after all this time?"

Vail glanced down at the letter, but didn't quote directly from it as he explained. "It appears Dyer was doing some missionary work at Fort Ridgely, trying to save the souls of captured Santee. Some of the officers gave him a hard time, saying he was wasting salvation on already damned souls the army was fixing to hang. But whenever Lieutenant Bedford was the officer of the day, he let Dyer into the stockade to help the condemned Santee pray for forgiveness."

Longarm smiled thinly. "Must have worked for some of 'em. I understand they had close to four hundred Santee on charges of murder, rape, and worse. Abe Lincoln spoiled a heap of fun when he pardoned all but thirty-eight of 'em. Indians I know say at least thirty-seven of 'em were mean as hell by Indian standards."

He flicked more ash, ignoring Vail's warning frown as he went on. "This Israel Bedford sounds like a charitable cuss, and would a paid-up Union officer want all that much truck with Confederate renegades who stole Union officers' mounts to head out west along the owlhoot trail?"

Vail suggested, "That's one of the notions you might want to ask him about. I ain't ordering you to huff and puff his soddy down and haul him all the way back in irons. I only want you to ask him, in your usual sneaky way, where he got that purloined treasury note. It's possible he sold something in good faith to an old army pal or a new neighbor, who'd be the next one you'd want to question, discreet but on your toes, lest you wind up in a mysterious fire as well. Henry's got your travel orders out front, if you're in such a hurry to miss that Sunday-Go. So what are you waiting for, a fatherly pat on the head or a boot in the ass?"

Longarm felt no call to argue with anyone as stubborn as Billy Vail. So knowing old Henry could play that typewriter faster than most could write by hand, he went out front and asked, "Would you be do me a favor, Henry? The boss don't seem to cotton to my carrying office files all the way to Minnesota. So I was wondering if you'd like to type up a thumbnail sketch of that payroll robbery and a list of names we might be interested whilst I run home to pack, send my regrets about that Sunday-Go to a couple of pals, and pick me up a fresh railroad timetable at the Union Depot?"

Henry handed him a bulky envelope and smugly replied, "I wish you wouldn't tell me how to do my job. You'll find everything you need in here, along with your travel orders, and I naturally looked up the times and places you'll have to transfer between here and New Ulm if you're leaving on the eastbound night flyer, as I'd say you ought to."

Longarm didn't argue with Henry either. He allowed he'd be back when he finished the field job, strode out of the office and over to his hired digs, then hauled his possibles to the Union Depot and bought a round-trip ticket to Durango on his own.

Chapter 5

Longarm wasn't being disrespectful of Billy Vail's ability to read sign. He knew nobody tracked better on paper than his pudgy paper-pushing boss. But sometimes sign read different in the cold gray light of reality, and old Billy had just said there wasn't a great hurry to head for New Ulm. For a suspect working to prove a homestead claim would be there if he wasn't worried about the law, and long gone if he was.

Meanwhile Durango, Colorado, was far closer than New Ulm, Minnesota, even though it got sort of hard to tell along the last leg of the tricky route across the very spine of the Rockies.

In the end, it only felt like a million miles of hairpin turns above sheer drops to ribbons of white water in the canyons way down below. It was still short of midnight when Longarm stiffly climbed off the train in Durango with his heavily laden saddle. He checked the McClellan with its bedroll riding across stuffed saddlebags in the depot baggage room, hanging on to his Winchester '73 saddle gun lest it prove too tempting, and went straight to the Durango office of the railroad dicks.

Pending more official incorporation as a township in the southwest corner of the fairly new state, the settlement was being policed by the railroad that had opened it to settlement once the Ute had been run off to less desirable water, timber, and range. The railroad didn't brag about it, but Longarm knew the silver smelters near the rail yards refined ore from up the valley a fair haul by freight wagon. So there wasn't much mystery about a gang that went in for payroll robberies drifting through Durango. They hadn't been out to buy any land-grant property off the D&RGW. Unless and until they laid the last of those narrow-gauge tracks up to Silverton, Durango would remain the transfer point where the three dollars a day of many a hardrock miner would be sent on by stage, in the handy form of treasury notes, over many a bumpy mile of lonesome mountain scenery.

But there hadn't been any recent stage robberies out this way. The purported leader of the gang, Calvert Tyger, was supposed to have died in an accidental fire, which would be easier to buy if yet another gang member, under the same name, hadn't been done to a turn much the same way in Denver, and if a bill from that earlier payroll robbery hadn't surfaced later more than thrice that far from whatever in blue blazes they'd been up to in Durango.

The railroad dicks, like telegraphers and such, stayed open around the clock because that was the way you ran a railroad. Longarm had met the older gent on duty that night as watch commander. He knew the old-timer had been a full-fledged U.S. marshal down Texas way at a time when good men and true had been forced to make their minds up on the double. Unlike a Ranger captain named Billy Vail, old Ross Gilchrist of West Texas had surrendered his U.S. marshal's badge to accept a commission with Hood's Texas Brigade, C.S.A. A railroad had been more forgiving later than the winning side.

Gilchrist seemed sincerely glad to see Longarm again. Things did get tedious late at night on a weeknight in Durango. But while he broke out a pint of what he swore to be real Scotch liquor, and offered Longarm a Havana claro from the humidor on his rolltop desk, the old-timer allowed he'd been there when that roominghouse had burned down less than two furlongs to the west, but couldn't seem to tell Longarm anything that Henry hadn't already typed up on onionskin for him.

Gilchrist said there'd been no autopsy ordered for a drunk who'd died screaming like a banshee behind a wall of flames the volunteer firemen hadn't managed to break through in time. When Longarm mentioned there was no record of the late Calvert Tyger having a drinking problem, assuming he was really all that late, Gilchrist shrugged and said, "I've read his yellow sheets, old son. There's no record of him signing the pledge neither. But leaving aside whether he burnt to death drunk or sober, he sure as shit burnt to death. You could hear him bitching about it for quite a ways and longer than I'd care to die that particular way."

Longarm asked Gilchrist if he'd seen the body afterwards.

Gilchrist grimaced. "What was left of it. Had he baked a mite longer we could have saved the expense of planting him over in Potter's Field."

Then, as if he'd foreseen the next obvious question, the war vet and experienced lawman volunteered, "He wound up on his side with his arms and legs drawn up the way most of us do when we're dying miserable. Used to see old boys like that in the hills of Tennessee. You could tell when a soldier boy had been killed instant or sobbing for his momma by the way he lay. Like I said, they should have let Tyger burn a mite longer and let the wind have his clean ashes. This way, his remains wound up the worst of a couple of ways. Halfway cremated and then left to molder in the wormy clay of Potter's Field. Ain't that a bitch?"

Longarm grimaced and sipped some more Scotch liquor. It was almost as good as Maryland Rye, save for a smoky aftertaste that he didn't really need right now, picturing what likely lay in the pauper's grave of a stranger charred beyond recognition. "I was wondering how I meant to get an exhumation order without a heap of tedious explanations. I'll take your word a cuss checked into that roominghouse as Calvert Tyger and died in that fire as a result of that fire. But as long as we're on the subject of my need to report this side trip to Durango, I'd as soon not bother. I get to file enough in triplicate as it is."

Gilchrist leaned forward to light the cigar for Longarm as he chuckled and allowed he knew the feeling. "I ain't about to write up this social visit for the Denver & Rio Grande Western, if that's what you were hinting at, old son."

Longarm put down the empty shot glass and helped himself

38

to a mouthful of less smoky-tasting smoke before he confessed he'd had such a shortcut in mind. Then he blew a thoughtful smoke ring and added, "I mean to ask around town, seeing I'm here, but might your company files hold anything on the other riders said to have been with Calvert Tyger when he somehow got the call to check into a mighty seedy roominghouse alone?"

Gilchrist shook his head. "I'd have said so if we'd noticed. Nobody working for the railroad knew any of 'em were here in Durango till that fire broke out a couple of weeks back. Since we do such police work as need be, we naturally took some interest as soon as we saw what we took for a handful of part-time laborers and full-time drunks had gone up in smoke. We'd planted 'em all in Potter's Field, like I said, before anyone put the name of one victim together with that of a wanted outlaw."

Longarm blew another thoughtful smoke ring. "My short and sweet notes on the case do mention other unfortunates who died in both mysterious fires, now that you mention it. So how come we know so much about that one particular screamer, seeing he was a stranger in town?"

Gilchrist poured another shot in the glass at Longarm's elbow as he answered easily. "Because he was a stranger, of course. Most of the drifters who'd checked into that roominghouse naturally got out in time. At sunrise they and some townsmen who'd hired various old boys for a few hours' work now and again were able to identify all but the one cadaver. Nobody came forward for him. But the night clerk at the rooming house had saved their books, and like I said, once someone noticed Tyger was wanted so often in so many places . . ."

"Get back to the part about him screaming so much before they found him in that fetal position," Longarm urged. "Didn't anyone else object to being burnt alive in there?"

Gilchrist shook his head. "The ones sober enough to yell got out sudden when the room clerk sounded the alarm. The same old clerk recalled Tyger as having paid two bits extra for a separate room, or cubicle, with a door you could bolt on the inside. All the others who failed to wake up in time were trapped further toward the back wall. The volunteers figured the bewildered cuss in that locked cubicle woke up in a strange place, blinded by smoke, and died trying to escape by way of the wardrobe against the back wall instead of the one real door at the other end. They found him in the ruins near what would have been the back of his bitty private cell had the plank walls still been standing. The poor bastard could've kicked his way out any way but through the stout oak wardrobe he was trying to escape through."

Longarm grimaced as he pictured it, and worse yet, sort of felt the bewilderment the trapped man must have felt when, flinging open what he thought to be the door of his cubicle, he'd stepped into that tall oak wardrobe against the wrong wall!

He started to ask another dumb question. He didn't, because it was obvious the volunteer firemen or railroad dicks would have made mention of any large sum of paper money they'd found miraculously preserved among the ashes of a burned-down and water-drenched frame structure. He swallowed the last of the liquor instead and got back to his feet, saying, "We both know why no pals of a wanted man came forward to identify his body, if that was his body. We're more certain that was the real Brick Flanders butchered and baked over in Denver more recently."

Gilchrist rose to walk him out front. "Glass eyes and gold teeth do say more about a well-done cadaver. How do you like a second in command using the name of his dead boss to confound us all further?"

Longarm didn't like it that much. But he never said so, lest he waste more time with a cuss, however agreeable, who didn't know one thing more about that fire in Denver or the note cashed in Minnesota than anyone else on the side of the law.

He allowed he'd see if the boys in the back rooms up the way knew anything about other strangers, the one called Chief in particular, who'd passed through Durango about the same time as the late Calvert Tyger. Then he asked when he could catch a train out. But Gilchrist said there wouldn't be another train in or out this side of sunrise, explaining, "The engineers are sort of unsure about the tracks ahead. So we have no call to cross the Divide by the dark of the moon."

To which Longarm could only answer, "Shit, I'll just have to study on finding me a room for the night then. Is it safe to say most new folks in town will have already booked their own rooms for the rest of the night by this late?"

Gilchrist agreed that seemed just about the size of it. So they parted friendly and Longarm ambled over to the one main street in no great hurry. For there was more than one primitive but brand-new hotel in the brand-new mushroom town, and if they couldn't fix him up at one he could always ask at another, or in a pinch, sleep sitting up in a lobby chair for the usual dime tip.

There was little going on in any of the four saloons and the one pool hall he dropped into long enough for a short beer and such few words as he could get out of anybody. It was the wrong night of the week and too far from payday for a town that tiny to show that much action along a public thoroughfare. It was tough for a new cuss in any town to find the high-stakes gambling and serious sinning the money folks indulged in behind closed doors and drawn curtains. So nobody he could get into a conversation with could recall much about that rooming house fire, even if they'd been in Durango a whole fortnight.

Longarm had a light supper of elk venison steak smothered in chili con carne under two fried eggs, washed that and the service-berry pie down with buttermilk instead of the usual black coffee—lest he find it tough to fall asleep sitting up—and headed for the nearest hotel with no baggage but his Winchester cradled in the crook of his right elbow with his thumb through the trigger guard.

It was easy to shift the saddle gun so its muzzle and fifteen-round magazine preceded him along the shadowy planking of the partly covered sidewalk as he walked with some interest in the direction of a gal complaining low and a male cussing loud in a drunken tone.

As Longarm drifted closer, unseen by anyone involved in the late night dispute, he saw the gal was in more trouble than he'd first expected. For the cowhand holding on to one arm of the gal in a dark velveteen riding habit was loudly

calling her an infernally stuck-up whore. The two riders with
him were just ogling her like hungry coyotes closing in on a
newly yeaned calf with its momma off somewhere else.

Longarm told himself gang rapes were more unusual than
lots of asshole remarks to an unescorted gal along Saloon Row,
even in the town of Durango. Then he told himself that even
if they were serious, the gal was likely partly to blame and
Durango dammit had a half-ass company police force that was
supposed to watch out for such rowdy behavior. Then he told
himself that he was the only peace officer in sight and that the
gal seemed really worried as she tried to get free, protesting,
"Unhand me, sir! I'm not the sort of girl you seem to take me
for, and I'll tell my husband if you get fresh with me!"

One of the ones just standing by, as if for his turn, laughed
dirty and jeered, "You ain't wearing no ring for the same
reasons you ain't got no man of your own, Amarillo Annie.
You must really take us for tenderfeet if you hope to fool us
with such a high and mighty act, you two-bit cunt!"

Longarm had heard enough. He stepped out of the shadows,
saddle gun aimed politely at the planking between them, as
he called out in a conversational tone, "Evening, Miss Annie.
They told me you'd lit out just before I arrived to escort
you . . . wherever it was you aimed to go."

The gal didn't answer. She was no fool. But the one who had
her by one arm sneered, "She aims to go with us and you'd be
well advised to stay out of this, pilgrim."

Longarm smiled pleasantly enough, considering how tricky
the light was, but let an edge of steel creep into his voice when
he softly but firmly replied, "I can see by the way all three of
you wear your guns that you could be headed into a situation
much like the one in that sad old song about the eastbound
herd bull and the westbound train. I don't want to brag, but
I am not a cowhand in town with a skinful, and even if I was,
I got more rounds in the tube of this one Winchester than you
could possibly have in the wheels of the two guns you seem
to be packing betwixt the three of you. So don't tell this child
whether he ought to stay in or out of anything, and Miss Annie
just told you to let go her arm, *amigo mio!*"

The other one, who seemed more sure of the gal's social

42

status, tried not to sound worried as he cautioned, "You don't want to get in a fight with three grown men over Amarillo Annie, pard. Don't you know what she is?"

To which Longarm could only reply in a dead-level way, "I do. She's the lady you all just heard me offer to escort on to wherever she may want to go. I'd sure hate to hear anyone call any lady I'm escorting anything less than a lady. For that would make me a sort of fool, in your eyes leastways, and that would mean I'd have to make you look even more foolish, wouldn't it?"

The one still holding the gal's arm, although not as firmly, tried a nervous horse laugh and blustered, "Hell, I see one of him and three of us, too spread out for him to get more than one of us as we both draw, Slim."

What the skinny one with the other six-gun might have answered remained a mystery. The gal they'd been tormenting wrenched her arm free and declared, "Now stop it this instant! Don't you silly kids know you're trying to scare the one and original Longarm, and him with the drop on you?"

The one who'd been about to grab for her arm some more crawfished back as if he'd just noticed a diamondback he'd been fixing to tread on barefoot. The skinny one with the other six-gun worn too high for a side-draw gulped and protested, "Nobody here never said nothing about scaring nobody, Miss Annie. Can't you take a little joke?"

The gal didn't answer. So he tried the same question on Longarm, who shrugged and quietly asked, "How about you, Miss Annie? Do we take all this as kid stuff and let 'em live, or would you like the three of them stuffed and mounted?"

By the time she'd grudgingly decided to let it go this one time, she and Longarm seemed to be alone on the walk. But he offered her a free elbow and suggested softly, "We'd best duck into this slot and let me carry you on from the far side of the block, ma'am. It's been my sad experience that some sore losers are inclined to wait up ahead in the shadows after you think you've backed 'em down."

The gal in dark velveteen slipped a gloved hand through the crook of his left elbow, and there was just room for the two of them to go side by side through some mighty dark shadows,

43

dogleg along that alleyway in line with the street out front, and then slip through yet another slot to the street beyond as he told her to hush every time she started to say something to him.

Once they'd crossed to the far side of the residential street he'd led her to, Longarm told softly her, "We can talk now, long as we talk soft and walk no louder. I'd be Deputy U.S. Marshal Custis Long, as you seem to have guessed, and you still have the advantage on me, ma'am."

She sighed. "I might have known you didn't remember me, Custis. You really were just being your gallant self, to a gal in trouble who was really what they said she was for all you knew."

She hugged his arm to her nicely padded bodice and added, "They said you were like that, when you and me and the world were younger over in Dodge."

There were no street lamps, and the moon was only a thin fingernail paring of light in the starry sky above. So Longarm had to stare at her upturned face a while, noting she was sort of pretty or at least not downright deformed, as he replied uncertainly, "Are we speaking of you and me in Dodge before or after I started packing a badge six or eight years ago, Miss Annie?"

"Annie Newton, back in '72," she replied wistfully, and went on. "You were still punching cows and I was a skinny chambermaid at the Drover's Rest that afternoon you saved my virtue from yet another trail herder who'd come back to the hotel early to catch me alone upstairs, he thought."

She laughed girlishly. "I can still see him flopping like a rag doll down those stairs you sent him, and I guess you did do it because you thought it was only right. For you never got fresh with me yourself, even after I'd called you my hero and got up on my tippy-toes to kiss you smack on the mouth!"

Longarm broke stride to spin her around and bend closer as he marveled, "You're that bitty orphan child that drunk from my old outfit was scaring that time? Well, I never, and Lord have mercy if you ain't growed some since that day in Dodge, Miss Annie."

She softly murmured, "I feel even older. For I've been scared a lot since. But they call me Amarillo Annie because

44

I was working there until recent. I was dealing blackjack, just in case that matters to you, Custis. I deal cards these days at that Pronghorn Saloon up the street a ways. Sometimes I have the sort of trouble you just got me out of with idiots who think a gal willing to lie down with them for money would stay on her feet like that, hour after hour, for the commission the house pays a dealer."

Longarm nodded. "I figured they were idjets too. So where would you like me to carry you from here, Miss Annie?"

She said she lived up the slope and a couple of corners to the south. So that was the way they walked in the faint moonlight, with her doing most of the talking as she caught up on the more recent career of a handsome cowhand she'd once had a young girl's dreams about. It was her idea to confide that he could have had her virginity, once she'd kissed a grown man for the very first time and noticed how exciting it felt. He wasn't cruel enough to tell her he'd paid little attention to the shy lips of a little orphan gal. But as if she could read his mind, as they got to the gate of her hillside cottage, she confided, "I've followed your fame as a lawman in the papers, Custis. I was so surprised to read about you in that shootout shortly after you'd been so sweet to me in Dodge. But then I read where you'd been in the war even earlier, and so I suppose that to you I was just a silly little kid, even kissing you as grown-up as I knew how, right?"

"Wrong," he lied gallantly, moving the Winchester out of their way to kiss her some more in her front yard the way he figured she'd want to be kissed good night, these days.

Then he suspected, from the way she was kissing back, good night was not what she had in mind just yet. For this time, while she still had to stand on her toes to get at him right, her kissing was nothing at all like he dimly recalled from that awkward day in Dodge. He was sure glad he smoked instead of chewed as her nosy tongue seemed intent on exploring his surprised mouth. She sucked his tongue deep too when he tried to return the favor, and it was just as well she seemed to be hauling him inside her unlit cottage, once he considered where she'd grabbed hold of him to haul.

It was black as a bitch indoors, but when he tried to strike

45

a light she blew it out, gasping, "No. Don't spoil it with the cruel teeth of time, Custis. Take me as if we were still a young cowhand and a maiden of fifteen!"

He allowed he'd be more than willing, if she'd lead him to some less vertical position. So she did, and they wound up across a bed in the blackness with her clutching at his duds and vice versa till he was in her, both of them still half dressed, and going at it with more enthusiasm than he'd thought he'd saved up aboard that train from Denver. She moved in a way no fifteen-year-old would have ever moved in, biting down hard with her vaginal muscles as she slid up and down his erection in time with his thrusts, gasping downright embarrassing love words as she pleaded with him to make a woman of her at last, after all these years. So he did his best, and managed to get them both entirely undressed by the time he'd come in her a second time. It was her fourth, according to her. When she shyly repeated she'd known it would be grand with him, although not this grand, he was too polite to observe she'd sure as shooting done it with somebody a lot to get that good at losing her virginity.

He finally got her to let him stop long enough to smoke at least one cheroot and maybe get his second wind. But when he thumbnailed a light with their naked bodies together across the rumpled sheets, she turned her head away, as if not wanting him to see more than the way her jet-black hair came out of the base of her skull mousy brown. He looked the other way, spied a candlestick on the bed table, and lit the candle along with his cheroot.

When she softly protested, Longarm got rid of the match and gently reached across her swell tits to take her small chin in hand and turn her face toward the light.

She sobbed, "Oh, Custis, you don't look like I remembered, and I've gotten so old and plain since then!"

He blinked in bemused delight. "I see what you mean about us both screwing somebody else just now. But it wasn't that long ago you were too young for me, and to tell the truth, I find you just about right and even prettier than I thought whilst I was coming with some other image just a moment or so ago."

She archly suggested they come some more by candlelight, and asked how long he'd be in town. Like most men, Longarm had found gals tended to freeze up on a man or demand a honeymoon's worth of humping when he told them they'd likely part by the cold gray light of dawn. So he answered, truthfully enough when you studied on it, "Ain't sure. My boss never sent me to Durango to begin with, and now that I'm here I ain't sure just what I was expecting to find."

She grasped his semi-erection firmly and forked a shapely and now full-grown leg across his naked flesh to impale herself on his suddenly inspired shaft, demurely demanding to know if he was disappointed in what he'd found in Durango so far.

Longarm laughed up at her sweet face and bouncing candlelit bosom. "I like surprises more than I can say. So I'll just have to show you. But no offense, Miss Annie, you wasn't exactly what I was expecting to investigate in Durango."

She allowed no offense was taken as he rolled her on her back to treat her right in a softer, more romantic way. They took turns puffing on the cheroot with half his weight on one elbow. He was pleased to learn she knew how nice it could be that way too, despite all her virginity bullshit. For once a man and woman got past the mad dash for eternal orgasm, it could be mighty nice to just drift together down the currents of togetherness with calmer but lingering pleasures.

She followed his drift, dilating and tightening her innards in time with his languid thrusts as they shared a smoke and conversed like pals over coffee and dessert. He told her more about his own reasons for being in Durango, and added, "Seeing a lady dealing blackjack sees more of life than, say, a schoolmarm, I don't suppose you'd have noticed if anyone had been flashing hundred-dollar treasury notes where the lights are brighter late at night?"

She shook her head, putting the cheroot back between his lips as she replied, "Betting a twenty in paper raises an eyebrow and calls for the floor manager, Custis. Most of the miners and railroad men out our way are paid in silver cartwheels. A top hardrock man draws a double eagle in gold. The boys don't cotton much to paper, and the house likes it even less."

She thrust her hips for a better grip on him as she calmly

47

went on. "Trying to cash a hundred dollars in paper would cause way more excitement in Durango than a Chinaman trying to marry that schoolmarm you just mentioned. What made you ask such a question to begin with?"

He got rid of the cheroot so he could roll her higher atop that pillow under her bare behind, and got deeper in the saddle with her soft thighs hugging his hips while he nuzzled her naked collarbone and explained, "Like I told you, that gang led by a cuss who seems to keep dying in one rooming house fire after another grabbed a heap of hundred-dollar treasury notes up Fort Collins way."

She seemed to be paying less attention as he continued. "Cashing hundred-dollar treasury notes attracts raised eyebrows no matter who tries to cash one, anywhere outside a bank, and you'd play the fool trying to cash a stolen hundred-dollar note in any bank worth its charter."

She murmured, "If you say so, darling. Could you move in in me a little faster?"

He could, and did, but whether she really cared or not he said, or panted, "I asked about somebody trying to cash such paper in a gambling house because I was on another case a spell back, on this same side of the Divide, where outlaws were trying to account for their ill-gotten gains by passing it off as gaming house winnings. But riding off to a remote mining town with the proceeds of that payroll robbery sounds even dumber when nobody seems to have cashed any of the proceeds and . . . Never mind, spread them sweet legs and come with Pappa!"

She did. It felt so good it almost hurt him, and seemed to cause her considerable agony, judging by the way she was moaning and groaning and carrying on till they somehow wound up with him pounding her even harder dog-style. She called him a brute for abusing her in such a beastly way and threatened to strangle him with her bare hands if he dared to take it out with her right on the razor's edge of infinite pleasure that would last for all eternity.

Then she came and said, "Shit. I was trying to make it last too. What was that about dying in one rooming house fire after another? I've heard of going back for second helpings

48

of this hot stuff, Custis, but wouldn't one rooming house fire be enough for anybody?"

He planted his bare feet wider on the rug, and got a friendly grip on either of her hipbones so he could keep it in half soft as he explained. "I don't buy the same Calvert Tyger burning to death more than once, if he ever burned to death at all. We know for a fact who one of the victims was. I ain't sure it matters who they buried here in Durango by the same name. The real mystery, as soon as you study on it, was why in thunder anybody would check into any rooming house as Calvert Tyger to begin with."

Amarillo Annie arched her spine to encourage his questing moist glans as she shrugged her bare shoulders and suggested, "Isn't it likely somebody checking into a place on the sneak would give them a false name, darling?"

To which he could only reply, with a friendly thrust indeed, "I just said that was the mysterious part. Why in thunder would even a wanted outlaw check into anywhere under the name of another wanted outlaw? Calvert Tyger was wanted more seriously than the late Brick Flanders. I'm still working on who the cuss here in Durango might have been. But no matter who he was or what he was hiding, would it make sense for him to register under a name appearing on all those federal wanted flyers?"

She thrust her bare bottom upwards and backwards to encourage him as she insisted, "Whoever they were, and whyever they did it, they did it, didn't they? Maybe they thought this Calvert cuss wasn't wanted as badly as they were. Wouldn't that explain it?"

He muttered, "Not hardly. The bounty on Jesse James is double that of the one on Billy the Kid. But could you see Jesse checking into some hotel as Billy the Kid, so the local law wouldn't check up on who might be bedded down upstairs?"

She agreed that sounded dumb, and asked if she could get on top again if he was going to take so infernally long while he chewed a poor girl's ear off. So he let her, and he was glad he had, once she'd braced a bare heel to either side of his naked hip and literally jerked him off with her shapely bounding body. For it was true what some kindly philosopher, likely French, had said about a man's mind never being clearer than right after a good lay.

He felt sane as hell as he lay there in the cozy candlelight with a pretty gal snuggled close and telling him how smart he was. His completely satisfied flesh let his brain drift any way it wanted to as it tried to make sense out of the little he really knew.

The only trouble was, thinking clear and detached as he was, he still couldn't make a lick of sense of anything he'd been able to find out so far.

Chapter 6

The *Durango Free Press* was set up across from the Western Union office near the depot. Longarm found a little gray gnome sticking type behind the counter blocking access to the presses and such in back of him. Longarm introduced himself, and the gnome looked sort of wistful and went on about his two-fisted chore as he asked what he could do for a cuss who didn't want to place an advertisement or even buy a damned paper.

Longarm said, "I've already read your swell paper over breakfast with a pal this morning. Read some back issues on the premises as well. I know you never run no photo-engravings of that jasper who went up in smoke as Calvert Tyger a spell back, but in the unlikely event you took any pictures of the dismal scene . . ."

"We never did," the gnome said. "We can't afford that newfangled Ben Day process, and if we could we'd have never wanted to run no picture of that mess they hauled outten that burnt-down rooming house across the tracks. I heard you was in town and considering an exhumation order. Take my advice and leave the well-done remains in the ground. His own mother wouldn't have recognized him as they were lowering him down, and the worms have had their way with him by this time."

Longarm nodded soberly. "A tad over six feet tall and weighing around one-eighty, the last anyone on our side saw of him alive and raw. Might have been harder to judge as they dug him out of the ashes curled up in a ball and baked like a potato, though."

The older man grimaced. "You'd do well to rake your spuds out of the coals before they bake that black. I was there and it could have been most any cuss, or critter, you'd like it to be. But your description of Calvert Tyger don't fit the Calvert Tyger we had here in Durango for a week or more before that fire."

Longarm said, "Neither did the glass-eyed cuss who died down in Denver under the same name. What did your Calvert Tyger look like, and how come you recall him at all, seeing he was here such a short time?"

The newspaper man wrinkled his nose. "You'd be as apt to recall a dapper dresser who favored a velvet frock coat and a lavender brocaded vest, and who lit up one of them violet-scented French cigarettes he smoked. After that he was just a tad taller than me but way under six feet, and couldn't have tipped the scales at one-fifty with his boots on. Some say he won at draw poker more often than such a sissy might find safe in towns as raw as Durango. So to tell the truth, I was set to publish his epitaph a good three days before he died in a more unusual way than I'd been expecting."

Longarm reached absently for two cheroots as he mused half to himself, "Tinhorns living dangerously have been known to use the name and rep of somebody more dangerous. But it's odd that you had him down as a gambling man from down this way when a certain blackjack dealer up the street couldn't tell me anything at all about such a spectacular sport."

The newspaper man accepted the offered smoke with a nod of thanks. "No mystery there. Tyger or whoever he was was a professional to begin with, and a sissy boy after that. He'd have never been interested in betting against them pretty gals at the sucker palace up the street. His game was draw poker, like I said, played in the back room of the Strand Saloon most often."

Longarm thumbed a matchhead aflame and lit them both before he suggested, "Run that part about him being a sissy boy past me some more. Were you talking about the way he dressed or the way he liked to make love?"

The older man took a drag, grinned dirty, and said, "Both. He dressed like a sissy, walked like a sissy, and while I never got to watch, he was seen more often in the company of young boys than any kind of gals. Some say he haunted the gin mills and rooming houses on the wrong side of the tracks because of the young drifters who've got less choice about such matters than a halfway lucky tinhorn."

Longarm blew a thoughtful smoke ring and cautiously observed, "A pal of mine who writes for the *Denver Post* keeps telling me a newspaper reporter hears lots of things and has lots of suspicions it's best not to print, lest somebody proves you wrong or sues your ass off."

The cruder version of the *Post's* more polished Reporter Crawford nodded. "That's true. There was heaps of gossip, vicious to common sense, when that sissy went up in flames. Are you asking me official or like a pal just smoking and bullshitting with you?"

Longarm agreed they were only bullshitting. So the newspaper man said, "I'll swear I never said this if you try to use it in court as my say-so. But try her this way. There was a handsome young cowboy and queer whore, according to some, who dropped out of sight the same time. I've never said this to a soul before, but we all like to play detective like Mister Poe, even when we don't write stories for a living. So what if a rich sissy took a poor sissy to his own bitty room and they had a lovers' quarrel?"

Longarm considered and replied, "Any serious wrestling in a small space lit by a candle or an oil lamp could get mighty heated, and an upset stranger would be more likely to charge into a wardrobe than somebody who knew his way out through the smoke."

The older man cackled. "I always figured I'd have made a good detective if I hadn't won that old hand press in a card game on my way West. Would you agree your average sissy boy who'd just about cremated a queer whore with friends in town would have felt any call to linger here in Durango?"

Longarm shook his head. "Most gents in such a fix would be

as worried about the local law, whether the victim had friends or not."

Then he blew another smoke ring and quietly added, "That's not to say a queer whore who beat, robbed, and roasted a customer had any call to hang around either. You'd better give me the name and some description of that wayward youth, pard."

The newspaper man did, as Longarm got out his notebook to take down the probably fake name of Jake Brown and the banal description: a slender youth, dressed cow and having nothing to set him apart from your average run-of-the-mill white cowhand or saddle tramp pretending to be a cowhand as he scouted for easier money in a land of opportunity.

Longarm put the notes away as he shrugged and opined, "It's sure starting to look like I've been chasing down a false lead. I wish we didn't have to do that so often. But the only way you can tell is by trying. So I thank you for your help in eliminating the late Calvert Tyger of Durango as any likely lead to the whereabouts of the outlaws I had in mind."

As he started to turn away, the newspaper man said, "Hold on, old son! Don't you care whether it was that boy-lover or the boy he was out to love who left the other to die in that fire and is still running wild?"

Longarm shook his head. "Not hardly. I'm packing a federal badge, and heated lovers' quarrels in local rooming houses ain't federal, praise the Lord. I got enough on my plate with those more serious outlaws who rode off with a federal payroll. As I put what you just told me together, it seems like a tinhorn who didn't even know how to dress sensible adopted the name of a more ferocious gunslick in the hopes of not having any gunfights at all. He got himself in a whole other mess entire. If he was the one who got out alive, like I said, it's a local matter. If it was that kid called Brown, it's still a local matter. I ain't packing no federal wants on a squirt called Jake Brown. I'll allow he describes like heaps of cow-town drifters, but there was nothing about queers in any of the yellow sheets we have on the real gang led by the one and original Calvert Tyger. So it's been nice talking to you, but if I don't get it on down the road my boss told me to take, I'm likely to get my own ass fried to a crisp!"

So they shook on it and parted friendly. Longarm would have felt even dumber as he boarded the train that morning if Amarillo Annie hadn't fried him up those swell scrambled eggs without crisping them at all.

Chapter 7

There was no way to run a railroad through the Rockies that didn't involve a certain amount of exciting scenery. So the two young gals seated behind Longarm were squeaking like mice by the time the eastbound D&RG combination was two hours out of Durango.

Longarm was tempted to turn and tell them the few hairpin turns and nine-degree grades on this line were kid stuff next to that new narrow-gauge they were running north to Silverton out of Durango. But he never did. The gals were kid stuff as well, neither was all that pretty, and it was a caution how expensive it could get to soda-and-sandwich three passengers on this infernal line.

He decided to read instead. His saddlebags and most of his possibles were riding up forward in the baggage car, but he had a recent issue of the *Police Gazette* and the onionskins of that payroll robbery to peruse as the train commenced to scare the wits out of those two young squaws with the mountains to the east getting a mite more dramatic. He failed to see why they insisted on staring out the downhill windows if they found the view so frightening. It was tempting to point out there was nothing to look at but walls of dynamited rock if they'd only move across the aisle and stare that damned way. But starting up with squeaky young gals was a lot like dipping into a cracker barrel. Once you got started, it was a chore to stop. So he just let them squeak as he read in the *Police Gazette* how some London society gal had been dropped by the old Prince of Wales and his set for getting too familiar with his nibs. That was what they called putting ice cream down the back of an old drunk's stuffed shirt, getting too familiar. The gal sounded like a mite more fun to Longarm than the prince's usual play-pretties. But on the other hand Longarm wasn't as old, stuffy, and married up. Fair was fair, and Longarm had to allow a prince might have a chore explaining all that ice cream in his underwear to his handsome but humorless princess once he got home.

Longarm didn't really care who got to drink with the Prince of Wales these days, and he failed to see what all that fuss about Miss Sarah Bernhardt was about. He'd met the Divine Sarah that time they'd asked him to bodyguard her on her Western tour, and she'd made no mystery of the simple fact she'd been born Jewish but partly raised by Catholic nuns and hence felt as comfortable, or uncomfortable, praying either way. The current dispute seemed to have something to do with Miss Sarah's unconventional ways with men and other pets she liked to lead about on leashes. Longarm had found her a good old gal who'd only kissed him like a sister that time he'd saved her life. But it seemed the French Jews and Catholics were having a serious row over her now, with the Catholics insisting she was Jewish and the outraged Jews insisting she'd been baptized by those nuns and so the Catholic Church was more than welcome to such a flashy thing.

Longarm didn't bother to finish the dumb news item. He found it mighty tedious that grown men could really care what an actress did or didn't do just to work up some curiosity about her show. Longarm had been too polite to ask, but the Divine Sarah had told him to his face she'd never slept in a coffin or kept a live crocodile in her bathtub like some said. But those Jew-baiters he'd had to save her from out Virginia City way must have believed even worse tales about her judging from the wild way they'd carried on.

This old world seemed filled with folks who carried on wild as all hell over nothing much. It was one of the reasons he was packing his badge and guns. He'd found some of the wildest bastards convinced of their own God-given right to raise hell in the name of some half-ass excuse, such as Frank and Jesse's conviction they were riding for a Confederate Army they'd never been enlisted in to protect kith and kin from the cruel advances of the Missouri Pacific, which ran way the hell over on the far side of their state but deserved to be robbed in any case, according to them.

Calvert Tyger's gang of Galvanized Yankees seemed to have worn their own fight for the Lost Cause a mite thin, to Longarm's way of thinking. The James boys, at least, could be said not to know any better, since their only military experience had been with half-assed guerrilla bands who'd never surrendered for the simple reason nobody had ever asked them to. But Tyger had enlisted in the real rebel army, been captured fair and square, and enlisted in the Union Army so he could get out of Sandusky Prison and fight the Santee.

That romantic bull about two flags waving at Little Crow side by side, as boys in blue and gray civilized him with butt stock and bayonet, was postwar twaddle. Calvert Tyger and his pals had foresworn the Confederacy a good spell before Lee's surrender, and would have been free to head home the same as any other Union vets had they not deserted both armies in time of war.

One of the young gals behind Longarm squeaked, "I can't look! Tell me when it's over!"

Longarm glanced out his own window as he set the *Police Gazette* to one side and dug out the sheaf of typed-up onionskins Henry had given him. The tracks wound gently alongside the brawling San Juan through the South Ute Reserve near the New Mexico line, and what the hell, most everyone aboard figured to live if this old car jumped the tracks and rolled no more than three or four times down that forty-five-degree slope. He wondered what those gals were fixing to squeak when they got to the really high hairpins further up the line. His own asshole had puckered some the first time he'd been over that series of sheer-drop zigzags along the Piños on the far side of the Divide, where the ranges rose more steep and craggy.

He'd read Henry's terse but thorough rundown on the Tyger bunch and their recent robberies a dozen times since leaving Denver on what seemed to have been a wild-goose chase. He read them again, with the breeze through the open window fluttering the corners of the thin pages as he searched once more for some pattern that made a lick of sense.

The double turncoat and his half-dozen followers had shot up that federal paymaster's office at Fort Collins as gleefully and senselessly as a wolverine raiding a box full of kittens. A stenographer gal they'd spared after some mock gallantry had given the same description as the one wounded clerk who'd not been hit as bad as he'd let on. The other four men on the premises had been gunned down like dogs after they'd opened the damned safe and given up the damned money. The paymaster in charge, who'd told the others not to put up a fight, had doubtless seen how tough a time they were going to have with those high-denomination treasury notes, intended to pay government expenses rather than salaries at that time of the year. The gal said Tyger had cussed her boss about those hundred-dollar notes before gunning him, as if it had been the poor paymaster's fault. Tyger had never been accused of deep thinking. Longarm was hardly the first lawman who'd wondered why a nondescript outlaw who was said to be fairly well educated insisted on being so famous.

Frank and Jesse, the Youngers, and that stubborn young rascal they called Billy the Kid down Lincoln County way tended to get named a lot because they perforce hung out in the same parts, where lots of admiring folks knew them and tended to gossip about them even as they were helping them hide out.

But nobody riding with Tyger, Flanders, and that more mysterious Chief had ever gone home after the war. They seemed to roam all over the Far West with no particular base the law had any line on. So why would even a mad-dog killer take such pains to let the law know just who they were after? Anyone you were robbing at gunpoint was just as likely to turn over the money whether you said your name was Smith or Jones, and the law would take far longer as they tried to figure out who'd done it.

"Oh, Dear Lord!" wailed the fatter of the two gals behind him as they rounded a turn at a speed even Longarm considered a tad sudden for a sheer drop of a good two hundred yards.

"Road company picking up extra actors!" Longarm suddenly said aloud as he rose from his seat and put the onionskins away so as to spare his ears what was coming next.

What was coming next involved a shaky trestle over a headwaters branch of an ominous river valley. Screaming gals had a way of distracting a man even when he was interested in them, and he was on to something he hadn't considered before as he strode on out to the forward platform where a man could smoke and think in peace.

As he cupped his big hands around a match to get a cheroot going in the cross winds of the platform, he thought back to that time on the road with the Divine Sarah's road company. He'd seen right off how they saved a heap of fancy salaries for French actors by just keeping the key players on the payroll as they traveled from town to town. Once they got to where they meant to put on another show, they could easily hire local talent, or even unemployed cowhands, to put on a costume and just stand around carrying a spear or waving a fan while the few professionals did all the real acting. Those Mormon gals in Ogden had made fairly convincing Egyptian slaves for Miss Cleopatra, or would have had not they insisted on wearing their special Mormon underwear along with their otherwise revealing stage costumes.

But getting part-time help to act convincing hadn't been Longarm's chore, and everyone agreed the Tyger bunch had been acting far more vicious than smart. So say no more than those three original deserters wandered from place to place, picking up extra help as needed amongst the drifting riffraff you found most everywhere. A down-on-his-luck drifter without the balls to pull robberies on his own would need some encouragement to join up for even one job. But a gang leader with a rep would have less trouble picking up a part-time gang. That accounted for the bragging, and it wasn't too tough to buy a tinhorn sissy boy trying to cash in on some real or fancied resemblance to a tougher gunfighter in the hopes of staying out of gunfights. But in that case, why in blue blazes had the late Brick Flanders been using the name of Calvert Tyger in that other rooming house?

Another passenger came out between cars. He was dressed

cow, and both shorter and younger-looking than Longarm. As they nodded and Longarm made room for the other man to pass, he wondered idly where the young cowhand thought he was going. He was fairly sure *why* another male passenger would want to head forward as those two young gals commented on the scenery shrilly, but the next car forward was the baggage car, with the mail and then freight cars beyond. Maybe the jasper was after something in his own saddlebags. He hadn't been anyone the law was after.

Or had he?

Longarm turned just in time. It was still a good thing he had a good grip on a boarding grab-iron as the total stranger hit him stiff-armed, with all his weight, to send Longarm over the side, or try to. Then the bigger deputy grabbed a fistful of shirt with his free hand and raised a long leg to knee the wild-eyed cuss clean off his feet.

His attacker swung wildly, even as he howled in agony. But Longarm caught most of the blow with a suddenly shrugged shoulder, as he hauled the lighter man in and butted him in the face with his forehead. Then Longarm's hat was gone, and so was the total stranger, who'd tried to shove him off the train as it rumbled across that high trestle those gals were doubtless screaming about in the car behind.

The stranger screamed too, all the way down to the narrow ribbon of white water, which blossomed pink for a moment before his shattered body and all that bloody foam were whipped downstream by the ferocious current.

The train hissed to a stop on the far side of the trestle, and Longarm had just recovered his hat from a far corner of the platform when the conductor came out to yell, "Some female passenger says she saw a man falling off back yonder, and another asshole pulled the emergency cord. I don't suppose you'd know who we're talking about, cowboy?"

Longarm shrugged and replied, "Can't say anyone I'd ever seen before fell off any train." He was in a hurry, and it was likely to take days or weeks before that body hung up on some damned something way downstream. And because what he'd just said was the simple truth as soon as you studied every word.

Chapter 8

The next nine hundred miles or more were tedious as hell. For while a flirty gal got on at Trinidad, and an even prettier flirt came aboard at K.C. to sit across the aisle as innocent as a mink in season, Longarm was as considerate a lover as other gals allowed he was, and it wouldn't have been considerate to risk either gal's innocent ass getting peppered with lead just because they both looked so tempting. That jasper who'd swan dove off the trestle had seemed mighty determined, and since Longarm was sure he'd never done a thing to a total stranger, it was even-money he'd been sent by somebody else with a personal hard-on for a lawman who simply didn't know who he, she, or it might be!

He had no way of knowing whether his unknown enemy or enemies knew how poorly their errand boy had done. So there was a good chance he had nothing to worry about but his virtue as he kept avoiding those arch glances shot his way by two very pretty gals. He could tell they were aware of one another by now, and there was nothing like a rival flirt to turn a gal prick-teasing for practice into an all-out and go-for-broke nymphomaniac. Gals that worked up over a gent had been known to go for a three-in-a-bed orgy, with each trying to outscrew the other, rather than let a pretty rival win the whole game. So a man of some experience in such matters was inclined to tingle in his crotch a mite as he tried in vain not to picture a saucy little redhead and a statuesque brunette fighting over him without all those high-buttoned bodices and flouncy skirts confining their movements or his view. Lord, that bigger one's ass swung like it was a saloon door on payday every time she went forward to the water cooler at the end of their car.

But Longarm concentrated on the far less interesting gloom outside as the small redhead almost cartwheeled up to that cooler as if to make certain he hadn't missed the way she filled out that bodice of summer-weight calico. So by bedtime both gals were sore as hell, and there was no sensible way he could assure two pretty strangers he was out to save their lives by not hauling them both into a sleeping compartment and making mad Gypsy love till somebody made another try for him.

Having ridden this line before, and having let the conductor win a few hands of penny-ante in the wee small hours after the club car was officially closed, Longarm was able to fort up in one of those fancy sleeping compartments without paying extra. His conductor pal allowed he hated noise too, and agreed a passenger who might have somebody gunning for him would be safer out of sight. Longarm hoped he'd be out of mind as well. For he'd spent more than one night in a coach car, sitting up and trying not to think about a piece of ass he'd just missed out on.

It was tough enough lying down in a comfortable bunk, trying to concentrate on payroll robberies instead of redheads, brunettes, and such who'd doubtless find the bunk mighty cozy.

He never found out where either got off. Having forted up so fine, Longarm sent out for coffee, sandwiches, and reading matter all the way to Minnesota. The name was supposed to stand for Sky Blue Water in Santee, if you wanted to be poetic. An Indian Longarm had asked the last time he was this far east had allowed it meant more like chalky or dishwater-gray water. The Indian hadn't known why either name might apply. They had all sorts of water, as well as some mighty arid range, in such a fair-sized state.

Lots of folks considered Minnesota an eastern state, since it had been a state before the war and had so many farms and farm folks. But in fact, lots of it lay west of the Mississippi. The Santee country Longarm had been sent to lay in the drier southwest corner, just a spit and a holler east of the Dakotas.

He had to stay aboard till they stopped at New Ulm, the seat of Brown County, where the tracks crossed the Minnesota River. So he got to see quite a few miles of the Santee hunting ground, and it sure was a caution how much pure hell the folks called Sioux by most everyone but themselves could raise in such natural cavalry country.

Whether the gently rolling swells out yonder were covered with a blue-stem prairie dotted with groves of hardwood, or a forest with a lot of open glades all through it, depended on who you asked or just what stretch you were both talking about. The sub-tropical term "savannah" was used to describe such parklike mixtures of grassland and groves, although nobody who'd ever seen how it snowed up here in the winter would describe the place as sub-tropical.

The bluestem was still blue-green, going to tawny on the windier rises, thanks to all the rain they'd had across the West that last greenup. The trees were mostly oak atop the rises, with crack willow, box elder, and such along the bottoms of the draws. Longarm spied a heap of cows and no buffalo at all as they rolled on through lands the white man had stolen, according to the Santee, or bought fair and square off Indian-givers, according to Washington.

Such matters were not for Longarm to adjudicate. He hadn't been riding for the law when Little Crow, or at least his young men, had brought a long simmer to a boil by killing three white men and two white women, the prize for this shootout being less than a full dozen eggs from the homestead they'd hit.

Some said, whites included, that old Tshe-ton Wa-ka-wa Ma-ni, as he said his name in Santee, had tried to head off what he knew was coming, warning his followers they just didn't know what they were getting into. But of course, being a Santee, he had to lead them when they insisted on an all-out war with the Wasichu, lest they get their fool selves killed even faster.

They'd gotten killed soon enough, once an outraged Great White Father showed he wasn't too distracted by the war in the East to do nothing about the blood and slaughter along the Minnesota Valley. Sibley's Minnesota militia were gleefully exterminating Santee, having gained the upper hand after some earlier and mighty frightening reverses, by the time old Pope had made it west with his Union regulars and columns of Galvanized Yankees in time to mop up.

The onionskins failed to say whether Calvert Tyger and his reb pals had lit out before or after Abe Lincoln told the army to take it easy and pardoned all but a tenth of the bunch the army had been fixing to hang. According to the little they had on Israel Bedford, the Union vet and local homesteader who'd cashed that one treasury note in these parts didn't seem connected in any way with Galvanized Yankees, whether they'd deserted in time of war or served with honor and just gone on home to brag on being a vet of both sides.

But Bedford had cashed that bill, not long after a mess of federal employees had been gunned for such ill-gotten gains. So Bedford would be the first one up ahead to scout for sign, discreetly as possible, just in case he turned out to be the one who'd sent that kid to shove a lawman off a train.

It had been Longarm's experience that jaspers with guilty secrets to hide tended to want lawmen headed off before they got close enough to uncover the secrets.

Longarm had no idea, after all this time to study on it, if there was some secret connection between a mad-dog outlaw gang and a sober settler everyone seemed to have down as honest and upright. But that was how come they called such connections secret.

Longarm knew the baggage-smashers he'd tipped in advance would run his McClellan and possibles over to the baggage room of the New Ulm depot for him once they got there. In case his unknown enemies had other secrets planned for him, he ambled back to the rear observation platform and swung over the rail to hit the cross-ties running when the train slowed down on the outskirts of town. He still came close to killing his own fool self for any sons of bitches laying for him around the depot. But he landed in a patch of sunflower and rolled lightly back to his feet, Winchester at port arms, after tripping over a switch point while the train was running fifteen miles an hour.

As long as he was still moving quickly, Longarm sprang across a trackside ditch, crossed the dusty service road on the far side at a dead run, and hunkered down in the shady angle provided by a box elder growing against the plank fence of somebody's backyard.

He wasn't planning on hunkering there any longer than it took to catch his breath and gather his wits a bit. The odds on the smartest crooks in the world knowing where he'd drop off so they could set up an ambush more than a mile from the depot seemed mighty slim. So he doubted the lady staring over the fence at him from under a polka-dot sunbonnet could have murder in mind. But she did sound determined as she scolded, "Get out of my tulips and explain yourself this very instant, young man!"

Longarm glanced down to confirm he had in fact flattened out a patch of cropped vegetation that might have sprouted as tulips a spell back. He grinned up sheepishly. "I doubt I damaged the bulbs along this fence, ma'am. But I'd be proud to buy you some new ones if you'd name your price. I'm U.S. Deputy Marshal Custis Long, on a government mission and allowed to charge anything within reason to my expense account."

The woman on the far side of the sun-bleached planks sounded doubtful as she replied, "You're likely right about underground bulbs surviving your silly behavior. But would you like to show me some identification? You look like a hobo in need of a shave, I just saw you drop off that passing train, and I could say I was Queen Victoria if nobody asked me to prove it!"

Longarm got to his feet, holding the Winchester muzzle down in his free hand as he got out his billfold and flipped it open with a practiced motion to display his federal badge and personal identification. He gallantly suggested, "Nobody would ever buy a lady as young as yourself for the Widow of Windsor, ma'am."

He hadn't lied. He doubted she could be past fifty, and he could see she'd been a real beauty in her day. She still had most of her teeth, and if the hair peeking out from under that sunbonnet was a mite streaked with gray, it was still

66

thick and healthy-looking. Gals who shaded their features with sunbonnets didn't prune up as fast in prairie country. So she looked downright comely when she smiled across the fence at him and said, "Well, I never. You come around to the front and let me coffee and cake you whilst you tell me all about it! Were you chasing somebody when I saw you leap from that speeding train, Custis? I didn't see anyone but you bearing down on me at breakneck speed, but then, I was cultivating my cabbages with this high fence between us."

"I wasn't chasing nobody, ma'am," he said, only hesitating a moment before he added, "I'll surely take you up on your kind offer. For anybody out to chase me round the depot figures to get discouraged when I don't get off that train and they don't see me anywhere downtown for a spell."

That would have roused most anyone's curiosity, and it turned out she was a woman who'd had few men to talk to since she'd wound up a widow three summers back. So he told her more or less why he was on the outskirts of her town, leaving out a few details. It was best to leave a certain amount of guilty knowledge to guilty folk, and far as Longarm knew, nobody in New Ulm was supposed to know about serial numbers one could backtrack to a payroll robbery but the bankers and the local lawmen who'd contacted Billy Vail about that treasury note. With any luck, the crooks who'd run off with them still didn't know the dead paymaster had listed the numbers on those larger notes. For nobody but a total asshole, or an innocent man, would try to spend any paper as hot as that.

His widowed hostess had shucked her sunbonnet in the shade of her kitchen as she'd sat Longarm at a pine table and rustled some coffee and cake for the both of them. Her comfortably lived-in face looked softer once out of the harsher sunlight, and light brown hair streaked with gray looked sort of nice pinned up atop her fine-boned skull that way. She said the raisin cake she'd baked herself was an old Swedish recipe, and he wasn't surprised, since her name was Ilsa Pedersson née Syse. She and her late husband had come to America from the Norwegian province of Sweden as kids, before Lincoln's Homestead Act cluttered up these parts with land-hungry Scandinavian folk. So that likely accounted for her natural English, although she confessed she could still talk her own sort of Swedish if push came to shove. She said most of the new American landowners were proud to be American now, and only talked their native languages during old-country festivals and such. She seemed surprised he already knew about Swedish children expecting a lady in a long white nightgown, with candles lit atop her head at Christmas instead of Santa Claus. Ilsa said it had to be fascinating to ride all over the country, meeting all sorts of folks and being allowed to question them without being called a nosy snoop.

He chuckled down at his coffee mug and confided, "I do get to ask about most anything I find interesting, Miss Ilsa. But seeing you know more folks around here than me, and couldn't be expected in advance to lie to the law, I've good reasons for asking if you've ever heard anything about a local homesteader called Israel Bedford."

The friendly old Swedish lady nodded, smiling. "Of course I recall Captain Bedford from that dreadful Sioux uprising during the war! You may have seen that famous photograph they took of all us women and children huddled together on a prairie rise, with the army guarding us, after Little Crow burned most of New Ulm and killed so many!"

Longarm nodded. "I've seen it. Some of you ladies looked sort of pretty despite your windblown and dusty appearances. But you all look sort of worried as well, and there's one pretty gal near the front, staring into the camera in sheer terror, as if it was a ghost."

The graying brown-haired woman across the table nodded gravely and said, "She might have been seeing ghosts. I know the face in the photograph you mean, albeit I've forgotten her name and exactly who in her family they killed. I was more fortunate. My man was riding with Sibley's Volunteers and we had no children. But the Sioux did some dreadful things to the young boy we had working in our dry-goods store at the time. They say they shoved wads of straw down the throat of one trading-post employee to swell his stomach like a balloon until it burst!"

68

Longarm nodded gravely and explained, "Trader named Andrew Myrick, in charge of the trading post at Redwood. It was Indians as told me about it. Seems that during a hungry stretch before the fighting got started, some starving Santee begged Myrick for food and he suggested they eat all the grass they liked."

He finished his coffee and dryly added, "Indians are inclined to possess sardonic notions of humor, as well as long memories."

She refilled his mug from her pot. "Pooh, neither me nor mine around New Ulm ever did anything to harm those Sioux. So why did they ride right through town, howling like wolves as they murdered, burned, and looted!"

Longarm suggested, "They were vexed with the Wasichu, ma'am. That's what they call us white folk, Wasichu. The Third Colorado figured a Cheyenne was a Cheyenne too, when they rode through that Indian camp along Sand Creek, howling like wolves as they murdered, looted, and burned. It's a mistake to consider such clashes to be melodrama, ma'am. Our relations with Mister Lo, The Poor Indian, make more sense as tragedy, with neither side all right or wrong, and we were talking about Israel Bedford, right?"

She shrugged her shoulders, perking up the small firm breasts he could just make out under her pleated calico in a surprising girlish way, as she told him flatly, "Captain Bedford was a kindly as well as gallant officer during the war. There was more to assisting hungry and homeless survivors than just chasing Indians away. I think he was in charge of the spare horses. I know he was in a position to issue supplies without the usual fuss and feathers others put us through."

She served him another slice of cake, unasked, as she went on to say, "My late husband and I were at the dance they staged to welcome the captain and his bride when they came back to Brown County about eight or ten years after the war. Life in the peacetime army hadn't agreed with an ambitious man and a farm-bred wife. So nobody was surprised when they bought the Bergen homestead and commenced to raise barley, ponies, and kids. Two girls and a boy, the last I heard, with another one on the way."

"Back up a ways and let's go over them *buying* a homestead claim, ma'am?"

She shrugged again, just as perky, and explained. "With money he'd saved up as a soldier, I suppose. Old Lars Bergen had proven his original claim and so the land was his to farm, let, or sell. They say the old man lost interest in his quarter section after losing one son in the war, another to prairie lightning, and then his wife coming down with the cholera and dying on him so nasty."

She grimaced, made a brushing motion, and continued in a brighter tone. "Suffice it to say the old Bergen place is a lot more cheerful these days. The Bedfords are good neighbors, even if they didn't come from the same old country. I still do business in town, so I can tell you their credit is good. Captain Bedford pays all his bills when due."

"That's what I heard," said Longarm thoughtfully. He had no call to tell her what he meant to ask at the bank. But she'd said at the start he looked sort of travel-stained, and he'd scare most bankers by striding in with a Winchester as well as a strange face. So he told her, "I sure could use some place to store my saddle gun for a spell, and you say you still have that dry-goods store in town, ma'am?"

She shook her head. "You can leave that rifle here with me if you like. We never rebuilt the place the Indians burned out. Since the railroad crossed the river I've done better taking orders for barbed wire, patent windmills, and such from this very house."

He allowed in that case he'd be proud to bring her anything she might need from town when he came back for his Winchester. When she asked when that might be he told her truthfully, "Can't say yet. I got some wires to send, some other errands to tend, and some calls to make around Courthouse Square. Then I got to find me a place to stay, hire me a pony to ride, and—"

"I've more than one spare room and two horses out back," she told him. "One of them draws my sulky, and I ride the other when I have to make time cross-country. So I can tell you it's a pretty good jumper, with my weight at least."

Longarm started to protest he didn't want to put her to that much trouble. Then he considered how tough it might be for a hired gun to find out which hotel a stranger in town had registered at if he was holed up in a private home a good quarter mile away instead. So he nodded soberly and said, "I can easily get away with putting down a dollar a day for room and board, and most liveries hire mounts at two bits a day plus deposit, ma'am."

She said she dealt in hardware, not room and board, and suggested they argue about it after he came home for supper. So, the day not getting any younger as they sat there staring thoughtfully at each other, he allowed that sounded fair, and they shook on it before he head on into town on foot.

It only took Longarm a few minutes to cover the five or six city blocks to the area around the depot he was more familiar with. That Western Union was still where it had been the time he'd stopped here in New Ulm on his way to Northfield, where the James and Younger gang had robbed that bank. When he strode in and identified himself to the older gent behind the counter, he was told they'd been expecting him because more than one wire had been sent to him in care of the New Ulm Western Union.

One was from Billy Vail, informing him that yet another of those hundred-dollar treasury notes had turned up at a Cheyenne bank, but that he was to go on with his investigation at New Ulm in any case, that you didn't investigate by running in circles, and that nobody in Cheyenne could say who'd broken that big bill in a local saloon on a Saturday night to begin with.

Another wire was from Pagosa Junction in the South Ute reserve, in answer to the earlier wire he'd sent them while changing trains at K.C. The Indian Police said they'd dragged a few likely stretches of the San Juan in vain and relayed his request to the Navajo Agency downstream. So he knew he didn't have to wire the Navajo Police after all. They'd find the body of that murdering young jasper for him or they wouldn't, and in either case it wasn't too likely anyone out to assassinate federal lawmen would be packing identification papers made out to his true name. But aliases turned up on the yellow sheets as well, if an owlhoot rider kept flashing the library card, voter's registration, or whatever he'd stuffed in his wallet.

Longarm hummed a few bars of "Farther Along" as he tore open the last wire from an old pal in Denver who screwed like a mink and rode herd over a library of war records, including Confederate, collected by a rich eccentric who, having avoided service in either army, seemed to have enjoyed the hell out of the war on paper.

The good old gal he'd wired for more details about Tyger, Flanders, and others who deserted about that same time, such as that scout he only had down as "Chief," had wired back she needed more time. For most of the Confederate records in that private library in Denver dealt with western rebs, such as Hood's Texas Brigade. But she said she'd keep digging and that she was looking forward to a personal visit as soon as he got back to Denver.

Longarm grinned as he put all the telegrams away, for after all those pure hours aboard those trains, even the memory of a sort of homely old gal could make a man feel sort of horny. He remembered how hard she tried to please with a rollicking rump despite her plain appearance.

Recalling what Ilsa Pedersson had just said about him looking like a hobo, Longarm scouted up a barbershop that served hot baths in the back as well. He borrowed a whisk broom and did what he could about the fly ash and dust on his duds as the tub slowly filled with only slightly rusty water. He had a fresh shirt and a change of underwear in his saddlebags, of course, but he didn't want to traipse all over New Ulm to get them. The dirt on his light blue work shirt wasn't all that awful anyway, once he'd washed his hide good with naptha soap and had the barber sprinkle him with plenty of bay rum after his shave out front.

The barber's business had been slow that afternoon, but a lawman who knew the ropes of a small town didn't press his luck by bringing up the subject of Israel Bedford. Old Ilsa had already told him the suspect enjoyed a good local rep, and there was no way in hell to ask about folks in a town this size without someone being sure to let them know there was a stranger in town asking about them.

There were only so many hours in a day to work with, but a strange lawman who didn't let the local lawmen know who he was ahead of time could sure have silly conversations about the six-gun someone had just noticed he was packing with no other visible means of support.

Billy Vail's opposite number in these parts worked out of the bigger twin cities further east, where the Minnesota joined the Mississippi. So the ranking law in New Ulm was the county sheriff, and fortunately the sheriff himself was out raising campaign funds for the coming fall elections. So Longarm only had to tell a senior deputy what he was doing in Brown County in a dirty shirt and with a .44-40.

The deputy said they'd been expecting him, and added that the boys from the Saint Paul Federal Court had already questioned everyone at all involved, without finding out too much.

When Longarm groaned inwardly and asked whether other deputies had called on Israel Bedford, lest he not know those serial numbers had been recorded, the sheriff's deputy said cheerfully, "Hell, you can't hardly ask a man where he got a treasury note without explaining why you're asking, can you?"

Longarm grimaced and growled, "Sometimes it don't pay to be quite so direct. I don't suppose anybody wondered what a suspect might do with other listed treasury notes he'd been fixing to spend once they told him how they'd spotted the first one?"

The local lawman shrugged. "There was no need to pussyfoot. Everyone knows Captain Bedford is as honest as the day is long, and your federal pals left content with his story."

"Which was?" Longarm asked.

The deputy sheriff answered, "Livestock transaction. Bedford has some of the finest riding stock in the county for sale. Serves his mixed mares with a pure Morgan stud these days. Told us he'd sold a saddle-broke filly and a promising colt for that hundred-dollar note. Said the buyer was an Indian, or mayhaps one of them Metis, or Red River breeds. Anyways, others out his way say they'd seen a whole family

73

of dusky wanderers around the right time. The one who paid cash for Bedford's stock was dressed like a white man. Had a more Indian-looking squaw and a mess of raggedy kids tagging along, from toddlers to kids in their teens. Us county riders tried to help your federal deputies cut the trail of the prosperous savages, but the sod's as thick and springy as it gets out yonder, and they were traveling with neither a cart nor travois so . . . What the hell, it ain't as if Captain Bedford is famous for robbing folks and wasn't there something about an Indian riding with that gang when they shot up that government office at Fort Collins?"

Longarm shrugged. "We can't ever get everyone to agree on how many there were in the gang. One witness figures five all told. Another counted six or eight as he bled on the floor. He may have just been excited. Nobody on the streets of Fort Collins seems to have counted shit as the gang left cool as cucumbers and slow as innocent churchgoers. But Tyger and Flanders did have at least one associate called Chief. I'm still working on his full name. The army sure kept casual records as they were chasing Little Crow with such informally recruited columns."

The somewhat older Minnesota man nodded. "Don't I know it. I rode with Sibley's Volunteers, and we had to laugh at those ragtag Galvanized Yankees when they rode tear-ass all over after Sioux we'd already shot the liver and lights out of."

He got up to stride over to a file cabinet as he continued. "We thought some of the regulars were all right, though. Captain Bedford was in charge of his column's remount and quartermaster detail. Not as picky as some West Pointers when it came to sharing supplies in the field with comrades in arms. Made hisself a heap of friends out this way."

Longarm nodded and said he'd heard as much. Then, since the son of a bitch was helping himself to a swig from that jug without offering to share, Longarm allowed he had other fish to fry, and got back out to the square before he found himself saying something unprofessional.

It wasn't easy, knowing half-ass federal men and selfish county men who openly favored his prime suspect had totally fucked up his original plan of action.

74

Chapter 9

The Granger's Savings & Loans was just off the square, and a handsome young gal peering out through the bars of the teller's cage didn't look scared of strangers as Longarm came in just as they were fixing to shut down for the afternoon. When he flashed his badge and told her what he'd come for, she vanished for a moment, and then unbolted an oaken door from the inside to run him back to the branch manager's private office.

The bank was run by a P. S. Plover, a portly white-haired cuss who rose behind his acre or so of desk in a neighborly way to wave Longarm to another padded chair and offer a cigar from his big brass humidor. "That was quick," he said. "I just posted my letter yesterday and I didn't expect Saint Paul to send anyone this side of Monday."

Longarm accepted the Havana claro with a nod of thanks, and took his seat before he replied. "I ain't from the marshal in Saint Paul, Mister Plover. I ride for Marshal Vail out of Denver, and I'm here in response to that purloined treasury note you all detected. You say you've written more since?"

As he lit his fancy smoke the banker explained. "I'm pretty sure I can name that breed who bought stock off Israel Bedford with one of those hot treasury notes, Marshal Long."

Longarm modestly replied, "I'm just a deputy marshal, but lots of folk make that same mistake. Just let me get out my notebook before you name the mysterious Indian for us, hear?"

As Longarm gripped the cigar with his teeth to break out his notebook and a pencil stub, the banker said, "He's not pure Sioux. Looks like a full-blood, if you ask me, but he claims to be white on his daddy's side and hence eligible to own land, sign contracts without a white sponsor, and in sum, make a perfect pest of himself with his full-blood squaw and platoon of trashy breed brats."

Longarm poised his pencil and cocked a quizzical brow, so the banker said, "His name's Chambrun, Wabasha Chambrun, for God's sake. Claims to be the spawn of a French-Canadian mountain man and a squaw of the Osage persuasion."

Longarm wrote down the name, mildly observing, "Squaw means woman in most Algonquin dialects. Osage, Santee, and other such Sioux-Hokan speakers say something like Wee-yah for women in general. Meanwhile, whilst they talk much the same lingo, real Osage range farther south than you'd have expected your average Canadian trapper to range in the Shining Times."

The banker shrugged. "I have them down as Santee Sioux too. But try to prove it, and even if you could at this late date, who but the Land Office has any say in the matter of their homestead claim?"

He took a drag on his own cigar before adding, "In any case, the rascal who stuck Israel Bedford with that hot treasury note came in here bold as brass just yesterday to open a savings and checking account with us."

Longarm grinned wolfishly with the cigar at a jaunty angle and asked, "With yet more of those treasury notes from the Fort Collins robbery?"

The older man splashed cold water on that. "Well, not in so many words. He presented four hundred and thirty-seven dollars to Magnusson out front, in bills of smaller denomination, but I had told all my tellers to watch out for prosperous Indians, and so they naturally asked him, in a cool and casual way, if he was by any chance the same Mister Chambrun who'd bought that nice riding stock off Israel Bedford. So guess what he admitted bold as brass!"

Longarm whistled thoughtfully. "Stupid as hell too, if he knew where that bigger bill came from. Could we have your

76

smart teller join in with the rest of this conversation, lest we drop even one detail in the cracks?"

The banker nodded and banged a desk chime near the humidor as he agreed, "Good thinking. I should have asked her to stay to begin with. She was the one who brought that hundred-dollar treasury note to my attention when a shopkeeper got it off another depositor last week."

The willowy-hipped but top-heavy blonde came in to join them with a puzzled smile. Her boss waved her to another seat and explained, "I want you to tell Deputy Long just what you know about both the Bedford and Chambrun accounts, Vigdis."

Longarm jotted down "Vigdis Magnusson," figuring that that might not get you teased as much by the other kids in your school if they'd been stuck with Swedish names as well.

The beautiful blonde explained in her educated but lilting English how they'd already known about the respectable Captain Bedford paying for seed and supplies with that hot paper a dark sinister stranger had stuck him with.

She said she couldn't rightly say why a polite breed or assimilate had struck her as sinister when he'd come in, dressed white and with a batch of innocent paper and specie.

She said the sinister stranger had given his name as one Wabasha Chambrun, had allowed he and his family were settled in and trying to prove their own homestead claim up the river a ways, and had said that he'd heard it was safer to keep his money in a bank and pay his bigger bills by check.

The big blonde sounded a mite puzzled as she confided to Longarm, "I'm not sure why such a simple story from such a polite homesteader simply asking to open an account with us made me feel all tingly and sneaky. But it did, and so I found myself asking if he was the same Mister Chambrun who'd bought that adorable colt off Captain Bedford. He admitted he was, with neither shame nor hesitation!"

P.S. Plover nodded sagely. "There you have it, young sir. I naturally reported what Vigdis told me, in writing, that very afternoon. When are you planning to arrest the thieving redskin?"

Longarm put the notebook away so he could take the cigar out of his mouth as he explained. "I ain't planning to arrest nobody right off. It ain't that I'm lazy. It's just that I've found it tough to start a fire with wet matches or keep a cuss in jail on weak evidence. And by the way, who's holding that treasury note at the moment?"

Plover blinked in surprise and said, "Why, we are, of course. In its own sealed and marked envelope, in our vault, lest we mix it up with innocent bills. I offered it as evidence to the sheriff as soon as I saw its serial number was on that list. But the sheriff told me I'd best hold on to it for the time being because he'd be reporting what seemed a purely federal matter to you federal officers."

Longarm nodded and said, "He did good. Put a man with a lawyer in a county jail on an interstate federal charge, and he'll be out on a writ and likely long gone before anyone like me is likely to be in town. I'd just have to find some safe place to store the evidence for now if I was to ask you to turn it over, so I won't."

The smart buxom blonde asked who'd get stuck in the end, knowing there was no way to exchange a *counterfeit* note for the real thing, once you'd been dumb enough to get stuck with it.

Longarm told her, "We're not jawing about queer money, ma'am. We're talking about stolen goods. Once that bill in your safe ain't evidence any more, the Fort Collins paymaster who replaced the murdered one will likely reclaim it."

She protested that it hardly sounded fair to stick her bank for funds stolen clear out Colorado way. So he said, "I hadn't finished. Didn't that merchant get the note from Bedford to begin with? And didn't *he* get that money from this Wabasha Chambrun?"

She clapped her hands like a delighted girl-child and exclaimed, "That's right! We can ask Captain Bedford to make good on the note, and then he can ask Wabasha Chambrun to make good on the note, and . . . where does it all end in the end?"

Longarm shrugged and said, "On the gallows, once we backtrack to the gang member as commenced such complicated cash transactions. The point is that this bank won't be stuck in the end for that hundred dollars. So I'd sure like it to stay put where it is for now."

P.S. Plover scowled across his desk and complained, "I'm not sure I like your tone, young sir! Are you suggesting we might try to pass that treasury note on? Have you forgotten it was I who brought it to the law's attention in the first place, when I could have just pretended to overlook it and passed it on?"

Longarm shook his head. "Nope. If I had you down as a party to that payroll robbery, I wouldn't be asking you to hold on to that evidence for us."

He leaned forward to flick cigar ash in a tray on Plover's desk as he continued. "I need more evidence before I go arresting anybody. I mean to talk to both Bedford and Chambrun as smooth as Miss Vigdis here might have. I ain't sure what I'll do after Bedford says he got that paper off Chambrun and Chambrun tells me he came by it just as innocently."

Plover asked what made Longarm so certain the mysterious newcomer to Brown County would be able to offer such a good excuse.

Longarm said, "He'll have to. Would you just admit your robbed and gunned a federal paymaster even if you had?"

Chapter 10

Somebody in these parts had to be lying. Until he was sure who it was, Longarm felt it best to play his own cards closer to his vest than usual. So once he'd checked out his saddle and possibles at the depot, he refrained from heading for a livery as he otherwise might have. He just braced the awkward load on his left hip, leaving his gun hand free as he headed back to the Pedersson place, with his eyes peeled and hugging the sunny side of the street because that was the side you met the fewest on when the afternoons got this hot.

Ilsa Pedersson looked a tad older than before, after all that eye-to-eye smiling at pretty young Vigdis Magnusson, but she'd tidied up her grayer hair and changed into a fancier gingham print and fresh apron by the time Longarm got back, as if to remind him how stale his own shirt must look, despite his bath and a store-bought shave with bay rum. But she allowed he looked way more civilized than when he had hunkered down in her tulip bed, and said she'd show him right up to his room so he could store that army saddle and such before she served him another snack out back.

He said he'd rather just tote his riding gear on back to her carriage house if she'd meant what she'd said about hiring him one of her ponies.

She said he'd be riding her jumper, Blaze, but pointed out it would soon be suppertime.

To which he could only reply with a wistful smile, "I can

smell what you got in your oven from here, ma'am. But they sent me here to put in a day's work for a day's pay, and I've just about time for a couple more calls before sundown if I start right now."

She didn't argue. But as she led the way around to the back she naturally wanted to know where he'd be riding, and seeing he'd be riding there on her stock, he felt obliged to tell her.

She gasped. "The Bedfords dwell a good six miles north of town, and you say these mysterious breeds are homesteading nine miles out beyond them?"

Longarm said soothingly, "We won't be jumping no fences loping either way, ma'am. I don't see how we'll get back before sundown either, but it's a county road and the moon will rise full tonight with no clouds worth mention."

So she sighed and said she'd put the ham she was baking in the warming oven up above, so it could cook much slower, but warned him his supper would be ruined if he didn't get back by seven or eight. He doubted he could, but he never said so as he followed her inside, agreed the black gelding with a white blaze she introduced him to was a handsome brute, and went along with her suggestion he use her bridle instead of his own because old Blaze was more used to the feel of the bit. He wasn't about to ride fifteen miles each way in her sidesaddle.

Seated astride an old McClellan, with his own Winchester back in its saddle boot, Longarm rode out the north side of town a little before four, and asking directions only twice along the way, rode into the Bedford dooryard around five.

The spread was a tad more imposing than he'd expected, even knowing Israel Bedford had bought a proven claim with a dozen years' worth of improvements on it before he and his younger family started work on their own. The main house and outbuildings, while sod-walled, were tin-roofed with all the wood-trim whitewashed. Handsome glass windows let in the light and kept out the winter winds. Less prosperous settlers tended to have glass bottles driven through the sod walls instead.

There were two pole corrals and a good-sized training paddock out back, with a patent sunflower windmill watering the whole shebang. It was too early in the season to say, from where he sat old Blaze, whether those forty acres of grain to the north of those new apple saplings were barley, like some said, or the oats Longarm would have drilled in if he'd been raising that many ponies. That deputy sheriff had been right about Bedford's stock having Morgan bloodlines, and it made a man feel swell just to look at those dozen or so pretty ponies staring back curiously from that one corral.

A dog was barking inside the house. The Bedfords had doubtless called their kids inside when first they'd spied a stranger riding in. For Israel Bedford stepped out a side door alone, a Greener ten-gauge in hand as he smiled uncertainly and called out, "You'd be just in time for supper if you're out this way on friendly business, stranger."

Longarm flashed his badge before he dismounted in order to talk softer as he introduced himself. "I don't mean to slight that swell chicken soup I can smell from all the way out here. But I got many a mile of riding left ahead of me. So I'll get right to my business with you, Captain Bedford."

The retired army man, a wiry individual in his late thirties wearing bib overalls, walked along as Longarm led his mount to the veranda steps and tethered it loosely to the cottonwood railing. Longarm broke out two cheroots and got them both lit up before he tersely brought Bedford up to date on his investigation.

Bedford had naturally figured some of it out already, thanks to earlier unskilled questioning by the local sheriff. He said he knew that Chambrun bunch better now than he had the day he'd sold Wabasha Chambrun a filly and a colt for that recorded treasury note. He said they'd met on the road out front a time or more and had some friendly talk about the weather, their crops, and such. He had no idea where the breed or assimilated full-blood had come by the money because, he said, he hadn't asked.

When Longarm asked whether an old soldier might by any chance recall his Sioux-Hokan-speaking neighbor from that big Santee uprising of '62, the retired Indian fighter shook his head as if he knew and replied, "If we ever swapped shots he'd have been just a painted kid loping past, and to be honest, most of such wild and woolly fun had ended by the time us regulars got across the Mississippi to tidy up."

He stared off across the range, now more peaceful, rolling gold and lavender in the late afternoon sunlight, as he added in a soft, bemused tone, "There wasn't much to tidy up after irregulars hit Mister Lo with everything but the kitchen sink and then shoved his head in the sink. But I have to allow Indians tend to stay down when they've been put down by others just as savage. You saw what the old Seventh Cav got for sparing so many women and children on the Washita. Old Hank Sibley and his fourteen hundred militiamen of the Sixth Minnesota didn't bother with such niceties as separating the sheep from the goats. Sibley had been an Indian trader, spoke Sioux, and just kept running down and butchering Sioux till they begged him to stop and agreed to peace on harsher terms than us regulars might have offered."

Longarm wrinkled his nose and muttered, "I'd have been scared of Long Trader Sibley if I'd been an Indian too. I understand he wound up with close to a hundred and fifty thousand in Indian funds in his own pocket before the Santee rose. But that's not what I was sent to look into. I'll take your word you didn't recall Wabasha Chambrun from your Indian-fighting days, Captain. But wasn't Wabasha the name of an important sub-chief under Little Crow?"

Bedford nodded. "I met *that* Wabasha. He was a rival as well as an earlier follower of Little Crow. They'd argued strategy from the beginning, and once they'd suffered some reverses Wabasha came over to our side as a sort of peacemaker."

"Or a sort of Benedict Arnold, to hear the Indians tell it," said Longarm thoughtfully.

Then he said, "I'll just ask this other Wabasha how come he took the name of a famous fork-tongue. Quill Indians are allowed to make up their own names with the aid of visions and such. But the son of a Christian, raised to wear Wasichu duds, might have been given his name without him having any say-so in the matter."

He blew a thoughtful smoke ring and mused, half to himself,

"Any way you slice it, though, a man named after a famous Santee chief and living on what used to be Santee hunting ground sure ain't all that convincing as a French-Canadian and Osage anything!"

Chapter 11

A good pony could carry a man thirty or forty miles overnight if he liked it, and over a hundred if he hated it. But old Blaze was not his to abuse, and Longarm figured spells of trotting and walking would cover the nine more miles to the Chambrun place in less than three hours.

The walking was easier on the ass of any man seated in a McClellan saddle. The old army ball-breaker had been designed with the endurance of the mount rather than the comfort of the rider in mind. But things could have felt worse. Longarm was smart enough to ride in tight pants and snug underdrawers, so his balls never got wedged in that open slit down the center of a McClellan that was designed to prevent chaffing or overheating the pony's spine no matter what new cavalry recruits wrote home about it.

The day was dying gently with a poetical sunset off to the west as the horned larks and redwings sang their harsh but not unpleasant evening serenades from either side of the dusty road. He could tell it more or less followed the trend of the river, not because he could see that much sky blue or chalky water through the denser cover to his right, but because there was so much of the cover. You never saw willows or cottonwoods that high unless they grew close to all-summer water. The scattered oak and thorn apple off to his left was reaching way deeper for groundwater on that side of the county road. But either way, the sunset made them all look as if they'd sprouted leaves made out of amber, butterscotch, and such, while sunset-gilded bees still foraged the wildflowers peeking up at him from amid the taller bluestem and needle grass. The grass didn't seem to have been grazed so much out this way, although those bees by themselves would have told an Indian, or warned him, there were white folks in these parts.

Indians admired honey as much as anybody, and so, as they had with the white man's tall-dogs, or horses, the Indians had adapted to what they called the white man's flies, or honey bees, despite the fact there'd never been any before white settlers brought them from the old country, along with other novelties, good and bad, from steel tools to smallpox.

Along about dusk, Longarm passed a homestead neither Bedford nor anyone else had mentioned to him. He wondered at first sight whether they'd gotten the distance wrong and he'd already made it to Wabasha Chambrun's. Then he saw that the folks waving at him from the front of their sod-roofed sod house seemed to be plain colored folks, not breeds or Indians. He reined in, waved back, and called out, "Ain't got time to stop and set a spell, no offense. I'd be the law and I'm looking for the Chambrun spread."

The colored homesteader rose from his barrel seat and pointed up the road as he called back, "About an hour's ride, at the rate you've been riding, Cap'n. What have them Sioux folks done?"

To which Longarm called back, "Ain't sure. Just want a few words with 'em for now. What makes you so sure they ain't French-Canadian and Osage breeds, like Chambrun says in town?"

The African-American called back, "Can't say for sure what Neighbor Chambrun might be. He never stops to talk as he rides by on his pony. But some of our kids have met up with his kids along the river friendly enough, and they say their mamma is one of them Santee Sioux you white folks had so much trouble with back when I was raising crops for somebody else, God bless Mister Lincoln and all his soldiers blue!"

Longarm didn't even want to refight the Indian Wars, so he thanked the thankful freedman and rode on through the gathering dusk.

The cloudless sky went from salmon pink and purple to star-spangled black velvet with little ceremony, as skies tended to when they had no clouds up yonder to catch any lingering rays. Longarm knew a full moon would be rising most any time now. But in the meanwhile it was a good thing horses saw better in the dark than humans. For Longarm had to take it on trust that Blaze wasn't trotting over the edge of an awesome drop as they forged on.

He told his mount, "You're doing fine. Just keep picking 'em up and clopping 'em down and there ought to be some sort of light in a window up ahead this early in the evening."

He failed to see any, and he'd spent enough nights with Quill Indians to know they turned in early and rose with the sun, like a lot of country folks save for Mexicans.

He had to chuckle as he recalled that pretty Comanche down on the Staked Plains who'd said if there was one thing her kind and his had ever agreed on, it had to be that Mexicans were natural night owls next to real Americans, red or white. She'd screwed agreeably, too, now that he thought back. But why in thunder was a man thinking back to Texas when he was riding towards . . . what, Minnesota?

As the moon rose at last, pumpkin yellow above the tree tops to the east, there was still no sign of lamplight ahead, and Longarm told his mount, "I ain't jerk-off hard. I'm piss hard. I usually get over horny dreaming as soon as I get up and piss too. So why am I just telling you all this when I got all this open country to just piss all over?"

The black pony didn't argue as Longarm reined to a halt and dismounted to suit actions to his words. But as he stood there unbuttoning with the reins in one hand, he detected distant hoofbeats and confided, "It's a good thing we stopped for a piss call, Blaze. For I doubt I'd have heard them, or vice versa, at this range with your big feet distracting my delicate ears."

He started to lead his mount off to the west through the tall grass afoot as he told the gelding, "They're doubtless on innocent business, such as making it home in time for their own suppers. But they sure are coming this way hell-for-election, and mayhaps we ought to just get out of their way and see what happens next."

He led his mount into the deeper shade of some thorn apple clustered around a blown-down or lightning-struck oak, and then took that leak, with a sigh of contentment, before he loosely tethered Blaze to an oak branch and broke out his saddle gun.

But even as he levered a round of .44-40 into the chamber of his Winchester '73 he muttered aloud, "Billy Vail would surely frown on my drygulching innocent travelers. On the other hand, it's a big boo to challenge strangers in uncertain light when they sound that excited about something!"

So he just stood there, a silent shadowy form amid bigger shadows, as the mystery riders—there were four of them—tore past at a horse-killing flat run, not pausing to tell him where they were headed or even to glance his way. But as they thundered on, Longarm told his own mount, "They want to be there sudden, but they can't be headed all that far. So the Chambrun place sounds about right."

When Blaze failed to answer, Longarm continued. "The question I'd like you to answer is whether they have such urgent business with old Wabasha Chambrun or . . . somebody else. So how many knew you and me were on our way to question him about that payroll robbery?"

The pony didn't answer. Longarm hadn't expected it to. Talking to yourself or other dumb brutes could organize your thoughts. But they said you were in trouble when you started to hear answers. So he undid his hasty half hitch and remounted, leaving his saddle gun thoughtfully primed and cocked across his thighs, as he walked Blaze back to the road, paused there a moment in thought, and then decided, "As old George Armstrong Custer found out in broad daylight, it ain't smart to charge into a place you don't know, where you may be way outnumbered, whilst pussyfooting can get you killed even quicker."

He swung the pony's head southeast, and heeled it back the way he'd just ridden, explaining, "It's neither polite nor smart to drop in uninvited when you just don't know who might be there. We can't shoot first, the way Hickok did that time he gunned his own deputy like a trigger-happy asshole. But it can take fifty years off your life to shoot last when it ain't a pal after all. So why don't we skin this cat another way entire?"

He felt no call to explain further to a pal who couldn't answer and might not care. So he just rode back to that homestead, where a worried-looking colored kid was just heading out to the road aboard a mule. When he spotted Longarm about the same time he called out, "My pap just told me to ride for town and tell the sheriff you might be dead, Cap'n! There was a bunch of hardcase white boys here just now, asking for you by name if you'd be Deputy Long!"

Longarm said, "You'd best thank your pap for me and let me deal with 'em. Did they say what they wanted of me, or where they might be headed from here?"

The kid replied, "Not in so many words, Cap'n. But they called you a mother, and Pap says he doubts they meant Mother Dear. When he allowed you'd just rode by, before they called you a mother, that is, one of 'em said they'd be able to get you as you came out of the Chambrun place if they hurried."

Longarm asked if it had sounded as if they were pals of Wabasha Chambrun, enemies of Wabasha Chambrun, or just using him and his spread as a point of reference.

When the kid said he didn't know, Longarm told him to get back to his own kith and kin and, if possible, forget this whole conversation. When the kid said he followed his drift, Longarm added, "I don't ask any man to burn himself trying to get my chestnuts out of the fire. You've done me a real service by telling me as much as you just did. If those others are smart enough to lean on any of you about the way I just backtracked, go on and tell them anything you need to tell them to keep from getting hurt, savvy?"

The kid nodded gravely, eyes wide in the moonlight, and said he surely did and assumed Longarm meant to ride in and tell the sheriff about all this himself.

Longarm didn't say yes or no. He wasn't sure as he thanked the helpful young cuss and rode on. He didn't see what the local law could do about some riders who, so far, hadn't done a thing to anybody. Meanwhile, it might be interesting to see who might know about any of this bullshit without being told.

89

Chapter 12

Night riders aiming to ambush a lawman along one stretch of the moonlit county road could be set up just as sneaky along another. So Longarm cut off across the moonlit grass as soon as he'd cleared the southeast corner of that fenced-in colored homestead. He let old Blaze have his head, since horses saw better in the dark than humans and Blaze likely knew the way to the stall he seemed so intent on reaching at an easy lope. But they were both saved by tumbleweeds, piled up in the moonlight against an otherwise invisible drift fence some son-of-a-bitching cattle outfit, most likely, had strung parallel to the road a quarter mile west, doubtless taking advantage of the wide-apart homestead fencing as well as their own. Drift fences were designed to prevent just what they were named after. A cow ranging wide from the water tanks and salt blocks of its home spread could wind up attracted by somebody else's, and road traffic tended to spook cows into drifting further.

Longarm consulted his mental map of Brown County as he dismounted to break out his small claw hammer from a saddlebag. The country hereabouts was getting crowded for free-ranging beef if they'd spent money on this much bobwire. For while the Minnesota shared Brown County with other streams such as the Sleepy Eye and Cottonwood, there had to be at least ten miles of high and dry grazing off to the west, meaning some other cattle outfit had laid claim, and likely had its own wire strung between here and the Sleepy Eye creek and wagon trace.

Tethering Blaze for the time being to a panel of four-strand he meant to leave intact, Longarm got to work with his claw hammer as he quietly explained, "It ain't neighborly to cut a man's fence if you don't have to. Since they were considerate enough to staple this murderous shit to cedar posts, we don't have to."

He used the claw of his hammer to pull staples like tin teeth, palming each one as he did so, until nothing but its own mild tension was holding the wire off the moonlit grass. Then he untethered his borrowed mount, lowered the loose wire far enough with a hand to hook the instep of a boot over it, and flattened it in the grass underfoot so he could simply lead the pony over to the far side.

One he had, he was considerate enough to retether Blaze, get back on the eastern side, and restaple the wire back the way he'd found it with the business end of the hammer. No four strands of bob were able to stop a man afoot who knew how to duck through it, of course.

He put the claw hammer away, untethered from the fence, and swung back in the saddle to ride on, knowing he'd be skirting the back forties of the Bedford place. He knew Israel Bedford wouldn't tell him anything he could be certain of, no matter what. He'd said he'd gotten that treasury note from Wabasha Chambrun. Everyone in town seemed to feel Bedford was less likely to fib than his new breed or full-blood neighbors. On the other hand, if those colored folks had heard those other sneaks right, they didn't seem to be in cahoots with Chambrun.

"Mebbe," Longarm muttered aloud as he held Blaze to a silent walk as they moved along the far side of the fencing. A white man with a tolerable rep could alibi himself easy as pie just by claiming he'd gotten a recorded treasury note off any number of neighbors. On the other hand, a newcomer of at least mixed blood would have enough on his plate without his pals gunning a federal deputy right on his own homestead claim. So innocent or guilty, he'd want to tell the local law he'd never laid eyes on any rascals gunning folks after dark along a public right of way.

"Chambrun can't be a full-blood," Longarm muttered to his mount as he reached absently for a smoke, warned himself against a dumb move, knowing a match flare could be spotted from three miles off on open prairie, and decided, "Not a *registered* full-blood leastways. Abe Lincoln's Homestead Act of 1862 was designed to fill this part of the country up with white folks. The government figured there were already enough *Indians* out this way."

Some said, even some white folks, that the Homestead Act, passed as it was in the early half of the War Between the States, had been the spark that lit Little Crow's fuse. The Santee Sioux, as Washington called them, had already moved west to get out of the way of progress more than once. So they'd doubtless felt sort of squeezed, west of the big chalky water and with their Dakota cousins to the west, when all those Swedes, less successful Midwestern farm folks and draft dodgers crowded across the Minnesota to raise cash crops and kids where the Indians had just put down fresh roots.

There was a lot of guff, from partisans of both sides, as to the exact details leading up to what could be described as a hen-house raid or a massacre, depending. But there was no doubt old Little Crow had known what the Wasichu would do to his people once Wasichu blood had been spilled, and he'd been enough of a general to hit first, hard as hell, even though they said he'd led his young men chanting his death song, cursing the killers from the Shakopee band as he promised them they'd all have the shit kicked out of them by wintertime, and promising true.

Longarm had been busy killing other young men at the time further east, but troopers who'd been out this way said the Santee had fought like wildcats, more often on foot than their Dakota kinsmen, and more inclined to wear flowers than feathers in their hair as they came whooping and hollering or, more often and more scary, creeping on their bellies through the bluestem like murderous animated pots of prairie posies. Likely cornflowers that time of the year. The fighting had broken out in early August. By late September a whole lot of red and white folks had died and the Santee were in one hell of a mess. It's tough to call off a war with pissed-off white

92

men when they're winning. Most of the real fighters had lit out for Canada or the Dakotas, along with all their fighting chiefs. The seventeen hundred rounded up by Sibley and Pope, mostly women, children, and sissies, got marched to Fort Snelling, pelted along the way with stones, horse apples, and worse, to join their white admirers in watching the mass execution of the Santee Lincoln just couldn't let off. Then they were moved to their swell new reservation at Crow Creek in the Dakota Territory. The few who'd drifted back to these parts over the years, such as old Little Crow himself, had been gunned down on sight as "wild" Indians. So that meant Wabasha Chambrun, even named as he was after a Santee who'd gone over to the whites, couldn't be a full-blood. No full-blood of any nation would have been issued a homestead claim by the Bureau of Land Management, which meant . . .

"Where is it engraved on stone that any cuss named Chambrun has been issued doodly-shit by anybody?" Longarm asked his mount conversationally.

When the pony failed to answer he explained. "You ain't *supposed* to fence in and improve no quarter section of public land without you file a homestead claim, wait for its approval, and pay the modest filing fee. But if you've never filed, who'd be likely to notice you ain't paid the fee on a claim you never really filed, right?"

The pony might have opined that sounded sort of raw, if ponies had any say in such matters. But Longarm had arrested folks for far more casual views on property rights, and folks were forever gutting a mountain, logging a forest, or raising cash crops without getting arrested, paying taxes, or even being noticed by Land Management.

A couple of dark masses off to the right jumped off to run off, cussing Longarm and his mount in cow. Longarm nodded and thought about cattle barons, filing or not bothering to file on a taxable quarter-section home spread so they could graze and often fence the surrounding range as far as they could see from high up.

He started to rein in, thought better of it, and rode on, muttering, "Let's eat this cake a bite at a time, and look at some records by the cold light of logic, before we go asking a man late at night whether he hold lawful title to his spread or not."

A man who'd lie about one thing would likely lie about others, and if the late Jacob Weber of Switzerland could claim a whole section of prime bottom land free as his private paradise, after proclaiming himself and his family The Father, The Son, and the Holy Ghost, it only stood to reason a squatter with Indian blood might say most anything.

A heap of such folks had started to. Squatter-traders such as William Bent of Bent's Fort and mountain men like Kit Carson had married up with all sorts of Indian ladies from all sorts of nations, friendly or not, to produce all sorts of kids who tended to live red, white, or however the spirit moved them. So it was tough to say what the civil rights of, say, the Bent kids ought to be, with one grown son scouting for the army, a second living purely Quill in a tipi with the Cheyenne, and the one daughter married to a French-Canadian trader living white, even though he was said to be part Cree.

Longarm decided the confusing ancestry of Quanah Parker was most relevant to whether Wabasha Chambrun might or might not hold a valid homestead claim. Old Quanah, born to a white captive woman and her Comanche husband, who'd done the right thing by the pretty little thing, had started out as a holy-terror Comanche war chief, scared the shit out of his white kin, and then, after they'd scared the shit out of *him* a few times, recalled he was half white after all and joined the winning side. This appeared to give old Quanah the right to a government allotment as a tame Comanche, and at the same time to wheel and deal in Texas real estate as a white or at least part-white Texican business man. Longarm figured that was as fair as the law letting the pure white Belle Shirley Starr live Cherokee at Younger's Bend in the Indian Nation, just because she screwed Indian moonshiners as well as white horse thieves.

One of those spooked cows came tearing along the fence line at him, bawling fit to bust. Longarm swung Blaze out of the way as the full-grown steer tore past, spooked by something at least as terrifying up ahead.

That was something to study on in light as tricky as this.

That ink blot a pistol shot away in the moonlight appeared to be a clump of coppice, or second-growth saplings sprouting from the stumps of more serious cottonwoods cut a few years back, for corral poles or other such use most likely. Cottonwood wasn't worth much as firewood or construction timber. Longarm swung his mount out to his right, meaning to circle wide. As he heard the brush of metal against springly twigs he rolled out of his saddle, Winchester and all, to flatten in the tall grass as Blaze loped on a ways, and then stopped as if to ask how come those reins were dragging on the grass like so.

Blaze could wait. Longarm addressed the inky shadows ahead in a firm but friendly voice, calling out, "Evening. I'd be Deputy U.S. Marshal Custis Long, out this way on government business with fifteen rounds in the tube of this saddle gun I can aim as polite or as rude as your answer might call for."

There was a long silence. Then a youthful voice with just a whiff of that Swedish singsong in it called back, "Well, I'd be Gus Hansson, riding for the Rocking R, which you've been riding across, and Miss Helga figured you might be over this way."

Longarm stayed put, keeping his guard up and his saddle gun trained as he called back, "Who might this Miss Helga be, and how come she figured anything about me, since we've never been introduced?"

The kid who'd been hunkered in the coppice broke cover, turning out to be in his teens with batwing chaps and a hat big enough to house at least a small Indian family. "My boss lady is Miss Helga Runeberg, who's owned the Rocking R since her daddy's pony hit a prairie-dog hole at full gallop a couple of roundups back. Her home spread fronts on the Sleepy Eye trace six or eight miles to the southwest."

Longarm started to comment on all the grass the mysterious lady seemed to think she held rights to, if this was her drift fence, but that was between her and Land Management. So he kept his mouth shut and his ears open, and sure enough, the kid explained. "Earlier this evening some strange riders came by, allowing they was federal deputies looking to ride with you, since they'd heard you'd ridden out to the northwest of New Ulm."

That meant at least the Bedfords and those colored folks were off the hook, if what this kid said was true. Longarm got to his own feet, gun muzzle trained politely but still ready for anything. He heard young Hansson say, "After we told 'em we hadn't seen any sign of you and they'd rid on, Miss Helga told us to fan out far and fan out wide, so's to tell you they were looking for you and telling whoppers about being on the same side."

Longarm answered cautiously, "As a matter of fact, some lawmen from Saint Paul could be headed this way. How come your boss lady cast such doubts on their reasonable-sounding tale, Gus?"

The young cowhand shrugged and said, "Miss Helga's smart, I reckon, or mayhaps she recognized one or more of 'em from somewheres else. She can be sneaky too, when she's giving a hand enough rope to hang hisself. But why not ask her your ownself, Deputy Long? Miss Helga said the rider as caught up with you was to carry you on back to the big house so's you could tell her what you wanted us to do next about the big fibbers."

Longarm thought before he decided. "It's a tempting invite. But I'm already invited to supper with another lady in New Ulm, and I'd as soon go over some records at the county courthouse before I say what I want to do next with, to, or about anybody."

Young Hansson was close enough now so they could converse in quieter tones as he shrugged and said, "Suit yourself, but don't you never say I didn't relay her invite after warning you about them odd riders. I swear I didn't know who you were when first I spied you way out here in the middle of nowheres. How come you ain't on the county road where I expected to meet up with you, Deputy Long?"

Longarm explained, "I was afraid somebody less friendly might be expecting me to head back to town that way. You ain't the first who's told me or warned me I have so many admirers out searching for me by the light of the silvery moon,

Gus. You know those colored folks a mile or so up facing that other road?"

The local rider calmly asked, "Which darkies, the Conway family or the Bee Witch?"

Longarm blinked uncertainly and replied, "The folk I talked with looked more like a family than any sort of bees, or even witches. I heard some riders had been asking about me ugly from a colored boy about your age. Your turn."

Hansson said with certainty, "That sounds like one of the Conway boys. They're all right. We've told all the nesters along the bigger river we don't object to no quarter-section claims along the county road. For as long as they don't string bobwire more than a half mile southwest of the road, it helps our own drift wire hold Rocking R stock back from that dangerous river and spooky road travel."

Longarm dryly replied, "I'm sure your new neighbors find that a generous offer. I thought those Conways had to be on my side when they warned me some rascals were talking mean about me. Try that Bee Witch on me some more."

The white cow hand explained. "That's what they call this crazy old colored lady who dwells on a house raft and ranges her honey bees all along the banks of the river. When they ain't out foraging flowers they live in these white boxes, right on the raft with the Bee Witch herself. Ain't that a bitch?"

Longarm shrugged and said, "Takes all kinds to work this land of ours, I reckon. Is this floating beekeeper supposed to be dangerous?"

The cowhand shook his big hat. "Not to grown folk. I hear she threatens to hex kids who pester her or her bees. That's how come they call her the Bee Witch. They say she can threaten kids sort of scary with chicken claws, African goofer dust, and such. What might you want with an old crazy lady who keeps bees, Deputy Long?"

"They likely sell her honey for her in town at some food shop," Longarm decided. "Wabasha Chambrun is the one I'd sort of like to talk to, without those mystery riders noticing. I reckon I might get straighter answers once I go over some courthouse papers in the morning. But seeing as you seem to know so much about nesters over on this side of your considerable range, what can you tell me about that bunch?"

Gus Hansson said, "They're Sioux, part Sioux anyways, no matter what they say. I was still a toddler when Little Crow and his cruel Santee rose against us that time, but I was big enough to see what they'd done to the Atterbom twins and poor Ann Margaret Tollgren, left all bloody and dead with her skirts up around her waist, and damn their two-faced lies, I remember what a damn Sioux smells like, dead or alive, and that lying Chambrun and all his lying kids smell the same way, no matter what he says about being mostly white with a part-Osage woman!"

Longarm said soberly, "Indians allow they smell us as something different too. I ain't sure my own nose is educated enough to pick out a Santee from a distant Osage cousin, but like I said, I mean to go over some records before I call any man a liar."

Gus Hansson asked, "What do you do when you prove a man's a liar?"

To which Longarm could only reply, "Depends on what he's lied to me about, of course."

Chapter 13

Since first things had to come first, Longarm was rubbing down the widow woman's saddle brute in her stable when she caught up with them, lantern in hand, to say, "Oh, I was hoping it was you I heard out here. I'd about given up on you for the night. You said you'd be right back. I sure hope you like cold ham, Custis."

Longarm smiled sheepishly in the lantern light, and explained how he'd gotten sidetracked without ever getting a chance to interview Wabasha Chambrun at all. When she said she could fetch her part-time stable hand, an old Finn who lived just down the alley, Longarm told her, "I'm better than halfways done here, and there's no need to pester anyone else. You can see I've run some well water in this trough, but where might you be keeping your oats, Miss Ilsa?"

She set the light on a keg and hauled a feed sack from another stall as she said, "Barley and cracked corn. Minnesota oats command a premium price back East, and I wasn't planning on entering the Kentucky Derby with either of these ponies."

Longarm allowed barley and cracked corn made for a fair balance as he poured some feed in with the twists of hay he'd already shoved in Blaze's feed box. It wasn't until his hostess moved to pick up her lantern again that he noticed her informal costume. She hadn't been whistling Dixie when she said she'd about given up on him getting in any time tonight. But it would have been rude to tell a lady he could see so much of her through a nightdress with a lantern on the far side of it, so he never did. But she sure had swell legs for a gal with that much gray in her hair. Her gathered-at-the-neck outfit of ivory cotton flannel looked more modest as soon as she was holding her wan lantern between them again. Old gals living alone doubtless got so used to flouncing about the house informally that they tended to forget they looked half undressed to late-night visitors.

She told him he was unusually kind to riding stock as he finished rubbing old Blaze down with some sacking while the pony put away some fodder after being watered first. Longarm went on rubbing as he just shrugged and said, "I ain't all that kindly. I'm just more country than some townsmen who don't ride as serious, ma'am. Me and old Blaze here warmed up pretty good with some cross-country lopings in chill night air, and I'd like to borrow him some more tomorrow."

She naturally said Blaze was his to ride as often as he liked. So he naturally replied, "That's how come I don't want him lamed up with poorly tempered sinews, ma'am. Ride a Sunday horse serious, and let him rest up without a good rubdown, and he'll wind up the next day the way we do when we're out of shape and cut a cord of stove wood or do a couple of loads of laundry in our first rush of enthusiasm."

She laughed and said she knew what he meant, although she couldn't picture him doing even one load of laundry. Then she said something about heating up the coffee, and left the lantern for him as she headed back to her kitchen.

He draped his saddle blanket over one of the rails of one stall and his McClellan over another. He hung on to his saddle gun as he picked up that lantern and followed after old Ilsa.

She'd been wrong about the ham turning cold. It was at least lukewarm, thanks to her warming oven, and the fried potatoes she served with it hadn't gone greasy yet. As he dug in at her kitchen table he wasn't sure he wanted too much of that reheated but strong-smelling coffee. For he had a busy day ahead, his head was still buzzing with events of the day just ended, and it was going to be tough to fall asleep in a strange bed under the same roof as such a sweet smelling female in any case.

He could tell, even as she sat across from him with her matronly curves covered modestly enough by soft ivory folds, that she'd just had a hot bath and doused herself with plenty of lilac water after using some white vinegar to get her hair, or something, clean enough to eat off. But she wasn't acting flirty as she demanded he bring her up to date on his moonlight ride. When he told her he meant to check Wabasha Chambrun's homestead claim before giving the cuss enough rope, she looked puzzled and said, "I know for a fact he bought enough Glidden wire and staples to fence a full quarter section, Custis. Wouldn't even an Indian have to be awesomely stupid to think he could get away with simply squatting along a well-traveled county road?"

Longarm washed down some chewed-up ham and potatoes with her fine coffee before he replied. "How often might you ask to see the title deed of a homestead you're riding past on a visit to somewhere else? I'll ask at the courthouse come morning whether Minnesota follows common law on squatter's rights. A lot of states still do, and we're only talking about two years' difference if your luck holds out."

She said she had no idea what he was talking about. She'd said her folk had hailed from a different old country. So Longarm had to explain. "Back when Ben Franklin and the boys were inventing a whole new country, they still felt the need for some law and order. So they decreed that until such time as they passed new laws that might read different, the courts could go along with the precedents of old English common law. That's what you call what some judge and jury have already said a time or more, a precedent. If you refuse to buy ignorance of the law as an excuse, you got to let folks sort of know what to expect if they do the same things the courts have decided on in the past, see?"

She said she did, despite the dubious look in her big brown eyes, so he continued. "The doctrine of undisputed habitation, or squatter's rights, goes back before King William's Doomsday Book. For as law and order came out of the Dark Ages, it was tough to produce a written title search on such property as you might or might not have held a spell."

The Minnesota gal brightened and said, "Oh, they tell about

such things in the Sagas! The Norse tradition held that land belonged to the first man who'd drawn water and built a fire on it, as long as he was man enough to defend it."

Longarm nodded and said, "Defending it against the claims of any others was the sticking point in any such notions of land titles. It was tough at times to say who might have been first on a particular plot of ground. So the early courts held that any man who'd held his claim for seven years or more, undisputed by any others, likely had as good a claim to it as anybody."

She asked, "What about Indians, in the case of land on this side of the main ocean?"

He grimaced and said, "Now you're straying from common law into a can of historical worms. Whether this corner of Minnesota became so civilized by Indian treaty or criminal trespass is moot, with all the original Indians marched off to the Dakota Territory. As of, say, 1864 this has all been federal open range or taxable privately held land, depending. If Chambrun's been allowed to file a proper home-stead claim, despite his complexion, so be it. Five years after his claim's been approved by the Land Office, providing he doesn't mess up entirely, the land is his to keep, cherish, or sell at a profit as far as Uncle Sam cares."

She nodded. "But if they never filed, and just fenced off some open land on their own?"

Longarm said, "I told you I got to look up the local view on squatter's rights. But unless Minnesota law reads different, and specific, Chambrun and his kin get to keep that quarter section as their own as soon as they've held it seven years with nobody else disputing 'em."

Ilsa stared wide-eyed across the table. "I can see why you said it was only a matter of two years either way. But would they let an Indian pull a stunt like that, Custis?"

To which he could only reply with a shrug, "Depends on what you can prove an Indian, or vice versa, in a court of law, should that be your pleasure."

She looked mighty puzzled, even as she picked up the coffeepot to refill his cup. So he said, "No more coffee for me, thanks. It's tougher for some folks to decide who might be an Indian than it can be to decide who's colored. I ain't sure

I follow the logic myself, but in those courts as enforce color codes, it seems a person known to have any colored ancestry is colored. But the same folks who won't rent a room to an octoroon, with one colored grandparent, seem just as able to classify anyone less than half Indian as a white person with a little Indian blood."

"Then this Wabasha Chambrun could be a white man in the eyes of the law?"

Longarm shrugged. "Depends more on the B.I.A. than his biology. Chief Ross of the Cherokee was seven-eighths Scotch-Irish, and there's many a blue-eyed blonde drawing their government Indian allotment just by putting on a fringy shirt and lining up like the rest of their nation. Folks listed as Indians by the B.I.A. are identified as such by allotment number, tribal agency, and such. But there's nothing to prevent a member of a so-called friendly band from just going into town, getting a job, and forgetting the whole deal, no matter how much Indian blood he may or may not have in him. So saying what Chambrun says about a French-Canadian daddy is true, and if he's never been listed on paper as any particular sort of Indian, he's about as white as you or me, at least as far as federal law can prove."

She said she'd never heard such nonsense, and made as if to pour him some more coffee anyway. So he put a hand across the top of his empty cup. "Waste not, want not, Miss Ilsa. It ain't as if I don't admire your coffee. I just don't want to toss and turn all night, as I'm apt to with my mind filled with caffeine as well as a heap of other distractions!"

She sighed and said she knew what he meant, murmuring something about it having been over a year since last she'd felt really fulfilled in her lonely bed.

That was what womenfolk called getting laid, fulfilled, and hadn't she said her man had been dead longer than that?

Longarm tried to ignore the sudden tingle in his pants as he tried not to wonder too hard whether she'd made a slip or was out to tell him something. For a man could mess up either way at times like these. He had a good thing going already, with nobody in New Ulm so sure just where he was forted up after dark, and the sweet old widow woman was likely to think he

103

was lower than a sidewinder's belly button if he abused her generous hospitality by grabbing for a dessert she wasn't really offering.

On the other hand, Hell had no fury like a woman turned down once she'd offered, however delicately. So he didn't dare say he'd had all the supper he cared for and just wanted to go to bed before he had a better handle on her own bedtime aspirations.

He figured it might be safest to ask her whether she knew that other Swedish gal, Helga Runeberg, out at the Rocking R. He sensed he might have been safer asking about somebody else when his hostess flared. "I've seen her around town in her silly hat and buckskin skirts, the self-satisfied young snip! I might have known she'd been flirting with you since you'd been riding no more than ten miles from her door!"

Longarm had to laugh. "Hold on, Miss Ilsa, I've never laid eyes on the gal in question. I was more interested in her common sense than her looks."

The older woman didn't sound too sensible as she snapped, "Helga Runeberg hasn't got any common sense. Her poor father would turn over in his grave if he knew how she rides all over, unescorted, as carefree as one of her cowboys."

Longarm said, "It was one of her cowboys as told me his boss lady had said she was able to tell a real lawman from a fake lawman at first sight. I was hoping to save me a ride out her way with some educated guesswork as to how a carefree cowgirl might know so much about lawmen."

The widow woman shrugged inside her loose nightdress and replied, "I wouldn't put anything past Helga Runeberg. They do say she was sparking a married deputy sheriff till Pastor Lindorm heard about it. Maybe she knows a lot of lawmen in the Biblical sense. I don't really care to know her at all."

Longarm made a mental note to drop by the Rocking R the next time he was out that way, and surprised himself by having to stifle a real yawn he hadn't been expecting.

The widow woman noticed and said, "Good heavens, it is almost ten o'clock, and I'm not usually such a night owl myself. I suppose you must be anxious to get to bed, right?"

He allowed that was about the size of it as they both rose

from the table. He started to help her move the dishes to the drain board of her modern wet-sink, but she told him they could wait till she felt more in the mood for housework. So he didn't argue as he started to follow her out of the kitchen, Winchester in hand.

As she moved just ahead with her candlestick, she laughed and asked if he always went to bed fully armed. He told her he hardly ever got all the way in bed without leaning the Winchester in a handy corner and hanging his gunbelt over a bedpost. He assumed she was leading him to some guest room. So he was mildy surprised when they wound up in a perfumed chamber with a lot of Irish lace draped around the big fourposter.

Ilsa set the candlestick on a nearby bed table and softly asked, "Do you mind if I get undressed in the dark, Custis? I know it seems old-fashioned, but as I said before, I don't get to do this much anymore."

He figured the safest answer called for simply pinching out the candle without saying anything as the room was plunged in darkness.

He leaned his Winchester against the wall behind the bed table as he heard the soft rustle of cloth coming off and that odor of lilac water and vinegar grew stronger. He waited for her to shyly suggest it was all right for him to come to bed before he shucked his own gun, boots, and duds as calmly as he felt able, rolled in under the covers, and took the warm cuddly nakedness he found there in his own bare arms. Then as she sobbed, "Oh, Custis, I feel so low. Whatever must you think of me?"

He ran a friendly hand down her naked flank as he suggested he feel her somewhat lower, and then he kissed her firmly as she tried to cross her legs and say something dumb about what he was trying to do to a poor defenseless widow. Then he was doing it to her, and she was doing it back with considerable skill, as her poor embarrassed lips kept murmuring all sorts of accusations and excuses for what just came naturally at times like these.

He knew better than to say anything before he'd made her climax and allow she just might like it. So he tongued her ear

105

and humped her hard, with her big bare breasts crushed against his naked chest and one hand under her tailbone as he helped her bounce in time with his thrusts. She suddenly wrapped both legs around his waist to hug him further into her as she sobbed, "Oh, Custis, I'm really trying to respond to you, but it's been so long and you have to give a girl time to warm up!"

He told her to take all the time she wanted, since he wasn't going anywhere but in and out of her for the foreseeable future. But he still had to wonder, even as he came in her and just kept going with no need to change positions, what a gal this tigress was jealous of might be like in her own right!

But of course he never said so. For even as he was pleasuring her dog-style a good half hour later, old Ilsa was purring, as she arched her spine to take it deeper, that he was never going to get away from her now that she'd caught up with him at last.

She seemed to think he had just what it took to satisfy her hungry ring-dang-do. But he didn't see why. She felt tight as a schoolmarm as he just went on doing what came naturally in anybody that passionate.

He could only hope she was feeling natural as she suddenly shot off his erection, rolled over on her back, and pleaded with him to finish in her the more romantic way.

He felt mighty romantic as well, coming with her softer warm flesh crushed beneath his excited heaving body. But then she sort of spoiled the afterglow by murmuring, her lips against his bare shoulder and her hand clutching his balls right firmly, "Oh, Custis, I'm so happy, and I can't wait to see how surprised everyone will be when we post the bans with Pastor Lindorm!"

He didn't answer. He sensed it could be considered impolite to tell a gal she was *loca en la cabeza* right after you'd come in her. There'd be plenty of cold gray dawn to go into why a man who packed a badge had no call marrying up with anybody young or old, for richer, poorer, or whatever, till Mister Death grinned that spoilsport grin at all concerned.

He was sure she'd follow his drift when he told her about those department funerals he had to go to all the time. A lot of gals had, and hell, some of them had been young enough to marry up with if a man was ready to *do* dumb things like that.

Chapter 14

It was a caution how some folks could think so smart with their heads and so dumb with their glands. But by the time she'd fed him a swell breakfast in bed, Longarm had convinced the hot-natured Ilsa it might be wiser to keep their understanding a secret until he found out who was gunning for him and how come.

It hadn't been easy. The strong-willed widow woman had said she'd be proud to share the fate of her newfound true love. She'd only given in after Longarm managed to convince her she was being downright sneaky in the name of the law. They said the glamorous Confederate spy, Miss Belle Siddons, had enjoyed the sneaky part of her services to the Southern cause even more than screwing all those Union officers half to death. Lots of men enjoyed it better sneaky too.

After breakfast, a tub bath, and a blow job, Longarm ambled over to the Western Union to see if anyone else was excited about him. He found some messages waiting for him there care of the telegraph office.

Durango and the South Ute agency were still working on just who that so-called Calvert Tyger they'd buried and the kid who'd gone off the trestle into the San Juan might have been. Longarm was even more certain someone had been fibbing about that charred body registered as Tyger when he opened a message from his home office to discover his fellow deputies, Smiley and Dutch, had found two other rooming

107

house registers that claimed, in different handwriting, Calvert Tyger had spent some recent nights in other parts of Denver at the same time, before somehow moving on alive and well as far as any fool records showed. So some damned body, for some damned reason, seemed to be going around checking in and out for the night under the assumed name of a wanted man. It made no sense to Longarm, but on the other hand, he wasn't the asshole doing it!

It got worse when he stopped by the nearby sheriff's office to ask if those other federal deputies from Saint Paul had by any chance arrived and asked for him the night before.

The same deputy sheriff he'd talked to before said nobody from Saint Paul had arrived at all. Then he handed Longarm a telegram they hadn't mentioned at the Western Union, since it had been addressed to other lawmen, and said, "Looks as if all you federal men could be barking up the wrong tree here in Brown County."

Longarm scanned the wire from the Texas Rangers, and heaved a vast weary sigh. For according to Texas, another of those recorded hundred-dollar treasury notes from the Fort Collins robbery had surfaced at a bank in Amarillo.

As he handed the message back, Longarm said, "Try her this way. A bank in any part of the country would have that list of serial numbers and money-changers who might give a shit. But nobody making change in a gambling hall or house of ill repute would have that list or care where the money came from as long as it was good."

The local lawman answered dubiously, "A hundred-dollar bill does stand out in a crowd, you know."

Longarm nodded. "I just said that. Any card dealer or crib gal presented with such paper would doubtless ask the floor boss or madam to okay it. But without that list, all the smartest eye could detect would be whether the note was genuine or not. Once they changed it for the high roller or low-lifer, they might or might not take it to their own bank for safekeeping. The odds are just as good they'd pass it on to some other business folks as rent, liquor-bill payment, or whatever. So there's just no saying how many hands any of these fool bills might have passed through before they were spotted by some sharp-eyed banker such as P. S. Plover around the corner."

The deputy sheriff shrugged and said, "I'll be damned if I see what we're arguing about then. I just said it may not mean a thing that a single one of them stolen treasury notes turned up here in New Ulm. I may have wax in my ears. But didn't you just agree with me?"

Longarm nodded soberly. "I surely did, up to a point. I can go along with that one note from Fort Collins just sort of finding its way here through a whole chain of innocent hands, if you'd like to tell me how come somebody seems so anxious to keep me from questioning your apparently innocent county residents about it. By the way, might either Israel Bedford of Wabasha Chambrun be registered to vote this fall here in Brown County?"

The deputy sheriff said the ones to ask about that would be over at the county clerk's across the square. So that was where Longarm turned up next. The older gent in charge reminded Longarm of what young Henry, back at the Denver office, was likely to look like in twenty years if he didn't watch out. But the skinny, balding, prune-lipped cuss seemed friendly enough as he scanned Longarm's badge and identification and said, "Figured you'd be along most any time now. Two other lawmen were here just this morning, asking if you'd been by."

Longarm put his billfold away with a puzzled smile. "It ain't considered polite to poke about another lawman's jurisdiction without letting him know you're in town, and I know for a fact the gents of whom we speak never checked in with the sheriff across the way. What might they have looked like and what sort of badges might they have flashed?"

The country clerk frowned thoughtfully and replied, "I never asked to see no badges. That might have been why they never offered to show me any. As to what they looked like, one was tall and the other short. They were both about your age and dressed like undertakers who punched cows or vice versa. Is that any help?"

Longarm got out a couple of smokes as he mused, half to himself, "Two deputies riding out of the same federal district court as me describe about the same way. But I can't see

Smiley and Dutch behaving so unprofessional. If my boss sent them all the way to New Ulm for a damn good reason, they'd have strode right into your sheriff's office to ask about me, knowing I'd have been there ahead of 'em if I was anywhere in this county."

He thought some more as he got both their cheroots going with a wax Mexican match. Then he shook out the light. "Well, since they seem to be looking for me, I'll let them worry about who they might be until they catch up with me and I can just ask. What I'm here about is voter registrations. To be specific, I'd like to know whether two different Brown County boys who seem to have handled the same suspicious money might be on your books as registered resident voters."

The older man proved he was worth what they paid him by nodding soberly and replying without hesitation, "I know who you mean and they are. Israel Bedford voted in the last election, here in Brown County. That Chambrun cuss just signed up this spring. We had to let him, even if he does look Sioux, because he packs a U.S Army discharge, honorable, and other government documentation indicating he must be a white man, or at least a U.S. citizen."

Longarm raised a thoughtful brow. "Regular army discharge, or one of those certificates they give Indian scouts after a single campaign?"

The old-timer snorted in disgust. "I fought under Pope in the east and west, dad-blast your respect for your elders, and I guess I know an honorable discharge, U.S. Army, when I see one they gave somebody else. Chambrun's says he did a postwar hitch with the Ninth Cav as a trooper, not a scout. Ain't the Ninth supposed to be one of those colored outfits? Chambrun don't look colored to me. He looks like a sonovabitching treacherous Sioux, and some old boys who know say they heard him talking to his woman in that very lingo one day here in town. Ain't that a bitch?"

Longarm blew a thoughtful smoke ring. "The complexion or conversational habits of a particular homesteader are none of my beeswax as long as he don't bust no federal laws they pay me to enforce. You say he had other official papers to show you when he was here to register to vote this fall?"

The clerk nodded. "His homesteading permit, from the Land Office. He had to offer some proof he had a legal address here in Brown County, didn't he?"

To which Longarm could only reply, "Reckon he did, and I reckon you just answered a whole lot of other questions I was fixing to ask about Wabasha Chambrun. Like I said, it's none of my beeswax how a homesteader who talks Santee to his *wiyeh* may or may not have convinced the War and Interior Departments he's more white than, say, Sitting Bull. If he holds a homestead claim he holds a homestead claim, meaning he does seem to have a permanent legal address, which leads to more interesting questions, such as which old boy, Bedford or Chambrun, would be hurt most by being unable to account for that hundred-dollar treasury note."

The county clerk showed he was up on county gossip by observing that he'd heard the mysterious bill they were talking about was good for its face value in silver specie. Longarm nodded grimly and replied, "That was doubtless why the robbers took it at gunpoint. I aim to ask Chambrun where he got it, then ask on back some more, till I meet up with somebody who just can't convince me he came by it innocently!"

They shook on it, and Longarm headed back to Ilsa Pedersson's to see if she'd loan Blaze out to him again. This time he meant to make straight for the Chambrun homestead, and the day was still young enough to make it well this side of sundown.

As he strode along the sunny side of the street an old colored woman with a wheelbarrow filled with garden truck came out of an alley to ask him if she'd make it to the river in time.

When he politely got out his pocket watch and asked in time for what, she explained she aimed to sell her swell fresh vegetables to the steamboat passengers headed on up the Minnesota to Montevideo. When she allowed the steamboat would be putting into New Ulm around three that afternoon, he assured her she was way early. It might not have been kind to tell her how early. She likely didn't know how to read and write either. Longarm got along better than some of his kind with folks who still failed to grasp the Victorian concept that time was money. Recent slaves, perhaps because they'd been

111

slaves, could usually grasp the notion something was fixing to happen this morning, this afternoon, or at least sometime today. Indians tended to get surly when you tried to pin them down to the exact week in a moon they'd agreed on earlier.

He figured the old colored lady might sell some of her produce by the landing, or at least sit in the shade, enjoying the change in her daily chores, for the next four hours or more. He wondered idly, as he strode on, whether Wabasha Chambrun and his family kept track of time the way he'd have had to in the army, or the way his wife had likely learned about such matters . . . where?

Growing up Indian had gotten complicated since the first squaw men had married up with gals such as Miss Pocahontas. She hadn't been the first such gal who'd liked to dress up like a white lady and wound up treated to a Christian funeral. On the other hand, some old mountain men who'd settled down with Indian gals had wound up more Indian than some Indians, fluent as hell in the lingo of their in-laws and taking Wakan Tonka more seriously than they'd ever taken the Wasichu Good Book, and even fighting against their own kin on the side of their adopted race. So when you got right down to cases, there was just no saying how much Indian blood old Chambrun or even his Santee-speaking wife might really have. For it wouldn't be polite to ask a suspect to open wide so you could examine his teeth, and that wasn't foolproof proof in any case. That anthropology gal who studied Indian skulls had told Longarm there were even full-bloods who didn't have those concave backsides to their damned front teeth. There was no one thing that could prove or disprove more than a general impression. Defining an Indian from, say, a Swede was a lot like defining beauty. You could say at a glance whether a gal was pretty or ugly, but there was no exact line you could draw with all the pretty gals on one side and all the ugly on the other. That was doubtless why they said beauty was in the eye of the beholder, or how a cuss some saw as an Indian could file a homestead claim as an old soldier with an honorable discharge and never mind who he wanted to raise his family with.

Turning the corner near the Pedersson place, Longarm noticed two cow ponies, saddled with double-rigged ropers,

112

tethered to a rose-covered picket fence in the sun when there was a thornless hitching post in the shade just a few yards down, closer to Ilsa Pedersson's front yard. Longarm glanced thoughtfully at the house the roses went with. He couldn't see any front door. The house faced another way entirely. So what were those two ponies doing there in a sort of uncomfortable limbo?

Longarm knew from his own romantic past that a gent paying a call on a lady with a rep to worry about might not want to tether a mount smack out front. On the other hand, he'd seldom come pussyfooting for some broad daylight slap-and-tickle aboard two ponies at once.

Moving catty-corner to the shady side, Longarm crawfished back to an alley entrance and did some serious pussyfooting of his own until he'd circled wide to approach Ilsa Pedersson's property on its blind side. He rolled over her plank fence, screened from the only window on that side by some white lilac, and moved in fast on his feet. He knew how tough it was to see out through that frosted glass since he'd been shaving on the far side of it. He hadn't thought at the time to see whether old Ilsa kept it locked or not. When he reached it, to find it level with his shoulders as he stood in yet another flower bed, he was able to slip the blade of his pocket knife under the sash and lever it up a crack.

As he did so he heard somebody else suck in their breath, too close for comfort, just on the other side. So he hunkered down and hugged the whitewashed siding as, sure enough, somebody inside tried to raise the same damned sash, muttering a puzzled remark about damned kids with sling shots.

The man inside gave up trying to raise the swollen wood sash as soon as he had it high enough to bend down and peer out the six-inch slit he'd managed, bawling, "I see you, you little shit! Cut it out or I'll tell you mamma on you, hear?"

Longarm didn't answer. He knew he was no little shit. So it seemed safe to say the cuss he'd startled with a sudden creak of window sash was just bluffing as he peered out at nothing much. Longarm's Stetson hat was just below his field of vision. Longarm knew he'd guessed right when the man

113

inside snorted, "Kids ought to go to school all summer, damn their eyes!" and slammed the frosted glass shut again.

Longarm figured he'd been in there taking a leak. He had no idea who the proddy cuss might have been. Ilsa had said she peddled bobwire and other hardware from her house. But why would, say, a retail merchant or homesteader tether catty-corner across the way instead of smack out front?

"Didn't want us to notice he'd come calling," Longarm muttered as he moved along the shady side of the house. "It gets even spookier when you consider that second pony. It don't add up as a rival for a pretty widow gal's favors, and a man on more innocent beeswax wouldn't worry about nosy neighbors while calling on a business woman during business hours with a chaperon in tow!"

Longarm eased around a rear corner, gingerly rose for a cautious peek, and saw nobody was in Ilsa's corner pantry. Better yet, she'd opened the pantry window from inside to cool a couple of fresh baked pies on her broad sill.

They were talking in the kitchen. They seemed to be talking about *him*. For one male voice was saying, "Of course there's been no sign of that Denver boy out back. You'd have heard this here scattergun going off if he was within range of yonder back door. Get back up front and cover the front door like we agreed, you nervous ninny!"

Another male voice sort of whined, "I guess I got a right to feel nervous, knowing they're expecting just the two of us to take out a gunslick with his rep, and I still say I heard something outside when I was in the crapper just now!"

The one who appeared to be the boss, the one covering the most likely entrance with a shotgun, raised his voice a tad as he insisted, "Get back to your damn post and stay there till I tell you different, whether by word of mouth or gunshot. I swear I was a fool to let them saddle me with such an itchy greenhorn!"

Longarm worked faster, taking advantage of the noise as boot heels clumped sullenly off through the frame house. He slid the pies silently aside and eased his long frame over the sill as smoothly, and as noisily, as a weasel slipping into a hen house.

114

Then he was over by the pantry door, six-gun in his big right fist as he gingerly inched the door open just a crack. The first thing he saw, with a stiffled sigh of relief, was Ilsa Pedersson in a far corner, bound and gagged but seated upright in one of her kitchen chairs. He could tell by her scared staring eyes that she saw him as well. There was no way to tell her not to look his way with such an interested expression. So he was more chagrined than surprised when some cuss he couldn't see gruffly demanded, "What are you staring at like that, pretty lady?"

Longarm had little choice but to kick the door all the way open and blaze away as the startled jasper near the stove with that ten-gauge tried in vain to swing its muzzle up in time. For nobody with a pistol and a lick of sense tried to take a man with a ten-gauge alive in a close-quarters fight. So Longarm nailed him twice in the chest to sit him uncomfortably on the hot stove while he blew a hole in Ilsa's pressed-tin ceiling without really knowing what he might be aiming all that buckshot at. Then he just fell forward off his hot seat, too dead to notice his pants were on fire.

Longarm didn't care either. For sure enough, just as he'd spun into another corner, facing the hall door, it popped open to let a somewhat taller and younger gunslick enter, a Colt '74 in each fist as he yelled, "Hot damn! Did we get him?"

Longarm put three rounds in him and got out his derringer backup as he wearily replied, "Not yet," then moved in to see what he'd done to that one. The younger one lay across the threshold with his spurred boots in Ilsa's kitchen and the rest of him making a mess on her hall runner. As Longarm hunkered to feel for a pulse his victim croaked, "Is that you, Alabam?"

Longarm softly replied, "Yep. How did we know that lawman might be staying here?"

The dying stranger sighed and murmured, "Don't you remember? It was your grand notion to ask around town about that black pony with a white blaze. When the kid heard it was kept by a widow who lived all alone, you were the one who said it surely sounded like old Longarm's wet dream!"

Longarm smiled thinly and muttered, "They told us true

about the horny rascal, didn't they? By the way, old son, who told us?"

There came no answer. Longarm felt the downed man's throat again and then, since the smoke was getting bad by now, he got back up to go pour a pitcher of what turned out to be fruit juice over the smoldering body spread out face-down by the stove. It sure smelled funny in the end. He threw open the back door as well as another window, and moved to cut Ilsa out of her pigging string bonds as he said, "Sorry about that dessert topping, honey. Thought it was water."

The widow gal, who'd been baking up a storm when they'd burst in on her, removed the wad of dishrag from her own mouth as she gasped, "I was afraid you'd never get to *me*, you brute! Let me up! I have to pee so bad my back teeth are floating!"

So he let her run for it, and just managed to reload and pin his own badge to his own chest by the time that deputy sheriff and a quartet of town constables showed up out back, their own guns drawn.

Longarm stepped out on the back porch, holding up a hand for some decorum as he saw other men, boys, and at least a few gals stampeding onto the Pedersson property. He declared, "I want you New Ulm lawmen to keep this growing crowd out of Miss Ilsa's flower beds." Then he motioned to the county deputy. "You'd best come on in and tell me whether two gents I just shot were the same ones as were asking so many questions about me earlier."

The deputy sheriff followed Longarm inside, marveling, "Whatever has Miss Ilsa been cooking in here? Smells like candied ham mixed up with burnt wool, for Pete's sake!"

Longarm said that was about the size of it as he rolled the short one over with a boot tip. The county lawman stared soberly down at the dead man's blankly staring face and firmly declared, "That's the senior deputy from Saint Paul. How come you shot him, Deputy Long?"

Longarm answered tersely, "Had to. Got an eyewitness. I got me another one over here by this other doorway. Miss Ilsa may have heard him confess they'd been sent after me by name. He died before I got him to say who they were working for. But I'm going to be mighty surprised if our Saint Paul federal office sent either. You naturally asked to see their badges and credentials when they called on you before?"

The deputy sheriff smiled down uncertainly and allowed, "This taller one was introduced as a junior federal man, but to tell the pure truth, nobody asked to see no papers, once that older one flashed what surely looked like a badge pinned to his wallet."

They went back in the kitchen. Longarm hunkered down to gingerly probe the charred pants of the dead man by the stove until he found a singed and juice-soaked wallet. As the local deputy watched bemused, Longarm opened it up to expose a badge of German silver and some rather official-looking identification. Then he muttered, "Mail-order badge. Sold by a Saint Lou novelty house for the use of kids, so-called private outfits, and pests like these. I see he filled out these lodge membership cards under the name of John Singleton Mosby. Reckon he thought Smith and Jones had been used up."

The Minnesota deputy frowned thoughtfully and asked, "Wasn't old Johnny Reb Mosby the Confederate raider we used to call the Gray Ghost?"

Longarm nodded wearily and said, "I arrested an owlhoot rider who said he was Paul Revere one time, and the hell of it was, the name on his birth certificate really was Paul Revere. But this old boy's not young enough to be named after the real Colonel Mosby of wartime fame."

The Minnesota lawman decided, "You'd still have to admire a rebel raider a heap to name yourself after him, wouldn't you?"

Longarm soberly replied, "That's about the size of it, and they've sent me to backtrack a gang of unreconstructed rebel admirers who've raided considerably, after starting out in these parts to begin with!"

The deputy sheriff removed his hat to scratch his head as he sighed and said, "I'm missing something here. I know they all say Calvert Tyger, Brick Flanders, and them other Galvanized Yankees started out in these parts years ago. But didn't you say yourself both them crazy rascals are supposed to have been burnt up in rooming house fires?"

Longarm nodded and said, "More than once in Tyger's case. On the other hand, the last I heard, Colonel John Singleton Mosby was still alive and full of piss and vinegar, no matter how dead this namesake at our feet seems to be right now."

Ilsa Pedersson seemed awfully pensive when she finally came back out. Longarm didn't see why. He was the only one who knew for certain where she'd just been, and it wasn't as if he'd never noticed she had the usual entrances and exits down yonder.

Some of her neighbors pitched in to help tidy up as the local law hauled the bodies off to be photographed and stored in a cool place in the hopes somebody might come forward to claim or at least hazard a guess as to who they might belong to.

Longarm didn't think a widow gal living alone would want all her neighbors to know she liked it dog-style. So he made sure nobody else was listening when he offered to spring for a new hall runner and some ceiling tin. But she just got all flustered and ran up front again with her apron over her red face. So he figured, as soon as he had the chance to do so quietly, it might be best to slip his saddle and possibles off her property and over by the boat landing. For it was getting late to ride Blaze clean out to that Chambrun place to begin with, and there seemed to be at least one member of the gang left in New Ulm. The one that dying jasper had only named as "the kid" was not only out there somewhere, but had the added edge of being the only one who knew all the faces involved!

Chapter 15

The Minnesota got a mite tricky to navigate above, say, Mankato. But the little sternwheel steamboat, *Moccasin Blossom*, carried some local freight and passengers every other day, and this turned out to be one of those days. And since two can keep a secret if one of them is dead, Longarm didn't tell anyone in town what he planned to do next. He found that same old colored lady over by the boat landing, and gave her four bits to smuggle his baggage on board, disguised as garden truck, once he'd had a sneaky conversation with the little tub's purser in the shade of a riverside sycamore.

The purser was the officer in charge of who got to ride upstream with them or not. He allowed his skipper would be proud to assist a federal man on a secret mission, and even suggested the best way for Longarm to board without that mysterious "kid" noticing.

So just before they shoved off again, a tall figure sporting a crewman's billed cap and packing a big gunny sack on one shoulder moved up the gangplank with the purser and some of his other men.

Longarm might have chanced the gang not thinking to plant anyone aboard a steamboat long before he'd even thought of using it to get past them on the northbound county road. But when the purser said he'd be safer from prying eyes on the Texas deck than in the passenger salon, Longarm was quick to take him up on it. But he didn't get to shake and smoke with the bewhiskered older skipper in the pilothouse until after they'd backed out into the main current and swung the *Moccasin Blossom*'s blunt bows up the main channel, such as it was. A steamboat skipper had too many other worries on his mind to stand at the wheel staring straight ahead. So once he'd warned his younger pilot to mind that slick to starboard they were already swinging wide of, he had the time to accept one of Longarm's cheroots and hear him out.

Once Longarm had tersely explained his desire to be put ashore where he could hire another pony and approach the Chambrun homestead from the unexpected upstream side, the skipper nodded and told him his best bet would be the Kellgren spread, a good-sized cattle operation just the other side of the county line.

When Longarm quietly replied that seemed a tad far, considering the hour, the skipper insisted, "It's less'n twenty statute miles and we'll have you there in no time."

Longarm smiled thinly. "Wasn't worried about getting that far by steam power. Still have to get back by horse power, and like I said, that old sun ball's already halfway down the sky bowl. Don't you reckon any outfits further down this river could have even a mule they'd be willing to hire out?"

It was the purser, who got to gossip more with the locals, who horned in from the other side. "Gunnar Kellgren and his outfit are all true-blue white. That's more than can be said for the trash along the west bank from the Bedford place up to the county line. I swear I don't know what's come over the Land Office, the way they let niggers and even Quill Indians file for whole quarter sections of those old Santee killing grounds!"

Longarm glanced out the glass to his left. He had to admire the rate at which the *Moccasin Blossom* was overtaking and passing willows, sycamores, and such along the chalky banks. Further out the land rose balder, with good-sized rises hither and yon in the near-to-far distance. He said he'd heard the Santee had held the west banks of the Minnesota from New Ulm to Big Stone Lake, close to two hundred miles upstream, before that ill-advised raid on that poultry farm.

The purser nodded. "Their strip was ten miles wide as well, leaving the shiftless redskins nigh two thousand square miles of hunting grounds, after which they were allowed to join their Sioux cousins over in the Dakota for the twice yearly buffalo drives. They threw that all away for a basket of eggs and some scalps to brag on whilst they fried them!"

Longarm doubted they wanted to hear there might have been a little more than that to the Santee Rising of '62. He asked to hear some more about the new nesters moving onto the lost Santee reserve.

They were rounding a willow-covered sand bar now, so Longarm had to look sharp out ahead as the skipper grumbled, "There's one of 'em, tied up to that snag near the bank, the crazy old crone!"

When the sun-silvered jumble of planking and shingles suddenly resolved in Longarm's eyes, he saw it was a tumble-down shack perched atop a log raft someone had moored in the backwater formed by a mass of waterlogged driftwood along the west bank. As a raggedy jet-black figure came out on deck to flap crow-like sleeves at them and scream like a rabbit caught in a bobwire fence, the skipper dryly went on. "That'd be the Bee Witch. Crazy old nigger gal. They say she keeps a young Santee breed in bondage, as if to make up for her own misspent youth as a slave."

The purser objected mildly. "They say that kid they call Sweet Sioux sells honey in town on her own. Paddles down to New Ulm in a painted canvas canoe about twice a month."

The skipper shrugged and said, "So I've heard. They still say the Bee Witch has some hold on the Indians. They call her something like *witch* in Sioux."

Longarm thought, brightened, and said, "Might that be more like *witko*, sir?"

The skipper decided, "Close enough. Do you speak Sioux, Deputy?"

Longarm modestly replied, "Not hardly. But from the little I have been exposed to, the Sioux-Hokan dialects ain't half as complicated as Na-Déné, or what you'd call Apache or Navajo. The folks who'd as soon call themselves Nakota, Dakota, Lakota, and such talk dialects with a heap of the same notions about vocabulary and grammar as we follow. So *witko* would come out as 'crazy,' not 'witch,' in Santee."

As they passed the dark figure shaking her upraised black fists at them, Longarm smiled gently and remarked, "She's sure acting *witko*, ain't she? Lord knows what a Navajo might call her. They don't abide by our notions of lingo at all. I mean, you ask a Santee or Omaha what his dog is, and he'll say right out it's his *shunka*. But a Navajo will want you to tell him exactly which of his dogs, doing what, to whom, you might be asking about. They got whole different words for a man's dog, a woman's dog, running, scratching, and so on, see?"

The skipper exchanged glances with his purser and replied, "If you say so. When Indians want to talk to me, they'd best talk plain American if they know what's good for 'em. But I can see why Uncle Sam might send someone who speaks some Sioux to question old Wabasha Chambrun. Lord knows you don't get straight answers out of the shifty-eyed cuss in English!"

Longarm asked, "You mean you know Chambrun personal?"

The skipper shrugged. "We've delivered some heavy hardware to him now and again."

As if to back his word, a distant sunflower windmill flashed a suddenly turning metal blade at them above the tree tops along the shore, and the skipper pointed the cheroot Longarm had given him and observed, "There's the Chambrun spread now, off to the northwest on the far side of the county road. You can't see anything but the new windmill we delivered this spring from here."

Longarm took a drag on his own smoke and let it all out before he observed, "Well, the Land Office does expect a homesteader to make taxable improvements on his claim before it's his to have and to hold free and simple. But them patent windmills cost more than your average pony, don't they?"

The skipper nodded soberly. "They do indeed and I follow your drift, now that you've told me about Chambrun paying for that riding stock with a hundred-dollar treasury note. I fear I'm simply not able to say how Chambrun paid for that patent windmill and all the other fancy trimmings we delivered there this spring. It was sent prepaid from Chicago Town. We just ran it up from the railroad back where you just came aboard. Hardly worth putting in."

The purser volunteered, "Rocks. Chambrun staked his claim along one of the worst places to put in along this already rocky enough old river. Ain't that just like an Indian? Even the other breeds and freed darkies in these parts know enough to consider river traffic as well as that muddy wagon trace along the damn bank."

The skipper nodded. "Damned right. Even dumb Swedes who can't speak English consider the lay of the land before they file a homestead claim along a damned river. Land near a good landing site is sure to rise in value as this valley fills up over time."

The purser said, "Lord, I sure wish I'd had the sense to file a claim across from that new railroad town called Fairfax! For nobody expects a man to waste time and effort plowing land where railroad and river traffic meet and grain elevators sprout like mushrooms!"

They were already passing that distant windmill. As Longarm kept staring at it wistfully, considering how far back he'd have to track as this day grew ever shorter, the skipper said, "Chambrun and his brood of Lord knows how many little Indians will get to plow until they're old and gray back yonder. Some of the boys who helped them haul that windmill gear and bobwire rolls ashore say the land the fool breed has claimed isn't much less rocky as you get back from the river. They spotted more than one outcropping in the forty-odd acres cleared so far. So it's safe to say that when you see rocks poking up out of a field, the soil can't be all that deep anywhere else!"

The purser suggested, "Mayhaps they're planning on a mining operation instead of cattle or wheat?"

Longarm didn't feel the call to chew that bone. He knew the old Santee reserve had been surveyed for minerals of any value before the B.I.A. had offered it to them in exchange for their original woodlands closer to the Great Lakes. The most valuable thing this corner of Minnesota had to offer was dirt, rich prairie dirt that grew crops better where it lay deepest, and surely even an illiterate would be likely to look over any land he meant to file a homestead claim on before he ever signed his X. So what in thunder might have made the oddly prosperous Wabasha Chambrun feel he just had to homestead a quarter section with rocks sticking out of it and no decent boat landing on the nearby river?

When he voiced his puzzlement, the skipper just shrugged and told him, "You just said at least some Indians don't think the way we do. The Santee could have kept all the land you see off to the west if they'd only behaved halfway sensible. The B.I.A. had built trading posts and even schools and dispensaries for 'em, at two different agencies, so's they wouldn't have to travel too far. Old Little Crow and the other chiefs got to live in fine frame houses, just like us white folks, only better. They paid no rent and got their roofs fixed free when they leaked. So what did they do, just because they had to wait a little longer for their government handouts in wartime, in the middle of summer after a good spring hunt, for Gawd's sake?"

The purser explained, "We were working together on an earlier and slower steamboat called the *Saint Anthony* at the time. We were the ones hauling army supplies up to Fort Ridgely after Little Crow and his warriors tried in vain to take it, the poor ragged assholes!"

The skipper snorted, "Flowers in their hair, for Gawd's sake. Hit all along the river treacherous and dirty, with most of the first whites killed the poor fools who'd thought they were on good terms with the Indians."

The purser grumbled, "*Trying* to be on good terms, you mean. The two-faced redskins got the first white settlers they killed into a friendly shooting match, then attacked the poor simps once their guns were empty and it was the Santee's turn to shoot!"

The skipper growled, "They slaughtered four hundred whites the first day. More than half of 'em women and children. Fifty-odd whites near the downstream agency, who'd never trusted Sioux they knew better, got away to spread the alarm. Just in time. Scared settlers flocked in to Fort Ridgely on the far side of the river. Forty-eight of the soldiers had already been ambushed and scalped, leaving a garrison of thirty troopers to protect over two hundred scared-skinny civilians with no earthworks or even a stockade betwixt them and the so-called friendly Indians!"

Longarm could read, and had read some about the events that were so vivid to the older men after all those years. So he was the one who said, "By the time Little Crow worked up the nerve to attack Fort Ridgely, they'd been reinforced by another hundred or more real soldiers, along with some twenty-odd civilian volunteers who did have time to throw up some breastworks, and let's not forget the modest but ferocious field artillery pieces on hand. I read someplace the bursting shells killed lots of Santee."

The skipper grumbled, "You'll have read in other books how the only white killed three days later down by New Ulm was a young girl caught in the cross-fire too. But old-timers who were there make it thirty-six whites killed and most of New Ulm in ashes by the time the Sioux gave up. The whites gave up too, and stampeded down the river to Mankato, at the big bend, as soon as they dared break cover!"

The purser, who seemed to enjoy figuring numbers, said, "Eight hundred or more whites killed outright, a hundred and seven whites captured, along with a hundred and sixty-odd breeds and friendlies who'd been treated just as rough by the time they were rescued. At least thirty thousand whites in all had been pushed off their homesteads, dead or alive, and they figure less than half the white gals raped ever owned up to it when they were taken back from the savage bastards!"

Longarm muttered he'd read there'd been some argument as to just how many of those hundreds of condemned ringleaders had deserved to hang or not. He knew what these old Minnesota white boys would have to say about the Episcopal missionary Henry Whipple, who got Abe Lincoln to commute the sentences for all but the likes of a brave called Cut Nose, who bragged from the scaffold how he'd killed Wasichu men, women, and children until his arm got too tired to kill any more. Old Billy Vail hadn't sent him over this way to find out how folks felt about the long-gone Santee. Although he'd have to take that smoldering hatred into account as he tried to decide the guilt or innocence of an odd homesteader with what seemed at least a few Quill Indian in-laws.

Chapter 16

The Kellgren spread had its own steamboat landing, man-made but natural-looking at first glance. They'd graded the slope gentler than the river current would have, and then paved it with cobbles to keep it that way. The *Moccasin Blossom* didn't tie up there to put one man ashore. They simply nosed in as far as they could, and swung the gangplank the rest of the way so Longarm could run down it with his saddle and possibles on one shoulder and make it to dry ground with a squishy skip and jump. Some passengers who hadn't known he was aboard came out on deck to watch bemused. But nobody seemed excited about his getting off out there in what seemed the middle of nowhere.

The skipper had told Longarm he'd find the Kellgrens a tribe of amiable Vikings playing cowboys, with anyone who wanted to play Indian well advised to stay the hell away from them.

But in point of fact they didn't turn out that odd. Longarm had no sooner toted his McClellan over to that country road than he was met by a couple of kids in their teens on cow ponies almost as blond as they were. When they asked who he was and why he'd come, Longarm flashed his badge and explained his need for the hire of a horse.

They said he'd have to ask their elders over to the house, where he'd be just in time for coffee and cake if he didn't want to upset their mamma. One of them took the McClellan from Longarm's shoulder before he could slip the Winchester from its saddle boot. But as it turned out, they were just trying to be helpful.

When they broke through the last of the riverside timber and got to the country road, Longarm saw the three-strand fence on the far side extended well over the usual quarter mile in either direction. The mighty small town or mighty big homespread atop the rise ahead was at least a full furlong from the gate. Being afoot, Longarm politely opened and shut the gate for the two young riders. When he commented on the size of their spread on the way up to the white-trimmed cluster of housing and outbuilding, the one packing his saddle for him bragged on how big their old man preferred his surroundings. The kid said they'd come west from a regular-sized homestead in Wisconsin after making it pay but getting to feeling crowded. When Longarm mildly observed they seemed to have way more than a quarter section fenced out this way, the other kid bragged on the open range to the west they grazed as well. The one with Longarm's saddle explained, "Pappa paid cash for already proven claims, half a dozen in all. It was just after Custer and his boys got wiped out further west. Pappa read in the same papers how these more Indian-free parts were getting wiped out by grasshoppers. So he figured nesters who'd been grasshoppered broke might be willing to sell out cheap."

The Kellgren kid who'd bragged on their herd chimed in. "Them bugs were still at it when we hauled in here back in '77. You never did see such hungry grasshoppers. They'd eat all the leaves off all them trees back yonder and grazed all the grass you see now, right down to the bare dirt. Mamma and the girls had to hang the laundry to dry indoors that first summer, lest them greedy bugs chew holes in the sheets for the starch!"

Longarm quietly observed he'd seen grasshopper plagues. They occurred about every seventh year between the Rockies and the Mississippi. The kid who'd bragged on their grazing told him cows were safer to raise than crops in grasshopper country. For in a pinch a hungry cow could graze on grasshoppers, and the grass grew back thick as ever once the plague had passed.

The kid packing his saddle waved expansively to the north

127

and said, "Both the Linderboms and Ericssons lost their newly planted orchards as well as cash crops by the time Pappa made 'em an offer. He paid 'em more than he really needed to, seeing they were our sort of folk. They were down to living on eggs, since chickens are the only stock that really thrives on grasshoppers alone."

Longarm idly asked who they'd bought out to the south. The kid with the saddle innocently replied, "Oh, we got the Alden and Marvin spreads for next to nothing."

Longarm didn't ask why. Anglo-Saxon country folks could be just as quick to take advantage of fool furriners.

By now they were close enough to the two-story shingled-frame main house to make out the four full-grown and gaggle of smaller figures watching from the front veranda. As they got within earshot, the Kellgren kid who wasn't packing any load rode forward at a lope to doubtless gossip some about their unexpected visitor.

So nobody asked to see his badge when they invited him to come on in and tell them all about it while he had some coffee and a slice or more of Momma's *ostkaka*.

Gunnar Kellgren looked a lot like Santa Claus must have before he got fat and his full beard had gone from wheat-straw to snow-white. His old woman, Miss Frederika, was a big motherly gal in blond braids and flour-dusted pinafore who looked as if she still liked to screw when nobody was watching. The two of them spoke tolerable English, but a tad more singsong than their pure American kids.

The cheerful kitchen of their stout frame house was painted in the pale sunny way most Scandinavians fancied, with everything that wasn't buttercup-yellow either mint-green or baby-blanket-blue. The coffee they served him at the yellow kitchen table was black as sin. The ominously named cake turned out to taste like cheese and cherries, only sweeter. As he enjoyed two whole slices Longarm told them more about his needs. Gunnar Kellgren said they'd be proud to lend the government a good mount, and that Longarm could just leave it in that livery near the landing in New Ulm when he was done with it. For his boys rode into town more often than their momma and the pastor of their church felt they ought to.

When Longarm said he was on an expense account and offered to pay for the hire of their pony, the expansive Swede looked hurt and asked, "Do we look like barley growers, Deputy Long? We don't keep our cows in the house with us but there are plenty out back, along with many a draw filled with firewood and running water across both our lawful holdings and the open range we graze almost entirely our own selves."

Longarm said he was sorry if he'd insulted anybody. Then, the free loan of that pony settled, he innocently asked who else might be sharing the open range off to the west.

Kellgren sounded just as unworried when he answered, "Other cattle folk named Runeberg. They're all right. Pretty little Helga Runeberg has been running the outfit since her own daddy died. It's a shame she'd be a tad too old for Junior here. If our two families ever married up they'd leave a grand cattle empire to our grandchildren someday!"

Longarm allowed he'd heard Helga Runeberg ran a mighty big outfit from her own spread along the Sleepy Eye. Then he added, "That would be better than a score of country miles to the southwest, wouldn't it?"

Kellgren nodded casually and replied, "I said it would make a grand empire. Like ourselves, of course, Miss Helga only holds a section or so she has to pay taxes on. But none of the farm families moving in along either our river or Miss Helga's claim more than a half mile back from the roads to market. Field crops can't be driven down off the rises on its own hooves, and after that, this part of Minnesota is laid out just right for cattle folks and farm folks to live and let live."

Longarm didn't need to be lectured on the advantages of drilling in spuds or grain on bottomland while grazing beef or dairy stock on the higher rolling prairie between river valleys. So he washed down the last of his second slice of *ostkaka* with the last of his coffee, and made a show of taking out his pocket watch to see how he was doing as to time.

The burly cattleman took the obvious hint and rose from his side of the table, suggesting they go have a look at the riding stock. So Longarm picked up his McClellan from the kitchen corner and trailed after Kellgren and his older boys.

All the ponies in the corral out back looked well fed and spunky. Longarm said so, and added that since they knew their own stock better than he did, he'd leave the choice to them.

One of the kids wanted to lend Longarm a chestnut with four white stockings. But old Kellgren snorted and said, "The man said he wants to cover a good bit of ground, a lot of it after dark, not rope or cut, Junior."

He pointed out a bigger blue roan and told Longarm, "You'd want old Smokey there. Sixteen hands at the shoulder to pack a man your size through thick and thin. There's only one thing, though. I see that bridle lashed to your saddle has a stock bit and Smokey is a lot of horse. Would you care for the loan of a meaner spade bit?"

Longarm said, "Not hardly. I got a lot of wrist, and old ladies call you names when you ride a pony into town foaming pink."

Kellgren said it was up to the rider to decide such matters, and told his boys to saddle Smokey up for their guest. As they were doing so, with the big blue roan objecting some, Longarm asked Kellgren more about his neighbors to the south, since he'd have to pass more than one on his way to the Chambrun spread.

The big Swede shrugged and said, "We get along. It's best to stay on neighborly terms. Whether they sneak some beef on you or not, it makes it easier to deal with them when the time comes to buy them out."

"You've been planning that far ahead?" asked Longarm thoughtfully.

Kellgren sounded as if his conscience was clear when he replied, "You have to, if you expect to leave this world better off than you came into it. I know the government was anxious to fill all this wide-open space with somebody that pays more taxes than buffalo or buffalo-hunting redskins. But we all know four out of five homesteaders fail, even when they're white folks who know what they're doing. The trashy halfbreeds and colored folks down the river as far as the Bedford freehold can't know what they're doing. They don't even listen when a well-meant white neighbor tries to tell them what they're doing all wrong!"

"What are they doing all wrong, and ain't any of them white?" asked Longarm with a puzzled frown.

Kellgren shook his leonine head and said, "Nope. All but those colored Conways down the other side of Chambrun seem to be breeds or poor-white squawmen married to kin of that full-blooded Chambrun woman, Miss Tatokee Something. Sometimes she's supposed to be this and other times she's supposed to be that. But Miss Matilda, who fetches and carries for the Bee Witch, says she's a full-blood Santee, and Miss Matilda ought to know, being part Santee in her own right."

"You all know this so-called Bee Witch?" Longarm asked.

Kellgren said, "Sure. She's not really a witch. Just an odd old colored woman who keeps bees. She acts sort of wild and crazy when mean kids tease her. But the honey she sells is so clean and clear my Frederika serves it straight from the jar. We mostly deal with her helper, Miss Matilda, a young breed gal who gets around better. Like I said, she's the one who says the Chambrun squaw's a full-blood Santee, no matter what the government said about moving them all out to the Dakota Territory."

Longarm somehow doubted even a part Santee would have called any other woman a squaw. But by now they had old Smokey saddled and bridled. In the meantime, it wasn't getting a lick earlier. So Longarm asked no further questions about the neighbors to the south, and just made certain he had that New Ulm livery right as he mounted up and rode out, with the sun agreeing with his pocket watch it would soon be suppertime.

But there were a few hours of daylight left as he rode the big blue roan down the county road, admiring the view as well as the easy gait of the long-limbed gelding. To his left, between the road and river, second- and third-growth bottomland hardwood grew so thick in places you hardly knew the water was there. Most such trees grew back from the stump as circles of saplings around the ghost of the original full-grown alder, cottonwood, willow, or whatever. All that gathering of free firewood since the Santee had been run out had made for a genuine jungle in summertime and doubtless good brush shelter for critters the rest of the year.

Off to his right, as the prairie rolled higher, whether as

131

slopes or rocky bluffs, such trees as still grew either marched in file down scattered watercourses, or circled up like a wagon camp atop otherwise bare grassy rises, with a cow peeking out from such cover every now and again. Longarm knew that when this had still been an Indian reserve the trees had grown far thicker, with real woodlands sometimes reaching clean to the river banks in some stretches. For unlike their buffalo-running cousins further west, or perhaps the way those cousins had started out before they'd met Tashunka, or Horse, the Santee had lived far more like their Ojibwa enemies, on the bounty of their original woodlands around the Great Sweet Waters, where Hiawatha had met his Santee sweetheart, Miss Minnihaha. Woodland Indians could be hell on trees with useful bark, such as birch or elm, but they liked to choose dried-out deadwood for fires, and had less call than white folks to chop down green and still-growing timber.

Someone had sure cut a heap of it since the Santee had been run out back in '63. Neither the Kellgrens nor the neighbors he'd said were at least part Indian would have had much call to log this seriously so far from their own woodpiles. It seemed as likely the more valuable red oak, rock maple, basswood, and such on the drier slopes had been cut and rafted downstream for fun and profit before many homesteads had been filed upstream from New Ulm after the land had been thrown open to white folks.

A horned lark was cussing about it from a bobwire fence and the shadows were getting longer when he overtook a raggedy kid driving a dairy cow on foot, likely homeward bound, along the far side of that fence with soft words and a big stick. Longarm reined in to stand in the stirrups and peer down the road ahead as he called out, "Evening, cowboy. That your homestead a furlong on with that smoke plume waving at us in the breeze?"

The kid called back, "I may not have me a pony to ride, mister. But that don't give you no call to mock me."

Longarm laughed lightly and replied, "Mocking was never what I intended. Anyone can see you're a boy in command of a cow. And as for you having a pony or not, any Mex matador can tell you it's a heap braver to mess with a cow afoot than mounted up. That particular cow looks pure Jersey as well. You'd never get that matador to mess with a Jersey in the bull ring. How come you're so brave?"

The kid replied, less pissed, "Got no choice. They sent me to fetch old Napin Gleska when she didn't come in to get milked with the others. You were right about her being a purebred. We got us a whole dozen milkers of the very best."

"Brand-new four-strand fence I see there too," Longarm noted in an admiring tone. "Your folks must be doing mighty well."

The kid whacked the milch cow's tawny rump with his stick as he shook his head and explained. "Ina Tatowiyeh Wachipi gave Pa all the money we needed to prove this claim. She's the one who's rich, and she don't sit on her money like an old broody hen expecting to hatch it neither! She's a real Nakotawiyeh! Not a stingy old Wasichu lady!"

Longarm nodded as if he understood everything they were talking about. "Others have told me Wabasha Chambrun's fine wife was a true-heart. Santee Nakota, right?"

The kid sounded smug as he stuck out his skinny chest to declare, "Just like my real *ina*. It ain't my fault I'm only half Nakota. They'd have never let us claim this land back if my *ina* hadn't married up with a Wasichu like you."

Then he jabbed the Jersey under her tail with his stick and shouted, "*Hokahey*, you lazy cow! *Iyoptey niyeh* or I'll never get any supper tonight!"

Longarm could see the kid was busy. So he said so and rode on, digesting the little he'd learned as he repeated their few words in his head. Others had told him the Chambruns weren't the only odd newcomers who'd filed homestead claims up here on what had once been the Santee Reserve. He'd meant what he'd said to that kid back there about fancy dairy breeds and one more strand of new Glidden Brand bobwire than most nesters strung. The more eastern dialect the kid had larded his English with was close enough to the little Lakota Longarm knew, despite it's being a tad more guttural with the L sounds transposed to N, for Longarm to figure the kid had likely meant to call the Chambrun woman his aunt instead of his real mother. A lot of the nations used the same

133

words for all the elders of their parents' generation. Tatowiyeh Chambrun, to keep it simple, could as easily be just a friendly older woman as true kin. Indians tended to be better friends and uglier enemies than some. So a full-blood married to a homesteader who had hundred-dollar treasury notes to spend would doubtless help out another full-blood gal married up with yet another nester.

The breed kid had innocently verified what others suspected about Chambrun having a Santee woman, whatever in thunder *he* claimed to be. The kid had called her a Nakotawiyeh, or woman of the allies, as close as it worked out in Wasichu. But he hadn't argued when a friendly stranger referred to her as a member of her own particular Santee nation.

Longarm ignored the yard dog and other raggedy kids who seemed so interested as he rode past their soddy. He had meant his remark about their chimney smoke a tad sardonically. For few white nesters could afford that much of a fire just for a summer supper, and Indians were inclined to burn less than a third as much fuel, left to their usual habits. But he knew that a prosperous *wiyeh*, living "Fat Cow" because her man was so successful, could be inclined to build such a fire as it drove everyone out of her tipi with their eyes burning so she could modestly brag on the way her man had been spoiling her.

He rode past the next fenced-in spread he came upon, knowing grown folks fibbed more to the law than their kids might and that suppertime was a rude time to come calling in any case.

The summer sun set later that far north than it might in some other parts. But the sky to the west was a crimson memory of the day, and the wishing star was winking down at him from the east when he saw a lamp lighting up a quarter mile ahead. As he slowed old Smokey to a thoughtful walk, he was sure that dark cluster down the road had to be the Chambrun place and that at least the lady of the house was a full-blood from a fighting nation.

Longarm had read that same crap about Sioux being afraid to fight after dark because the Great Spirit might not be able to find their ghosts if they were killed. Old Ned Buntline said Calamity Jane had ridden with the Seventh Cav as well. But the simple truth about the fighting tactics of the Horse Nations was that nobody with a lick of sense, red or white, ever ordered a full cavalry charge after dark because it simply smarted to ride into a solid object at full gallop.

After that, Wakan Tanka (or Wakanda) translated more like Great Medicine or Big Mystery than Great Spirit, which would have been Wanigi Tanka if any old-time medicine man thought he knew who was running his own world. Nobody was supposed to come looking for your four ghosts when you got killed. *Some* of you went looking for your enemies to haunt them, which was why they maimed your corpse to cripple your ghost, while another part of you went to live with Old Woman in her lodge beneath the Northern Lights. Longarm agreed with his Indian pals that it might be more fun to roam with those other ghostly parts of your dead self in what some translated as the Happy Hunting Ground, although no Indian thought his ghost would have to hunt very hard, where it was never too hot, never too cold, you always felt as if you'd just eaten, and all you had to do was ride forever on a fast immortal pony.

Meanwhile, back here in the living world, dusk was considered a swell time to raid an enemy, and knowing this, most Quill Indians could be more proddy about sudden bumps in the dark than a stranger riding at them in broad daylight. So Longarm reined in a furlong out and drew his .44-40 to peg a shot at that wishing star.

As he sat his stationary mount reloading, that lamp winked out in the window of the soddy in the middle distance.

A long time later a cautious voice called out, "Who's there and what might you want?"

Longarm called back, "I'd be Deputy U.S. Marshal Custis Long, and I'd like a few words with Mister Wabasha Chambrun. I fired that shot lest you take me for a thief in the night."

The man in the darkened doorway of the soddy called for him to come on in in that case. But nobody struck a light inside before Longarm had dismounted in the dooryard and was tethering his mount to their hitching rail in plain view. That lamp inside was relit as he approached the front door, hands polite and Winchester still in its saddle boot for anyone to plainly see.

Wabasha Chambrun, after all that talk, turned out to look mighty unremarkable in his checked shirt and bib overalls. He could have passed for a fairly clean-cut Mexican in town, if he'd said that was what he was.

The same could not be said for the moon-faced old gal over in a corner near that lamp. Nobody but Buffalo Bill wore fringed buckskin in the summer when they didn't have to. But her blue print Mother Hubbard didn't disguise her long slick braids or the red line she'd painted along the part of her greased black hair. It wasn't true a full-blood always kept a poker face. Her smoldering sloe eyes were driving mental splinters into him where it really hurt a man as her husband said something to her in her own lingo.

She muttered, "*Ohiney!*" and turned her back on them as Longarm noticed that the four half-grown kids peering through a doorway at him seemed a tad less Indian and not quite as sore at him.

Chambrun told Longarm, "You got here too late for supper, and I know better than to offer you any of her chokecherry and lard dessert. But I told her to put the coffee on and she will, in a while, if she knows what's good for her. I ain't talking Santee to her to be rude. Tatowiyeh Wachipi's a good old girl in many ways, but she refuses to even try and learn Wasichu."

Longarm almost asked if Tatowiyeh Wachipi might not translate as something like Dancing Antelope Gal. Then he wondered why he'd want to ask a dumb question like that. Chambrun already knew what his woman's name meant in her lingo, and it was often surprising to hear what people might have to say when they didn't think you knew a word they were saying.

As his sullen woman cussed some more and threw a length of pitch-pine in the firebox of their cast-iron corner range, Chambrun waved Longarm to a seat at the table in the middle of their main room cum kitchen. As Longarm removed his hat and sat down, the somewhat older and burlier breed said easily, "I know why you've come. But just as I've told everyone else, I can prove I was right here in Brown County when they robbed that government office over in Fort Collins!"

Longarm nodded amiably and replied, "Nobody thinks you

136

took part in the holdup itself. You'd know better than the rest of us how you came by that hundred-dollar treasury note you gave Israel Bedford in exchange for that riding stock."

Chambrun shook his head and said, "I came by it as honestly as Neighbor Bedford. I sold some stock of my own for cash to yet another farmer whose name was Tom, Dick, or mayhaps Harry."

"Might we be talking about dairy stock?" asked Longarm innocently.

Chambrun, caught off base, nodded before he decided it might be smarter to say, "We don't milk any cows on this spread. That's one of your customs none of us have ever bothered to learn, so I reckon you'd as soon have you coffee black than creamed our way, with flour?"

Longarm said he always drank his coffee straight. Then he took a breath, held it so his voice would come out dead level, and told the breed dead level, "I know at least one part-Santee family who keeps some dairy stock and milks 'em, just before supper and doubtless once before breakfast whether they're creaming their coffee or just selling the produce to Wasichu. I was never told they bought a fine Jersey purebred off you, Mister Chambrun. I was told they'd been given a helping hand from a generous . . . aunt?"

Chambrun sat down across from Longarm with a confused whoosh of wordless breath. Longarm leaned back and didn't press him. Sometimes the fibs you gave them time to make up could reveal as much as half truths you slapped out of a worried mouth.

But it wasn't Chambrun who broke. He seemed at a total loss for words as his wife came over, slamming two empty tin cups down on the bare wood as she snapped, in perfect English, "Your damned coffee will be ready in a minute. My Wabasha has done nothing wrong, nothing. It was I who gave him that paper money. All of it. Are you going to take me down to Mankato so they can hang me too as my children watch and weep tears of blood?"

Longarm answered quietly, "Not hardly, ma'am. Possession of stolen property ain't good for much more than a year in jail, and that's only when they can prove you knew it was stolen.

So if I were you and I'd come by that recorded treasury note honestly, I'd just tell the law the truth and have done with it. The fine print on that note allows you had every right to spend it, any way you saw fit, as long as you broke no laws to come by it, see?"

She said something about that coffee, and went back to her range to consider his offer. Chambrun asked which one of those windy kids up the road had blabbed to the law about family matters.

Longarm smiled thinly and replied, "Would you want me to tell on you after I'd tricked a bitty dab of gossip out of you?"

His wife turned around to stare thoughtfully down at him, her dark eyes filled with worried wonder. She said, "You say you don't care where people might get money as long as they have broken none of the laws they pay you to enforce. But hear me, what do you have to do with the regulations of the Bureau of Indian Affairs?"

Longarm answered honestly, "Nothing. I don't ride for the B.I.A. and Brown County ain't an Indian Reserve no more. If you're hinting you might have saved up or even re-invested some B.I.A. allotments, when everyone knows you spend it all on white flour and ribbon bows before it's time for another handout, that's between you and your B.I.A. agent. If you had a B.I.A. agent. Since you seem to be living off the blanket on your Wasichu homestead claim, I fail to see what beeswax of my department it might be."

She stared long and hard. Then she nodded and said, "I think I know who you must be. They spoke of a man like you at the Crow Creek Agency out in the Dakota Territory. Our western kinsmen called you Wasichu Wastey and said you spoke as straight as you could shoot. Are you not the one Mahpiua Luta calls his Medicine Grandson?"

To which Longarm could only modestly reply, "I reckon old Red Cloud and me are on friendly enough terms considering. He's one wise old gent, and likely would have kept his own bands out of that dumb Custer fight whether I'd warned him that time or not. It hardly took as much medicine as some said I must have had to predict the way things were sure to come out

138

in the end. Red Cloud got invited back east to Washington after he'd won his war along the Bozeman Trail with the U.S. Army back in '68. So he knew what Tatanka Yotanka, Tashunka Witko, and the others would be up against if they opposed old Terry's advance on their Paha Supa treaty lands. All I told the big chief that he hadn't heard was how certain members of the crooked Indian Ring in Washington were hoping for a nice big battle, because that would give them the excuse to just tear up the Treaty of 1868 entirely and grind the whole Lakota Confederacy up like sausage meat."

Tatowiyeh Wachipi sighed soulfully and said, "You spoke the truth. After the good fight at Greasy Grass along the Little Big Horn, they said we were savage children it was pointless to bargain with, and they took away the powers of all our chiefs and moved us off all the good lands, all of it. Do you think that was fair, after signing the Treaty of 1868 with Mahpiua Luta in ink?"

Longarm shrugged and said, "Depends on how you read a treaty, I reckon. The Five Civilized Tribes lost their rights to self-government in the Indian Nation after they chose to fight on the Confederate side in the war. There was nothing in any treaty about the government granting perpetual scalping rights to anybody."

Chambrun said, "Hold on! My own *ina*'s folk were Osage and they fought on the Union side in the War Betwixt the States!"

Longarm nodded and said, "That's doubtless how come the Osage got their own strip in the Indian Nation, carved out of Cherokee and Creek holdings along the Arkansas. I'm glad to hear you really have Osage blood, Mister Chambrun. But how come we're jawing about such ancient history when all I ever asked was where you all got that one infernal treasury note?"

She pouted, "How can you prove the one we paid Israel Bedford for some stock was the one they say somebody stole from that payroll? A Wasichu who hates us would find it easy, very easy, to switch the paper we paid a neighbor in good faith with another he knew to be stolen. Did we think to keep a record of the serial numbers on our own money?

Did Israel Bedford? Does anybody, unless they have a good or bad reason?"

Longarm started to say something that might not have been perfectly fair. Then he nodded soberly and said, "*Hokahey*. Let's try that on for size. Let's say Banker Plover had already short-stopped one of those red-hot treasury notes and was keeping it on ice for some devious reason. Let's say he just waited until an innocent party came in to deposit a plain old innocent hundred-dollar note. Then let's say the banker switched 'em and called the law on a customer."

Chambrun said that worked for him. His wife agreed it only confirmed what she'd always thought about Wasichu who dealt in treacherous written words and complicated numbers that always left you owing the trading post more than you'd expected.

Longarm shrugged and quietly asked, "How could Banker Plover have known where Bedford got that recorded note before he had the chance to ask him?"

The breed and his wife exchanged puzzled glances. She said something too fast for Longarm to follow in their private lingo. Then she turned away to see about that coffee.

Chambrun chuckled and said, "She says you must be Wasichu Wastey because you chew your thoughts so good before you spit them out. Now that you've put it that way, even I can see how unlikely it was that old P. S. Plover could have had it in for us in particular."

As his woman brought the coffeepot back to the table, Longarm asked either one who cared to guess, "Then what might that banker have had against Bedford? There's the old boy who'd have been in a whole lot of trouble if he hadn't been able to point to you, and you hadn't owned up to giving him that mysterious treasury note."

Tatowiyeh Wachipi poured the reheated coffee as she told Longarm in a weary voice, "There is no real mystery about where I got that money, and other money. From Wowinapa, you call him Mister Thomas Wakeman, and others of our people who now live as if they were Wasichu and, as you suggested, invest allotment funds for some of our people still drawing them from the B.I.A."

Longarm whistled softly and asked, "Ain't Thomas Wakeman, also known as Wowinapa, the surviving son of Little Crow?"

Dancing Antelope Gal nodded soberly and replied, "Just as I am a niece of Wamni Tanka. You called him Big Eagle and sent him off to the state penitentiary as if he'd been a common thief instead of a great war leader!"

Longarm shrugged and said, "He got off light. The state posted a twenty-five-dollar bounty on Santee scalps and a heap of burnt-out homesteaders got new starts by collecting quite a few. But weren't we talking about Little Crow's grown son, who lives respectable these days?"

She nodded soberly and said, "As Thomas Wakeman, Wowinapa is now an Episcopal deacon and an official of the Y.M.C.A. Other Santee who never wanted to go to that Crow Bend Agency have done as well. Hear me. Some of them have done very well, very, off the blanket and under a Wasichu haircut."

Her husband volunteered, "A gent can get hurt asking a stranger drinking next to him in a saloon how he might have come by that deep tan and sort of high cheekbones."

Longarm nodded impatiently and said, "I drink regular with such old boys, and a fellow deputy out of the Denver office makes no bones about his Indian blood. Could we stick to that hundred-dollar treasury note?"

The lady of the house nodded and said, "A group of Indian or former Indian businessmen have formed a syndicate with the quiet intent of getting back as much of this ancestral Santee land as possible the Wasichu way!"

Her husband chuckled fondly and said, "We ain't had much luck in trying to hold it Indian-style. No matter how the damned treaty may read, somebody on one damned side or the other always seems to trip over some damned provision. You were the one who just said what happens when Washington gets the excuse to scrap an agreement on the grounds of breach of contract."

Longarm laughed incredulously and said, "Let me see if I got this straight. You treacherous Sioux, having failed to lick the U.S. Army and take this continent back by force of arms, mean to take at least some of it back by way of the Federal Homestead Act?"

Chambrun asked smugly, "Why not? The government lets freed slaves and Swedes who speak even worse English than us file homestead claims before they've bothered applying for citizenship. Where in your Constitution or Good Book does it say a human being born on U.S. soil to families that go way back before Columbus can't call his or her ownself an American farmer, as long as he or she can abide by all your fool rules?"

"And pay all bills in legal tender?" the moon-faced wife of the otherwise normal homestead added as her breed kids snickered from the next room.

Longarm didn't want to compound the confusion by making objections or asking questions that had no direct bearing on that Fort Collins robbery. So he sipped some bitter brew to compose his own thoughts. He knew it could look either way to that kid with the cow, and it really cut no ice whether the Chambruns were using other folks' money or acting as distributors for that mysterious syndicate. So he put down his cup and got out his notebook as he quietly said, "If I take your word how you came by that recorded hundred-dollar note, I'm still going to have to backtrack it all the way to Fort Collins, or at least to someone criminal for certain. So you'd best give me some other names I can check out. You say these sort of retired Santee have been advancing you homesteading kith and kin the money it takes to make a go of a government claim?"

Chambrun nodded, and might have said something if his moon-faced wife hadn't cut him off with a rattle of Santee Longarm couldn't keep up with.

It was tough enough to follow a Mexican conversation in rapid-fire Spanish when you knew most of the words but didn't think in Spanish. The folks you were trying to listen in on tended to run on to the next paragraph while you were still translating the first in your own head.

It was even worse when you only knew some baby-talk Indian. The Sioux-Hokan dialects weren't as confusing as some others, but that didn't mean the grammar was simple as English. The nouns and verbs changed enough, depending

142

on who was talking about whom, while the singular and plural could stay the same. So while Longarm was still brushing up on the little he knew of their lingo, the Chambruns had come to some agreement on how they meant to talk to him in Wasichu.

It was Chambrun who spoke up, although Longarm suspected that none of these white or breed squawmen had the final say when they'd been funded by the kith and kin of their purebred wives. The burly breed said, "We're not going to tell you, Deputy Long. Didn't they ever tell you that tale about the golden goose?"

Longarm nodded soberly and replied, "They did, and I follow your drift. *I'd* be sore if I'd advanced somebody the money to start a sort of agricultural experiment and they called the law on me too. On the other hand, looking at it from my side of the checkerboard, I've been ordered to trace that treasury note all the way back to the cuss who took it from that government payroll at gunpoint, and so far the trail seems to end at your very doorstep."

Chambrun shook his head stubbornly and said, "No, it don't. Israel Bedford is the one who presented a thing to the bank that was listed as stolen. Banker Plover read the number of that particular piece of paper off his official list. Nobody never read shit off nothing when I paid Bedford for that riding stock."

Longarm frowned and said, "Hold on. Bedford says the note he took to the bank was the same one he got from you."

Dancing Antelope Gal cut in. "*We* can say we got it from Old Man Coyote as long as we didn't have to prove it. Why do you take the word of Israel Bedford over that of my husband? Because the Wasichu has blue eyes and thus his heart must be pure?"

Longarm wet a finger and drew an invisible chalk mark in the air between them as he said, "I'll give you that point, even though they say in town that Israel Bedford has a good rep."

Chambrun grumbled, "What's wrong with *my* rep? Has anybody said I steal from my neighbors or fail to pay my bills on time? It's all the fault of that Mark Twain, making Indian Joe the halfbreed the villain. I know what they say about us two-faced snakes in the grass, but was Simon Girty who led all those raids along the old frontier part Indian? Was Benedict Arnold or Judas part Indian?"

Longarm grimaced and said, "I just said I conceded that point. But they still expect me to make some arrests in connection with that hot paper, old son."

Chambrun shrugged and said, "Arrest Bedford then. He's the one who spent that treasury note in town for certain. It's my word against his that I handed him that particular treasury note and no other. But if you want to arrest me, on no more than a white man's sacred word, I reckon I'll just have to take my chances with the grand jury if it goes that far."

His wife said, in a less teasing tone, "We know none of the people we are . . . fronting for would hold anybody up. It would only upset them, very much, if we told you who they were and let you bother them. If they knew anything, anything about stolen money, they would never pass it on to people of their own nation."

Then she crossed her arms and quietly added, "So hear me. I have spoken."

Longarm finished all but the dregs in his tin cup as he composed his words carefully. "I know nobody would knowingly pass on a recorded hundred-dollar treasury note if they knew about those lists of serial numbers, ma'am. But you've just now convinced me an innocent person could accept and pass one on in ignorant good faith. So can't you see how some perfectly respectable businessman of the Santee or part-Santee persuasion could have accepted some of that hot paper in trade, and might be able to tell me just who in thunder stuck him with it?"

The Indian woman didn't answer. Her husband rose from the table to say, "I reckon I have spoken too."

So Longarm shrugged, got to his own feet, and put his hat back on as he replied, "In that case there's nothing left for me to say but *pilamiyeh*, or is that *pinamiyeh* in Santee, and in either case I'll be back if your story don't hold water, hear?"

Chapter 17

The darkness had finished falling by the time Longarm mounted up to ride on, the bitter taste in his mouth only partly inspired by that dreadful coffee back yonder. The moon was up and out to shine bright, but a herd of big black clouds were stampeding across the sky from the southwest to make the night air taste like electric tingles felt and make the moonlight mighty tricky. But as he rode old Smokey downstream, Longarm could tell the road under them lay at a nine- or ten-degree grade, and they'd told him aboard that old steamboat how Chambrun had claimed high rocky ground instead of richer bottomlands up and down the river for the taking. For folks trying to live off the blanket like white settlers, they sure had some mighty odd ways, maybe left over from the vision-seeking notions of less advanced times. Indians were always camping way up in the middle of the air, and starving themselves on top of rock outcroppings, until a friendly *wanigi* took pity on them and sent a vision from the spirit world. Longarm had never heard of anyone having a vision in the warm comfort of a really swell campsite.

As they followed the gentle grade down to more sensible cropland, shifting shadows made everything to either side of the county road wriggle and writhe in the ghostly moonlight. Longarm had figured out as a kid why folks felt proddy moving past a graveyard when the moon was full and the hoot owls were feeling amorous. So he told old Smokey not to believe in ghosts, even if they were smack on the very warpath those Santee had come boiling down once the pot had boiled over up at the lower agency. Of course, they'd hit that military post on the far side of the river first, likely fording the Minnesota at some handy crossing and . . .

"That's it!" Longarm assured his mount as he chuckled and added aloud, "Old Chambrun was right. It might not be smart to assume a man can't think sensible as anyone else just because he's got some Indian blood!"

He reined in to light a cheroot as he expanded on his inspiration. It made just as much sense as he got his smoke going and shook out the match. It only stood to reason a well-funded breed, scouting earlier than the rest of his bunch for a good spot to claim, might see the advantages of a place along the river where they'd never build any steamboat landing but might surely build a bridge, or even a railroad trestle, once this valley commenced to fill in some more!

Longarm blew smoke at a sycamore making obscene gestures at them in the shifty light and told Smokey, "They call it the law of eminent domain when they want to run a railroad or bridge approach across your property. You got to let 'em. But they got to pay you a fair price, or as much as the land would be worth under, let's say, corn and taters. So if I had my homestead on the best bridge site for miles, I reckon I'd let them force me to sell the acres they needed at their price, and then I'd set my own price on what I had left, once I'd cut 'em up into building lots for the crossroads settlement you generally find where a serious river crossing intersects a county road!"

He heeled his borrowed mount to ride on. Then he suddenly reined in some more, and sure enough, those other riders he'd only thought might be echoes reined in themselves after they'd noticed he had.

He rode on at a comfortable lope, knowing for certain there were four or more riders about a quarter mile back. It got less easy to say for certain once there were more than three.

Longarm figured he could take up to half a dozen with his Winchester if he could surprise them from good cover. There were plenty of shifty-lit trees to his left, between the road and riverbanks. If he turned old Smokey loose to run on for some oats, as ponies were inclined to behave by nature . . . Shit, the gelding would doubtless head back to its familiar fodder and water at the Kellgren spread, meaning an empty saddle passing those other riders on the road to give them plenty of warning someone had dismounted up ahead to lay for them!

"I reckon we'd best stick together," Longarm told his loping blue roan as he hauled out his Winchester anyway with a hell of a night ride still ahead of them.

He knew the big gelding was made out of flesh and blood, like he was, and only a steam-driven machine, whether afloat or on wheels, was about to swallow that much distance in one gulp. So those others, who had to know that much, would likely wait until he took a trail break before they . . . what?

"Let's find out," Longarm growled as he neck-reined old Smokey off the road to burst into the second growth off to their left. The gelding didn't like it much, and it was tough on Longarm's knees without chaps as well. But he forced the blue roan through the springy jungle as far as a little moonlit cove, where he dismounted on the drier side and tethered Smokey to an alder, saying soothingly, "You got plenty of browse and all the water you can drink. So keep your voice low whilst I work back a ways with this saddle gun and see if I can find out what this is all about!"

Old Smokey didn't argue. Longarm found it far easier to move his own smaller frame through the tanglewood on foot. Closer to the sometimes-moonlit road he found a fallen sycamore with a swell clump of box elder sprouting just right to break up his own outline as he lay behind it in the grass with his Winchester propped across the mottled sycamore bark to cover the road.

Nothing happened. It felt as if the Ice Age had come and gone, to be replaced by the rise and fall of the Roman Empire at least. The moon was now overhead, but the night kept getting darker as those clouds got thicker, and he could only hope a night bird had just shit on his hat brim in passing, because otherwise it was starting to rain and he'd left his damned slicker by the river with his damned saddle on that damned gelding!

Another drop hit his left wrist, closer to the muzzle of his

'73. There was nothing he could do about it. If it rained hard he'd get wet. If it didn't, he wouldn't. Those other riders doubtless had slickers handier on their damned saddles. They were likely back up that road a piece, putting them on. They'd be along directly, the dry and comfortable sons of bitches.

But still they didn't come, and now it was starting to really rain. Longarm lay there, getting soaked, as the raindrops pounded out yonder on the road as if intent on muffling the sounds of any approaching hoofbeats. He considered whether that could be what had inspired the mysterious riders on his trail to hold back. He knew that same rain made it tough for him to judge whether anyone else was out there in the dark or not. He doubted he'd want to ride in on anybody with his own loaded gun, not knowing just where the rascal was in shifting darkness with all but the loudest sounds drowned out.

It was even possible they'd never been after anybody to begin with, Longarm decided, as he went back over various conversations he'd had in recent memory.

He hadn't told anyone in New Ulm where he was headed or how he meant to get there. It hardly seemed likely anybody aboard that steamboat could have followed him on horseback. The Kellgrens had had the drop on him earlier and acted friendly as hell after he'd told them who he was and where he was headed. So why would any of their riders be trailing him?

He'd passed other spreads without stopping. But that didn't mean nobody had spotted a stranger riding by in broad daylight and gotten to fretting some. County folks living alone with all sorts of oddities on their consciences had given Longarm some anxious moments in the past. Just hearing a lawman was in his neck of the woods had been enough to set off that old prospector living in sin with his daughter up a canyon that time, poor old bastard.

But it was just as likely the Chambruns had been unsettled by his unexpected visit and personal questions. It was true they'd acted as civilized as he'd had any right to expect. But they'd had more than one boy back yonder big enough to pack a gun, and who but a total asshole would gun a lawman on his or her own property when the poor cuss had a good eight- or twelve-hour ride ahead of him on a damn-near-deserted county road?

"Meanwhile I'm as likely to die of a summer ague if I don't get out of this cold rain!" Longarm grumbled, even as he forced himself to just stay put and take some more while he counted to a hundred for at least the hundredth time.

Then he hauled in his gun muzzle and rose back to his soggy feet, knowing that even if they were still out there in the stormy darkness, they couldn't begin to guess where *he* might be in the dark.

He made his way back to his rain-soaked mount, untethering it but not remounting just yet as he said, "I'm sorry about this too, pard. I was spooked over Lord knows what, and whatever it was don't seem to be after us no more. So what say we get back to the road and move on at least as far as that Conway spread? Them colored nesters ain't on our list of suspects, like the Bedfords further on, so we'll ask for shelter there, all right?"

He started working their way through the dripping tanglewood. It wasn't easy. The saplings and sticker brush seemed even thicker in the direction he'd chosen. Then he spied light through the branches ahead and marveled, "We can't be that close to the Conway place or any other I remember from the pilothouse of the *Moccasin Blossom*."

Then he thought back harder and decided, "That crazy old colored lady they call the Bee Witch! It has to be a lamp in a window she has facing the shore, and she was tied up right by the bank. So how do you feel about asking our damned way at least?"

He led the gelding after him through the riverside growth as the moon winked on and off through the scudding clouds above them. That rain had blown over and it seemed to be clearing up, if that was how you wanted to describe soggy footing and dripping leaves all about. So the moon had burst through to beam down on the rambling shanty out on that log raft as Longarm spotted the plank stretched ashore and politely called out, "Ahoy, yon houseboat! This here would be a mighty wet U.S. Deputy Custis Long, bearing neither warrants nor malice for anyone on board. Now it's your move."

He'd been expecting most any move than the one busting out of the shanty, wailing like a banshee and flapping what seemed to be big old buzzard wings at him as his mount spooked and fought the bit while Longarm stood his ground and just called, "Howdy, ma'am."

The raggedy black apparation moaned in a spooky voice, "Go away or I'll turn you into a toad and have you for my supper!"

Longarm chuckled indulgently and replied, "I thought it was frogs, or their legs leastways, some folks ate, ma'am. Far be it from me to call a lady a big fibber, but I'm more worried right now about catching my death in this wet outfit than I am about getting turned into a toad."

"Don't you think I can do it? Don't you know I'm the Bee Witch?" the spooky shadow cackled.

Longarm gently replied, "I heard your Santee admirers called you something more like Sapaweyah, ma'am," figuring that it might sound needlessly familiar to toss in that part about her being *witko*, or crazy. Indians looked on being crazy with more respect than white folks or, as in her case, colored folks. Some Indians, though not all of them, considered insanity a sign of at least a possible meeting with a *wanigi,* good or bad. No medicine man would go out on a limb and say for certain a raving lunatic was in good with the spirits, but on the other hand, it might be just as safe to treat such a confused and confusing person with respect.

This one waved her wings, or sticks threaded through shaggy black tatters, anyway, and desperately moaned, "Go away! I have spoken!"

That wasn't exactly the way an old colored lady, sane or insane, might have put it. So Longarm nodded and said, "Evening, Miss Matilda. You say the Bee Witch is feeling poorly tonight?"

The dark figure out on the raft let her fake wings drop and stood frozen in confusion, or perhaps fear, without answering. Longarm let it ride until he saw it would be up to him and gently said, "I ain't using *wakan sapa*, Miss Matilda. They told me your old boss lady had a younger orphan gal out this way helping out, and no offense, you talk more like an Indian

150

lady than a colored lady, even trying to talk spooky. Would you like to talk more sensible now?"

She didn't answer, but it sounded as if she might be crying out there under that raggedy witch outfit. But Longarm insisted, "I told you I was federal law, and you seem to be afloat on a federal waterway instead of private property. So I could likely make it stick if I was to board you without a fussy search warrant."

He let that sink in before he added, "On the other hand, I told you true this pony and me are cold and wet. So would you like to talk a mite more sensible about that and give me less cause for suspecting you of Lord knows what?"

The small spooky figure sobbed, "I have done nothing wrong, nothing! If I show you where to shelter your horse and give you both food and water, will you keep my secret?"

Longarm almost asked what her secret was. Then he decided he'd cross that bridge after he made sure old Smokey wouldn't cool lame on him and the Kellgrens. So he said he didn't ride for the B.I.A. or anyone all that interested in bee culture, and that brought her ashore, showing more of her head in the moonlight as she murmured, "We can't keep our pony cart and burro aboard the raft. I'll show you where I pitched the tent this time."

Longarm followed her along the bank a ways to where, sure enough, an old army perimeter tent stood back in the sticker bush screened over with cut branches. The small gal had explained along the way how much safer she felt out on that raft after dark with all sorts of Wasichu moving up and down the river or that county road to the west.

It was far warmer inside the thick beeswax-dubbed canvas because a small burro had been in there, giving off dry heat through all that summer rain. It got easier to see in there after Longarm struck a match and lit an oil lantern hanging handy on the center pole. The two-wheeled cart she'd mentioned took up close to a third of the remaining space. But he saw the blue roan would have enough room if he tethered it next to the burro. Both brutes being geldings, they just nickered at one another while Longarm exchanged the bit and bridle for a more comfortable rope halter and peeled off the wet saddle and sopping blanket.

The gal said he could drape both over the side rails of that pony cart. So he did as he saw she was pouring cracked corn in the elm-bark trough the two brutes were close enough to share. In the soft lantern light the head sticking out of the raggedy black costume she had on wasn't spooky at all. The fine bone structure under her tawny complexion and raven's-wing hair said she was at least part Wasichu. She hadn't painted the part in her braided hair Santee-style either. Dressed up more sensibly, with her hair pinned up more fashionably, she might have passed in town for a high-born Mexican gal had she wanted to. He was still working on why she wanted to be taken for a crazy old colored lady.

He never said so. He said he'd sure like to wipe old Smokey down with some dry sacking if they had any.

She nodded, and worked her way around the far side of the pony cart to fumble out some feed sacks and, better yet, a tattered but clean and dry horse blanket. Longarm wiped the blue roan as dry as he could manage while he told her she was an angel of mercy and asked if she'd like to tell him some more about the Bee Witch now.

She started to cry. He went on wiping until he saw no improvement for the effort, and then he fastened the horse blanket over the corn-munching critter and quietly suggested, "I met up with another beekeeper down to the Indian Territory a spell back, preserved in wax like a bug in amber. Of course, the slow learner he had working for *him* when he died naturally wasn't bright enough to just bury the poor old gent, or did you sink her in the river?"

The young breed gal wailed, "Hear me! I did nothing, nothing at all to Sapaweyah Witko! Come with me and I will show you she is not aboard her house raft dead or alive. I don't know where she is. I have not seen her since the moon when the wolves run together."

Longarm frowned thoughtfully down at her and demanded, "Are you saying she's been missing since the other side of our New Year's Eve, Miss Matilda?"

The girl nodded. "She said she was going into New Ulm to tell her own people something on the talking wire. If you wish to call me by name, I am called Mato Takoza."

152

Longarm nodded soberly. "I stand corrected and I sure am wet. You wouldn't have a stove, or at least a peg to hang some of these wet duds on, aboard that house raft, would you, ma'am?"

She said she had both, and asked him to douse that lantern before he followed her outside. So he did. Neither his mount nor her burro seemed to care. As he followed her back along the same path Mato Tazoka explained, or bragged, how her grandfather had been a war chief almost as important as Little Crow himself, before the blue sleeves had killed him in the fight at Birch Coulee. Longarm had already figured her name meant something like Grandchild of the Bear. It might not have been polite to point out none of the ranking chiefs the milita or regulars bragged on had been called Mato. It was possible he'd been a Big Bear, a Medicine Bear, or some other sort of Bear. It was even more likely he'd been an enlisted Santee remembered as more important by his kith and kin. Longarm had yet to meet anyone whose daddy had been killed as a Confederate private, the C.S.A. records being sort of scattered since the war, and Indian war records had been hampered by neither modesty nor words on paper.

He followed the proud Santee beauty across that springy plank and into the lopsided shingled structure that took up most of the raft.

She'd left a candle lit inside. So he could see the front room was a work shed, smelling strongly of honey and devoted to the extraction gear and mason jars of her trade. Most of the jars seemed to be filled. When he commented, she said she'd been saving all the money she got in town from the Bee Witch's regular customers. She said she hadn't tried to drum up extra business on her own.

When Longarm said he hadn't noticed all that many beehives in the woods, she explained she'd set out two score that spring, along the edge of the trees to the west, shaded by the trees from the hot noonday sun but offering her bees plenty of flowery foraging on the far side of that county road. Longarm was country enough to know she was talking straight when she said more kinds of flowers grew, in greater numbers, where Wasichu had messed with the original lay of the land. Her kind had set grass fires late in the season to keep their hunting grounds open and lush for the critters they ate. But even had they wanted more posies they'd have had to wait till white settlers brought a whole Noah's Ark of extra old country greenery such as alfalfa, chickory, clover, dandelions, and even that Kentucky bluegrass everybody thought as American as apple pie, which was Pennsylvania Dutch in the first place.

The center of the surprisingly roomy shanty was taken up by a main room where, bless her heart, the pretty little thing had lit a combined cooking and heating stove against the damp chill. She seemed as anxious to show him the whole layout as he was to inspect it. He had to allow the two bedchambers opening into the far end of the main central room smelled too clean for her to be hiding a corpse on board.

Mato Takoza sat Longarm at a plank table and rustled up a length of cotton line and a cheesebox of clothes pegs. She strung the line catty-corner across the top of the hot stove, from hooks screwed into the two-by-four framing just right, and told him to shuck his wet duds so she could dry them for him as she whipped up some fresh coffee and scrambled eggs.

He was willing enough, till he got down to just his dank pants, soggy undershirt, and gunbelt. By this time she'd shed her raggedy black spook dress, and it was surprising how womanly a gal with such a young face could look in a thin cotton shift. She didn't have to hang her black rags to dry. As she pegged his to the clothesline she asked how come he was ashamed to take off his gun and pants. She said, "Hear me, you are much bigger than me and you can see I am wearing no gun under this flour sacking. Hang that gunbelt over the Winchester in the corner behind you, and we can have a lot of fun watching one another for false moves!"

He chuckled and replied, "You might suspect me of plotting other sorts of moves if I was to sit here in my birthday suit so close to anybody pretty as you, no offense."

She was too dusky for a blush to show in such dim light, but she fluttered her lashes and sounded a tad flustered as she stammered something about being just a halfbreed, sakes alive. Then she fetched him a blanket from another room, saying, "Wrap this around you if you're afraid I'll peek. But get out

154

of those wet clothes if you don't want to catch a summer cough. It will get colder before it gets warmer here on the water."

He knew that was true. So he ducked into one of the bedrooms to strip down to his bare feet and come back out, wrapped in the dark blue blanket with his free hand holding his gun rig and boots as well as soggy duds. She took everything but his six-gun, saying his boots would dry safer if she stuffed them with newspaper and didn't stand them too close to her stove. He went and hung his gun rig on a nail above the Winchester he'd stood in the angle of some framing. He'd found it could be as educational to pretend you were completely disarmed as it could to pretend you didn't know a word of Spanish or Indian dialects. So the less said about the derringer under the blanket the better.

By this time she had everything hung and she'd rustled up the makings of that light supper she'd offered. As she put the pot on to boil, under his dangling duds, and greased a cast-iron spider for the eggs, Mato Takoza told Longarm more about herself.

She said she'd been a girl-child during the big Santee Scare of '62 and the long forced march to Crow Creek that had followed inevitably after that much bad blood between her two races.

Both her ma and pa had been breeds, raised Indian by pure-blood gals who'd been married up with Wasichu trappers while they'd been out this way. Mato Takoza's momma's clan had fought more and hence lost more under Little Crow. But later, out at the Crow Creek Agency, the young gal's daddy had taken to strong drink and wife-beatings in spite of, or maybe because of, never counting coup in the short but savage uprising. Mato Tazoka was too smart to call it "The First Sioux War" the way some old soldiers and even civilian volunteers put it when they got to bragging.

She busted half a dozen eggs into her greased spider and got to scrambling them, along with some chopped-up wild onion grass, as she told him how her homesick momma had brought her back to the old Santee Agency at Redwood Falls, only to find Wasichu, many Wasichu, living there now. She sounded mighty steamed as she complained, "Hear me, my mother's people were not woodland creatures. We had learned long ago to build cabins and plant fruit orchards by watching you Wasichu. Out at Crow Creek they expected us to winter in tipis where the wolf wind howls across open prairie from the Moon of Many Colored Leaves to the Geese Nesting Moon. We had built nicer houses here than a lot of Wasichu, and now Wasichu had moved into them. All of them."

Longarm shrugged his bare shoulders under the blanket and resisted the obvious observation about the spoils of war. He knew they'd never admitted starting a war, and he didn't want her to lose the thread of her own story.

She didn't. She dished out the eggs on tin plates as she told him how she and her late momma had gotten by as hired help to homesteader housewives, since both had looked half-white and it had been easy enough to say they were friendlier "Chippewa" when no real Ojibwa were about to call them fibbers. After Mato Takoza's ma had died of the consumption or some other lung rot, she'd heard tell of the Bee Witch, a crazy old colored lady who lived free and easy up and down the river, and so, being less afraid of the white man's flies than some purebreds might have been, she'd tracked the Bee Witch down to ask her for a job.

It hadn't been easy. Mato Takoza had learned that spooky crow-flapping act from the old colored lady, who was more worried about being robbed or pestered than really *witko*. The Bee Witch had tried to scare the Santee breed off, and when that hadn't worked they'd got to talking enough so they could finally cut a deal.

Mato Takoza said the Bee Witch had been an easygoing boss, once she'd taught her young apprentice how to herd bees without getting stung too often. Mato Takoza said the older gal had been way more educated than she'd let on to strangers. As she motioned him to dig in and moved back to her stove to check the coffeepot, she told him how the old colored lady had read herself to sleep with big old books, and how she'd liked to sketch with pencil and ink on a drawing pad as she let her younger helper do most of the simple chores that went with a mighty carefree life.

Longarm said the old gal sounded as if she might have been a house slave in her younger days, explaining, "Most slave states had laws against teaching bondservants to read or write, since they thought a little knowledge could be a dangerous thing after a slave called Nat Turner read a copy of the Declaration of Independence and thought *he* was included in that part about all men being created equal. But lots of easygoing slaveholders didn't mind, and even taught some of their people, as they called 'em, to read. For one thing, it made a house slave more valuable if he or she could read written instructions."

Mato Takoza said, "I wish I could read. Miss Jasmine, that was her real name, left heaps of books under her bed and it's been lonely, lonely, since she never came back from town last winter."

Longarm thought about that as he ate. He hadn't known he was this hungry, and her scrambled eggs with onion grass would have tasted swell if he hadn't been. Her coffee was grand too when she poured it to go with their dessert of only slightly stale fruit cake. When he asked if it was store-bought, she fluttered her lashes and modestly allowed she'd learned to cook Wasichu-style sometime back. She might have taken it wrong if he'd pointed out she was still Indian enough to know about onion grass. She might have learned that from some settler gal in any case. All country folks tended to learn what grew tasty, for free, wherever they might wind up. A heap of what folks back East took for old-fashioned American cooking had been invented by Indians.

In the meantime Billy Vail hadn't sent a senior deputy all this way to search for lost, strayed, or stolen colored ladies. But after his worried young hostess brought up that part about the telegraph office again, he said, "I'll ask if they recall your Miss Jasmine at the Western Union in New Ulm. I got to ask 'em about other folks who may or may not be getting wired money orders fairly regular, and how many colored ladies by any name do you reckon they've sent lots of wires for as well?"

As he washed down some fruit cake, Mato Takoza recalled the Bee Witch had once said she'd hailed from one of the

157

Carolinas. Longarm assured her they'd remember her or not, no matter where she'd come from, adding, "Every railroad town has at least a few colored folks. But I'll be asking about someone they ain't used to seeing around town. How did she get into New Ulm to begin with, by the way? You run her in with that pony cart?"

Mato Takoza shook her head and explained the Bee Witch had her own riding pony, or *had* had one leastways. She'd already asked in town about the older woman's pony. Nobody in New Ulm had owned up to having seen it coming in or going out. Longarm agreed that had him stumped. He said, "An old colored lady in touch with kith or kin in other parts could be inspired by a sudden wire to hop a train without dropping a line to an illiterate, no offense. But she'd have had to leave that pony she rode to town with somebody."

"What if she fell in the river, or got murdered along the way?" the younger gal asked, owl-eyed.

Longarm shrugged and said, "Either way, we wind up with a leftover mount. A pony suddenly riderless for any reason would tend to run home to its familiar feed trough left to its druthers. So since it's been gone this long, it's safe to say somebody else has it, with or without the old lady's approval. What did this pony look like and was there anything at all unusual about its saddle or bridle?"

Mato Takoza said, "She rode bareback with a rope bridle, the Indian way. It was an Indian pony she'd traded for honey with one of your own kind who couldn't seem to break it your way. Miss Jasmine knew enough to mount an Indian pony from its right side. It stood about thirteen hands. It was a red and white paint with white mane and tail. It was pretty, and just the right size for a small woman too modest to sit it astride. She called it Mister Jefferson Davis. I don't know why."

Longarm said he did. He had no call to make a written note of a description so simple. As he'd told her, folks in town would remember or they wouldn't. He wasn't unkind enough to say his own boss hardly expected him to dig any deeper than a few routine questions when it hardly seemed likely anyone had paid for a jar of honey with a hundred-dollar treasury note.

That reminded him of more suspicious folks out this way and so, as she refilled his cup and allowed she didn't mind if he smoked, Longarm asked her what she knew about that other Santee lady, Tatowiyeh Wachipi Chambrun.

The younger and prettier Santee made a wry face and told him, "She says she is related to Wamni Tanka. Maybe she is. Or maybe she is long joking, the way my mother and I used to around Redwood Falls."

Longarm wasn't certain he followed her drift. As he rose to pad over to his dangling vest for a damp cheroot and those hopefully waterproof matches, he cautiously asked, "Might this long joke involve folks pretending to be what they ain't?"

She nodded innocently and said, "It is not hard for Absaroka to pass for their Oglala enemies, and a lot safer when they are outnumbered. At the Greasy Grass fight some of Custer's Absaroka scouts saved themselves by throwing off their blue coats and playing the long joke. Nobody knows why a band of Ree told everyone they were Pawnee for many years, many. But they did, and those two nations don't get along much better than Santee and Ojibwa!"

Longarm came back to the table and sat down to light up as he said he saw why they called it a long joke. She marveled at his waxy Mexican matches, and he said he had more he could leave her in his saddlebags. Then he asked what point there might be in a lady from another nation trying to pass herself off as Santee on the old Santee killing grounds.

When the admitted Santee looked puzzled, Longarm explained. "You just said you and your late momma had to say you were Chippewa to get around old grudges left over from all that bloodshed back in '62. So why would anyone who wasn't a true Santee brag on being a Santee in a neck of the woods where Santee still ain't all that popular?"

The Santee breed said she didn't know. Longarm said it made little sense to him either, but might be worth checking once he got back to New Ulm.

She asked when he meant to ride on. Longarm glanced at his hung-up duds and decided, "Not too sudden, at the rate that tweed's drying out despite your swell stove. It's already getting late and to tell the truth, I ain't too sure of my welcome once I do ride in, early or late. I don't suppose I could impose on you further by just bedding down out here for the night?"

She sucked in her breath and really looked flustered. He started to assure her he meant he'd noticed they had at least two beds in as many separate rooms. But then she came around to his side of the table to grab hold of his head by both ears and bury his face against her heaving marshmallow breasts, sobbing that she'd been so afraid he was never going to ask. So he just scooped her up and carried her in where he'd noticed the biggest bed. When she giggled and said her room was the one next door, he said he didn't care and just lowered her down to shuck his blanket, lift the hem of her shift, and lower his naked hips into the soft love saddle formed by her welcoming tawny thighs. When she giggled and asked him if he really thought he needed that derringer in his own fist, he shoved it under the head of their mattress and murmured, "Not hardly, but remind me to haul up that old plank and fetch both my saddle and six-gun back here once we've, ah, got more relaxed."

As she felt him entering her, Mato Takoza gasped, "Oh, *hinhey*! You call what you are doing to me *relaxing*? What do you and your Wasichu girls do for *excitement*? Not so fast yet! You're so *hanska*, and it has been many moons since the last time I did this with a boy much smaller, in every way!"

So Longarm slowed down and thrust less than he really wanted to, delighted by the surprising ripples of her almost too-tight but responsive love maw. It was her own idea to wrap her short muscular legs around his waist and hug him closer for some kissing she'd never learned off any Indian boys. Few regular Americans French-kissed with that much abandon as they tried to bust a man's spine with a leg-hug and literally sucked on his old organ-grinder with their smooth wet innards. So Longarm assumed she was warmed up enough for more serious action, and he knew he was right when she flung all her limbs to the four corners of the universe and war-whooped, "*Hokahey! Iyoptey!* Why are you holding back? Don't you *like* me, you big sissy?"

Chapter 18

The river water was warm enough, but the night air was chilly
when they went for a moonlight swim to cool off their bare
behinds. Longarm saw why Mato Takoza had suggested it
when they wound up in a mighty interesting position with
her hanging on to the edge of the raft facing away from him.

Then the moon ducked back behind the clouds and thunder
rolled up and down the river, so they got out, dried off, and
were huddled for warmth under the cover of the Bee Witch's
bed by the time heavy rain was pounding on the shingles above
their entwined bodies.

It warmed them up fine. But it was tough to fall asleep
in a bed neither was used to after all that coffee. So after
they'd shared a cheroot and talked about the missing Bee
Witch some more, Longarm lit the reading lamp on the old
gal's bed table while her naked student beekeeper rolled across
him to rummage out some of the expensive tomes the so-called
crazy lady had kept under her bed.

Longarm doubted any lunatic would have spent much time
with such dry but educational reading material. There were
books on geology, civil engineering, and such, along with an
atlas and a folder of even more detailed survey maps put out
by the government. Longarm sat up in bed with his cheroot
gripped between his teeth as he looked over a large-scale
contour chart of just Brown County, Minnesota, and a few
square miles of other counties that fit into the space left over on

the rectangular chart. Mato Takoza snuggled her naked charms closer as she confided, "Miss Jasmine liked that drawing. She used to thumbtack it to her drawing board and trace it on this funny stuff that might have been very thin flour sacking or maybe wax paper. When I asked, she got cross with me. So I never asked anymore."

Longarm lightly rubbed the fingertip of his free hand over the stiff manila paper as he murmured, "Draftsman's tracing silk. Costly and won't bear careless handling. The slick sizing over the mesh of fairy-dust weaving is meant to hold and to cherish traced lines, drops of spit, or moist fingerprints. So that might explain why she didn't even want an illiterate reading over her shoulder, no offense, but what in thunder would an old colored beekeeper be doing with contour maps and tracing silk?"

"Making her own maps?" the breed gal suggested innocently.

Longarm hugged her closer and said, "Bless you, my child, and as soon as I can get it up again I aim to kiss you. But let me have my arm back right now. I need both hands to investigate this further."

She sat up long enough for him to haul that arm out from behind her bare shoulders, but as she grasped what he was doing she protested, "Don't get that paper all dirty! Miss Jasmine will be angry, angry!"

Longarm went right on rubbing tobacco ash all over the survey map with gentle fingertips as he said soothingly, "It'll all brush away in the end. In the meantime this is an old trick we use when we find paper somebody's written or traced something else on top of."

As the pretty breed watched in wonder, the tobacco ash, blacker where it stuck in the grooves left in the thick paper by a heavier hand wielding something sharp, proceeded to draw lines across parts of Brown County where no government surveyor ever had. Indians made pretty fair maps on their own. So even though she didn't know how to read or write, Mato Takoza was able to follow the drift of the missing Bee Witch when the hitherto invisible line reached the Minnesota the two of them had just been swimming in.

"That line crosses the river just above the driftwood jam

162

this raft is moored below!" she decided.

Longarm soberly replied, "I noticed. Whether your Bee Witch had another wagon trace or a railroad in mind, she figured it ought to cross the river up by the Chambrun place."

He took a drag on the cheroot to produce more ash before he went on. "I'd have to agree with her if somebody asked me to survey yet another trestle site. These contour lines show higher ground to either side of the river, meaning a mid-stream span high enough for the bitty steamboats up this way to sneak their stacks under."

He rubbed in more ash as he mused, "Any engineer worth his salt could figure that much out in bed with his true love and this public knowledge. Did your Miss Jasmine ever drill holes in the ground as she barged her beehives up and down the banks?"

Mota Takoza started to say no. Then she thought and decided, "Hear me, it would be rude to follow anyone into the trees when they took along a shovel and a mail-order catalogue. Everyone digs at least a little hole to squat over if they intend to camp more than a night in the same spot."

"Unless they crap in a handy river," Longarm objected. He didn't ask how often she'd done that. Her sudden silence spoke louder than words. He just said, "Either way, you wouldn't have to dig far to be sure there's as much granite under the Chambrun claim as more local folks keep saying. When you plant foundations for a trestle you want to make sure they don't shift. Foundations planted in granite bedrock ain't about to shift, even on the flood plain of a somewhat whimsical river, so, yep, Chambrun knew what he was about when he up and claimed that high, dry quarter section. Or should I say his Santee wife and her secret pals picked it *for* him? Did your Miss Jasmine ever go over to borrow a cup of sugar or mayhaps sell a jar of honey at the Chambrun place, kitten?"

Mato Takoza thought before she said, "Not while I was with her. I told you I don't know that Tatowiyeh Wachipi who thinks she's such an important person. What are you afraid the Chambruns might have done to Miss Jasmine?"

Longarm frowned thoughtfully and replied, "Don't know and, damn it, I wish there wasn't so much stray sign across the trail Billy Vail sent me over this way to follow. But if what I'm commencing to suspect about a harmless colored crazy lady pans out, the Chambruns would be the last ones along this river to want her harmed or hampered in any way!"

She naturally wanted to know more. So Longarm explained how easy it had been for Miss Harriet Tubman, a lady of color, to pass herself as a silly old Negro mammy searching for her missing owners like the faithful darky of Dixie mythology, while acting as one of Allan Pinkerton's top Secret Service agents behind Confederate lines. He said, "The South was too proud to use colored spies. So they never looked twice at a dumb darky, when they might have asked what a white person they didn't know was doing in that particular place at that late hour. They say Harriet Tubman talked her way past a reb patrol close to Robert E. Lee's headquarters late one night by allowing she was searching for mushrooms. Every country boy in that patrol knew it was the wrong time of the year for field mushrooms, but they figured a dumb old nigger woman wouldn't know as much as them."

"I told you Mother and me played the long joke on Wasichu women to get work," the pretty breed replied. Then she asked, "What do you think Miss Jasmine was trying to hide by pretending to be *witko*?"

Longarm shrugged his bare shoulders and said, "Who she was working for, most likely. Nobody planning to run another rail line across the Minnesota would want it to get out ahead of time. It takes a year or more just to plan your route, grease the right political palms, and get title to the right-of-way you finally decide on. Railroads and even wagon routes have had to swing wide over greedy folks holding out for more money than a detour might be worth. Folks go *witko*, building *tipi tankas* in the sky, when they consider all that money they'll wind up with if only they can hang tougher than the rich folks trying to buy 'em out. So I doubt anyone in these parts knew, any better than you, what the so-called Bee Witch was really up to."

He took another drag on their shared cheroot, but began to brush the survey chart clean as he added, "Might as well keep her secret for her. It's easier to see now how come she took so much trouble to keep strangers well clear of this raft."

As if to prove his point they heard a cascade of tinny clankings, inspiring Longarm to say, "What the hell?"

His bed companion murmured, "That's how I knew you were moving along the bank before. Miss Jasmine showed me how. You tie one end of a dark fishing line to a sapling someone moving along the trail has to push aside. Then you run it, tautly, through a hole in the work-room wall, and hang some tomato cans up inside to—"

"Never mind the details! Let's worry about who in thunder it might *be* at this owlhooting hour!" Longarm trimmed the lamp to plunge the interior into darkness as he rolled off the bed to silently slip into the other bedroom for his Winchester. She followed close, whispering, "Nobody ever comes this late. Nobody!"

As if to prove her a liar for certain, somebody yelled in the near distance, and Longarm was glad they'd hauled that plank in. The male voice hailed them again in English, and when nobody answered he switched to Santee. Longarm was able to follow the coldly correct "*Hokahey!*" meaning something like "Get the lead out, damn it!" But then Mato Takoza went outside, and she and the strange Indian lost him as they rattled back and forth in their usual mixture of soft pleasant vowels and strangled or hissed consonants. Longarm, crouching behind her, had no way of controlling the parley, and could only hope Mato Takoza knew what she was doing as she seemed to be talking sweetly to the son of a bitch. Then, as yet another voice chimed in ashore, it seemed there were at least two sons of bitches!

Longarm followed just enough to figure she was inviting them to come aboard for coffee and cake, Indians having the same notions as other country folks when it came to *offering* leastways. But even as he hunkered low with his Winchester, Longarm heard one of the men on shore call the pretty little thing his Unshi, or grandmother, and respectfully decline.

As the two or more of them went crashing back along the bank through the tanglewood, Mato Takoza hugged her naked breasts to his bare back and sobbed, "They were looking for you! They said they were your friends and just wished to tell you something. But you had already told me about someone following you along the county road, and I didn't think you wanted them to know where you were!"

Longarm rose, getting a better grip on her as he shifted the cold-steel Winchester to his other side, saying, "You thought right. Did you get any line on who they might really be, and how did you manage to get rid of them like so?"

As they moved back inside, her naked hip rubbing his bare thigh, Mato Takoza said, "As I told you, they said they were friends of Wasichu Wastey, but neither offered me his name, not even a fighting name one offers a respected enemy, so I knew they did not want me to know who they were and I thought it might not be wise to press that."

She reached coyly down to grasp his flaccid manhood in the dark as she added, "I invited them to come aboard for the rest of the night. But then I had to warn them I might be *tehinda*, if they still followed the *wakan* of their elders."

Longarm started to ask, then he recalled what *tehinda* meant and had to laugh. He'd heard Sandwich Islanders considered a gal having her period taboo, as they put it, although few Indian nations got that excited, and were content to just stay the hell away from a gal and her quarters until the bad medicine passed on and she could make herself acceptable again with a smoke bath.

But since they both knew that in this case Mato Takoza had only been fibbing, Longarm found it surprising when she insisted in proving she wasn't anywhere close to that time of the month by shoving two pillows under her brown bottom and having him hold the lamp close as she spread her legs invitingly again. He didn't really care as he found himself rising to the occasion.

Chapter 19

It got tougher to ambush a rider when you didn't know when or which way he'd be coming. So Longarm left early and rode high and wide for New Ulm, working his way through more than one drift fence as he circled out across the upland prairie between the bottomlands of the Minnesota and the more modest Sleepy Eye.

There were other less famous draws and a mess of tree groves a drygulcher might have found right handy, and a thoughtful rider had to consider each as he approached, his own saddle gun across his lap. But as Longarm had surmised from the start, nobody was laying for him where he hadn't told a soul he was headed, and he met nobody out that way but cows, mostly longhorn stock with a dab of Angus or whiteface to tender up their beef for the eastern market, now that the Depression of the early '70s had faded to bitter memory and housewives could act fussy about the meat they put on the table again.

The aptly named Sleepy Eye met up with the even more logically called Cottonwood around ten miles west of New Ulm. So Longarm cut east across higher rolling range and, as far as he knew, made it all the way into the bluffs just west of town without being seen by a soul.

He rode old Smokey down a deserted pathway past a brick kiln nobody seemed to be working that morning, and drifted into town at a walk, occasioning no more than casual glances from the townsfolk he found up and about. For thanks to his long detour it was well past mid-morning, and even the residential streets were fairly busy.

Gunnar Kellgren had told him he could leave old Smokey in the care of that livery near the boat landing. But the blue roan was a pretty good mount, and Longarm wanted to make sure he still had the use of old Blaze before he cut himself entirely afoot. So he rode first to see if old Ilsa Pedersson had recovered from her awkward feelings about two dead bodies in her house to explain to the neighbors.

She hadn't. Longarm found her raking under the shrubbery in her front yard when he reined in and dismounted. But as he was tethering to her hitching post the widow gal came over, rake in hand and face all flushed under her sunbonnet, as she flustered, "Good grief, Custis, what are you doing here in broad daylight?"

He frowned down at her uncertainly and replied, "I sort of thought I was staying here. Correct me if I'm wrong, honey."

She shot an uneasy glance up the maple-shaded street and murmured, "Come back after dark, on foot, no earlier than ten, and we may be able to sneak you in the back way, darling."

Longarm started to say it made little sense for a man to pussyfoot clean across town after he'd had to find another place to leave his saddle and such. But she might have thought he was acting proud, and a man just never knew before noon how he'd feel about going to bed with a particular gal after dark. So he just nodded and said he might or might not be back, depending on what they had for him over at the Western Union by the depot.

Ilsa almost put an anxious hand on his sleeve before she remembered her own rep and softly pleaded, "Promise you'll come back for at least one proper good-bye before you leave town for good."

"What about the neighbors?" he gently asked.

To which she replied with a Mona Lisa smile, "Let them get their own friends to say good-bye to. I'm not cross with you, darling. It's just that I have to live on this street and, well, it isn't every day a respectable widow has to explain three strange men shooting it out in her hitherto respectable residence!"

Longarm had to smile at the picture, but assured her he followed her drift, and would have kissed her before mounting up again if he'd thought she wanted him to. For she'd been a good old gal, and it was making him wistful already to think of her as no more than another fond memory.

But that was the way things had to be when a tumbleweed cuss wore a badge and a gun in this old uncertain world. So he rode on over to the river, where, sure enough, they knew the Kellgrens at that livery and said old Smokey would be welcome out back in their corral until such time as somebody rode in to pick him up.

Longarm asked what they charged to leave a man's saddle and possibles under lock and key instead of their more casual tack room. The elderly Swede who ran the place said it depended on whether he was a customer or not. So Longarm told him truthfully he just didn't know whether he'd need to hire another mount or not, and they settled on ten cents a day as a fair rate.

Longarm was glad. Toting his Winchester all over town could be a bother, and there were other things worth stealing in his saddlebags.

Being he had the time as well as the small room in the back to change in, Longarm left the livery in clean but faded jeans and an old darker blue army shirt he sometimes used when he wanted to look a tad different at a distance. For sometimes the fractions of shooting time it could take a shooter to make up his mind could make one hell of a difference in the outcome.

There was little a man could do about walking taller than average, and changing the Colorado crush of his sepia Stetson hardly seemed worth the bother. So he simply kept his eyes peeled as he made his way back to the Western Union afoot.

They'd been expecting him. There was no word yet on that stranger who'd gone off the railroad trestle into all that white water. But a long night letter from Billy Vail was waiting there to order him on back to Denver. According to Longarm's cagey old boss, one hell of a tracker in his own right, he'd sent his senior deputy on a wild-goose chase and he was sorry as hell.

Longarm told the telegraph clerk he wasn't ready to wire back just yet. Then he put the night letter in a hip pocket and headed up to the sheriff's office. This time that deputy was able to introduce Longarm to the sheriff in person, a potbellied but strong-looking old cuss called Verner Tegner. He said to call him Vern, and might have reminded Longarm of Billy Vail if he hadn't smiled so much.

As they lit up the cigars the sheriff handed out to guests in an election year, Longarm asked what they'd found out about those two gunslicks he'd had to lay low at the Widow Pedersson's. The local lawmen exchanged embarrassed glances, and the deputy said, "We're still working on them. Sent out an all-points by wire yesterday. Ain't had any nibbles as yet. Hired guns are most often from somewheres far and wide, you know."

Longarm took hold of the back of the bentwood chair the sheriff had pointed out for him, spun it around, and sat astride it so the two of them would consider it polite to sit. Then he sighed and told them, "There seems to be a lot of that going around. My boss back in Denver just wired he's cut the trail of that Tyger-Flanders gang way closer to the scene of their last known crime. Some of that hot paper's turned up in other parts as well. A bank in Salt Lake City stopped one, and then somebody got arrested trying to break a hundred-dollar treasury certificate in Chicago. They had to let the suspect go when he was able to prove he'd been dealing faro at the time of that Fort Collins robbery. Being a professional gambler, he naturally disremembers just who he might have won the infernal money off of."

The sheriff nodded sagely and said, "We never thought Israel Bedford was an outlaw. That Chambrun cuss likely got the hot paper as innocently. When a gang pulls a robbery, they generally have spending the money in mind. So by this time there's no saying how many innocent hands the purloined payroll has been scattered through far and wide."

Longarm took a drag on the cheap cigar, noting it burned hot in its own right the way such flashy political handouts were inclined to, as he quietly observed, "Chambrun naturally told me he'd come by the money honestly, and even suggested somebody might have switched a good note with a wicked one. Can either of you gents come up with a motive for Banker Plover wanting to get a halfbreed in trouble?"

The two lawmen looked blank. The sheriff was the one who suggested, "I don't know what sort of a name Plover might be, and he's not likely to vote for me this fall, the Republican cuss, but I fear I can't see why he'd want to frame any nester for anything. I don't think his bank could hold a mortgage on the Chambrun place, could it?"

Longarm shook his head and said, "The Chambruns won't own the land to mortgage it before they prove their claim, and now *there's* something I hadn't even considered until just now, bless your hearts!"

They naturally wanted to know what he was blessing them for.

Longarm explained, "I got an interesting line on that Bee Witch you gents may have heard about."

Tegner laughed and said, "Oh, her? She's crazy but harmless enough."

Longarm said, "I'm not so certain she was crazy, but she surely seems to be missing. Worse yet, I suspect she was working a secret survey for somebody planning yet another bridge across the river, up by Chambrun's claim."

The two local lawmen agreed they'd never heard such an outlandish suggestion about the crazy old Bee Witch.

Longarm insisted, "She was charting proposed crossings on a sort of fancy tracing paper out to her house raft. I looked for the tracings by lamplight and broad day. They weren't on board. Neither was she. I don't know whether she just abandoned her false identity because she'd finished what they'd sent her to do, or whether somebody waylaid her and destroyed her work to delay her employers considerably."

Sheriff Tegner frowned through his own tobacco smoke. "What good would that do anyone trying to keep somebody from building another span across our river? Lord knows we could *use* more this side of the one way up by Fairfax, and a good site is a good site. So why wouldn't they just send some other sneaks to survey the same way?"

Longarm replied, "I just said that. Meanwhile, a homesteader with an unproven claim smack in the path of a railroad wouldn't be able to hold out for a fraction of what a landowner free and simple could demand and likely get!"

Sheriff Tegner gasped, "Hot damn! It's an election year as well, and none of my white pals like those trashy Sioux to begin with. I'll get right out there to arrest the son of a bitch in person and—"

"I'd wait till I had a better case." Longarm said. "For all we know for certain, there's no case to begin with. I'd hate to have a murder victim turn up alive and well if *I* was running for sheriff this November."

Tegner called him a spoilsport, and asked why Longarm had brought the whole mess to his attention to begin with.

Longarm explained, "I got to. I promised a lady I'd find out why her Miss Jasmine, the Bee Witch's given name, never came back from an errand here in town. I'm handing you some other odd doings on a plate before I have to leave as well."

"You're going somewheres?" asked the sheriff's younger deputy.

Longarm nodded. "Since the two of you are real lawmen, you know real life don't work the way it seems to in those detective yarns by Mister Poe, Mister Twain, and such. In real life it seems one damned crook after another is pulling off some crime with no consideration of the cases we're already working on."

They agreed that was for damned sure. So Longarm explained, "My own Marshal Vail sent me here to New Ulm when that money from that payroll robbery turned up in the old stamping grounds of at least the leaders of the gang involved. I seem to have stumbled over other odd doings, and I mean to leave you a full report on paper before I leave. But as you just pointed out, that payroll seems to have been spread all over, meaning there's no particular significance to the transaction that brought me here, albeit you'll notice some assimilated Indians seem to be up to some mighty murky real-estate dealings."

The local deputy said, "You got to *watch* Indians once they learn to read and write. I hear old Quanah Parker's wheeling and dealing in Texas real estate since he decided to live white."

Longarm shrugged and said, "That's my point. A lady friend of mine down Texas way calls Chief Parker her Uncle Quanah, and seems to think he's sort of cute in his long braids and stovepipe hat. Meanwhile, like a heap of slick-talking Indians, or *official* Indians, such as Miss Belle Starr of the Cherokee Strip, Uncle Quanah can be as Indian as need be to draw his government allotments, and as Parker from Texas as he likes when it comes to making deals with other white cattlemen."

The deputy nodded sagely and said, "Charges a dollar a head if you want to drive your herd to market across Comanche land, or six cents an acre if you want to graze there, now that most of the buffalo are gone."

Longarm said, "Let's stick to your own Santee of fond memory. I was told flat out that a good many local Indians you ran out of these parts years ago mean to come back, living white, after gaining legal title to some of their lost Santee Sioux reserve."

"That ain't fair," Sheriff Tegner protested. "I rode with the Sixth Minnesota, and don't try to feed me that shit about Mister Lo, The Poor Indian. I was there when we had to bury white men, women, and bitty babies, all swelled up and flyblown, out on the prairie after the savages scalped 'em, stripped and raped 'em, the men and babes included! I heard that whining shit about them Sioux not getting their rations on time with a war going on back East, and I neither know nor care whether crooked traders short-stopped hard cash as well. Hardly a white person they butchered in revenge could have known doodly-shit about the government's dealings with Indians they'd been assured were friendly. It was that same old refrain you hear from every sniveling crook, red or white, once he's caught!"

The deputy nodded and chimed in falsetto, "Honestly, Sheriff, it was all my cruel landlord's fault! He evicted my poor momma for not paying her rent, so I naturally raped that lady across the street for revenge!"

Longarm grimaced and said, "You don't have to convince

173

me. Like I said, right or wrong, this syndicate of breeds and pure-bloods seems interested in local real estate and may or may not be up to something worse. I'm going to have to leave it up to you, interested as I found it, because my boss feels I'm wasting time around here."

He nodded at the deputy he'd talked to before and explained, "Like I told you earlier, we had too many Calvert Tygers burning to death in rooming house fires. My boss figured, correctly as it just turned out, somebody was trying to convince us Calvert Tyger was dead out Colorado way. So when he got word about that payroll money turning up here where Tyger commenced his shady career, he added two and two to come up with a wrong number."

Longarm took the vile cigar out of his mouth to hold it over the back of the chair and let it smolder politely as he sighed and continued. "I wasn't the only deputy working for Billy Vail, of course. He had a half-dozen others poking about closer to home. So the day before yesterday Deputy O'Foyle out of our office came across yet another Calvert Tyger registered as a guest of the Colfax House near the Overland Terminal in Denver. So that night, Billy Vail had deputies at the hotel, and sure enough, they caught a son of a bitch fixing to set fire to the place after midnight, and never mind all the innocent men and women upstairs, whether they were married to one another or not!"

Sheriff Tegner whistled and declared, "Hot damn! If I caught me a firebug out to cremate yet another Calvert Tyger, I vow I'd soon make him tell me why!"

Longarm nodded soberly. "Old Billy did. It takes him a tad longer, since he hates to leave bruises, but he usually gets the straight story with his gentler means of persuasion. The unfortunate they caught, who's facing a good jolt in prison even with the charge reduced from attempted murder to arson, was a well-known petty thief with a serious drinking problem. He says—and Billy Vail believes him—he was recruited for the job by a more prosperous sinister stranger who gave him a hundred up front with the promise of another hundred after the hotel went up in smoke with yet another Calvert Tyger."

The local lawmen looked blank. It was the younger deputy

who asked, "But how did they murder another such gent if the plot to set his hotel on fire failed?"

Longarm said simply, "They couldn't. We have the supposed Tyger in protective custody too. His real name's Peppin, and he'd never heard of Calvert Tyger before someone who describes a heap like the cuss who recruited the firebug offered him drinking money and a free room if only he'd play a little joke."

Longarm took a thoughtless drag on that cigar before he remembered why he'd taken it out of his mouth. "The generous sneak told Peppin he was working for a rich mining man who wanted his wife to think he'd checked into the Colfax House alone during a business trip down to Denver."

Sheriff Tegner decided, "Sensible story. Just sneaky enough for an average drunk to buy. The plot was for this Peppin to die as another Calvert Tyger, a famous outlaw, whilst he thought he was covering up for some rich dog and his play-pretty at another hotel in town, right?"

When Longarm nodded, it was the local deputy who demanded with a puzzled frown, "To what end? What's the point of somebody letting you find Calvert Tyger dead over and over again?"

Longarm said, "That's one of the things Billy Vail wants me to look into as soon as I get back to Denver. The first notion that comes to mind would be that the real gang leader wants us to think he's dead so he can settle down and enjoy all that payroll money. I can go along with old Billy's thesis that the real Brick Flanders, with his red beard, glass eye, and gold front tooth, would be better off drugged and burnt up in a fire than tagging along with a leader those two bums from the Colfax House describe as sort of smooth-talking but bland-looking. Another member of the gang could have changed the rooming house register easy enough before his fire burned up the already dead Brick Flanders."

Sheriff Tegner whistled again. "I can see why you ain't as worried about land grabbers who might or might not waylay a colored lady now and again. Anyone who'd burn folks up in his own name, over and over again, has to be just plain mad-dog *mean*!"

Longarm shrugged. "Billy Vail feels, and I'm inclined to agree, the surviving members of the gang have some motive, nasty as it may seem. It ain't as if Calvert Tyger ain't been at it as long as Frank and Jesse, you know, albeit he's been way more cautious and not half as active. So why would a careful occasional cuss who's always allowed things to cool down betwixt jobs suddenly take to burning his own self up in fire after fire, whilst still on the dodge for that big Fort Collins job?"

Sheriff Tegner said, "I follow your drift. You'd think that once he and his pals got away, clear with all that money, they'd leave Colorado entire instead of trying to convince you their leader was still in the state, albeit burnt to a crisp."

The younger local deputy volunteered, "I'd let that money I took cool down before I spent it too. I forgot to ask about the hundred dollars they gave that one cuss to set fire to that hotel the other night."

Longarm shook his head. "Billy Vail didn't forget. It was in ten- and twenty-dollar silver certificates. We just don't know whether the crooks who stole the money knew those serial numbers had been recorded. It ain't the usual routine. But the paymaster up there in Fort Collins did it, poor bastard, and now nobody will ever be able to ask why. Suffice it to say it's one of the few breaks we've had on this case. Had the money been untraceable, and had Calvert Tyger simply left the state, as you suggested, we'd be sniffing a mighty stale and musty trail by now."

He got back to his feet, saying in a brighter tone, "Meanwhile we ain't, Lord love all crooks too slick for their own good, so like I promised, I'll put all I know about your local mysteries on paper before I leave town. I've just a few more errands to tend in New Ulm before I do. So I'd best get cracking."

They rose as well to shake and part friendly with him. Longarm strode out front and headed next for the bank. Some cynical sage had once written, doubtless in French, that a stiff prick had no conscience. But even after he'd cooled off, he'd promised the poor worried Mato Takoza he'd see what he could find out about her missing Miss Jasmine when he got to town. So here he was, and now that he knew the Bee

Witch had sometimes called herself Miss Jasmine Smith, as unlikely as that sounded, there was an outside chance she'd cashed checks or money orders at one bank or another. The folks she worked for would have hardly funded her with cash or money orders she'd have to cash less discreetly at the post office or Western Union.

By this time it was going on noon, and the streets of New Ulm were starting to get hot as well as less crowded. For folks working in a town this size tended to go home for their noon dinners.

So Longarm spotted the cuss keeping pace with him, a pistol shot back, sooner than he might have had the walk been more crowded when he glanced at window glass in passing. A man with a job such as his learned to do that every chance he got. So Longarm was pretty certain the dark figure on his ass was really on his ass, once he'd crossed the street, actually out of his way to the bank, and spotted that same mysterious cuss at the same distance, behind him, in the plate glass of a dress shop.

The cuss wasn't reflected sharp enough to make out in detail at that range, but Longarm could see he was dressed cow, although a tad fancy, in a silver-trimmed black charro vest and shotgun chaps. His features were a dark blur under his big black Stetson Buckeye with its high crown pinched army-style. That didn't mean near as much to Longarm as the fancy Cleveland twelve-gauge the cuss had cradled casually over one forearm, as if he might be after duck or quail in the center of town.

Certain the cuss was tailing him, although uncertain about the motive, Longarm strode on as if he hadn't noticed, and swung the next corner as he might have if he'd been headed for somewhere down that side street to begin with.

It worked even better when, just around the corner, Longarm spied a service entrance in the brick wall of the corner store and crawfished into it, casually drawing his .44-40 but holding it down at his side politely. The man on his tail with that scattergun swung the corner wider, as a trained gunfighter was supposed to.

As he spotted Longarm and broke stride, Longarm called

out an easygoing howdy, and never raised his own gun muzzle until he saw he had to.

They fired as one, the dark stranger's twelve-gauge blowing a big dusty crater in the cinder paving between them as Longarm's round of .44-40 punched him in the gut to jackknife him out from under his large hat and lay him low.

Longarm managed just in time not to squeeze off the extra round or so that seemed safest on such occasions. He covered his downed foe thoughtfully instead as he strode over to smile down, saying, "I was admiring that fowling piece you just dropped, pard. English made over to London Town, right?"

He could see now the man he'd gunned seemed almost pure Indian despite his duds and short haircut. Longarm hunkered down, six-gun in hand but held politely, to quietly ask, "Where are you hit and, just in case, who would you like us to get in touch with for you?"

The dying man just glared spitefully as his lips moved silently in what could have been a curse, a prayer, or a death song. By the time Longarm had pinned on his federal badge and Sheriff Tegner had joined the gathering crowd, the black-clad stranger's jet black eyes had commenced to film over and he wasn't moving his lips or breathing.

As Tegner hunkered beside him, Longarm quietly said, "I ain't sure what just happened. He was tailing me from your office to here. But he had the drop on me earlier, and never got really hostile until I challenged him."

The sheriff said, "Remind me never to challenge you, Longarm. I think I know this old boy. He looks a mite older now, but don't we all, and he reminds me of a scout we had with the old Sixth Volunteers. If it's the same cuss, his name was Baptiste Youngwolf. Last I'd heard, he'd run off to his reservation. Lots of 'em were like that when it came to taking orders, you know."

Longarm softly said, "I've ridden some with full-blood scouts. If this was one who rode with you, Vern, might he by any chance have been Santee?"

The sheriff shook his head and replied, "Hell, no, Chippewa. Even if you could get yourself a Sioux to scout Sioux for you, you'd not be sure you could trust such a two-faced cuss yourself. Him being Sioux could complicate hell out of things!"

Longarm grumbled, "Not hardly. This would all make more sense if I could be more certain this was a Santee-speaker I may have overheard just last night."

"He was Chippewa," another old-timer in the crowd decided. "I recall that same hatchet face and the cavalry crease of his big black hat from earlier days as well. I never rode with the Volunteers, but I used to drink with some. This old boy was one of their scouts like the sheriff here says. The soldiers called him Chief, as I now recall, and now that I think back, they did say old Chief deserted with some white boys and never hung about to draw his last pay."

Longarm got wearily back to his feet, muttering, "A lot old Billy Vail really knows! I got to go send him a wire, Vern, if that's all the same with you."

The sheriff got to his own feet, saying, "As long as you wasn't planning on leaving Brown County before we can tidy this up with the coroner's office. I doubt there will be any fuss, you being a lawman and him coming after you with that scattergun and all. But they are likely to want some more details for the death certificate and bill of mortality book. You reckon he was really that cuss called Chief who ran off with them Galvanized Yankee deserters that time?"

To which Longarm could only reply, "That works better than any Objibwa working in cahoots on something else with folks he'd have been raised to call Nadowessioux and hate like sulfur and molasses!"

Then he added, reloading his six-gun, "After that, like your county coroner, I sure would like to have some-damned-body fill in some of the damned details! For I'll be switched with snakes if I can make one lick of sense out of all this bullshit!"

But before he could elbow away through the gathering crowd, one of the newcomers loudly demanded, "Jesus H. Christ, who tangled with the Chief and what's the Chief doing there on the ground?"

It was Gus Hansson, that young cowhand Longarm had met the other night on the open range west of the county road.

Longarm turned to the surprised-looking kid to declare,

"He's dead because he tangled with me. It was his own notion. I'm still working on how come. You say you knew him more recent than these older gents, Gus?"

Hansson nodded, but stared at Longarm as if he'd just been caught jerking off in church as he replied, "Well, sure I knew him. We was riding for the same outfit. Miss Helga Runeberg hired him as a top hand not two weeks ago, and she ain't going to like this at all!"

An older local in the crowd proclaimed with a more noticeable Swedish accent, "Yumpin' Yesus! Helga Runeberg has always been as mean as she was pretty and she has more than a dozen riders! If I wass you I'd get out of town before she finds out, no matter who I wass or why I yust shot one of her boys!"

Longarm smiled thinly and announced for all who had any interest in the matter, "I did what I had to and I'll leave these parts when I've finished what I came to do. If anyone wants to build what just happened here into a blood feud, be advised I can get just as mean as pretty too!"

Chapter 20

Longarm spent more time than he felt he had to spare at the Western Union office near the depot. First the fuss in charge had to argue with him about rates, seeing he wanted to send more than three full pages of close-set block lettering to his home office at day rates collect.

The clerk pointed out they charged way less than a nickel a word after midnight, when the moonlit wires might otherwise hum idle in the wind. But Longarm said he'd have told them to send it as a night letter if he hadn't wanted his boss to get the damned report directly.

They didn't argue, since he paid up front for the shorter wires he sent to the Indian agents at Crow Creek and Leech Lake, hoping to get a better line on that dead Indian, whether Ojibwa or Santee. Then he had a longer argument over their prior telegraph traffic, with the old fuss in charge insisting Mister Ezra Cornell would rise from his grave to haunt them if they betrayed their sacred trust to all their customers.

Ezra Cornell had been the rich old bird who'd gotten richer than old Sam Morse on the telegraph by founding and stringing the Western Union Telegraph Company just in time for the Civil War. He'd made so much money he'd had enough left over to build a university and get his son elected governor of New York, after Ezra had died, by setting down some company rules in stone. One that had given Longarm a pain in the past was that nobody who didn't work for the company was ever to read a private message sent by a paying customer.

Longarm explained, "I've had this argument with you boys before and, so far, I've usually won. Old Ezra never intended his employees to obstruct justice. He just didn't want small-town gossip emanating from his scattered offices."

He let that sink in and added, "I ain't interested in whether an elderly colored lady who might have called herself Smith was sending or receiving dirty messages. I only need to know if anyone like that availed herself of your services at all, damn it!"

The clerk sniffed and grudgingly allowed, "We have very few darkies in New Ulm to begin with. I suppose it's safe to tell you no elderly colored women by any name have availed themselves of our services in recent memory."

Longarm nodded. "Now we're getting somewheres. As you'll see whilst you're sending that tedious report to my boss, Marshal Vail, I just had to shoot me an Indian they called Chief Youngwolf. Santee, or what you'd call Chippewa. I described him in more detail in them wires I just asked you to send to the Sioux and Chippewa B.I.A. agents. You'd know if a pure-blood wearing a black Stetson Buckeye had been in and out of here all that much by any name, right?"

The Western Union man declared that as a matter of fact they had fewer Indians sending or receiving telegrams than colored folks, the Great Sioux Rising of '62 having left Indians unpopular as hell in this particular corner of Minnesota.

Longarm started to ask a dumb question about breeds. He decided an Indian gunslick laying low in a county so crowded with blue-eyed blond Scandinavians would as likely recruit a pure white to front for him if he was shy about dealing with Western Union in person.

Longarm confided to the clerk, as much to diagram it in his own puzzled mind, "Somebody communicating by wire with Colorado pals on a fairly regular basis would doubtless be using some slick code if he was too slick to just wire back and forth naturally."

The Western Union clerk asked how Longarm knew his mysterious red outlaw had been trying to communicate with anyone by wire to begin with.

Longarm said, "That's easy. I never put an ad in your local paper to announce my arrival. Youngwolf has been laying low on a cattle spread closer to Sleepy Eye than here to begin with. I'd have never thought to look for him there if he hadn't come looking for me with a twelve-gauge just now, if that was his true intent. I'd sure like to ask the white pal he must have had fronting for him just what in blue blazes this is all about. For up until a few minutes ago I was inclined to agree with my boss that there wasn't all that much going on here in New Ulm!"

The somewhat mollified telegraph clerk agreed it seemed a real poser. Longarm didn't want to get him het up again by asking to go over all the wires they'd sent or received for, say, the past seventy-two hours. He knew that even if he won the fight, he'd have a hell of a chore just reading that many messages without a clue as to which ones might be in code.

Folks who hadn't had to try decoding tended to mix codes up with ciphers. A cipher was kid stuff next to a code. The cipher everyone since the ancient Greeks tried first involved simply switching the letters of the alphabet around, so an *X* might stand for an *A* or a *Z* for an *E* and so forth. But any signal corpsman worth his salt would know right off that a message reading something like "UIF RVJDL CSPXO GPA KVNQFE PWFS UIF MBAZ EPH" had to be cipher, and once you knew that, it wasn't too tough to figure the letter used most likely stood for an *E*, the next most an *A*, and so on till you got a few words to make sense and could fill in the rest.

But a simple pre-arranged *code* could be almost impossible to break because it worked the way kith and kin might talk when they didn't want the kids to know just what they were saying. It was just as easy and less shocking, for instance, for the lady of the house to suggest they put the kiddies to bed and go for a stroll in the moonlight than it was to say, "Let's lock the kids up and screw," although her man had as good a notion of what she really had in mind. Crooks tended to use messages such as, "Aunt Edna sends her regards," when they wanted to say a robbery was off, still being planned, or all set to pull off. There was simply no saying how a gang leader back in Denver or Durango could have wired the Chief he was coming this way, or what to do about it once he arrived.

He mulled the recent events in his own mind as he legged it over to the post office. The Indian they called the Chief had surely been following him, to whatever purpose, when he'd forced the issue. Those other Indians who'd mentioned him by name, in Santee, might or might not have been working with an outlaw everyone had down as a blood enemy. Crooks had no shame. Or what if those Santee trying to get a foot back in the doorway of their old hunting grounds were not in cahoots with the Indian he'd just shot it out with, but worried about something else he might uncover on them?

The wheels were still spinning within wheels inside his head when he hit pay dirt, sort of, at the post office. A mousy but not too bad-looking mail sorter recalled a nicely dressed colored lady who'd picked up more than one bulky letter from Chicago, she thought, addressed to one Judith Jones in care of General Delivery, New Ulm. Longarm said that sounded close enough to Jasmine Smith.

Longarm had no call to pursue how such a lady might *send* mail to Chicago, since there were public mail drops all over. It added up to the sneaky so-called Bee Witch sending her tracing-silk drawings by mail and getting paid for them the same way. Whether she'd sent all they'd wanted and she'd just left for other parts, or whether someone else had committed foul play to keep her from finishing, was still up in the air. He'd told pretty little Mato Takoza that, either way, he saw no reason why she shouldn't just go on herding bees out yonder for fun and profit until further notice.

He had to go next to the county courthouse, where, just as Sheriff Tegner had said, they were holding a meeting in the cellar to see how they wanted to record that dead Indian.

As the older lawman introduced Longarm to their coroner and his pals, Longarm learned they'd already determined the cause of death had been internal bleeding, occasioned by a .44–40 round busting the old boy's aorta all to hell inside him. Longarm said he'd aimed low in the fond hope of getting more out of the son of a bitch than he had. Nobody there disputed the right of a lawman, or any white man, to fire on an infernal Indian pointing a twelve-gauge anywhere near him.

184

The coroner said he'd already sent a rider out to talk to the dead man's female boss, in hopes Miss Runeberg could shed some light on what one of her riders had been doing in town with that Cleveland to begin with.

Once that meeting was adjourned pro tem, Longarm walked Sheriff Tegner and his deputies back to their nearby office, and borrowed a desk to write up as detailed a report for Brown County as they had any right to expect. He suggested Tegner keep a friendly eye on the breed gal running that honey and wax operation in the absence of the missing Bee Witch. Since everyone else was acting so sneaky about a possible bridge site up the river, Longarm put things plain enough for a cuss as friendly as old Tegner to make some profitable real-estate deals if he felt like it. Old George Washington had been decent enough in his day, and nobody had begrudged him a little land speculation near the end of the Revolution. Doing well for oneself while doing good for others was a grand old American custom. Longarm didn't care what others did as long as they didn't break federal statutes on purpose or hurt a soul he had any use for.

But just in case he was missing something important, Longarm went next to that bank, arriving just in time to see them shutting the big front door from across the way.

He hurried on across, muttering about banker's hours, and ignored the "Closed" sign hanging behind the medium-sized glass door panel to knock on the shellacked oak as if he really meant it.

That pretty blond gal, Miss Vigdis Magnusson, came to the door to wigwag her finger at him chidingly. Then she recognized Longarm and popped the door inward, gasping, "Hurry! Get in here before anyone catches us being naughty! We've been closed nearly an hour and I was just about to duck out the back way. Everyone else has already left for the day and I'm not supposed to open up to anybody for any reason!"

He started to say he'd come to see her boss, old P. S. Plover. But she'd just said the cuss had left for the day, and sometimes a lawman could get more out of a bank employee who knew less about the law as it applied to running a bank. So he smiled sincerely at the buxom blue-eyed blonde, admiring how different she looked next to the gal he'd had breakfast with at dawn, and said, "Mebbe it's just as well your boss ain't here, Miss Vigdis. By the way, do any of your personal pals call you Viggy?"

She fluttered her lashes and allowed that sounded cute as she led him back to that office they'd been in before. She didn't seem to care why. As they passed the time-locked vault she said she'd sort of hoped he'd drop by again. Once they got all the way back, Longarm noticed the blinds had been drawn and everything looked sort of gravy-brown in the light still getting through from outside.

Vigdis, or Viggy, motioned to an overstuffed leather chesterfield against one wall and said, "Sit right down and tell me just what you wanted from me, Custis."

So he sat, smiling up at her a mite awkwardly as he chose his words and decided to take the bull by the horns, beginning, "You look like a sensible gal a man can just level with, Miss Viggy. I don't have too many friends here in New Ulm I can turn to for help and, well, to tell the truth, I'd like you to get even more naughty for me than you were by letting me in after closing hours."

She blushed hard enough to make out from where he sat, despite the dim daylight, and declared, "Certainly not! Just because a girl smiles sort of warmly at a nice-looking man, it hardly gives him the right to come right out and ask her to be naughty!"

Longarm laughed out loud as he grasped her meaning and protested, "Hold on, Miss Viggy! I never meant I wanted you to get *really* naughty with me once we wound up alone back here."

She answered demurely, "Well, in that case, you're forgiven. But I warn you, I don't go in for any of that really naughty stuff some girls say they like, and you promise you won't *tell* anybody, right?"

He started to tell her she had him all wrong. But then he noticed she seemed to have had nothing on under the summer frock she seemed to be shucking. So he just hauled her down on the tufted leather to treat her right as the two of them got

186

him out of his own gunbelt and most of his duds. She didn't ask him to shuck his army shirt and boots until they'd gotten to know one another better on that old chesterfield. But once she'd come, on top, with him kissing her big creamy tits in turn, she even decided she didn't want her shoes in the way. So a good time was had by all, and she declared she'd seldom been ravaged so romantically by such a grand kisser. It was her notion to call what they were doing "ravaging." Longarm wasn't certain he'd had any say in the matter. He believed her when she said she'd found it lonely working in a stuffy old bank with all her school chums clean down the river in the bigger town of Mankato.

After they'd screwed, kissed, and smoked a spell, Longarm decided it was safe to tell her what he'd really come for. He told her about the Bee Witch, or a sly old colored lady acting as some sort of secret surveyor for Lord only knows who. He explained he knew it was against banking regulations to release such information without a court order, but that he'd been hoping, seeing they were such pals, she might see fit to bend the rules a tad.

She did better than that, for a gal who said she didn't go in for any of that naughty French or Greek stuff. Smoking his cheroot in the gathering dusk, without having to strike a light or even get off his bare lap, Viggy said, "I know who you must mean. She had a savings account with us under the name of Janice Carpenter. She was getting these monthly checks from the Chicago and Northwestern, or was it the Minny Saint Lou? We cash so many railroad payroll checks. I'd have to look it up to be sure. But I do know she withdrew all her savings back around Christmastime, and now that you mention it, I don't think I've seen her around town since then."

Longarm took the smoke back for a thoughtful drag as the naked lady in his lap reached down to adjust his semi-erection for more comfort, to her, and coyly asked, "Can't it wait, darling?"

He leaned his bare back harder against the tufted leather to thrust up into her at a friendlier angle as he said soothingly, "No need to put you to that much bother, you sweet little Swedish doll. The most eccentric beekeeper fixing to get herself murdered would hardly have known she wanted to close her bank account first. The timing sounds right, and I don't suppose you'd recall how much she had with you at the usual rate of interest?"

Viggy writhed her bare bottom to take it even deeper as she told him in a surprisingly conversational tone, "I'd really have to look that up. All I recall at this late date was Mister Plover swearing because it was the last day of a busy week and he had to send for more cash after she and several others withdrew better than four-figure amounts during the holiday shopping season."

Longarm nodded and said, "That's all I really needed. In figures, I mean. Let me get rid of this fool cheroot and see if we can't do this right!"

They could, dog-style, with her bare belly hooked over one softly padded arm of the chesterfield and her big pale rump thrust up at an interesting angle.

As he watched his old organ-grinder sliding in and out of her, he was reminded, by the contrast, of the smaller darker gal he'd had at dawn in a similar position. Good old Mato Takoza was likely to make out well enough on her own in the beekeeping business. That handsome withdrawal by her Miss Jasmine likely meant the so-called Bee Witch had left for good without bothering to sell off her ramshackle raft and beehives. She'd doubtless been paid so much for her secret railroad survey she could have given that pony to some kid in town for a Christmas present.

Viggy arched her spine and moaned that she was coming again. So he buckled down to serious screwing for a time. But then he was out of wind and recovering his conscience. So leaving it in but sort of soaking, he told her, "Tempting as it may be to drift with the easy answers, I like to wrap things tight as I can. So now I'm fixing to ask you to be *really* naughty, Viggy."

The beautiful blonde sighed and thrust her tailbone higher as she said, "Well, if you really can't be content with the way we've been coming. But only after we've both had a bath at my place and if you promise not to low-rate me as a queer-girl afterwards."

He started to assure her that hadn't been what he'd had in mind.

Then he asked her how far her place was and what sort of a place they were talking about.

She explained how, being an out-of-town gal with a warm nature, she'd boarded here and boarded there in New Ulm until she'd found herself a carriage-house loft fixed up as furnished flat with its own indoor plumbing as well as a bitty kitchen and all.

Longarm caught himself starting to thrust some more, and forced his bare ass to hold still as he soberly warned her, "I could sure use a place to stay that nobody else in town knew about. But I got to tell you there could be one or more hardcases hunting for me even as we speak and, well, I'd sure hate to see any bullet holes in hide so fine, honey lamb."

She moaned, "If you're not going to move it, take it out so's we can get dressed and out of here before dark! What would it look like if others spied us slipping out the back door in the gathering dusk, as if we'd been up to something like we've just been up to?"

He chuckled and withdrew, saying, "I admire a natural gal who's good at acting innocent. But as to other transgressions I had in mind, if only you'd hold still and let me tempt you, I'd like you to rustle me up the bank ledger that would have the last transactions of Miss Janice Carpenter now."

Viggy rolled into a nude seated pose on the tufted leather as she gasped, "Good heavens, I'd feel less wicked taking it Greek-style! Mister Plover would have a fit if he knew I'd been screwing you in his private office, but he'd fire me for sure if he ever caught me letting an outsider go through our books!"

Longarm slid down beside her. "I only want to have me a peek at that one doubtless filed-away and inactive ledger, honey lamb. What if I was to just slip it under my arm, escort you home, and mayhaps take some notes from it on your kitchen table—when we weren't in bed, I mean. That way, nobody could possibly catch me at it here in the bank after business hours."

She sighed and said, "I swear I'm going to wind up Frenching you before this night is over, you persistent thing. Even one such ledger is heavy and awkward, and what on earth do you expect to find that I haven't already told you?"

He said, "Exact numbers, for one thing. If there should be any record of just whom she was getting regular checks from, I know some railroad dicks I could wire to make certain the old colored lady got out of here alive and rich instead of dead and robbed."

Viggy gasped, "Good heavens, you *do* deal with a rough crowd, don't you? But I'm sure the poor thing was never robbed. Now that I recall, she made that Friday withdrawal late in the day. So who but I could have known she was carrying that much money and . . . Surely you don't suspect *me* of any crime, Custis?"

He patted her bare thigh and assured her, "Not federal leastways. I ain't sure what Brown County has on its statute books on cohabitation, and you just made me promise never to tell."

He bent over to gather up the shirt they'd thrown to the floor and rustle up a cheroot and a light as he explained. "Eating the apple a bite at a time, I don't mean to worry about the old gal getting in any trouble around here before I figure out where she would have gone from here and whether she ever got there."

So while he lit the smoke, the big buxom blonde went bare-ass into another room, and soon returned with her big firm tits draped over the spine of an oblong ledger bound in slate-gray buckram. When she asked why he couldn't just jot down the little they had on one depositor, Longarm explained, "Might spot something interesting about others who put money in or took some out around the same time. I once caught a crook so dumb that after he'd held up a bank with a mask on he deposited the exact same amount with them, doubtless figuring it was the safest place in town to leave his money, knowing he was the only serious bank robber about."

Viggy laughed and said she couldn't believe any crook could be so stupid. Longarm had to chuckle fondly before he agreed. "Leavenworth ain't exactly a rival of Yale or Harvard. If the average crook was half as smart as he thought he was, he'd go into some safer line of work. You take that morose Indian

I met up with earlier today, for example. He's been wanted for years. But he'd found himself a job as a cowhand well clear of town, and I'd have likely never considered looking for him out at the Runeberg spread if he'd only had enough sense to stay put. I don't have anything on Miss Helga Runeberg, or didn't until this very day. But old Chief Youngwolf couldn't leave it at that. He had to come looking for me with a sissy English shotgun, and now look where he's spending the night."

He took a drag on the cheroot before he added, "They don't aim to plant him in Potter's Field before we can verify who he was air tight. I'm pretty sure he had to be the same Ojibwa who ran off with some white army deserters years ago to stop trains and rob banks for a living. Why don't we get dressed and talk about the wages of sin some more at your place?"

She dimpled sweetly, and allowed she'd like some supper as well as more sinning. Then, as they were getting dressed, she casually asked how come the mean Indian had been gunning for him like that.

Longarm shrugged and said, "They asked him to, I reckon. I had less luck at the Western Union than here. Reckless as old Chief may have been, he was too slick to visit the telegraph office in the dusky flesh, and his white confederate must have been sending and receiving some innocent-looking code."

The beautiful blonde innocently asked how Longarm knew the hatchet-faced Indian had a white confederate.

Longarm hauled on his jeans, saying, "I just told you. Nobody at your Western Union office here in New Ulm remembers anyone at all like Youngwolf, and his Colorado pals must have warned him I was on my way or he wouldn't have come to town to . . . Hmm, they might have only told him to keep an eye on me whilst they tried to figure just what I knew by whomsoever I met up with."

He began to button his shirt as he decided, "Too late to ask him now. My point is that they must have been communicating by wire. It'd take too long by longhand. Not only that, but to keep in touch by wire he'd have either had to ride into town more than your average cowhand could afford or have somebody here in town in cahoots with him, see?"

She didn't, bless her. She asked innocently, "Why would

he have to ride into town to pick up a telegram from Denver? I heard Western Union will deliver one for a modest extra fee."

He laughed and said he could just picture a crook getting secret telegrams by messenger in a bunkhouse. Then he suddenly stared at her thunderstruck and declared, "Jesus H. Christ, speaking of dumb bastards, I sure take the cake! For you're right! He wouldn't need much help, or even a slick code, if he'd never been using the Western Union here in New Ulm at all!"

Chapter 21

It wasn't too late to ride, but Longarm had other questions to ask there in New Ulm before he did. So he went on home with Viggy for the night.

They met nobody as she smuggled him in the back way from the alley. She'd already told him on that chesterfield that she didn't smoke. So the lingering smell of another brand of tobacco in her otherwise tidy quarters in the carriage-house loft helped Longarm understand how any gal so young could know so many interesting positions.

He hadn't told her he was a virgin either, and he'd already seen she kept her buxom blond body clean and tidy too, so what the hell. And there was a lot to be said for such a comfortable port in a storm with an easy lay who wasn't likely to piss and moan about it when a man just had to get it on down the road.

Screwing, scrubbing, and sweeping seemed to sum up the big blonde's household skills, though. They'd have wound up supping on weak tea, burnt toast, and jam if Longarm hadn't found some buckwheat flour and sorghum molasses in the back of her cupboard. She said a man who could make flapjacks after screwing a gal so fine would make a swell catch for some lucky lady who was ready to settle down.

Fortunately, she didn't seem ready to settle down just yet. She'd read those books by Miss Virginia Woodhull, advising ladies young and old to get on top and never marry up with any skunk who didn't think a woman ought to have the right to vote.

After she'd been on top enough to settle her nerves a spell, she said she didn't mind if he left the lamp lit and sat up to read in bed, as long as he didn't expect her to. But after he'd gone through that bank ledger more than once, taking notes, Viggy rolled over in bed to prop herself up one bare elbow, a pretty sight, and demand he explain what he was muttering about.

Longarm pointed at an entry with his stub pencil, but she didn't seem that interested in the tight handwriting as he explained, "That Wabasha Chambrun said he had no notion where that hundred-dollar note he gave Israel Bedford came from, and this far back leastways, he had no account with your bank. But here's an entry saying one of your tellers cashed a thousand-dollar check for one Antelope Chambrun just before Christmas. Miss Tatowiyeh Wachipi, Chambrun's pure Santee wife, must shorten her name when she signs it in Wasichu."

Viggy shrugged a bare shoulder and said she didn't recall either redskin around her bank all that much. Then she asked how he knew the check they'd cashed for them had anything to do with that hot treasury note.

Longarm smiled gently and replied, "It couldn't have. The Tyger gang hadn't pulled off that robbery in Fort Collins yet. The point is that the Chambruns seem to be telling the truth about big checks coming their way from other prosperous Indians. Your New Ulm bank had no problems with the out-of-state check, made out to the female or full-blood branch of the Chambrun family by the Pipestone Bonemeal & Fertilizer Company of Omaha, Nebraska."

Viggy observed she'd heard Pipestone was a place in Minnesota.

Longarm chuckled fondly and agreed. "Not too far from here, as a matter of fact. Pipestone, Minnesota, is named for the sacred red cliffs where the old-time Santee, amongst others, quarried the red catlanite or pipestone they carved into calumets, or what we tend to call peace pipes. The Indians smoked 'em for all sorts of medicine. I reckon it was only natural for some breed or assimilate going into a profitable business in Omaha to name his new venture after old-timey

194

good medicine. I suspect I passed their trackside operation the last time I was in Omaha. There's a heap of meat-packing going on around there these days, and a smart gent who ain't afraid of hard work and dirty hands can make a heap of wampum on the fringes of meat-packing by disposing of the leftover blood, crud, and bones at a profit."

Viggy repressed a yawn and asked what on earth grubby redskins in Omaha might have to do with anyone in New Ulm.

He told her he liked to know when folks were fibbing to him or not, and added, "Your boss, old P. S. Plover, caught the serial number on that later treasury note as it was passing through his bank. So it's unlikely the Chambruns got even one such note from you folk. But I see here you charged 'em one percent, or ten dollars, when you cashed that earlier check from Omaha."

Viggy nodded innocently and replied, "Well, of course we did. One percent is about the least any bank charges for cashing a check drawn on another bank for a person with no regular account with them. Would you have us go to that much trouble for nothing at all?"

Longarm said, "Not hardly. I never said you were bilking check-cashers. On the other hand, ten dollars is a week's salary for a top hand, and old Tatowiyeh Wachipi might well have scouted up some banker willing to cash a sure thing for less."

He wrinkled his nose and added, "That opens up a whole other line of questioning, and I just don't want to take the time to canvass every infernal bank in the county!"

She lay back down and coyly asked what he did feel like doing now that they'd rested up a spell. He laughed and said he wanted to take just a few more notes, since he doubted he'd have the strength or the interest in dry numbers once they got weak and wet some more.

He was right. Despite that weak tea, they fell asleep in each other's arms an hour later, to be awakened at dawn by rain on the roof and a distant rumble promising there was more to come.

The buxom blond banking gal said she was glad it was such

a dreary morning. After breakfast in bed, with toast and jam making more sense with the two of them in more of a hurry, Viggy told him she wanted him to give her a good head start down the alley with her umbrella and macintosh. So he did, hoping the infernal rain would let up as he smoked at her kitchen table and went over his notes. She had of course hauled out with the ledger itself under her rain gear.

It was still raining when Longarm couldn't stand sitting still up there anymore. He was wearing his thin practical range denims, but it was only wet outside, not cold. So he let himself out Viggy's back gate around eight-thirty, and damned if there didn't seem to be an old biddy out by the hen house in her yard across the alley just as Longarm tried to slip past. It would have looked more sneaky not to tick his hat brim at a lady, so he did, but she just sniffed and looked through him at the rear windows of old Viggy's little hideaway. Longarm didn't ask her who that other heavy smoker might be. With any luck the cuss might not find out about him.

Good and wet by the time he got to the livery, Longarm knew from sad experience he didn't want to break out his own rain slicker and put it on over wet denim in summertime. So he just dickered with them for the hire of a buckskin mare who didn't mind muddy roads, they said, and got even wetter riding her over to Courthouse Square in the steady summer drizzle.

The sheriff was off kissing babies some more. Longarm called on the coroner's clerk to tell them he had to ride over to Sleepy Eye, but meant to return before leaving for good. He handed the clerk a damp but legible sheet torn out of his notebook and added, "Whilst I'm scouting the Western Union over by that other railroad stop, I sure wish you'd check this modest list of bank depositors against the bills of mortality this side of, say, Christmas."

The clerk allowed he would, but naturally wanted to know how come. So Longarm explained, "An old lady keeping her money in the bank as Janice Carpenter vanished from the face of this earth just after she drew it all out. I got some pals in railroading circles who may or may not be able to tell me where she went from here. Meanwhile, going over the bank ledger with another pal last night, I noticed more than one

196

additional depositor cleaned out all or most of their savings around the same time."

The clerk nodded, but proved he was good with facts and figures by submitting, "Wouldn't it be natural for folks to withdraw lots of money during the holiday season, Deputy Long?"

Longarm proved how smart he was by replying, "It would, and we'll say no more about what folks might or might not have done with their own money then as long as they're alive now. But I'd sure like to know if anyone else wound up dead, or missing, just after cleaning out their bank accounts. Wouldn't you?"

The clerk allowed he might, but objected, "That jasper we've been holding at Oland's couldn't have robbed anybody as early as Christmas or even New Year's, Deputy Long. He only came back to these parts a few weeks ago."

Longarm wasn't sure who they were talking about and said so. The clerk said patiently, "Baptiste Youngwolf, that Chippewa cowhand you shot your ownself. We had him on display on the cellar doors around to the back until some cowhands who'd been riding with him over at the Runeberg spread identified him for certain and naturally told their boss lady what you'd done to one of her boys."

Longarm muttered, "Damn it, he came after me. I never even knew he was in town until he was swinging a shotgun muzzle my way!"

The clerk said, "That's the way the corner, sheriff, and district attorney see it, Deputy Long. Miss Helga Runeberg still rid into town on a broom last night to arrange for her Uncle Chief, as she called him, to be embalmed and gussied up in a genuine mahogany casket by old Ivar Oland and his crew. We allowed it wouldn't hurt as long as they kept him above ground and on display at their funeral parlor until we closed the books on the dead rascal."

The clerk sounded more annoyed as he continued. "Miss Helga's made arrangements to plant the red heathen in the hallowed ground of our Saint Paul's Lutheran Church, ain't that a bitch?"

Longarm allowed it was up to the church to decide whether

a dead Indian had been a good Indian, because he was more interested in how they knew how long the jasper had been in these parts.

The clerk said, "Miss Helga told us, and some of her hired hands back her story. She said she hadn't seen her Uncle Chief for quite a spell, but that she'd naturally signed him on when he showed up less'n a month ago, saying he'd been handed a shovel out Colorado way."

Longarm knew a top hand preferred to say he'd been handed a shovel, or asked to do work afoot, and naturally quit, in place of admitting he'd been fired mounted up. Longarm frowned thoughtfully and told the clerk, "A man on the dodge after a payroll robbery would be way more likely to tell an owner he knew he'd been fired off another spread. But how come this Helga Runeberg called Youngwolf her uncle? Is she a breed?"

"More like pure Swede," the local resident replied with an amused grin. "The Runebergs came from Vasternorrland in their old country, to hear them tell it. I understand Miss Helga and her little sister, Miss Margaret, are pure Hellstrom on their late mamma's side."

He read Longarm's puzzled expression right and explained. "That Chippewa you shot rode with their late daddy against the Sioux back in '62. Before he went bad and deserted with them Galvanized Yankees, he saved Axel Runeberg's bacon in a skirmish up by Yellow Medicine. So over the years he's always had a place on the payroll and at the chuck table with the other Runeberg riders, rain or shine and wanted by the law or not. Miss Helga told us she knew her Uncle Chief was laying low because he'd been accused of something he hadn't done, again. She seems to think that happened to him a lot just because he'd been a mite wild in his younger days."

Longarm rolled his eyes heavenward and snorted, "They say much the same about some old boys named James and Younger down Missouri way."

The clerk nodded and said, "Miss Helga can be stubborn as any old Missouri mule. When the sheriff pointed out that one treasury note from the Fort Collins robbery showing up in these parts about the same time as her daddy's old comrade in

198

arms, she allowed they'd heard and been thundergasted as the rest of us. She said her Uncle Chief had told her how he'd been out Colorado way at the right time and close enough to the right place, but hadn't known beans about that payroll robbery and figured we'd just never tried to understand him."

Longarm thought before he cautiously decided, "We could likely stick her with aiding and abetting if she's admitted right out she knew she was hiding an owlhoot rider wanted by the federal law."

The clerk nodded and said, "The sheriff's already warned her not to go around making war talk about lawmen only doing their damned job. She said she has no idea why her Uncle Chief was tagging after you with her dear old dad's fancy Cleveland twelve-gauge. She said she was still sore at us, and at you in particular, but willing to concede it might've been a tragic misunderstanding. That's what some call it when Indians go bad, a tragic misunderstanding. Only us white boys are allowed to be just no damned good."

Longarm didn't want to get into that. He shrugged and said something about letting Sheriff Tegner deal with his own constituents, and added, "Like I said, I got to ride over to Sleepy Eye. With any luck I ought to be back this afternoon."

The clerk glanced out the nearby grimy window and suggested, "If I were you I'd take the train. It's still raining outside and we're talking about wet hours in the saddle versus minutes by rail."

Longarm shook his head and replied, "No, we ain't. I already looked at the timetable I picked up free off the railroad conductor who brought me here. You'd be right if I was only going one way. There's a westbound stopping here in New Ulm today, around ten, and like you said, the flag stop of Sleepy Eye ain't but a few minutes west by rail. But after that I'd be stuck in Sleepy Eye till after sundown if I missed today's eastbound coming through just short of noon."

The clerk agreed it hardly seemed worth going to Sleepy Eye at all if a man didn't have several hours to visit there.

Longarm didn't know how long he might want to stay in that smaller railroad stop. He felt better about his means of transportation when, just as he was untethering his livery

199

mount out front, the sun broke through and he declared, "I'll be damned if I don't believe it could be fixing to clear up."

Both his jeans and his saddle were still sopping wet, of course, and neither would dry as fast in contact as they might if he let the sun and wind get at them. So instead of mounting up as he'd meant to, he told the mare, "There's a chance we got some answers to wires we sent earlier from here in New Ulm. So why don't we mosey on over afoot and sunbake that saddle some?"

The buckskin didn't seem to care. Others stared at them from all sides as Longarm led his mount deliberately down the sunny side of the muddy street, although he was sure the more experienced riders they passed knew what he was doing.

A quartet of riders coming the other way deliberately crossed over as if to give him more room than he really needed. Longarm kept the brim of his Stetson low as he kept a wary eye on them from its shade. All four of them were cowhands at first glance, but Indians as soon as one looked closer. Full-bloods. One of them still wore his hair in braids, although none seemed to feel the need for feathers, beads, or other fringes you saw on some old boys living off the blanket. So it was safe to assume they weren't out to advertise their ancestry in a county where many a Wasichu family was still mourning kith or kin who'd gone under in the Great Sioux Scare.

The four full-bloods, who could have been Ojibwa as soon as one studied on it, passed on uneventfully, leaving Longarm to wonder if they could have been the Santee who'd been asking about him personally out at that raft the other night.

Longarm was as puzzled by them asking Mato Takoza in Santee. For the late Baptiste Youngwolf, or Uncle Chief, had either been Ojibwa or one hell of an actor in a part of the country where most everyone knew the enemy nations apart. You didn't have to be fluent in either lingo to tell "Sioux" from "Chippewa" apart. They were as unrelated as, say, Spanish and English, and sounded like they were, whether one could follow the drift or not.

Neither pretty little Mato Takoza nor her mysterious night callers had been speaking the Algonquin dialect a "Chippewa scout" known to one and all as Baptiste Youngwolf would have spoken when talking to other . . .

"Hold on!" Longarm told the buckskin. "An Ojibwa paid to scout the Santee for the army might have learned at least as much Sioux-Hokan as the rest of us, and a man who'd desert any outfit in time of war, in the company of white outlaws, might not take his membership in the nation of his birth too seriously!"

The mare didn't answer, so Longarm explained, "A renegade scout of any nation could be riding with Santee who don't want to be Indians anymore. But damn it, that answer raises more questions that I can hear it answering!"

They trudged on, Longarm's wet duds starting to feel stickier as the sun warmed that rain to the temperature of sweat. He started to feel for a smoke, but decided to wait till his cheroots dried out all the way as well. They were almost to the Western Union near the depot by then, and who might that male and female be, coming out of the telegraph office and pretending so hard not to notice a tall man afoot with a buckskin mare at easy pistol range?

Longarm knew right off the young cuss he'd met the other night, out on the open range, had to be Gus Hansson, who'd bragged he rode for Miss Helga Runeberg. So the slightly older and far meaner-looking gal had to be the same Helga Runeberg who'd told everyone how sore she was at him for gunning her dear old Uncle Chief.

Longarm never broke stride as he just kept going the way he'd been going. So the two of them had to scurry some to mount the two cow ponies they'd tethered out front, still pretending not to notice him as he led the mare catty-corner across the muddy street.

Gus Hansson was blushing like a schoolmarm who'd been invited to elope with a whisky drummer. So Longarm assumed it was the gal who'd given the order to ignore a lawman she detested. Longarm was able to look her over all he liked as she pretended not to notice.

She was dressed for her business, which was raising stock, in an expensively tailored but practical outfit. The split skirts that let her ride astride were the only distinctly female notions to her dark gray outfit. Her dark hair matched her black pony.

Longarm had been expecting lighter features to go with her Swedish name. She wasn't as tall as either Swedish gal he'd met on friendlier terms in New Ulm. But Longarm knew some Swedes were naturally short and dark, just as some Spanish folks were tall and blond. The local folks who knew her better would have said so if she'd been a breed. Her profile was turned to him as they rode past him at a trot, her with her nose in the air, so he decided she just missed being pretty, although her whipcord-skirted rump, as he turned to boldly watch the two of them ride off, bounced shapely enough in her double-rigged roping saddle.

He chuckled, tethered the buckskin to the hitch rail they'd just been using, and moseyed on inside to see if anyone had sent any wires meant for him.

They had. Old Billy Vail had wired from Denver that yet another of those recorded treasury notes had surfaced at a bank back East in Boston, for Pete's sake, and hence old Billy wanted Longarm to come on home. He'd considered Longarm's reports about the member of the gang he'd apparently caught up with, or vice versa. But he still thought Longarm could be chasing his own tail.

For as the older lawman tersely pointed out, it stood to reason a member of the gang with local connections might have headed for New Ulm after they'd divided the proceeds of that payroll robbery before they'd split up in every known direction. Some of the hot paper had shown up around the renegade scout's old stamping grounds for the same reasons he had. But as far as anyone knew, none of those Galvanized Yankees who'd led a young Chippewa astray had been Minnesota boys, and other treasury notes from the same robbery kept turning up all over creation. So what was a senior deputy doing where he'd already run one of the rascals to the grave?

Everything his boss had wired made sense. But so did another wire from the Navajo Agency at Shiprock. The Indian Police had finally spotted the bloated body of that cuss Longarm had sent flying into the San Juan from a couple of railroad transfer points back.

Better yet, they'd matched some scars and a silly tattoo with a couple of wanted posters, state and federal. So the young cuss who'd lost that fight with Longarm as they'd been crossing the white water of the San Juan had been a known road agent called Mermaid Morrison. Or else there'd been two pallid youths with the same bullet scars and a mermaid tattoo who might have felt they had just cause to tangle with a paid-up lawman aboard moving trains.

Longarm got out his notebook to make certain. Then he tore off a telegram blank to wire Vail he might not be finished in New Ulm yet. For another suspect they had down as a possible member of the Tyger gang had sure been anxious to prevent him from ever reaching New Ulm, and come to study on it, why had Youngwolf been trailing him with a shotgun like so if he'd been the only member of the gang for miles?

Longarm wired he'd have never spotted the gang member he'd nailed if the fool Indian hadn't broken such fine cover, as if to prevent him from spotting something else. Then he allowed he'd head home after he'd found out what they both seemed to be missing so far.

Chapter 22

Longarm's crotch still sat sticky in the saddle, but the rest of him was dry enough, by the time he'd topped the clay bluffs west of New Ulm to follow the rail line's service road with the morning sun at his back.

The same sun was only commencing to dry the rain-smoothed mud of the service road. So it seemed easy at first to read the sign of the one two-spanned carriage or wagon, most likely, preceding him towards Sleepy Eye after that short but serious shower.

Then he spotted a hoofprint overlapping a wheel runt to the right of the center strip of grass, and knew two horses had been pulling the wheeled vehicle while the other two, although moving stirrup to stirrup as if a team, had been packing two riders. There'd have been better than one set of wheel ruts if he'd been reading two buckboards, and a lone rider leading a pack brute would have left most of the hoofprints of both critters along one or the other dirt-strip.

By this time Longarm's tobacco was dry enough to smoke. So he lit up without reining in as he idly wondered why he gave a hoot about morning traffic along a public right-of-way. A one-span carriage or buckboard had left New Ulm first, followed within a few minutes or a whole heap of minutes by a couple of riders, with all concerned no doubt headed for Sleepy Eye, where the rail line crossed another northwest-to-southeast county road, meant to serve the folks along that side of the higher ground between the Minnesota and Sleepy Eye.

The horse apples he spied on the road ahead from time to time were of more import to the bluebottles and buffalo gnats buzzing over them as he passed. He'd gotten back to pondering more serious puzzles. So he'd almost put the ordinary signs of ordinary travelers out of his mind, but not all the way out of his mind, when he spotted sign that wasn't there.

A less experienced tracker, or even an Indian who didn't give a hang, might not have noticed something that wasn't there. But just the same, before there'd been four steel-rimmed wheels and four sets of steel-shod hooves heading down that same road. Now he only read the sign of four wheels and three critters.

Longarm casually drew his Winchester from its saddle boot as he rode on, sweeping the range ahead with his thoughtful gun-muzzle-gray eyes as he tried to come up with innocent reasons for that one rider to hive off across the gently rolling and grove-speckled prairie all about. The most logical reason involved a shortcut for a nearby homestead after keeping company with that other rider a ways.

Had they in fact been riding side by side to begin with? Wasn't it possible that one-span vehicle had left first, followed by a lone rider headed for Sleepy Eye, followed by yet another who'd cut across yonder grass at an angle after . . .

"Anything's possible," Longarm said aloud to his own mount. Then he asked the buckskin, "Would you walk more than halfways to Sleepy Eye along this muddy wagon trace if you were really headed for another place from the beginning?"

When the buckskin failed to answer, Longarm reined her to his left, towards the railroad tracks, as he observed, "I've seldom seen you critters match your strides so tight unless the pal you were striding with was right close. But why are we arguing, when it's so easy for us to just swing clear of any sneaky bullshit?"

The buckskin balked a bit at crossing the loose railroad ballast and snaky steel rails. But Longarm rode with his knees tight and a firm as well as gentle hand on the reins. So they got across with no more than a little crow-hopping, and she settled down as soon as they were on soft ground again and he'd whacked her a couple of times with the barrel of his Winchester.

He rode due south, away from the rails at an angle, till they were better than an easy rifle shot from the tracks. Then he reined to his right some more, explaining, "It's better to be safe than sorry. That mysterious rider who dropped out of our parade couldn't have expected us to do what we just done. So even if he's hunkered off the road up ahead behind some sticker brush, he's going to have a long wait before he bushwhacks *this* child!"

Thanks to the clearly visible telegraph poles along the railroad right-of-way, it was just as easy to find the railroad flag stop ahead while riding most of the way across wet bluestem and more kinds of wildflowers than you saw on the higher and drier plains further west. When he saw a church steeple and grain elevator out ahead, Longarm had no call to cross the tracks a second time. He just kept riding until, sure enough, he came to that country road serving folks to the south as well as the north of the flag stop.

Sleepy Eye was called a flag stop because cross-country trains only stopped there if someone on board wanted off or the station master at Sleepy Eye flagged down the train because somebody wanted on. Freight and livestock were usually taken aboard on a more formal schedule, maybe once or twice a week.

To someone riding in from any direction, the overall impression of Sleepy Eye was that its name sure fit it, even though it must have been named for the watercourse way off to the southwest on its own tanglewood flood plain. The just as aptly named town was mostly sun-silvered frame, dozing like a big dried-out buffalo chip in the late morning sun as Longarm rode in.

That clerk back in New Ulm had been on the money about the tedious ride, and jam on toast would only carry a man so far. So first things coming first, Longarm asked directions from a couple of kids shooting marbles in a dooryard, and dismounted out front of the only livery in town.

An old geezer wearing overalls and a Swedish accent came

206

out to see if Longarm really wanted anything. Longarm told the hostler he didn't know how long he'd be in town, but that his buckskin pal could doubtless do with a rubdown and some fodder and water while she waited for him to finish his business in town. The old Swede said nobody had ever stolen anything from their tack room. But Longarm held on to his Winchester just the same.

So he was carrying it, muzzle aimed down as peaceably as he knew how, when he strode into the restaurant the old-timer at the livery had recommended. It stood handy to the Western Union and across from the open platform and stock loading ramps of the railroad. Longarm figured he'd fill up on stronger coffee and more solid grub than he'd managed for breakfast.

The drably pretty young waitress who seated him at a round table with a checkered red, white, and gravy-stained cloth didn't seem upset by his faded denims and Winchester '73. But he sure was getting dirty looks from the only other patron at that hour.

That small brunette he suspected of being the hot-tempered Helga Runeberg was seated at another table in a far corner, spitting venom at him with her big blue eyes from under the brim of her dark gray Stetson Carlsbad. Longarm had no call to nod at a lady he'd never been introduced to. He wasn't ready to question her about her Uncle Chief before he found out a bit more about the dead rascal. He'd come in here to settle his gut before he enjoyed the usual duel of wits with a small-town telegraph operator. So he didn't want to argue with the dead Indian's boss before he had a better line on whether Youngwolf had been taking advantage of an old pal's kin or the mean-eyed little gal had been aiding and abetting a cuss she'd known to be a charter member of a serious outlaw gang.

The drably pretty and dishwater-blond waitress said they didn't go by printed menus, but suggested the special for the day might be better for his health than anything their cook would ever whip up as a special order for some fussy eater.

When she added their special, as usual, offered him his choice between fried or mashed potatoes with his roast beef and succotash, he said he'd go with fried and asked if he could have his coffee with his grub.

She looked surprised, and asked how else anyone might ever drink their coffee. So he knew he was in a place that catered mostly to his own sort of country folk. The small brunette in the corner looked a tad stuck up for the place, and likely sipped her damned demitasse with a whiff of creme liquor, with some bittersweet dessert. She looked as if she could smell the crotch of his jeans clean across the room, and thought it unseemly to sweat in the saddle like a human being.

The air was still damp from all that rain as it started to warm up. So Longarm could smell that waitress pretty good as she returned in no time with his order. But he could tell she'd had a bath the night before, if not that morning, and it wasn't her fault she had to sweat a tad at honest work. He decided he liked her far better than the snooty sass in the corner, although the brunette would likely win in a beauty contest, where each feature got measured on its own.

Neither gal was a raving beauty, or even pretty enough to win the third prize, when you got down to brass tacks. But neither the pallid young waitress nor the somewhat older brunette cattle queen would have been thrown back in the sea if they'd washed up on Robinson Crusoe's beach.

Longarm figured he'd rather lay the waitress, although it wasn't going to bust his heart if he never laid either. The waitress seemed just a good old country gal who'd give a man a tolerable ride he might recall for as long as another payday in another trail town. The more finely featured but bitchy-looking brunette would likely scratch and bite, or just lay there like a slab of beef from the icehouse, depending on which way might make a man feel worse. He wondered idly who she kept reminding him of. She didn't look like any gal he'd even considered kissing lately. Yet he was almost certain he'd seen that almost pretty face and that elfin turned-up nose before. Meanwhile, the grub the much sweeter-natured gal had served was good, and the coffee was even better. Arbuckle Brand, if he was any judge, and percolated in one of those high-toned pots as well to taste *this* good!

Arbuckle Brand was roasted and ground to be sold in the Far

West with such complications as high altitudes and primitive brewing in mind. So a mountain man or cow camp cook could make a tolerable mug of Arbuckle Brand in a tin can, over an open fire, a mile or more above sea level with alkali water. The stuff turned to strong black ambrosia that would wake a man up grinning when you made it in a percolator on a real stove. So Longarm put away his first cup pronto, and asked for a second before he'd finished half his grub.

The friendly dishwater blonde got even prettier in Longarm's eyes when she allowed he could have all the coffee he wanted at no extra charge. For she was surely used to serving cowhands, and it was only natural to wonder how fine she might be able to serve them in other country ways.

But he never came right out and flirted with the good old gal. He hadn't ridden all this way to spark a waitress, and even if he had, that other gal was watching and he could tell she thought all men were beasts. Or leastways, *he* was. But he resisted the temptation to get up and go over to assure he didn't mean to mess with their waitress, and hadn't set out to murder her Uncle Chief back in New Ulm.

Longarm had just finished the last of his special, and was fixing to ask what they had for dessert when he heard considerable galloping out front and glanced through the glass to his right to watch a dozen and a half riders reining in and dismounting by the railroad platform across the way. When he recognized one as Gus Hansson, Longarm smiled thinly and nodded in satisfaction. For now he had a better handle on just how long it took to ride out to the Rocking R and back. It was obvious the snip at that other table had sent the kid to fetch her other riders as she'd ridden on into town.

So he wasn't surprised when Helga Runeberg suddenly rose to her not-too-imposing height and swept grandly past him on her way out the front door. Longarm figured she had an account with the best beanery in town. So he was more surprised when that waitress scurried after her, waving a riding crop.

Then he realized the distracted cattle queen had left her crop at that other table. He'd thought that dishwater blonde looked honest.

He watched her chase the shorter but more imperious gal across the street and hand over the crop. On the way back, the waitress seemed to be in at least as much of a hurry, and her dishwater-gray eyes were wide and worried as they met his own through the glass.

As she came back in, Longarm asked what they had that day for dessert. The waitress asked if anyone had ever called him by the name of Longarm, and when he allowed some had, she looked really upset and said, "If I were you I'd skip dessert and let me show you another way out the back. We don't want trouble, I don't like noise, and even if I did, they just said something about you being a *lawman*!"

Longarm asked what else they'd said, and when she replied Miss Helga had called him a murderer who deserved to be punished, Longarm sighed and said, "I reckon I'd best skip dessert at that. But you never want to duck out the back way unless you're certain someone ain't been sent around to the alley with just such an event in mind."

He asked how much he owed them. When she told him not to talk dumb and for heaven's sake get going, Longarm put a silver dollar on the checkered cloth by his empty plate, drank the last of his coffee, and got to his own feet, removing the Winchester from his lap to cradle it over his left arm as he headed for that same front door.

The waitress gasped, "Are you crazy or just deaf? Didn't you hear what I just told you?"

Longarm said, "Every word, ma'am. I know you're curious, but I'd be obliged if you stayed away from all this window glass for the next few minutes. Things are likely to get a mite tense out front for a spell."

Then he opened the door, stepped out in the sunlight, and things did. One of the younger hands across the way softly hollered, "Hot damn! The little darling must want to dance with all of us!"

An older and meaner-looking hand growled at him to shut up. All of them but their boss lady, standing with her boots apart a pace or more closer, were packing six-guns on their hips, and more than one, just like Longarm, had hauled out his saddle gun as well.

They were all a tad out of his way if the Western Union had been his next intended stop after all. He decided a beeline in any other direction but one could have the same effect on the wolf pack as a running deer fawn might have on the four-legged kind. So he strode straight across to where the only female in the bunch seemed intent on standing her ground. Then he stopped, just short of stepping on her booted toes, and softly said, "Allow me to introduce myself, ma'am."

Before he could she snapped, "I know who you are and why have you been following me?"

To which Longarm could only reply, "I ain't been. If I wanted to I reckon I could, lawful enough, on public thoroughfares across open federal range. I wasn't expecting to question you, on your own land or anywhere else I wanted to, before I had more to ask about. For now I choose to take your word you thought Baptiste Youngwolf was a misunderstood comrade in arms of your late father. I don't care just how you take my word it was him or me the other day when he came my way with that Cleveland twelve-gauge."

"Killer!" she snapped. "Cold-blooded killer with a bounty-hunting badge and not a fair bone in your body! Uncle Chief would have *won* if he'd really been after you with my daddy's shotgun in his capable old hands and a Navy Colt Conversion on his hip!"

Longarm shrugged and quietly asked, "Were you there, ma'am?"

The same young rider who'd sounded off so silly earlier called out, "Just say the word, Miss Helga! Just say the word and stand aside whilst we fix him good for our pal the Chief."

Before anyone could get even sillier, Longarm told their boss lady she'd better explain why such gunplay would hardly be wise.

She stared up at him, sidewinder friendly, and quietly asked why it might be unwise of her to just stand aside and let nature take its course.

He said just as softly, "You ain't that dumb. You're just pretending to be that dumb to scare me. I'm still working on why you feel a need to scare me. But suffice it to say, it ain't working."

211

Another rider, this one ominously older and more serious, pleaded, "Move clear and let us at him, Miss Helga. If there's one thing I can't stand it's a loudmouth trying to bluff his way out of a fight he brought on himself!"

Longarm waited, saw the gal wasn't going to say it for him, and raised his voice loud enough for all to clearly make out as he declared, "There's one of me and seventeen of you, as I feel sure you've all been feeling swell about. So good as I like to feel I am, I doubt I'd be able to take even half of you with me on my way out of this old world. But what would the survivors do for an encore?"

He let that sink in and continued. "It's possible to gun a federal deputy and make it to Canada or Mexico before Uncle Sam can hang you. But you'd play hell starting over anywhere in these United States with a federal murder warrant hanging over you. John Wesley Hardin was only wanted on a Texas murder charge, and they tracked him all the way back east to Alabama. But let's say at least some of you are smarter than old Hardin must have felt when he took to gunning lawmen. Killing this one would still mean the eternal end of all Miss Helga's late kith and kin ever worked for."

The dangerously smart-looking hand growled thoughtfully, "I fail to see how they could outlaw Miss Helga here for what some others might do with or without her full approval."

There came an ominous rumble of agreement from all along the line, and sixteen men lined up a surprisingly long way, even as they commenced to circle some from both ends. So Longarm quickly pointed out, "They don't have to prove toad squat in any court of law, once you make the boys *I* ride for sore at you. For openers, my having poked a few cows in my own time, let's talk about grazing fees. Or has the little lady here been paying any for all that federally owned bluestem you've been turning into beef for her?"

Helga Runeberg looked stricken and gasped, "Range fees? Nobody has been asking me for any range fees, you fool!"

Longarm said, "That's my point, and you'll find out who the fool might be if ever my boss, Marshal Billy Vail, takes it into his head not to like you, ma'am. Indians have recently been demanding and getting six cents an acre per month, or two bits per year, just by telling their B.I.A. agents they wanted it off white folks grazing odd corners of their reserve."

He reached for a fresh smoke as he quietly asked, "How much do you reckon a mighty sore white government agent might think an acre of prime long-grass prairie was worth? Oh, I forgot to mention the new fencing regulations up before Congress."

He let the worried murmur die down before he explained. "It ain't been passed yet, but we figure it will be within this decade. Seems a heap of self-styled cattle kings and queens have taken to fencing off public lands as if they owned it their fool selves. The Bureau of Land Management has a whole list of new regulations about drift fences, free access to water, and so on pending before Congress, like I said."

He thumbnailed a matchhead and lit his cheroot before he added, "I suspicion us federal lawmen will enforce such new regulations in accordance to how we feel about particular cattle folk grazing public land we might be most interested in. My particular boss worries more about the green grass closer to our Denver office, unless, of course, somebody in other parts gives him a real reason to send in other deputies, and then other deputies, for as long as it may take to settle the matter to his satisfaction."

Nobody said anything. Longarm let some tobacco smoke run out his nostrils and decided, "I came over this way to pay a call on Western Union's Sleepy Eye office. It's been grand discussing my future with you all, Miss Helga. But now I'd best be on my way. So you go ahead and back-shoot me all you want, if you're really ready to retire from the beef industry."

She must not have wanted to. Longarm heard some ominous muttering, and his spine commenced to itch like hell as he turned around to walk away from the spiteful gal and her surly bunch. So how come the street was suddenly so wide and he was moving so slow through air that felt as thick as glue until, suddenly, he found himself indoors again, breathing natural again as he muttered, "Son of a bitch. I *made* it!"

Chapter 23

As was often the case in such small towns, there was more behind the yellow-on-black Western Union sign out front than the occasional sending or receiving of telegraph messages. The balding old bird who ran things for Western Union in Sleepy Eye doubled in brass as their postmaster and sold feed, seed, and hardware on the side. He was neither Swedish, German, nor breed, and he was starved for gossip and knew Mister Cornell had never meant the law when he'd forbidden Western Union employees from repeating messages sent by paying customers.

That westbound train Longarm had been advised to take to Sleepy Eye came though, without stopping, as he was winding up his main errand there with the agreeable older gent. So Longarm would have been happy about that buckskin waiting for him at their livery even if it had still been raining and that waitress had been prettier.

The telegraph clerk confirmed that, just as Longarm had suspected, the late Baptiste Youngwolf had been using this telegraph office closer to his bunkhouse on the Runeberg spread a lot. The friendly but only part-time telegrapher hadn't kept any telegram blanks, seeing he'd found the Indian's communications with some other redskin out west sort of tedious. He agreed as soon as Longarm pointed it out that dull remarks about kith and kin no outsider could identify worked good enough as a code with nobody else really trying to break it. The telegrapher recalled most of the wires had been sent back and forth between Sleepy Eye and a place called Aurora, Colorado. After that he just couldn't nail things down any tighter. Longarm soothingly explained Aurora was a town about the size of Sleepy Eye an easy ride east of Denver.

He said, "One or more of that gang I told you about could lope out to that Aurora telegraph office and back before anyone in Denver even thought about it. I'd best send a wire to my Denver outfit from here, advising my boss how come he hasn't been intercepting too many wires sent to or from downtown Denver."

The older gent handed him a yellow blank. As Longarm was block-lettering his terse advisory, adding there'd be more from New Ulm in a spell, he asked the older local whether Youngwolf had been the only Indian out at the Runeberg spread.

The Western Union man seemed sincerely annoyed by the suggestion as he replied, "Jess H. Christ, Deputy Long, how many infernal Sioux do you want?"

Longarm suggested Youngwolf had been Ojibwa. The clerk nodded his balding dome and said, "Chippewa are about the onliest Indians still allowed in these parts, and Chippewa are bad enough. We've just agreed that red rascal calling his fool self Baptiste, as if he was some sort of Red River breed, was a wanted outlaw who tried to blow you away with another man's shotgun without asking. You want me to find you more?"

Longarm smiled thinly and explained, "Don't *want* more Indians. But I *need* more Indians if I'm to make heads or tails out of the last few days or nights."

He told the helpful old-timer about those other Indians asking about him by name, although in another lingo, out at the Bee Witch's floating shanty. The telegrapher hadn't heard that much about any Bee Witch, proving the eccentric colored beekeeper had been better known up and down the bigger river to the east. They both agreed an Ojibwa who'd fought Santee in his salad days would have to be mighty broad-minded to be working with a bunch of the Santee, even this late in the game. The old-timer knew his Indians well enough to agree it would be impossible to mistake the one lingo for the other, and told Longarm, "You got to remember the Sioux and Chippewa were going at it hammer and tongs before any of us white folks ever got this far west. Being both sides had similar views on religion, whether they prayed to Wakanna or Manitou, they tortured one another way worse than they ever tortured us. You see, there was more to it than personal dislike and—"

"I know about honoring a brave enemy by giving him the chance to die slow and stoic, singing his death song whilst you poke out his eyes and shove glowing embers up his ass," Longarm said, waving aside the theology of another breed of humankind as he suggested they stick to more recent events. "The blue and the gray fought more recent, with considerable enthusiasm, and yet there's been northern and southern malcontents riding the owlhoot trail together for fun and profit. So the real mystery would be where those other redskins have been hiding out all this time, whether they were in cahoots with that dead Ojibwa or not."

The telegrapher suggested he'd heard tell of breeds, full-bloods, and even colored folks filing homestead claims in these parts just as if they were real Americans or dumb Swedes. Dumb Swede was said by non-Scandinavian settlers in these parts as if it was one word, the way Damn Yankee was said down Dixie way.

Longarm shrugged and said, "I know. I've met some colored and Santee settlers over by the Minnesota lately. I can't make Youngwolf fit in with any of them, though. Aside from him hailing from an enemy nation, why would an Indian on the dodge hide out in a white bunkhouse and stick out like a sore thumb if he had even one family of Indians he could blend in with as, say, a *real* uncle who'd been further west for a spell?"

The telegrapher allowed he'd never hide out with a mess of Mexicans or Swedes if he had a whole bunch of his own kind to hide out among. Then he asked, "What if those other Indians were after you for some other reason entire?"

Longarm grimaced and said, "I was afraid you'd say something that smart. What do I owe you for this telegram to my boss? I want it to be delivered direct to his office with no argument about who had to pay, lest that gang slip another wire past us by way of that Aurora connection!"

The clerk rapidly counted off the words, and allowed a dollar and six bits ought to have the message on old Billy's desk before quitting time that afternoon. So Longarm paid, up, and they shook on it and parted friendly.

He found his hired buckskin rested and raring to go when he and his Winchester made it back to that livery. So he settled up, saddled up, and was on his way back to New Ulm under the noonday sun, with enough of a prairie breeze to dance the wildflowers all around and dry their sweat enough to keep them comfortable.

This time Longarm followed the service road north of the tracks, to see whether his warning to Helga Runeberg and her boys had sunk in. He decided it might have, once he was sure nobody, red or white, was following him or laying for him out ahead.

It was tough to either trail or ambush an experienced plainsman on such open range, once he was on the prod and watching for either.

Longarm took advantage of the breeze at his back and gentle slopes ahead of them to make better time going back than he had coming out. So it was still fairly early in the afternoon as he rode into New Ulm again, keeping to the narrower back ways on purpose lest someone ahead get word he was coming before he wanted to advertise he was back to pester them.

He wasn't even thinking about good old Ilsa Pedersson as he cut through a residential block a couple of streets over from her place. But she seemed even more surprised when they almost crashed into one another on horseback, with her riding good old Blaze at a smart trot. The comely widow woman smiled and howdied him, so Longarm had to tick his hat brim to her. But he felt no call to tell her where he'd been or where he might be going.

She must have wanted to know, for she swung her smaller black mount around to fall in place at Longarm's left, gazing archly at him over a calico-clad shoulder with her shapely rump aimed his way while she told him she'd just been over at the river landing on business and that she'd surely missed him at

217

her supper table, once those pies had cooled and things had quieted down along her street.

He knew exactly where she'd really been missing him, after suppertime, because he'd been thinking about females all the way back from Sleepy Eye, although in the line of duty, of course.

He asked old Ilsa how well she really knew Helga Runeberg, both of them being Swedish as well as Brown County gals. The somewhat older but far prettier widow woman made a wry face and demanded, "Have you been sparking her as well? I suppose you think I haven't heard about you and that Vigdis Magnusson at my very own bank!"

Longarm managed a poker face as he quietly replied, "I don't see why they bother printing a newspaper in this gossiping county seat. It's true Miss Magnusson has been helping me out with my investigation. I told you, late one night, how I'd been sent here to look into that hundred-dollar treasury note, and that lady happens to be a material witness. As to Miss Helga Runeberg . . ."

"What has that silly young Vigdis got that I haven't got?" the visibly upset Ilsa asked.

It would have been needlessly cruel to tell her. So Longarm said, "We were talking about Helga Runeberg, and you have my word she don't like me at all. I just crawfished my way out of a fight with her and a bunch of her riders. They all seemed to feel I should have let an Indian who rode with them pepper my hide with number-nine buck."

Ilsa said she knew all about Longarm's rough ways with both her sex and his own, adding, "It's about time some girl said no to you. You're too smug about your looks by half!"

Longarm shrugged and just let her fuss a spell as they rode side by side along the cottonwood-shaded back street. Then he saw a chance to slip some words in sideways, and said, "I know I ought to be hung as a menace to womankind, Miss Ilsa. Meanwhile, I'm still a lawman, and I keep feeling I've seen that surly little face of Helga Runeberg at some other time and place, mayhaps on somebody else. Somebody told me she had a kid sister. What about brothers or other male kin that might have the same distinctive eyes and nose?"

The older county resident thought, shook her head, and decided he couldn't have ever met Helga's father or real uncle, Jarl, both of whom had died years before. She added, "The last I heard of the younger Runeberg girl, Margaret, she'd run off to Chicago with a cattle buyer. Somebody told us later they'd really gotten married and settled down fairly well off."

Longarm thought, then said, "I've been to Chicago Town more than once. But I reckon I'd recall any Swedish gals married up with either crooked or halfways honest cattle buyers. There's no such thing as a totally honest cattle buyer."

Thinking of Chicago Town and the meat-packing trade made Longarm think of another widow woman, the younger and even prettier Kim Stover, who'd met up with him there, sort of like this afternoon, after they'd agreed to part friends out Wyoming way. A man could sure raise himself an erection astride a split-seat saddle, thinking about women whether he'd ever split their seat or not.

Then Ilsa coyly murmured that she had to turn off at the next cross street, but that she'd baked another pie and she could save some for him if he'd like to come calling after dark, well after dark, by way of her alley gate.

It was tempting in more ways than one. If the gossips up that other alley knew about him and old Viggy, it made no never-mind who he called on after dark as far as his own reputation went. After that, seeing he had to disappoint one or the other, this older gal doubtless had more delicate feelings, and it was sort of nice to pillow-talk afterwards with somebody who might really care about what you thought about something besides her.

On the other hand, if breaking up with a gal made a man feel sort of dumb, breaking up with the same gal a second time made a man feel downright stupid. He was still pissed off at himself about all those tears and recriminations after that grand night in Chicago with good old Kim Stover, after the both of them had just about gotten over an earlier sweet night of madness and some cold gray empty mornings.

So when they came to Ilsa's corner he said he'd study on it, once he carried out some uncertain chores in town. For there was no need to burn a bridge behind him, and another way to feel dumb as hell was to make double certain you'd have no other gal to turn to if something unexpected got a beautiful blonde sore at you.

He left the buckskin, McClellan, and most of his gear at the livery near the river, and legged it back to the center of town with his Winchester and six-gun on foot.

He stopped first at the New Ulm Western Union. It was a tad early to expect answers to anything he'd sent from Sleepy Eye, but they were holding replies to some earlier wires he'd sent from New Ulm.

He put them away and legged it on over to the courthouse, where he found that clerk in the coroner's office had one, but only one, death certificate of any interest to either of them.

As the county man explained, "None of the others on your list seem to have fallen on greater misfortune than needing money at Christmas time. That one old gent who died after drawing out his life savings won't work as a murder victim either. As you can see from all this paperwork, signed by a town constable and half a dozen witnesses as well as his attending physician, old Jacob Thorsson was run over by a brewery dray in front of God and everybody whilst full of the holiday spirits, which would have been pear brandy in Jake's case."

Longarm studied the papers the helpful clerk had dug out of their files as he softly mused, "Gents have been run over deliberately, and this one had just drawn close to ten thousand dollars at his bank to just about clear his account entirely!"

The clerk nodded and said, "I mentioned your notion to my own boss. He'd like to know what ever became of the money too. But the trail is over six months cold, and as you see, old Jake lived long enough to absolve the brewery dray driver, allowing he'd been drunk as a skunk and not paying attention when he stepped off the curb. His dying words were backed by those witnesses interviewed on the spot by the constable. So how might a murderer get a drunk to stagger so conveniently?"

Longarm didn't answer until he'd finished scanning the neatly handwritten doctor's report. Then he sighed and said, "Poor old coot was cold sober when he died seventy-odd

220

hours later, of internal injuries your own autopsy confirmed. So you're right, a man taking more than three painful days to die, with his kith and kin keeping him company, would have surely mentioned it if someone had pushed him in front of that dray. Running over a man with six draft horses and a load of beer seems an awkward means of assassination as well. But ain't it odd nobody seems to have wondered where all that money might have gone?"

The clerk agreed. "He sure as hell never got to spend it, seeing he drew it out of the bank the same day he got run over. Of course, he had time to spend at least some of it, and must have spent enough on brandy to get that drunk before sundown."

Longarm started to ask what time of the day the old man had been run over. Then he saw the town law had reported it as around six P.M., or about the right time for that brewery driver to be pushing for home after his last deliveries of the afternoon.

Longarm decided such details as whether the dray had been carrying full kegs or empties hardly mattered, since busted innards were busted innards and the dead man's missing withdrawal was more mysterious than what read as his fairly obvious cause of death.

Stuffing the new documentation in a hip pocket with those yellow telegram forms, Longarm thanked the helpful coroner's clerk and got on over to the county sheriff's office.

He found Sheriff Tegner seated at his desk talking to a stranger dressed about the way they made Longarm and his fellow deputies dress around the Denver District Court. So it came as no great surprise when Sheriff Tegner said, "We were just talking about you, Longarm. Meet Deputy Marshal O'Brian out of your Saint Paul office."

As they shook, O'Brian allowed his friends called him Sean. He and Longarm were about the same age, with O'Brian about two inches shorter and a good bit broader, with big red fists that reminded Longarm of sugar-cured hams sticking out of black broadcloth sleeves. The man from Saint Paul wore his own .44-40 lower and side-draw under his somber frock coat. There was a lot to be said for that rig, if a lawman worked mostly afoot and wanted that extra edge a side-draw might give in an alley fight.

Longarm naturally assumed O'Brian was there about that recorded treasury note and the death of one known member of the gang who'd ridden out of Fort Collins with it.

O'Brian shook his head and replied, "Not exactly. Those stolen notes of noticeable denomination have been turning up all over this county, and I don't see how I could arrest an outlaw you've already put in the ground for us."

Longarm shot a thoughtful glance at Sheriff Tegner, who nodded and said, "Well, sure we let them bury the dead bastard. There was never any mystery about who he was, was there?"

Longarm allowed he was satisfied if the county was satisfied, and asked O'Brian what else they might be talking about.

The beefy O'Brian said, "You. They sent me to warn you and back your play should a rumor picked up by a reliable informer in Saint Paul pan out. You ever hear of an owlhoot rider called Laughing Larry Lucas, pard?"

Longarm started to say no. Then he nodded thoughtfully and asked, "Homicidal maniac from the copper country along the shores of Lake Superior? Sent away to a lunatic asylum instead of the gallows after he blew up his own kin with dynamite?"

O'Brian nodded grimly and said, "He escaped last fall. Blew a lock with homemade explosives he'd put together from playing-card shavings, matchheads, and such. There's some argument as to just how crazy the man might be. But there's no doubt he's out, and working of late as a paid killer. Cheap, the way I've heard it."

Longarm whistled softly, and seeing the older Sheriff Tegner seemed more confused, explained, "We're talking about a maniac known as Laughing Larry because he thinks he's so damned comical. He likes to leave droll notes when he blows a safe, which he's good at, and play what he calls practical jokes, which he's not so good at, in my view leastways, because his victims tend to wind up dead."

O'Brian volunteered, "He said at his sanity hearing he was only trying to teach some Canadian in-laws about our Fourth of July when he touched off all that sixty-percent Hercules under

222

their outhouse. He said he hadn't expected his brother-in-law to be taking a crap when the dynamite went off."

Longarm grimaced and said, "They'd have hung him if he'd offered a less loco excuse for killing an in-law and business partner after a string of more sensible robberies. But be that as it may, whether he knows he's crazy or thinks he's fooling us, Laughing Larry can be injurious as hell to one's health."

O'Brian said, "We heard he was after you. Nothing personal. Somebody who knows you better must want you dead awfully bad to send for help as dangerous as Laughing Larry Lucas!"

Longarm sighed and said, "That's for damn sure. Did your informant say whether Laughing Larry was out to blow me out of my boots or shoot me down like a dog from behind, since he's been known to do both?"

O'Brian shook his head and said, "We're not even certain of the rumor. You know how they clam up on you as soon as you press them for details about word on the shady side of the street."

Longarm nodded and replied, "I seldom ask 'em how they learned a bank was about to be held up, if I put any trust in them at all. It makes more sense to watch the infernal bank."

O'Brian nodded grimly and said that was why he was there, adding his own office couldn't afford to tie up more deputies unless and until they had more proof Laughing Larry Lucas was anywhere in Minnesota. For as in the case of all that hot paper, tips about escaped lunatics seemed to come in from all over.

Longarm said he thought Lucas was a Scotch-Irish name, and asked if an Irishman named O'Brian might confirm his guess about Calvert Tyger's odd last name.

O'Brian nodded soberly and said, "It's Irish. Sometimes spelled Tiger, like the big striped pussycat itself. But I believe the family name derives from something like McTaggart to begin with. Why do you ask?"

Longarm said, "Tougher to see a first- or second-generation Swede or Santee sending for a killer of uncertain temperament and another breed entirely. Folks ought to know better, considering neither Judas nor Brutus were recent immigrants, but most of 'em still feel safer trusting secret plans to their own kind. Tyger and Flanders both tend to be Irish names, and whilst they did have at least one Indian riding with 'em, they sent a squirt named Morrison after me earlier."

O'Brian nodded thoughtfully and said flatly, "Morrison's another Scotch-Irish name, and I'm beginning to follow your drift!"

Sheriff Tegner, being of Swedish ancestry, said he didn't and that he wished they'd make up their minds whether this discussion was about Scotch or Irish outlaws, damn it.

Longarm smiled and nodded at O'Brian, who explained. "The true Scotch-Irish hail from the Protestant north of Ireland, where they tend to have names of Scotch, Irish, Welsh, or even English origin, since divide and conquer was the name of the game. But now we're all American, so what the hell."

Longarm volunteered, "Folks are funny about feeling less natural when they change their ancestry than when they only change their names. Billy the Kid, as they now call him, started out named McCarthy or McCarty. Then he said his last name was Antrim, and after that he decided he was William H. Bonney. Notice all three last names are Irish, and that *H* likely stands for Henry, the Kid's real first name."

O'Brian nodded and said, "One doubts Frank and Jesse have been using James as a last name since that narrow escape over at Northfield. But I'd bet money that when we finally do catch up with them neither will be calling himself Gonzalez, Morgenstern, or even Flannery!"

Sheriff Tegner got to his feet and went over to a filing cabinet to break out a tall bottle, muttering, "My breed calls this aquavit. You're not supposed to drink it neat on an empty stomach, and don't let the caraway flavoring fool you. But I just hate long dry conversations, and you two federal boys sure have a lot to talk about this afternoon!"

Longarm and O'Brian both laughed. As the older lawman rustled up some six-ounce tumblers and poured three heroic drinks, the man from Saint Paul suggested he might guess better if he knew just what the deputy from Denver had been up to in these parts.

Longarm brought them both up to date. It took them all more than one aquavit to make it as far as that old cuss being run over just after withdrawing all his savings from the bank. Longarm politely refused a third one, saying, "You were right about them caraway seeds. I'm starting to feel 'em in my legs now, even sitting down like so!"

O'Brian said he'd had enough for now as well, turning back to Longarm to ask, "How do you think the death of this Jake Thorsson ties in with the missing colored lady called the Bee Witch?"

Longarm stared soberly down at the two cheroots he'd apparently taken for three, or had it been five, as he said sort of thickly, "Might not be any connection at all. A mess of folks made withdrawals from the same bank about the same time. The only thing mysterious about that old drunk's death is where his money might have wound up, and I doubt that could be a federal matter."

Sheriff Tegner stared owlishly and demanded, "Don't you boys look at me! I recall old Jake getting run over last Christmas. But nobody never said nothing about any missing money, damn it."

Longarm said soothingly, "I know. I've sent wires about that beekeeper I suspect as a railroad spy to a couple of railroad pals in high and low places. A railroad dick I know, called Whispering Smith along the U.P. right-of-way, might have heard about such a sneaky old gal. I wired an even sneakier railroading man called Jay Gould about sneaky plans to run yet another railroad line through these parts. Old Jay owes me a favor, and the stock-manipulating rascal would have surely heard about anyone planning to lay one damn mile of track most any damn place in this land of opportunity."

O'Brian whistled softly and said, "My boss was right, Longarm. You do know your business, and I'd sure hate to be trying to hide anything as big as a railroad from you. But what on earth could some secret railroad plans have to do with the Tyger and Flanders gang or those missing treasury notes?"

Longarm figured he was seeing straight enough to hand out a pair of cheroots and light one for himself as he was explaining. "Might not be any connection at all. At the rate they've been turning up, those notes from the Fort Collins robbery might not all be missing much longer. I sure wish I knew how they spread so far and wide before being spotted. Meanwhile some local settlers, some of 'em Indians trying to go straight, seem to have been banking on that Bee Witch they admired sending them a railroad line to improve their fortunes. It's possible there was no connection at all betwixt the late Baptiste Youngwolf of the Ojibwa Nation and those Santee or whatever following me about for reasons of their own. Have you ever noticed, in real life, how complicated this job can get next to that of one of Mister Edgar Allan Poe's lawmen?"

The sheriff asked what in blue blazes Edgar Allan Poe had to do with all this flimflammery.

Longarm said, "In them murders along the Rue Morgue, Mister Poe's lawmen had enough on their plate with this giant ape tear-assing over the rooftops of Paris, France, to kill ladies in a confusing way. But think how confusing it might have been if there'd been even one other monster, or mayhaps just a murderous asshole, killing others in a different way, although in the same part of Paris, France."

. Sheriff Tegner snorted, "You think *two* lousy crooks acting up at the same time are confusing, old son? Shit, you ought to be here at roundup time when the cowhands are flush and the farm boys ain't been paid for the fall harvest yet!"

O'Brian ignored him too, and nodded at Longarm. "Two sets of crooks working at cross-purpose could confuse us all without really trying. I still think some members of that Tyger and Flanders gang had to be worried about you uncovering something about them here."

Longarm shrugged and said, "Hell, I did. His name was Baptiste Youngwolf and they just now buried him."

O'Brian nodded, but said, "Somebody else must be as worried about you catching them at something just as serious, pard. Why would known outlaws who've already tried for you directly send away for a hired killer more famous around here than out yonder where they robbed that payroll office and might still be hiding for all we really know?"

Sheriff Tegler objected, "Youngwolf wasn't hiding out in Colorado when he tried to back-shoot Longarm here. Them two who came after him at Widow Pedersson's place weren't local boys neither."

O'Brian insisted, "Doesn't matter exactly whom a particular gunslick might have been working for, once you see there could be more than one mastermind behind all these attacks. So 'fess up, Longarm, don't you have any ideas at all about someone right here in Brown County having something of their own to hide?"

Longarm blew a thoughtful smoke ring and morosely stated, "I have more possible things to suspect than I could shake a stick at. But I don't know a damn thing we could arrest anybody on! I told you I suspect, but only suspect, that old colored lady pretending to be a crazy beekeeper was really running a railroad survey. That wouldn't be a federal crime. Killing her to prevent or delay her work, then dumping her body in a federal waterway, might be. We'd have to know for certain someone had done that before we could arrest 'em, though."

"What about those unusual banking transactions?" O'Brian asked in a thoughtful tone. "Don't you find it unusual that the same bank president who reported that stolen payroll note was the one who paid out all that other money to at least two elderly people who wound up dead or missing within hours of their last withdrawals?"

Sheriff Tegner laughed gleefully and said, "Hot damn, let's all go arrest Banker Plover. He ain't a Swede and it's an election year, dad-blast his murderous eyes!"

Longarm laughed and said, "I ain't sure it's against the law to manage a Minnesota bank without being Swedish, Sheriff. After that, leave us not forget old P. S. Plover would have been awesomely dumb to report a stolen government payroll note in his possession, knowing it had been stolen, if he hadn't come by it honestly. I'm still working on where Wabasha Chambrun got that hot paper in the first place. His Indian sponsors have been sending him, or his Santee wife, innocent checks drawn on an honest Omaha bank. Not all of them have been cashed here in New Ulm. Those cashed Lord knows where may or may not have stuck the Chambruns with that one and only suspicious hundred-dollar note. The damned things have turned up so many places I have to agree with my boss it would be a waste of time, even if we *could* backtrack that one bill to yet another poor soul with no apparent connection with the robbery."

"Then why are you still here?" asked O'Brian. "Do you suspect Plover of having those two elderly depositors murdered for some other reason?"

Longarm chuckled and said, "You're as cynical as me about bankers. As a matter of fact, I did have something like that in mind when I asked the coroner's office to compare a list of heavy withdrawals with sudden deaths in this fair city. But as we've all been saying, Jake Thorsson seems to have died natural, and nobody knows what happened to that old lady yet."

O'Brian insisted, "That still leaves close to twenty thousand in untraceable bills unaccounted for, right?"

Longarm shook his head and said, "Wrong. We still don't know the depositor calling herself Janice Carpenter at the bank is really missing. She could be anywhere else, with her money in some other bank or, hell, under her mattress. So all we know for certain is that a man called Jacob Thorsson died in front of witnesses, including a doctor, in a manner I'd hate to have to arrange ahead of time. As for his missing money, who's to say it's really missing? You know what a fuss they can make in probate court about money left behind with no will to probate. They charge the kin for letting them have their own money too. So who's to say somebody around the old man's deathbed, maybe the old man himself, never got the grand notion to just avoid all that bother? Had anyone with money coming felt they'd been screwed, they'd have doubtless let the whole world in on it by now."

O'Brian ran a thoughtful thumbnail along the stubble of his fleshy jaw as he mused, half to himself, "That only works if nobody there had any idea the old man had drawn all that money out of the bank."

Longarm nodded, but demanded, "Would you lay there for three days without mentioning you'd been robbed if you'd been robbed?"

When O'Brian said he didn't think he would, Longarm went

on to say, "Damned right. But if you'd still had the money on you, or anywhere on or about the premises, somebody would have surely found it as they cleaned up after your demise. You get to clean up a heap after a man spends three days dying of internal injuries."

O'Brian nodded soberly, said he'd been in the war too, and asked how Longarm felt about a maid, or someone from the undertaker's, helping himself or herself to a bundle and never reporting it.

Longarm shrugged and said, "Happens all the time. It ain't nice, but it ain't a federal crime. I doubt the sheriff here would take your suspicion as a gift in an election year, unless there was some complaint by some damned citizen to go with it."

Sheriff Tegner muttered, "Damned right. Gotta have a corpus delicti before you can arrest anybody. Jake Thorsson's corpse wasn't delicti. He was run over by a brewery dray!"

Longarm suggested, "What I think he means is that you have to be able to show the body or substance of a crime to the grand jury."

O'Brian sniffed, "I guess I know what corpus delicti means, and I fear I follow your drift. Whether either of those old folks lost any money after they took it from their own savings accounts, we'd have a time proving anyone at their bank took a dime of it."

Longarm said, "That's about the size of it. I like to arrest as many bankers as I can too. But I don't see how even a banker could know in advance."

"Know what in advance?" asked O'Brian with a puzzled frown.

Longarm replied, "How even an old drunk would be sure to get run over by a dray *after*, not before you cleaned out his bank account."

"There must be a way," Sheriff Tegner suddenly decided, spilling almost as much as he was pouring as he insisted, "Never trusted that P. S. Plover. Never will. What sort of a name might Plover be? It sure sounds odd for these parts!"

Longarm gently took the bottle from the befuddled older lawman as he said, "You got to watch them Anglo-Saxon bankers, Sheriff. But I'm a peace officer, not a bank examiner."

O'Brian suggested a bank examiner might be able to figure a way to fiddle the books in order to show withdrawals taking place *after* rather than before a depositor died.

Longarm shrugged and said, "You gents feel free to examine all the bank ledgers you want. Meanwhile, I'd rather work on suspects, red or white, who've threatened me directly. Marshal Vail never sent me here to investigate Banker Plover, and Plover surely couldn't have been expecting me to. Yet sinister cusses have been trying to stop me ever since I left my home office, and to tell the truth, it's getting tedious as hell."

Sheriff Tegner didn't answer. He put his head down on his desk and commenced to blow small caraway-scented bubbles.

O'Brian grinned at Longarm and murmured, "I thought it was Irishmen who couldn't handle the creature. Where do we go from here, pard?"

Longarm said, "You go anywhere you like. One of us has to stay here until at least one of this old gent's own deputies shows up."

O'Brian seemed sincerely puzzled as he demanded, "How come? Neither of us ride for Brown County, and it was his own grand notion to get drunk on duty."

Longarm sighed and said, "Neither of us are running for re-election this fall, and he was trying to be friendly. What do you have to do that's so all-fired important with the afternoon sun so low?"

O'Brian said, "Send a wire back to my real boss for openers. Now that we've talked I ain't sure whether they want me to stay and back your play or head on home. No offense, and I know you're supposed to be good, but you don't seem to have any play in mind."

Longarm only shrugged. He didn't want another lawman, or any man at all, backing his play with pretty Vigdis Magnusson, now that the bank had closed for the day and most everyone but Viggy would be on their way home before long.

Chapter 24

After the man from Saint Paul was gone, Longarm helped himself to some wanted flyers, took another seat, and smoked and read the ugly statistics of wanted men and women until, a million years later, that senior deputy he'd already met came in, nodded morosely at the top of the sheriff's gray head, and muttered, "I see we've been into that old aquavit again. Thanks for holding the fort, Longarm. I can handle it from here, as long as nobody sets fire to the church or robs the bank!"

Longarm rose so they could shake hands and part friendly. Then he picked up his Winchester and headed for the Western Union himself.

He hadn't heard from old Jay Gould as yet. The railroad robber baron was doubtless already dining on fish eggs and green turtle back East, where it would be suppertime by now. But good old Whispering Smith, riding herd on gold shipments out of the Black Hills for the U.P. line, had wired he knew the Bee Witch well. Only her real name was Miss Judith Wright and she'd been a Union spy for old Allan Pinkerton's Secret Service.

But Whispering Smith said she hadn't stayed with Pinkerton when the gruff old Scotsman started his private agency after the war. Smith said the sly old colored gal worked free-lance for both railroad and land-developing outfits, having been taught to make pretty good contour maps when she wasn't pretending to be a laundress, a midwife, or some other sort of harmless dumb coon.

Longarm had already figured what the sly old gal had been up to in these parts. He wired Whispering Smith an urgent request to ask all about and find out whether the dusky old detective gal was alive. He explained he wasn't interested in any other secrets she or her real outfit might want to keep.

After that, knowing in advance how Viggy's notions of supper were doubtless better for her waistline than his own, Longarm stopped at a stand-up beanery to down some Swedish meatballs and potato pancakes with two mugs of black coffee.

Feeling refreshed by his light snack, Longarm consulted his pocket watch and decided it was safe to take his saddle gun to the bank.

Viggy let him in, as he'd expected, but giggled at his saddle gun and said, "I surrender, dear. Everyone else has been gone for some time, so where do you want to come, on that same chesterfield in the rear office?"

Longarm chuckled, hauled her in, and kissed her with enthusiasm inspired by chastely thinking of other women all that damned day.

But then he said, "There's no sense having to get dressed over and over when it's this close to sundown to begin with and I got some bank examining to do whilst there's still some daylight."

The beautiful blonde sighed and said, "Pooh, I thought you were only after my body. Didn't you go all through that ledger for last December last night, darling?"

He said, "I did, and I'm pretty sure I made out no more than two styles of handwriting. But I'd like to make certain, so . . ."

"I can tell you who made each entry, dear." She led the way around to the backs of the teller's cages as she continued. "You just missed them. I thought it was me you were interested in. But we have two more tellers, and we naturally transcribe all our daily transaction in the day book for that month at the end of every working day."

As she hunkered down to rummage for that ledger from the year before, Longarm said, "Hold on. Did you just tell me old

232

P. S. Plover would have never made any entries in his own handwriting?"

She panted, "Here it is. I thought you'd finished with the clumsy old tome. Why would Mister Plover be making entries in deposits and withdrawals, dear? He's the manager."

Longarm started to make a dumb objection. But he could see without asking how the front office would tally all the real cash on hand in person before locking it in the vault overnight.

Viggy rose to full height and flopped the heavy gray ledger atop the long work counter running the length of the teller's hidey-holes. As she opened it for him she idly asked what they were doing. So he brought her up to date on that old drunk and the missing colored lady as he found the entries dealing with the both of them. Then he sighed and muttered, "Thunderation! Neither withdrawal seems to have been tampered with, other entries above and below them confirm the dates for both of them, and worse yet, the two withdrawals on different days were recorded in different scripts!"

Viggy put a polished nail to the paper, saying, "This would have to be Mister Spandau's handwriting. Isn't it pretty? Mister Quinn writes clear enough, I suppose, but he's not as tidy a penman as Mister Spandau."

Longarm said he didn't care, and asked if any one teller got much time alone back there.

Viggy thought and decided with a giggle, "Playing detective is a lot of fun, albeit I'd still rather play house. I see what you suspect one of us sneaks of doing, dear. I suppose it would be possible for one teller to alter the books whilst the other was out of the cage to heed the call of nature or run some other quick errand. But he'd have to be awfully fast as well as awfully clever, don't you agree?"

Longarm swore under his breath and nodded. "I sure wanted to arrest me a banker too. Another lawman I was just jawing with had the same motive for my demise figured out. But old folks do withdraw all their savings and leave town or get run over by a dray."

She asked if he was through back there. He kissed her again and said he was ready to play house instead of bank examiner. So she led the way back to that chesterfield.

But once they got to old Plover's office the sunset was peeking fire-engine red through the drawn blinds. So Longarm repeated what he'd said about just getting undressed once the right way, with her grand old bed to play on once they had.

She dimpled and stopped trying to unbuckle his gun rig as she told him she agreed it was time they got out of this ridiculous vertical position.

They slipped out the back way and moved along a back street in the gloaming. Off in the distance, a train whistle seemed to be mourning the death of another day. But Longarm knew it was that eastbound he'd have had to wait for if he'd taken that clerk's suggestion about modern transportation. When Viggy asked what he'd just chuckled about, he told her, "I'd be crossing the Sleepy Eye trestle aboard that train about now if I hadn't checked today's timetable and met up with a buckskin pony that was more convenient. Don't know whether they'll be stopping at Sleepy Eye or not. Either way, they'd have been letting me off here even later."

As they approached the entrance to her own alley Viggy hesitated and murmured, "I might have felt better leading you and that rifle to my back door after dark, dear. It's not that I'm ashamed of anything exactly, but it's still awfully light out, and . . ."

"I know about small-town gossip," he said, not wanting to upset her by telling her a widow was talking about them clean across town. But he never argued when she shyly suggested he let her go on ahead and then come on down that alley alone after it got a mite darker.

He said he'd hold up a cottonwood with his back and smoke a couple of cheroots while she went on ahead to turn down the covers.

She glanced about, then stood on her toes to kiss him some more before she turned and scampered off in the gathering dusk like a kid out for mischief on Halloween.

Longarm chuckled as he turned his back to that cottonwood, cradled his Winchester over one arm, and reached for a smoke. But he'd barely lit it, and taken no more than a half dozen drags on it, when the soft gloaming light lit up with a hellish glare and the earth underfoot was shaken by a horrendous blast that

234

just had to be dynamite, a heap of dynamite, going off too close to keep Longarm from wailing, "Aw, shit, don't let it be that, Lord!"

But it was. Shattered wood had been set ablaze down the alley, and he could see the empty smoke-hazed gap where Viggy's carriage house had stood long before he got that far. So he didn't join the crowd of confounded neighborfolk gathering like flies around a cow pat as he spun and tore the other way, with the Winchester '73 at port arms. He levered a round of .44-40 in its chamber as he heard that eastbound train's huffing and puffing off to the west. He beat it into the New Ulm depot with time to spare, though, and was only half surprised to find the so-called Deputy O'Brian alone on the open platform.

O'Brian didn't act surprised to see him. He said, "Howdy, pard. I figured the bastard who set off that bomb would head for here to catch that train too."

Longarm said, "Well, sure you did. How did you know someone just rigged a mess of dynamite to go off when a lady I was escorting home tried to open her damned door?"

O'Brian tried, "I heard the explosion, of course. Just like you, I figured Laughing Larry Lucas had blown some damned something up and that he'd naturally have his getaway planned in advance."

"You're under arrest for the murder of Miss Vigdis Magnusson, a gal who never done no harm, you son of a bitch!" Longarm swung the muzzle of his Winchester to cover the impostor, adding, "Go for that side-draw, please, if you think I'm fooling. Otherwise you'd best give me some answers pronto. Who sent for you and how come?"

Laughing Larry lived up to his nickname by laughing like a fool hyena and demanding, "What if I tell you to just guess?"

Longarm said, "I reckon you'll get gut-shot trying to escape. You don't seem to grasp this situation, you comical cuss. I am mad as hell and I'd rather kill you personally, gruesomely, than let you die quick and painless on the gallows or even talk your way back into another nut house. But I'll still take you in alive if you'd like to say who else I want to arrest for what you just done!"

Laughing Larry looked really loco as the headlight beam of that train pulling into the station etched his grinning features in harsh yellow light and shadows black as sin. But Longarm was still trying to reason with the half-crazed killer when Laughing Larry suddenly spun on one boot heel like an awkward ballet dancer and bolted for the far side of the tracks just as the locomotive's big barn-red cowcatcher was about to plow between them.

Longarm fired, of course, and hit the fugitive felon low in the right hip, to send his holstered six-gun flying as he spun again to land spread-eagled on his back, both boot heels hooked over the far rail as the big locomotive hissed to a stop to block Longarm's view.

So he was tearing around the front end of the train as he heard a voice from the engineer's cabin wailing, "Lord have mercy! I think I just ran over a passenger!"

He was right, Longarm saw, as he moved down the far side of the big steel drivers through clouds of hissing steam. For he found the killer he'd just shot stretched out on the ballast, spurting blood from both severed stumps while he laughed like hell.

Longarm lay his Winchester aside on the ballast and whipped off the dark bandanna he'd been wearing in place of a sissy tie as he told Laughing Larry to lie still. He was knotting the now-bloody calico as tight as he could around the killer's right shin when the amused or more likely hysterical cuss laughed some more and asked if Longarm wanted to race him down to the far end.

Longarm reached for the killer's own shoestring tie as he told him not unkindly, "I feel your footracing days are done. But we may be able to stop the bleeding, and weren't you fixing to tell me who else I have to thank for all this tomfoolery?"

Laughing Larry just giggled, lay back, and closed his eyes. Longarm still knotted the tie around his left shin, even though it wasn't bleeding that hard now.

Sheriff Tegner and two deputies came around the front end of the locomotive with lanterns. As they joined Longarm and Laughing Larry, the older lawman said, "Thanks for standing by as I recovered from them caraway seeds. Somebody just blew Vigdis Magnusson to bits all by herself, despite the old biddy across the alley, and how come I see Deputy O'Brian laying there so still? Is he dead?"

Longarm nodded soberly and said, "I reckon. He wasn't the real Sean O'Brian from our Saint Paul office. He was the one and original hired killer he'd come all this way to warn us about!"

Sheriff Tegner swung the beam of his lantern over the blank face of the figure at their feet, marveling, "*That's* Laughing Larry Lucas? How come? Why would he go to all that trouble warning you he was in town if, all the time, he meant to blow you up the way he did Miss Vigdis and all them other victims?"

Longarm said, "He wasn't out to tell me. He was out to tell you. Would you have tried to stop a friendly fellow lawman from reporting my murder federal after you'd already said yourself you suspected they were worried about me at the bank a fellow victim worked at?"

Sheriff Tegner allowed he might not have.

Longarm continued. "He'd have come to New Ulm aboard that earlier westbound today. He'd have had plenty of time to scout around and pick up some gossip about the man they'd hired him to kill before he ever paid that false courtesy call on you. When I got in like a big-ass bird with his saddle gun already out, Laughing Larry grabbed the chance to throw me off guard whilst casting suspicion on Banker Plover, see?"

Sheriff Tegner grumbled, "Not really. Them same gossips said that blonde you were sparking had been sparked by her boss in the past. So who's to say he might not have sent away for a tougher cuss because he was jealous but afraid to take you on man to man?"

Longarm shook his head and said, "The hired killer. I was wondering about cigar smoke and how such a sweet little thing wound up in position to outrank and supervise two full-grown bank tellers. But had Plover been that serious about his part-time play-pretty . . ."

"How do you know they were only playing part of the time?" asked the county deputy Longarm knew best.

Longarm was aware of others drifting in for a closer look

237

now, so he kept his voice down as he replied. "I happen to know she had heaps of playtime of her own. This dead dynamite expert knew it as well. He slipped over to her known place of residence to set up his infernal device with me as the intended target. But there was a chance the other gent you just mentioned could have come calling and been as unpleasantly surprised. So how often does a hired killer either lay suspicion on a true client or blow him all to hell with dynamite?"

The sheriff said that made sense. But his senior deputy pointed out that Laughing Larry had been a homicidal lunatic.

Longarm shrugged and said, "Anything's possible, once you toss out all the remotely sensible reasons to kill folks. It's possible anyone here in Brown County could have sent for a hired killer just to see whether I died with my eyes shut or open. But if it's all the same with you, I'll start with more logical suspects."

Sheriff Tegner blinked and asked, "You mean you got some good as Banker Plover?"

To which Longarm could only reply, in a weary tone, "How would you like me to list 'em, alphabetical or numerical?"

Chapter 25

It was just after midnight when Longarm finally made it back up the river to that raft and told Mato Takoza not to flap those raggedy buzzard wings and moan at him like that.

The spunky little breed acted mighty happy to see him, once she knew who'd come calling at that hour. But she'd have likely acted as happy whether she'd meant it or not. So Longarm held a few things back until she was making him happy inside the shanty, bare-ass with her on top. Then he told her he had some other happy surprises for her, and rolled her on her back to open her wide and probe her deep as he told her he'd been scouting her old Bee Witch, as he'd promised her he would.

Long-donging anyone that pretty would have been easy in any case, but she'd been extracting honey all afternoon and smelled like she had, even after an afternoon swim in the chalky river water. She took all the organ-grinding inspired by all those Wasichu gals through a long chaste day as a personal compliment. So when she threw both her arms and legs around him to crush him tight against her tawny tits, he kissed the side of her neck and murmured, "I like you too. Now I have some questions to ask, and before you answer, I want to give you a couple of tokens of good faith."

She demurely asked what he wanted to know, and assured him she would never lie to him, never.

He murmured, "Don't see why not. We lie to you folks all the time."

As she stiffened under him he quickly said soothingly, "Always for your own good, just as your kind tells us things we'd like to hear instead of things that might upset us. Meantime, what's a little lying betwixt friends, and I hope you understand how awkward it would be for me to testify in any court of law against a sweetheart I just shot my wad in."

She started to cry with her legs up around his waist, and it sure felt interesting inside her. So he began to move in her just a mite as he said, "I'm fixing to tell you everything I know about your Santee plot and its likely outcome first."

She said she didn't know what he was talking about, gripping him tighter with her strong brown thighs. But he didn't move any faster as he insisted, "Sure you do. The Chambruns and those other breed homesteaders have only been leaving a little out. Nothing any of you have done is go-to-prison illegal. If it was, a land and railroad speculator I know would have been in jail a long time ago."

She pleaded, "Faster. Do it to me faster, Wasichu Wastey!"

He kept teasing them both with long, measured thrusts as he calmly said, "Someone in your Indian land-development syndicate figured out who the Bee Witch really was and what she was really up to. They sent you to beg her for a job, pretending to be a poor little orphan with no connections with those other Santee moving in up and down the banks she was surveying for her railroad."

She sobbed, "Hear me, I *am* an orphan! I have nobody. Nobody. Not even a man of my own kind to keep me company on this lonely raft!"

It was starting to feel too good again to talk. But as Longarm started pumping faster she demanded, "Have you ever met any other men out here with me, red or white?"

He kissed her, came, and moaned. "We'll get to that part in just a minute. First I'm telling you right out that the old railroad survey gal got back East all right with all her money and a bonus for a job well done. I got two wires in a row this evening from a railroad dick who'd know about such matters.

Neither me nor Whispering Smith have any idea where she got rid of that pony."

Mato Takoza groaned she was coming too now. So Longarm pounded her over the pass to Paradise, and let her get some breath back before he said, "I got a later wire from a Wasichu who delights in scalping other Wasichus, so listen tight."

When he was certain she was, he told her, "A robber baron who pulls such tricks all the time must have thought I was about to invest in a railroad stock manipulation. That's what they call crooking widows, orphans, and wise-ass Indians, railroad stock manipulations."

She proved how dumb and innocent she really was by demanding more details. "Why would anyone survey a railroad right of way if they didn't mean to build a railroad?"

He kissed her some more and replied, "To sucker folks into buying railroad stock, of course. The one and original Jay Gould assures me the whole thing's pie in the sky. They have railroad trestles enough down to New Ulm and up by Franklin. Nobody needs a third line between. So they ain't really fixing to build one."

She wailed, "Oh, *hinhey*! Now you Wasichu have really done it to us! Even when we play by your own rules you screw us, screw us, screw us!"

Longarm said, "Later, after I get my second wind. Meanwhile, I've told you what's really going on so's you can come out on top for a change. Jay Gould assures me the clever flimflam has some time to go as they sell more watered railroad stock at ever higher prices, thanks to carefully placed secret tips about secret surveys and such. Meanwhile, even homestead claims clouding title to future townsites must be worth something to the greedy speculators who've just started to hear about that swell new railroad line."

She nibbled his earlobe pensively as she pondered a mite before deciding, "But my Ina Tatowiyeh Wachipi's high and rocky claim will be worthless, worthless, once no river crossing is ever developed up her way!"

Longarm said, "Tell your aunt to sell such rights to the claim as they have for whatever they can get. Then tell them to buy stock in that feeder line the Bee Witch was surveying for."

"You said the stock was worthless, worthless!" she shouted.

Longarm hushed her with a kiss on the lips and told her, "You have to learn to pay attention if you're out to flimflam folks as slick-talking as mine. I said that railroad stock was watered pie in the sky. Stock is only worthless when nobody else wants to buy it from a poor ignorant redskin, who bought it earlier, before us wise-money boys heard about that trestle across the Minnesota, cutting hours off the regular railroading east or west."

This time she got it. She laughed incredulously and said, "Hear me, my *ina* and her friends have a lot of money to invest. What if we bought as much of that railroad stock as we could this month, and sold it for as much as we could get for it next month?"

He said, "Jay Gould tells me he figures to dump his own investment at the end of this month. I wouldn't hold on to any a day longer than that. For what goes up must come down, fast, when it has nothing but hot air lifting it anywhere to begin with."

She said she understood, and loved him so much for being so nice to her and her people that she wanted to give him a French lesson.

He said, "Before you find it tough to talk with your mouth full, I want you to be nice to me in another way. We both know I had to take your word about that conversation you had in Santee the other night."

She nodded and said, "I told you what those strange riders asked about you. Are you suggesting I knew them better than I told you I did, Wasichu Wastey?"

He said, "The thought had crossed my mind. A man tends to get sort of suspicious after he's been trailed by Indians for a spell, no offense. But if I take your word you weren't flimflamming me about some pals who only wanted to know how you were doing with the sucker, let's try and slice it a couple of other ways. To begin with, that was really Santee the bunch of you were speaking, right?"

She shrugged her bare shoulders, making her tawny breasts move in an interesting manner against his bare chest as she replied, "It was a Nakota dialect at least. I'm not sure it was

242

pure Santee. The stranger I spoke to could have been from some distant band."

"Or an Ojibwa who'd gotten fluent enough in Santee to talk to the folks he was scouting," Longarm decided. Then he asked how sure she was all four or five of them had been any sort of Indian.

She started to tell him she just knew. Then she stopped. "Hear me, it was dark, and while I thought I heard two voices, it could have been one trickster. But why do you think one Indian with Wasichu friends would want me to think them a band of Indians?"

Longarm replied, "You just suggested he was a trickster. Which means that I can account for one assimilated Ojibwa, riding with some cowhands off the same spread, better than I can account for a whole Indian band neither you nor your Santee pals would know about."

He told her as much as he knew about the late Baptiste Youngwolf or Uncle Chief as she made good on her offer to French him hard some more. She couldn't comment all that much with her mouth full, but as soon as they were going at it in a more conversational manner dog-style, Mato Takoza said, "*Iyoptey wanagi*! I love it this way! But hear me, I don't think you want to ride on to ask that Helga Runeberg more than you already know about her pet Ojibwa."

Longarm clasped the breed's firm tawny hips to aim it up her right as he muttered, "I know I don't want to. But I got to. She allowed she was sore as hell at me, but she never let her boys shoot it out with me over in Sleepy Eye when they had the chance."

Mato Takoza arched her spine and moaned, "Deeper! As deep as you can got! For Wakanna only knows when I'll ever find another man like you after that Wasichuweynh Witko gets another crack at you on her own land, with nobody else there to sing of the way you died!"

Chapter 26

Longarm had felt no call to sound foolish or show off, and he was almost certain he'd eliminated Mato Takoza and her Santee pals by the time they kissed for the last time the next morning. On the other hand, he felt no call to lay out all his future plans for her whether she was in cahoots with the ones he was really after or not.

So he was mildly chagrined when Wabasha Chambrun and a son in his teens overtook him on the road near the Bedford homestead to volunteer some backup. The burly breed reminded Longarm he'd ridden with the Ninth Cav in his day. "My wife's niece just told us about you going up alone against all them Runeberg riders. She told us how you took the time to rustle us up them swell stock market tips too. My oldest boy, Kangi Ska here, can hit a prairie dog's head at four hundred yards with that Big Fifty he begged to bring along."

Longarm sighed. "I reckon her heart was in the right place. I wasn't fixing to go up against at least seventeen guns alone, gents. I told your county sheriff and his own boys to meet up with me at Israel Bedford's this morning. Riding in on a sod-walled home spread in the dark can be injurious to one's health, and I wanted to talk to Miss Mato Takoza first, to make double sure my process of eliminating made sense. That's what you call it when you whittle away the less likely suspects, process of eliminating."

Chambrun smiled sheepishy and said, "She told us how

244

you'd wormed so many family secrets out of her. The two of you ought to be ashamed. But how did you figure out who the real criminal mastermind was?"

As the three of them rode on, Longarm made a wry face and made sure Kangi Ska followed his drift as he told the two of them, "Criminal mastermind is a contradiction of terms. Nobody smart enough to be called a mastermind would ever become an out-and-out outlaw. You take that old Jay Gould your wife's niece may have just mentioned to you all. He spends more on fancy food, drink, and diamond shirt studs than the Reno and James-Younger gangs combined ever took from anybody at gunpoint. Old Jay don't bother with robbing trains. He helps himself to whole railroads legally by way of dirty stock-market tricks. So the murderous gang leaders we're after ain't half as slick as they think they are. They've just been confusing the shit out of me with unexpected moves."

He spotted the breakfast smoke from the Bedford place ahead and said, "I'm saddled with a halfway logical mind. So I sometimes catch myself playing chess by the rules, when the game is really checkers with ornery illogical crooks." Then he heeled his livery mount to a trot.

Sheriff Tegner had seen them coming of course. So he and his good-sized posse had mounted up in the dooryard of Israel Bedford, as had Bedford, another ex-cavalry rider himself.

Longarm and the breeds reined in close to him. The older lawman leaned closer to ask if Longarm had any objection to Neighbor Conway and his own kids tagging along.

Longarm was too thoughtful to stare at the three colored riders staring his way as they shyly sat their ponies a tad apart from the others. Longarm said, "It's your posse. It's been my experience a bigger posse packs more firepower than a smaller one."

Sheriff Tegner said, "That's the way I see it, and I already have the Swedish vote sewed up. So let's ride."

They did. Tegner was too smooth a politician to come right out and say the Conways had his kind permission to get shot by Rocking R boys of uncertain temperament. Such mutterings as Longarm picked up on during the fairly long ride across open range seemed to be directed at Chambrun and his Santee breed kid. Hardly anyone had ever lost a scalp to colored folks around New Ulm.

Longarm hoped such neighborly affairs as this one might help the reformed Indians fit in as sort of half-ass Wasichu in times to come. It would likely have reservation life beat. For those still living on the Great White Father's blanket had already started to look sort of sad to a man who remembered the way they'd been living just a short spell back. Some Indians seemed able to stay Indian as wards of the government. Someone like a Hopi could still prove his worth as a man by bringing in his swamping crop of blue corn, while a strong and smart Ojibwa could still show off with his wild rice, and even sell it. But it was tough to live the life of a buffalo-hunting professional horse thief, providing one's wives with household help captured from lesser nations, without getting one's allotment cut off by an old fuss of a B.I.A. agent. So maybe young Kangi Ska would make out better in the end as a prosperous farmer rather than a charity case, pissing and moaning about good old days he didn't really remember.

Posse riders dismounted along the way to carefully flatten and restaple such fences as they had to pass through. They saw more and more beef critters as they approached the road running north out of Sleepy Eye. But they saw none of Helga Runeberg's cowhands before they topped a rise to see her home spread waiting for them, silent as if it was late at night instead of mid-morning.

Sheriff Tegner ordered his men to spread wide, with two of his full-time deputies leading their own bunches to circle the sprawl of buildings and empty corrals as the main party closed in.

As Longarm and the local lawman in official charge rode into her barnyard, Helga Runeberg came out her back door, alone and unarmed in a more feminine outfit of polka-dotted gingham, and stated sarcastically she'd have baked a cake if she'd known so many of them would be by to court her so early in the day.

Sheriff Tegner stared soberly down at her from the saddle. "You know blamed well why we're here, Helga Runeberg. Last night we found Miss Vigdis Magnusson scattered all over creation. Dynamite wired to the other side of her back door blew off all her clothes along with her right arm, her head, and both tits when she went to let herself in after an honest day's work at her bank!"

The smaller, darker, and plainer gal didn't seem too upset as she nodded. "I know. Gus Hansson told me all about it when he got back from New Ulm late last night. Are you suggesting anyone out our way had anything to do with it?"

Longarm asked where young Hansson might be that morning. She met his gaze boldly as she calmly said, "He and a few of the other boys are out hunting strays. I can't say exactly when they'll be back."

Sheriff Tegner snorted. "I can. Never. We saw all that new drift wire you've strung to the east, and you've had your frontage along the Sleepy Eye road fenced solid for some time. I reckon I'd better arrest you for murder before you decide to go hunt stray snipes or great horned jackrabbits your ownself, Helga Runeberg!"

She went a shade paler, but didn't look too scared. Then Longarm suggested, "Maybe we ought to go in out of this hot sun and have a more confidential conversation with the lady, Sheriff."

Longarm was already swinging out of his saddle as he said this. So Sheriff Tegner dismounted as well, even though he grumbled in a lower tone, "Damn it, Longarm, it was you who pointed out this very suspect and that missing Hansson boy availed themselves of Western Union's services in New Ulm when they had a perfectly fine telegraph office way closer in Sleepy Eye."

Helga Runeberg snapped, "So this fancy federal man says. But he's right about how high that sun stands right now. So come on in if you want to make total fools of yourselves with this dumb line of questioning!"

She waited until just the three of them were alone in her kitchen before she poured herself and herself alone a cup of coffee and asked the sheriff, "Did he tell you how he followed me all the way to Sleepy Eye and threatened my poor inexperienced cowboys with a repeating rifle in front of witnesses?"

The sheriff planted his old bony butt on one corner of her

247

kitchen table as he replied, "He did, and how he thinks you put on such a show for witnesses as well!"

Longarm remained standing by her back door as he nodded at her and explained, "Laughing Larry Lucas went through a charade to encourage the sheriff here to look somewhere else once I was dead too. You'd made too much public war talk to take back, right after I gunned your dear old Uncle Chief, and you were too sore to consider he was the only really experienced killer on your payroll. So after you wired for outside help from Saint Paul—"

"That's your word against mine!" she interrupted, eyes blazing.

Sheriff Tegner snapped, "No, it ain't. I questioned the Western Union clerk who served you, and he backs Longarm's tale of seeing you and young Hansson coming out just after. Before you even think of saying it was Gus Hansson sending that wire to that boardinghouse in Saint Paul, the clerk said it was you who wrote the telegram, no doubt in some tricky code, since we know you never had no Cousin Anna, but that don't matter. Tell her about the real deputy marshals over in Saint Paul, Deputy Long!"

Longarm smiled thinly at the defiant little thing, still trying to recall where he'd seen those eyes before, and explained, "It only took my pals in Saint Paul one visit to determine Laughing Larry had been boarding at that same address under the very name you evoked in your telegram, which would still be on file by the way."

She said, "All right, Uncle Chief gave me the name of another old army pal to call on if I needed help and he wasn't around. Uncle Chief traveled a lot. I don't know anything about any code. I was just told to wire Uncle Leroy that Cousin Anna was getting married and let his old army pals take it from there, see?"

Sheriff Tegner stood up, reeling some, as he snarled, "I see you think I'm just a dumb Swede you can brush away from your guilty fresh face like a housefly! But you can't fool me with your slippery answers, Helga Runeberg! I'm arresting you in the name of the people of Brown County for murder in the first degree and . . ."

248

Longarm moved with surprising speed to catch the older lawman as he lurched the gal's way, but seemed to be fixing to go another. The tall deputy said soothingly, "I told you to go easy on them caraway seeds. You're too upset to question the witness calmly. So why don't you step outside for some fresh air and let me see what I can find out from Miss Helga, Sheriff?"

The older man muttered, "Hang her, I say! Hang her as high as she blew poor Vigdis Magnusson's pretty blond head!"

But Longarm still managed to ease him outside. Helga Runeberg was frog-belly sweaty and pale as he turned back to her. But she managed a brave enough front as she said, "Drunken old fool! He hasn't a thing on me, and he'd know that if only he'd stay out of the aquavit!"

Longarm smiled knowingly and nodded, but warned, "He is the sheriff, and that gal Laughing Larry killed in my place was mighty popular in New Ulm. I'd hate to face a local jury, stuck with even the circumstantial evidence we have on you. That's what they call it when nobody saw you actually pull the trigger. Circumstantial evidence."

She said, "Damn it, I was right here on my own land, miles away from New Ulm, when that stuck-up blonde was killed!"

Longarm soberly informed her, "Miss Viggy wasn't *stuck* up. She was *blown* up. Laughing Larry would have been miles away by now had not I beat his train into the depot. I didn't know it was him before I got there. I ain't that smart. I only figured whoever it was would want to get out of town suddenly, and seeing I did know a train was about to pass through . . ."

"I don't know who or what you're talking about," she said. "You were there when I told my boys not to gun you down like the dog you were born. Were you there when somebody instructed a killer from out of town who his target might be and with whom he'd be planning to spend the night?"

Longarm sighed and said, "I sure hate small-town gossip. But I do thank you for tying up that loose end, ma'am. You see, I solve these tougher ones by tying up one loose end after another until none seem to be left and I get to make my own arrests. I'm a tad more scientific than Sheriff Tegner."

He let that sink in. Then he told her, "I want you to listen tight and weigh all the words of either of us before you toss more sass my way, Miss Helga. Sheriff Tegner's up for another term in the coming elections, and he needs an arrest and conviction so bad he can taste it."

He let that sink in before saying, "I'm sore about poor Miss Viggy too. Since you seem to have heard some gossip, I have no call to tell another lady why. Suffice it to say I am out for blood. But I can be flexible, not having to produce anyone for a local court. I want the big fish, on federal charges. I want him so bad I may just see my way clear to toss a few smaller fish back."

She hesitated, looked away, and bitterly replied, "Forget it. I have this family spread to think of. We both know I'd have to move far away and change my name forever if I ever turned state's evidence on a man like Calvert Tyger!"

Longarm nodded pleasantly and said, "*Pinamiyeh*, as your Santee neighbors would say. That's exactly the sort of loose end I like to tie up, and we've been wondering how come Calvert Tyger keeps dying all over this country. Would you like to try for the way those hot hundred-dollar notes got scattered even wider, ma'am?"

She hesitated, then softly murmured, "I have your word I won't have to sign anything or repeat one word of this in front of anyone else in this world?"

He hesitated in turn before cautioning her, "I can only bend the law so far. It's my duty as a potential witness against you to warn you I can't turn my back on a serious felony. But if I'm right about you only aiding and abetting, and you'd like to tell me just what in blue blazes has been going on, I see no reason to drag your name all over the arrest warrants once I know who I really want to arrest."

She poured another cup of coffee, this time for him, as she choked back a sob and confessed, "You were right about my sheltering Uncle Chief and, all right, a couple of other boys who might have been a bit wild. But I swear I've never taken part in any felonies myself, and that was no lie about Uncle Chief knowing nothing about that robbery in Fort Collins."

She waited until he'd sipped some coffee without calling her a liar to her face, and then she added, "He was never after you when you shot him either! I can see now how you might have thought he was. But he and some other boys he rode in with a few weeks ago were only following you about in hopes of finding out who'd sent you after them. Uncle Chief never bought that story about a bank note from that payroll robbery attracting you all the way to New Ulm. He said he'd heard they were turning up all over, and besides, he didn't know about any robbery in Fort Collins. He was afraid someone was trying to frame him and his friends."

Longarm asked where the rest of the poor framed gang might be. She shrugged and said, "Uncle Chief never told us. He did say they'd all agreed to split up and lay low for a while after the last big job they pulled. He never said what that one had been. Just that he found it awfully surprising that you and your own pals were after him for that Fort Collins robbery he knew nothing about, see?"

Longarm must not have looked as convinced as she wanted him to. For the next thing he knew she was standing mightily close as she put both hands on his upper sleeves, smiled timidly up at him, and asked if he thought she was out to give false testimony. She smelled so fine he had to smile back, and up this close she didn't seem quite so plain after all. Her perky nose was sort of cute, and her eyes were downright naughty as he stared down into their smoky blue depths.

Then something clicked in the back of his skull and Longarm put his coffee cup aside to soberly say, "I reckon I can go along with most of what you just said, Miss Helga. I'll see if I can get the sheriff not to arrest you this morning."

She looked so grateful he was afraid he'd never get out of there with his pecker in his pants. But he managed, and catching up with Sheriff Tegner outside, murmured, "It worked. Albeit not the way we planned. She lies like sin, and you're going to need way more evidence before you haul her before any grand jury, pard. But I'll send you what we have once we wrap the fool case up. Meanwhile, I fear arresting her might tip her pals off that I'm on their trail at last!"

Tegner shrugged and said, "I reckon she'll keep here on her

own place for now. But what did she tell you if she was lying so much?"

Longarm replied, "Nothing. I took every word she said with a peck of salt. Then I suddenly figured out who she's been reminding me of ever since I first laid eyes on her mean little face!"

Chapter 27

Later that week Longarm had an even less friendly conversation in the chambers of Judge Dickerson of the Denver District Court. Then he legged it over to the Tremont House to relieve Deputies Smiley and Dutch, who looked mighty relieved as they lit out a full hour before they'd expected to that afternoon.

As soon as Longarm found himself alone with the voluptuous honey-blonde they had down as a soiled dove known as Elvira Carson, he came right to the point, saying, "I've cleared it with my own office, which was easy enough, but the prosecuting attorney had a fit when I suggested he let you off scot free, Miss Margaret. He seems to think you were going to testify in court against your lover, Frank Keller, of the notorious Keller gang, which only goes to show how much they teach such dudes at Harvard Law."

The buxom half-naked blonde, wearing only a shantung kimono that late of a summer's afternoon, and not bothering to sash it all that modestly, leaned back on her hotel bed to smile up at him dreamy-eyed and purr, "I haven't had any lover in a coon's age, and what was that funny name you just called me, handsome?"

Longarm remained planted in the middle of her bedroom rug as he calmly replied, "Margaret, ma'am, Margaret Runesberg of Brown County, Minnesota, before you went wild. The real Elvira Carson died of the clap mixed with yellow jack over a year ago, and I reckon one of her admirers told you the name was up for grabs, just as the old boy they were expecting you to testify against must have heard about the real Frank Keller getting shot by the Mounties trying to rob the Canadian and Pacific even earlier. I just found out about that myself by including some old boys I know up at Fort MacLeod, even though the current Canadian government is sore at President Hayes, as the bunch of you were banking on."

She stared up at him thunderstruck, the wheels in those familiar blue eyes ticking visibly as he gently continued. "I never would have strained that hard, this not being my case at all, had not I gotten to know your older and uglier sister better back where you both hail from, and suddenly recalled where I'd seen such wickedly innocent eyes before. Once I had the least notion who you might really be out this way, it became a heap plainer what you were up to."

She said, "I don't know what you're talking about. Why would any girl adopt the name of a notorious trail-town whore if she was really some innocent child off a cattle spread in . . . Minnesota, did you say?"

He smiled thinly and replied, "I did say Minnesota. I never said a thing about no cattle spread. You got to develop a good memory to be a good liar, ma'am. I'd like you to put some duds on now. I'm taking you over to Curtis Street, where I mean to check us into another hotel as man and wife."

She laughed incredulously and declared, "This is so sudden, dear!" as she sat up to calmly shrug out of her thin kimono.

She shrugged mighty temptingly, and Longarm hadn't met anybody half that willing on the long train ride back from New Ulm. But he told her, "Maybe. I'm only human. But first we got to get some more serious matters settled. Like I said, I'm checking into that other hotel with you, and so it won't matter in court whether we did anything else or not. As a lady who's ridden the owlhoot trail as long as you have, you know what a pickle I'd be in, trying to testify against you in court, after you had documented proof I'd slept with you within an easy walk from the courthouse!"

He could see she did as she rose to her feet naked anyway and moved over to a corner wardrobe to start dressing herself with skill and speed to make one suspect she was used to

254

getting in and out of her duds at short notice.

As she sat back down, still mostly unbuttoned, to pull on her high-button shoes, she asked with a puzzled frown, "You say a federal judge and prosecutor wanted you to be so good to me?"

Longarm chuckled and replied, "They wanted to lock you up and throw away the key, should you go back on your promise to testify against the cuss they've been holding as a dead train robber. I convinced them how tough that could be, if you had any sort of lawyer of your own, once you threw the case so comically, with members of the fourth estate in court to describe the hilarity on the front pages of the *Denver Post* and *Rocky Mountain News* in an election year."

She stood up and asked him to button the back of her bodice for her while he told her where he got such wild ideas.

He managed to keep his hands steady, with some effort, as he got her fit to be seen on the streets with, saying, "I've seen a hostile witness throw a case before. It's even happened to me. I could be a hair off as to your exact moves, but as soon as I figured out who you had to be, I saw how easy it was going to be for you to wait until they were trying to swear you in as a woman of ill repute with an arrest record going back to Sodom and Gomorrah. I'd laugh too if I saw a bailiff trying to swear in another lady entirely as a long-dead trail-town hooker. I'd likely wonder how much attention the prosecution had been paying to its other homework."

She said he surely had a vivid imagination, and asked who he thought the prisoner they had down as Frank Keller might be.

He said, "We'll get into that after I get into you, or at least compromise myself forever as a witness. You see, I ain't just doing this because you're concave where I'm convex. I know plenty of gals here in Denver. I'll tell you what I really want as soon as you have me over a barrel. Let's go."

They went. She brought along her purse and carpetbag, saying she could hardly wait to get him over a barrel after she took the usual precautions.

They walked arm in arm in broad daylight to a more affordable but fairly clean hotel on Curtis Street, and she

255

stood there pretending butter wouldn't melt in her mouth as he signed them in as U.S. Deputy Marshal Custis Long & Spouse. The room clerk, who knew Longarm of old, looked surprised but said nothing as he handed over their key.

Longarm helped her upstairs with her carpetbag, and she said the hot stuffy room needed airing. So he locked the door and opened a window while she naturally bolted for the door.

When he told her, not unkindly, "I locked it with the key, which I hold in my hand," she just shrugged and commenced to get undressed again, murmuring, "Oh, well, I haven't had any for weeks, and it's not as if you're deformed or busting out in boils."

He didn't see any reason to stop her from undressing. For openers it might make a gal think twice about unexpected dashes down the hall outside. He shucked his own hat and frock coat as well, saying, "My first hunch was that we'd picked up the more notorious Calvert Tyger after that less exciting robbery by Keller, and so you meant to surprise us with, say, Canadian newspaper clippings, proving they'd booked him wrong as Frank Keller. But as soon as I studied more on that, I saw it was just plain impossible. The cuss we're holding as Frank Keller, whoever he is, ain't old enough to have ridden in the war on either side. Besides, somebody in a leadership position has to have been issuing a heap of orders, and paying at least something to have them carried out. So an alive and kicking Calvert Tyger still at large works better than Tyger in jail, or the late Brick Flanders, albeit the third in command called Chief might have issued one or more orders before he wound up just as late more recently."

The big blonde gasped, "Brick and the Chief are dead?" Then she recovered and asked who they were talking about as she sat naked on the bed to take off her shoes.

Longarm hung his gun rig on a bedpost, and commenced to unbutton his shirt as he replied, "We've been sitting on both stories up to now. But the evening editions of both the *Post* and *News* ought to be reporting the deaths of Brick Flanders, Baptiste Youngwolf, and of course Calvert Tyger— many, many times, in fact. We figure he just meant to go on dying all over this country until he was sure we had him down as dead, and he sure seems a murderous cuss."

She purred she didn't know any of those people he mentioned, and didn't want to talk about such silly boys, alive or dead. So once he finished stripping down himself, Longarm joined her on the bed, on top of the covers, to see if they could get on a more trusting basis.

She parted her big creamy thighs with joyous abandon, but as he entered her she stiffened and hissed, "My Lord, you might have warned me! I told you I hadn't been getting any for weeks, you overdeveloped stallion!"

He nibbled her ear as he told her he was sorry he'd thrust home with the first stroke, explaining, "I've been doing without aboard a mess of trains, and you have been acting like a gal who liked it barnyard style."

She raised her knees coyly to brace them against Longarm's bare chest so she had more control over the depth of his thrusts as she grinned up at him like a mean little kid and said, "I do, within the limits of my anatomy. I know I'm a big-boned woman of mature proportions, but I've always been a tad tight down there."

He allowed he'd noticed, in an admiring tone, as he began to move more cautiously in her surprisingly child-like privates. Few if any schoolgals would have gushed that wet or moved so fine while being ravaged by some older boy with a full-grown hard-on. So a good time was had by all, and toward the end she'd wrapped her big old legs around him to take it all the way as she sobbed he was killing her and that she loved it. He was afraid they'd heard her down in the lobby when she came in broad daylight at the top of her lungs.

She wanted to come some more, and begged him to let her get on top. So he did, and that felt even tighter, with her bare heels dug into the mattress on either side of his naked hips as she bobbed all that lush meat up and down.

He told her a couple of dirtier jokes as he made her come some more. Then, while they were cooling their loving-flushed naked flesh in a lazy dog-style way, he felt it safe to ask her if she could see how dumb he was going to look in court if he ever repeated anything he heard in such relaxed surroundings.

She arched her spine with her cheek pressed to the covers as she crooned, "Oh, just keep that up, lover man. You've already figured out who I really am. I was going to admit the man you're holding as Frank Keller had to be somebody I'd never seen before, so—"

Longarm faked a dramatic sob. "You women are all alike. You get what you want from us poor weak men and then you feel free to taradiddle us with sweet dumb lies."

She groaned, "Never mind the taradiddles. Just diddle me some more, and could you do that a little faster?"

He could have. He felt like it. But he stopped with it deep inside her, bracing his weight with a palm on each of her broad hips as he said, "Let's see if I can convince you of my good intentions with a bit more of what I've already got, seeing you don't seem convinced by all I've just given you. Mayhaps we'd better lie down and share us a smoke as we see whether we can come to terms."

She gasped, "Don't you dare! I was just about to come again and I'll say anything you want if only you won't take it out too soon!"

Longarm wasn't sure he could have. So he just started thrusting again, with his bare feet spread wide on the rug by the bed to ram it up into her at an angle they both found mighty satisfying.

After he'd satisfied them both Longarm lay side by side with her, propped up on pillows as they shared that cheroot and he told her, "Once upon a time, as you've doubtless heard, there were three big outlaws who'd come West together to stop trains, rob banks, and such. For reasons I'm still working on they must have had a serious falling out. Brick Flanders was murdered by one or more of his old pals, and they tried to make it look as if he'd died in a rooming house fire under the name of Calvert Tyger. I reckon the game ain't as much fun after you've ridden the owlhoot trail a spell. Frank, Jesse, and The Kid are all laying as low as they can this summer."

He took a drag and passed the smoke to her, then continued. "By a serious of pure coincidence proving what a small world or small outfit I ride for, I stumbled into Denver P.D.'s investigation of that deliberate rooming house fire. Then to make matters more nervous, a boss with limited manpower sent me first to guard you for a shift, and then assigned me to look into that hot paper turning up around their wartime stamping grounds, where old Youngwolf had just decided to hide out some more with your older sister."

She started to say something. Longarm figured it would be another lie. So he growled, "I ain't finished. I know this sounds like tooting my own horn, but facts are facts, and they must have figured I knew a heap more than I did when I kept stumbling around so close to their trail. So things have been noisy as hell, even with me shooting in the dark and just aiming lucky a few times."

She handed back the smoke and snuggled closer, purring that she really did enjoy bedtime stories when she wasn't half ready to go to sleep just yet.

Longarm swore, got rid of the cheroot, and sat up to shake her by both shoulders as he warned, "Can't you see you're done for, unless we get them before they get you and doubtless your sister Helga as well?"

She stared owlishly up at him. "Why should Cal be after my poor innocent sister, or even me?"

Longarm said, "For openers, in case you ain't noticed, he's a crabby cuss running scared. He's been busting a gut pretending to be dead, and both you and your sister know him on sight!"

She said, "Pooh, it's against the code of the trail to turn in a pal and Cal knows it."

Longarm said, "No, he don't. Whatever the original game was, he's been acting like a homicidal lunatic ever since I dealt myself in. He tried to stop me, but I got through, and how's he supposed to know I got all those pals, including Chief, by beginner's luck? Wouldn't you be worried about someone telling tales out of school if you were the leader of a gang already suffering from some internal struggle and the law kept foiling plan after plan on you?"

He saw those wheels going round in her big blue eyes again. So he said, "I'd be lying if I said I knew for sure whether those two he sent to the Tremont House were out to kill you or get you safely out of our clutches. Either way, I took 'em both so neat and tidy, it must have occurred to their boss that someone had tipped us off. With Flanders dead and Chief hiding out back in Minnesota, if you take my meaning."

She had turned a shade green around the gills before he continued. "It gets worse. Whatever you and your sister had agreed to, I nailed his second in command, Chief, whilst he was supposed to be hiding safe and sound with Miss Helga at your family spread. Then I nailed Laughing Larry, no matter who'd sent for him to do me in, as neatly as if I'd been tipped off he was coming. You want some more? I just left your sister free as a bird, despite an easy chance to nail her on aiding and abetting, if not criminal conspiracy."

The younger and prettier Runeberg sister reached down between them with a Mona Lisa smile as she murmured, "My, you *have* been busy, and so here we are, alone at last."

He let her fondle his semi-erection. Most men would have. But as she did so, he smiled thinly and said, "Yep. With you screwing the same lawman who seemed so easy on your sister back in Minnesota. You can see, of course, how I'd never be able to hold you as either a prisoner nor hostile witness after getting on such friendly terms with you. So you're free as a bird to leave this little love nest as soon as you can get dressed, unless you'd rather get even friendlier."

He could see she surely did when she rolled over on her plump knees and one hand to lower her blond head to his lap. He didn't try to stop her. Few men would have. But as he grinned down at the bobbing part of her hair he said, "That sure feels friendly. But what I meant was that I could get you out of Colorado in one piece, with no charges pending against you and mayhaps a pocketbook full of bounty money, if you'd only help me make the bad dreams of a bad man come true."

She took her lush lips from his raging erection to impale her tiny twat on it instead as she pleaded, "You're so right about how mean old Cal can be when he thinks he's been crossed. But roll me over and do this to me *right* before I tell you the whole dumb story!"

260

Chapter 28

The next morning, having hidden the repentant outlaw gal with Madame Emma Gould, a real soiled dove who owed him some favors, Longarm got down to the less amusing chore of seducing a prosecution team and at least one senior judge.

The meeting was held in Judge Dickerson's smoke-filled chambers, with Longarm's superior, Marshal Vail, naturally on hand to back his play unless it sounded wilder than usual.

Once he had everybody sitting down and lit up, Longarm declared, "Before I tell you gents what I want you to do for me, I'd best tell you a bedtime story, as amended for me in bed last night."

Vail growled, "I was just fixing to ask you why you registered at another hotel with that material witness. You told me you were out to get her to tell the truth, not go to bed with you, damn it!"

Longarm smiled sheepishly and said, "Sometimes you catch more flies with honey than with vinegar, Boss."

The fair but firm Judge Dickerson snorted, "Never mind how he got what out of a hostile witness and let the man tell us what he got!"

Longarm nodded thankfully and said, "Once upon a time there was this outlaw gang. Much like what we know about the James-Younger ways of pulling similar jobs, the three experienced leaders—Tyger, Flanders, and Youngwolf or Chief—stuck together and made plans, but picked up such extra help as they might need for a particular job from a way wider circle of kith and kin."

A lawyer who'd doubtless read a recent edition of the *Denver Post* said, "What has any of that got to do with Elvira Carson, or with you letting her go after a night of slap and tickle?"

Longarm said, "We call it giving them enough rope, and I got more'n slaps and tickles out of a gal who's really Margaret Egger née Runeberg, the common law wife of the Fulton Egger you've been holding for trial as the late Frank Keller. But this would still make more sense to you if you'd just shut up and let me tell it from the beginning."

Judge Dickerson warned everybody to be still and told Longarm to proceed. So Longarm said, "All right, moving closer to our own time, the three old pals hid out from time to time on this cattle spread close to their old stamping grounds, where they'd met as half-ass Indian fighters. The spread was owned and operated by the Runeberg sisters, at least until the younger one, pretty Miss Margaret, fell for the exciting bullshit of a part-time gang member called Fulton Egger and told the neighbors she'd be living in Chicago with somebody not quite as exciting."

"You mean it was the Tyger gang, not the Keller gang, who tried to rob that train and—"

"The judge just told you to be still," Longarm told the lawyer. Then he relented enough to explain. "We all know what a piss-poor train robbery that was. Young Egger got treed by the posse, and threw lots of sand in your eyes by confessing he was the leader, Frank Keller. And then you picked up a reluctant witness, coached in advance to blow the case sky high in court when the defense proved she'd been held as a trail-town whore instead of the innocent Minnesota miss she could be if she wanted. After the jury finished laughing about that, they were fixing to spring the death certificate of the real Frank Keller on the prosecution."

There came a rumble of discontent. But Judge Dickerson, who'd had folks trying to laugh in his court in the past and didn't much approve of it, ignored his own injunction to gravely observe, "It wouldn't have worked. Horseplay in court may or may not amuse the jury. But I've been over the briefs and I'd say the prosecution has young Keller or, very well, Egger, as charged. If giving the arresting officer a false name was enough to get you off, nobody would ever be convicted. Who came up with such a sophomoric scheme to disrupt the majesty of my damned court?"

Longarm said, "Brick Flanders, Your Honor. He was the big spender of the bunch. Tyger and Chief wanted to keep laying low, and told him his proposal to stop that train was dumb. But he tried to do it on his own, or with only his own fraction of the gang, at any rate, and we all know how that turned out."

He saw nobody had any objections and continued. "It got worse. The murderous but somewhat cooler heads heard the gang they'd thought they were leading had robbed that payroll office up to Fort Collins, and that the high-denomination treasury notes were hot as a whore's pillow on payday night because the government had a list of all their serial numbers."

Billy Vail just couldn't help but ask, "Which one of them was fool enough to spend one of those very treasury notes in the very county they'd always felt safe to hide out in, old son?"

Longarm said, "Tyger and Chief were sure it was Brick Flanders. The red-bearded and glass-eyed wonder had been identified by survivors of that robbery. He denied having pulled the robbery. So he naturally had to deny spending the hot paper like a drunken sailor, and this got Tyger and Chief so mad they beat and shot him, not far from that rooming house he was found in well toasted. Margaret Egger couldn't say just how they managed to smuggle his body in and register it as the late Calvert Tyger. But she agrees with me that Tyger might have made a habit of dying in fires because he's an ordinary-looking cuss who feels better off with us not looking for him above ground. Chief ran back to the old Santee country where, being Ojibwa, he didn't have to worry as much about being recognized by anyone who'd known him of old. Nobody from the gang bought any riding stock with a note from that payroll job. So you can imagine how chagrined they felt when I showed up as well."

He let them all chuckle and summed up with, "Like I told the gal who told me so much, I'd just fallen in the dung heap and come up with sweet violets. But if the truth be known, I never caught but one of the three leaders with barnyard luck, and the bad one of the bunch is still at large, twice as smart and not looking half as unusual. That gal who admits to knowing him personal tried to describe him, and it sure adds up bland. I doubt any lawman would look twice at a middle-aged cuss of medium build in a not-too-plain-or-fancy business suit unless he acted unusual. So here's what I want you officers of the court to do for me. I want you to drop the charges against Fulton Egger, alias Frank Keller, for lack of evidence. Anyone who reads the *Post* or *News* ought to be able to see how that material witness running off on us leaves us with no case and—"

"The hell you say!" one of the prosecution team declared. "We have the whole posse he surrendered to, along with the train crew they threw down on, and Jesus H. Christ, what sort of a federal prosecutor would throw in the towel over one hostile witness lighting out?"

Longarm said, "A federal prosecutor with bigger fish to fry and an eye for an unethical but simple deal, of course. We can hold Borden and Wagner, the two gunslicks I arrested at the Tremont House, for what—twenty-four hours after we turn loose the material witness they were menacing?"

Judge Dickerson said, "Seventy-two, on suspicion of anything. But you'd better make your other proposal a good one, Deputy Long. Why on earth would this court even consider turning loose a known member of a dangerous outlaw gang?"

Longarm nodded and replied, "Why indeed, Your Honor? What might you think if a bunch of sneaky lawmen turned a member of your gang and his gal loose, whilst still holding other pals they had less to charge with?"

Judge Dickerson smiled wickedly and said, "I like it. Let's try it."

Chapter 29

So later that afternoon, as Longarm and young Fulton Egger were coming out of the Federal House of Detention, a shady lawyer they'd both talked to in the past met them on the granite steps, looking a tad upset, to demand of Longarm, "Where are you taking my client now, Deputy Long? I warn you, he's never agreed to waive extradition on that old Kansas state charge!"

Longarm smiled thinly and said, "You ain't been keeping up, Lawyer Culhane. I ain't taking this innocent child to Kansas or anywhere else as a prisoner."

Egger stared back at his confounded lawyer, just as confounded, to say, "Don't look at me. I don't know neither. They just now told me they were dropping all charges and I was free to go."

"With one proviso," Longarm explained knowingly. He pointed west along the busy street as he said, "Just because we don't want him on train robbing doesn't mean we want him spitting on the sidewalks of our fair city. So I'm escorting him down to Union Depot, from whence he'll be catching a Burlington Flyer clean out of my court's jurisdiction. His little woman will be waiting for him when he gets there, and I hope this has been a good lesson to the two of them."

Lawyer Culhane stared thoughtfully at his client. "What did you and Margaret have to do in return, Fulton?"

Egger answered truthfully enough, "Nothing. They never asked for anything."

Longarm purred, "What might anyone want to ask a couple of pure innocent kids, Lawyer Culhane? Haven't you ever done anything from the goodness of your heart? Has dealing with the sort of clients you seem to deal with blinded you to the rights of an honest citizen? It says early on in the Bill of Rights that the accused shall be granted a fair and speedy trial. You've pestered me personally with enough writs of habeas corpus to know why we can't hold this pest."

The short and respectable-looking member of the courthouse gang shook his derbied head. "No, I haven't. You have a way of making arrests stick, Longarm. We both know I've never pried a client loose from you for lack of evidence unless you had damned little evidence, or unless you were throwing a little fish back in exchange for . . ."

"I never! I swear!" Egger shouted with an expression of dawning fear on his simple face.

Longarm said, "Believe the boy. He's telling you the pure truth. He can write to you and settle on what he might owe you, after I get him aboard that flyer and on his way out of our hair. We'd love to stay and chat some more, but the kid's train will be leaving around sundown, and he'd be better off eating in the depot beanery than aboard that night train. You care to come along and ask more questions? Neither one of us has anything to hide."

Lawyer Culhane said he had some other late errands. They both knew he didn't have to say any more. So Longarm never asked what they were.

As Longarm and Egger headed off down the street without his cheap lawyer, the unsettled outlaw suddenly confided, "Listen, we'd better not go to that depot just now. I follow your drift about my not being welcome here in Denver. I've been run out of town before. So why don't you just let me find my own way over to . . . You say old Margaret will be waiting for me in Omaha?"

Longarm said, "Mebbe. I told her that would be where you'd be getting off the train I'm putting you on. I'm putting you on that train and no other because I told Judge Dickerson I would when he signed your release papers. I don't think he wants you finding your own way to the city limits, no offense."

As they kept on walking, with Egger spooking at storekeepers sweeping the walk or passing riders dressed cow, the stockyards a few blocks away accounting for such riders innocently enough, Longarm told himself not to start tensing up before that tinhorn lawyer had had time to report to other clients. Then he considered how quickly one could whip around a corner to consult with another client at, say, a shoe-shine stand, and tensed up quickly.

Egger tried to hold his own cards close to his vest. But as the red brick walls of Union Depot loomed just ahead the outlaw pleaded, "I don't want to wait for no train in there. You as much as told Culhane where this child would be during tricky gloaming light, and I guess Margaret told you Culhane acts as lawyer for all of us here in Denver, right?"

As a matter of fact, she had. But it would have been dumb, as well as needlessly cruel, to tell a man who'd just lost his woman that she'd even told the law how big his dong got. The big blonde, who could easily satisfy a modestly endowed man but said she'd learned to like a hung one better, could meet old Egger farther along if she wanted to, assuming he lived through what was about to transpire.

When Egger suddenly asked why Longarm was grinning that way, the lawman said, "Just thinking how often I've caught a crook I'd have never known about had he only had the sense to leave me alone."

As they crossed the street through the horse-drawn traffic, Egger started to make a break for it. But Longarm caught him by one elbow and spun him around, saying, "Careful, old son. You don't want to get run over by a coach an' four. I don't want to handcuff you neither, but I can and I will if you try that again!"

Once on the sandstone walk in front of the depot, Egger sputtered, "You bastard! You're using me for bait! You never meant to turn me loose at all. But you figured Tyger would hear you had, suspect we'd made a deal to do him dirty, and come for me, right?"

Longarm said, "Yep." He hauled the frightened man into an archway and hauled out a folded length of linen bond paper, handing it to Egger as he continued. "I told your Miss

Margaret I don't play dirtier than I need to. If you want the whole truth, I think you're a useless punk. But she assured me you've never killed nobody or even stolen apples without somebody leading the way. So I can afford to let you run loose, until somebody kills you or you get a little sense. Meanwhile, there's no accounting for taste, and one of the conditions Miss Margaret made was that both of you went free in exchange for Tyger. I never said I wouldn't wire Brown County they could pick up her older sister, so remember that in days to come when and if she says I double-crossed her. For when I make me a deal with the likes of you all, I dot every I and cross every T. After which you are on your own."

Egger hadn't heard that last part. Even as he put his walking papers away he was weakly gasping, "Margaret made a deal to turn Cal in? Oh, Dear Lord, where can we hide?"

Longarm led him inside the crowded depot by one arm, leaving his own gun hand free, as he said gently, "Your gal never told me where he was. She didn't know. Neither of you will have to hide from him if he gets caught. So I want you to keep a sharp eye on the folks all around and let me know if you spot Calvert Tyger, hear?"

Egger moaned they were both going to be shot down like dogs. So Longarm led him into the depot dining hall, and bought them some chili con carne with mince pie and coffee. When Egger said he felt too sick to his stomach to eat, even seated in a corner, Longarm ate both of their orders and drank all the coffee.

Then he consulted his pocket watch, saw it agreed with the wall clock, and said, "Pay attention lest you wind up feeling even worse, Egger. I can only watch so many ways at once, so there's an outside chance you'd get away from me if you made a break for it in the near future. After that it would be a toss-up whether I caught up with you and kicked the shit out of you, or Tyger got to you first and you wound up wishing you were only getting the shit kicked out of you."

The pale-faced crook whimpered, "Cal's got it all wrong. Nobody I was pals with robbed that payroll office behind his back and got him so famous out this way!"

Longarm said, "Tell him that as you lay dying. I hadn't

268

finished your instructions. We'll be going out to the open platform now. It's early. There shouldn't be too many innocent targets in the way. I can watch you or I can watch for more important rascals. So like I said, you could likely make a dash for freedom if you weren't already free and had anywheres safer to dash. Can I bank on you acting sensible?"

Egger said he just wanted to be safely far away with his sweet little Margaret in his arms after all those lonesome nights in a cell.

Longarm didn't comment on how a gal that big-boned and buxom could be described as small, or where she really was just then. He rose to leave some coins on the table and muttered, "Let's move out."

They did, and sure enough, the open platform out back was sunny and unoccupied, with no train expected for a good forty-five minutes and the late afternoon sun glaring uncomfortably hot through the dust and coal smoke of the rail yards to the west. Longarm led Egger to an open stretch near the north end of the platform, and told him he doubted too many passengers would come crowding up this way to get on the Burlington Flyer's cowcatcher once it arrived.

Egger glanced nervously about and protested, "We're easy targets out here, and that dazzle off the boards and bricks will make it even tougher to spot Cal in time!"

Longarm stared soberly at the switchman's booth forming a cul-de-sac to the north as it almost met the sun-washed bricks of the depot's rear wall. "The light will be just as tricky for him. How come you're expecting Calvert Tyger in the singular flesh, Egger? He sent a whole swarm of lesser lights after me and we're still working on some of their true names and addresses."

Egger sighed and said, "You just answered your own fool question. You don't send a boy to do a man's job, and he wants us both bad if he suspects I rode with Brick Flanders against his orders and just now made a deal with the law!"

He glanced down the other way and added, "Aside from that, he must be finding good help tougher to find these days. We were all running low on pocket jingle when Brick took it in his red head to stop that train on his own."

Longarm started to ask how the gang could be throwing around all those hundred-dollar notes if they were so broke. But the punk had told him more than once that Calvert Tyger and his faction hadn't taken part in the Fort Collins job. That had doubtless made Chief sound mighty sincere when he'd told Helga Runeberg he'd been framed for a job he'd never done.

Egger sucked in his breath, and Longarm turned the same way to see a familiar figure, missing his chaps but wearing a six-gun, slowly coming up the platform from the cover of those baggage carts to the south. Egger said, "It's Gus Hansson. He's supposed to be riding for my sister-in-law back in Brown County! What could he be doing way out here in Colorado?"

Longarm said, "Move back and off to one side and I'll ask him." So the unarmed Egger crawfished back and off to one side indeed as Longarm just stood there, smiling sort of wistfully.

As the Minnesota kid came within pistol range Longarm called out, "That's far enough and don't try it, Gus. Can't you see you're being used as a cat's paw by a sly old mouser who doesn't give a fig for your future?"

Gus Hansson stopped, only to drop into a gunfighter's crouch as he bitched, "We just got word from New Ulm, you son of a bitch! The sheriff just arrested Miss Helga and half of my pals on the Rocking R!"

Longarm nodded amiably and replied, "I know. I wired them earlier and allowed it was about time we commenced wrapping up. Somebody has to pay for hiring Laughing Larry Lucas to blow pretty ladies up, and I'm sure the big boss has told you it wasn't his dumb notion."

Gus Hansson snarled, "Fill your fist by the time I count to three. For that's when I mean to draw, you smirking know-it-all!"

Longarm thoughtfully threw his frock coat open to expose the grips of his cross-draw .44–40, but called out in a calm reasonable tone, "You don't want to try it, Gus. This ain't one of them Wild West yarns in Ned Buntline's magazines. Life is real, life is earnest, and I've got an edge on your skills and experience."

Gus Hansson grimly answered, "One!"

Longarm snorted, "Aw, shit, this is getting silly, Gus!"

To which the determined-looking kid answered, "Two!"

So Longarm, being a grown man instead of a kid who'd read too many dime novels in the bunkhouse, fired the derringer he'd been palming all this time before the fool kid could slap leather as he counted to three.

Then all hell busted loose, and Longarm let the double derringer dangle from his watch chain as he dropped to the platform and rolled over the edge to bob back up with his more serious six-gun in hand as he called out, "Smiley? Dutch?"

"Over here," came a jovial reply from the narrow dark slit between the switchman's booth and depot wall.

A second voice Longarm recognized as that of the more somber cuss called Smiley called out, "It didn't work quite as well as you planned though. We tried to get him to drop his damned gun and grab for the sky as he was fixing to throw down on your back. But he paid us no mind and, well, you know Dutch here."

Everyone who worked with the jolly but murderous Dutch knew how he was when suspects didn't do exactly as he said. But first things coming first, Longarm rose to his full height, brushing his tweed pants with his Stetson as he holstered his unfired six-gun and put the warm double derringer away for now. He moved over to the nearer of the two figures sprawled on the platform. Rolling Gus Hansson over with a boot tip, he could see at a glance the bravely stupid kid had no need for a sawbones. You aimed for the dead center of a man's trunk when you only had two derringer rounds to work with.

But as he turned on Egger, the pallid punk raised his head from a puddle of puke and sobbed, "Am I still alive? Is it over?"

Longarm muttered, "All but some loose ends," as he saw his boss, Marshal Vail, coming out from the depot waiting room on his stubby legs, his own gun out.

Vail announced, "O'Foyle and Cohen will only be able to keep that crowd inside a few minutes longer. They keep saying they got a train to catch. Who's that lying yonder so dead?"

Longarm said, "His name was Gus Hansson. We met earlier back in Santee country. He was one of 'em. You already

271

know Egger here. So let's see who Smiley and Dutch have yonder."

They moved to the far end of the platform. Despite his height, Longarm found it easier to move through that narrow slit than his shorter and stockier boss did. But they both managed, and sure enough, the tall grim Smiley and short jolly Dutch were standing over another corpse. This one was older, wearing his gun rig under a snuff-colored store-bought suit, and wasn't familiar to either Longarm or his fellow lawmen.

Longarm called Egger through the slot and demanded, "All right, is that the real Calvert Tyger, or has he faked his damned death some more?"

Egger gulped and marveled, "It's Cal. You got him! I didn't think it could be done! He was such a sly old dog!"

Longarm shrugged and said, "I figured he'd be more cautious than a villain in one of Ned Buntline's gentlemanly duels. That's how come we staked out all the handy cover he'd have to work with, after I'd made sure he'd know of a good time and place to nail the two of us."

Billy Vail chuckled fondly and said, "There was never a rider that couldn't be throwed or a slicker who couldn't be snowed. It's sort of sad about his young sidekick. But we got him. So that's about it, right?"

Longarm said, "Wrong. We have an even slicker bastard left, Boss."

Chapter 30

Fort Collins, sixty-odd miles north of Denver, had commenced as a military outpost on the Cache La Poudre or Powdercache River. But by this time it had grown into the seat of Larimer County, with a new land-grant college and all. The federal government offices had all closed for the day when Longarm paid his call on Miss Lorena Fenward, the surviving female witness to the horrendous events at the payroll office closer to the center of town.

The stenographer gal roomed with an even more maidenly older lady, who sniffed at Longarm's badge and identification, and allowed he and her roomer gal might be more comfortable out on her front porch as the warm shades of a summer evening crept down from the Front Range to the west.

When she fetched Lorena Fenward, the mousy little thing looked sort of pleased with him. As she offered Longarm her tiny hand, she told him she and Clifford, the other survivor of the robbery, had just read the newspaper reports about the capture of those notorious outlaws.

As they sat down together on the nearby porch swing, with somebody inside doing a piss-poor job of peeking through lace curtains without moving them, Longarm told her, "The three leaders and a heap of their followers are dead, not captured, ma'am, and notorious was just the word I wanted to talk to you about."

She seemed to be paying attention. So he explained. "Most

273

outlaws tend to be notorious after the fact, ma'am. I know it don't seem like it now, but hardly anyone had ever heard of Frank and Jesse James before they tried to rob a bank in Northfield, Minnesota, along with the unknown Younger and Miller boys. I was just back yonder in Minnesota, thinking about notorious outlaws in general, and it struck me, lighting a smoke one day, how Frank and Jesse got so famous all at once by riding out of that wild shootout alone, leaving the shot-up survivors of a robbery gone sour to be interviewed by all those reporters and get famous themselves."

She demurely asked if he'd like her permission to smoke. He chuckled and said, "I wasn't hinting, ma'am. I was explaining. That Tyger gang might have gone on robbing hither and yon if they hadn't started to get so notorious within just the past year or so."

She said she hadn't really been following Calvert Tyger's criminal career before he'd burst into that payroll office like a maniac to murder all the men but poor Clifford and scare her half to death.

Longarm had gone over his notes before he'd come calling, so he nodded and said, "That would be Clifford Stern, the bookkeeper who played dead after he'd only been grazed?"

She nodded and said, "You should have seen how bloody his shirt was after that evil Indian they called Chief creased his poor chest with a pistol ball. I was the one who described that Indian member of the gang in some detail. I only caught a glimpse of that other one's red beard amid all the gunsmoke and confusion. Clifford remembered that scary glass eye and gold tooth more vividly because that one—Flanders, wasn't it—was the one who bent over him to say he was done for and not to waste any more time."

Longarm nodded and said, "Riding with a full-blood and a red-haired cuss with such distinctive features did cause folks to remember who might have robbed them, once they made a more serious habit of it. From gang members we've interviewed since, the less distinctive-looking Calvert Tyger was getting broody about reading his name in the papers, albeit we all know it was his wilder-looking sidekicks folks described while laying the blame on his doorstep. So he'd given the others orders not to rob anybody for a spell. It must have really put his nose out of joint when he read in the papers about his gang, or a close facsimile, robbing your office and killing federal employees in the process!"

The mousy stenographer gal gasped, "My heavens, are you suggesting that wasn't the Tyger gang robbing us in broad day and murdering poor Mister Godwynn and those younger clerks?"

Longarm nodded grimly and replied, "That's about the size of it, ma'am. If it's any comfort, the gang had a furious falling out over it, with Tyger and Chief deciding to get rid of fellow riders they had down as big fibbers. Brick Flanders and his bunch kept saying they had nothing to do with any payroll robbery, and tried to excuse a train robbery that went wrong by complaining they were broke and needed the money. Tyger and Chief, trying to lay low, must have had conniptions when hundred-dollar treasury notes taken from your payroll office kept turning up all over the country as if Santa Claus was on a spending spree. An outlaw who went on spending such hot paper after learning from the papers it was hot would have to be awesomely stupid. We tried to keep the papers from reporting how your boss, the late Paymaster Godwynn, had made that list of serial numbers. But once they'd turned up all over, getting all sorts of folks hauled in to say where in blue blazes they'd come by the money . . ."

She nodded primly and said, "That was why Mister Godwynn made that list of serial numbers. It must be very difficult to cash a hundred-dollar treasury note recorded as stolen from the government!"

Longarm said, "It sure is. Brick Flanders had his faults, but he'd been riding the owlhoot trail better than a dozen years, and he'd have never tried to spend big bills he knew we had records on. He'd have fenced them for, say, two-bits on the dollar to a money-washer willing to sit on 'em for a couple of years and cash them in once they'd had a chance to cool down. I'm sure Calvert Tyger knew as much as we do about disposing of outlaw loot. He must have felt mighty vexed at his old pard when Flanders naturally kept saying some other red-haired cuss with a glass eye and gold front tooth had held up a government office and gunned a federal paymaster in cold blood for no good reason. Or did they offer some explanation why they shot all the male witnesses and let you live, Miss Lorena?"

She stared owlishly at him in the purple twilight. "How should I know? Clifford and me agreed at the time they'd been awfully mean. As they were leaving the leader did say something about leaving nobody to tell the tale. But mayhaps the last young boy out the door just didn't have it in him to shoot a girl."

Longarm nodded thoughtfully. "That works. So does somebody pretending to be a more famous outlaw, using theatrical makeup or a mighty fine wax mask. Another lady who's gotten to chatting with me about a former beau says Chief, Baptiste Youngwolf, was with his boss in Denver at the time of your robbery up this way. Tyger must have been willing as me to figure one Indian would be recalled much like yet another by a robbery victim. Unfortunately for Flanders, Tyger was way more certain it had to be *him* pulling jobs on the sly and making an outlaw laying low more famous than he'd ever mean to be."

Longarm shifted his weight in the swing and removed his hat so she could see his grave features more clearly as he placed his hat in his lap. "There's no call to go on with that comedy of errors and coincidence. Suffice to say that gang's no more, and now I want to talk about the money, Miss Lorena. I can promise you won't hang by your pretty little neck, and you'll still be fairly young when you get out if you'd care to turn state's evidence now."

She stared at him thunderstruck. "State's evidence of what? Are you accusing me of being in on the robbery with that gang?"

Longarm said, "Nope. Accusing you of making false accusations. A grievously grazed bookkeeper and miraculously unscathed stenography gal sold everyone but me a titanic taradiddle about an inside job, and now you'd best tell me where the two of you hid the money."

She wailed, "What money? Those outlaws rode off with all the money we had after they'd murdered everyone but Clifford and me! Haven't you been paying attention to the newspapers? Treasury notes with serial numbers recorded by poor Mister Godwynn have been turning up all over creation!"

Longarm nodded pleasantly. "It had that gang confused as well. For which I reckon we ought to thank you. But since I see you still think you can fib your way out of it, here's what I'm fixing to testify at your trial."

He leaned back more comfortably and continued. "Everyone knows how handling large sums of money can tempt our weaker brothers and sisters. So outfits that deal in such temptations set up all sorts of checks and balances to make it nigh impossible to embezzle funds without being detected."

She protested, "You can't mean that! Neither Clifford nor I were ever left alone with the contents of that office safe!"

Longarm replied, "I just said that. Funds coming in or going out have to be noted in the daily ledgers as well. I was recently going over some bank records in New Ulm, and it hit me then how tough a time a thief would have cooking books kept in more than one hand by more than one money-wrangler. So I don't doubt the ledgers of your payroll office would tend to go along with your fairy tale about red-bearded ogres with glass eyes and gold teeth, Miss Lorena. But that other list, kept separate in block lettering but purported to have been the notion of Paymaster Godwynn, is a whole other kettle of fish."

He gave her a chance to comment. When she just went on staring at him bug-eyed, he said, "Your boss had no call to keep such a list. There was no question the money coming in had just been printed for him by the federal mint. There'd have been no point in recording the serial numbers on notes to be paid out within days to honest folks the government owed money to."

She said, "We were asked about that at the time. Neither of us could say why Mister Godwynn had been extra-cautious. Perhaps he'd been tipped off about a planned robbery, or . . ."

"Or perhaps it was one or both of you two survivors who'd made up the list, over a period of days or weeks, by writing down numbers of high-denomination notes being paid out in good faith to honest folks."

She laughed incredulously and demanded, "Why would anyone want to do that, whether they were honest or not?"

He sighed and said, "You sure stick to your guns, considering how far down in the water you are right now. We both know the two of you knew that even if you gunned your boss and fellow workers to leave no witnesses, someone was sure to consider all that money leaving the office safe another way. So you made up that list in advance, to let notes with those serial numbers spread far and wide, before the two of you just smoked up your own office one Friday around closing time. Then you told your whopping fish story to the first lawmen on the scene, and produced that list you said your late boss had made, just to throw suspicion off your ownselves as all that stolen money turned up here, there, and everywhere but around *you*. So I figure the two of you have been waiting for that impressive but *unrecorded* money to—"

Then the front door of her rooming house burst open, and it was a good thing Longarm had already drawn his .44-40 and covered it with his Stetson. Because it was still too close for comfort as the dark figure in the doorway threw down on them, but had to watch where he was aiming as his doxie screamed, "Get him! He knows!"

Longarm didn't have to worry about his own fusillade, so he got three rounds of rapid fire off in time to stagger his foeman back against the doorjamb, and put a fourth round in him when he took a full extra second to drop his own six-gun and slide silently down to the doorstep while Lorena Fenward wailed like a banshee and might have scratched Longarm's face off if he hadn't stiff-armed her back on that porch swing.

He was standing over them both, reloading, when that same old landlady joined them, yelling "What is the meaning of all that noise and, oh, my stars and garters, who shot poor Clifford Stern in the breast like that?"

Longarm said, "It was me, ma'am. I told you I was the law. Would you kindly go down to your front gate and wave in any other lawmen as they come running? Miss Lorena and me still have to talk about some money, if she knows what's good for her."

If you enjoyed this book, subscribe now and get...

TWO FREE

A $7.00 VALUE–

If you would like to read more of the very best, most exciting, adventurous, action-packed Westerns being published today, you'll want to subscribe to True Value's Western Home Subscription Service.

Each month the editors of True Value will select the 6 very best Westerns from America's leading publishers for special readers like you. You'll be able to preview these new titles as soon as they are published, *FREE* for ten days with no obligation!

TWO FREE BOOKS

When you subscribe, we'll send you your first month's shipment of the newest and best 6 Westerns for you to preview. With your first shipment, two of these books will be yours as our introductory gift to you absolutely *FREE* (a $7.00 value), regardless of what you decide to do. If

you like them, as much as we think you will, keep all six books but pay for just 4 at the low subscriber rate of just $2.75 each. If you decide to return them, keep 2 of the titles as our gift. No obligation.

Special Subscriber Savings

When you become a True Value subscriber you'll save money several ways. First, all regular monthly selections will be billed at the low subscriber price of just $2.75 each. That's at least a savings of $4.50 each month below the publishers price. Second, there is never any shipping, handling or other hidden charges—*Free home delivery*. What's more there is no minimum number of books you must buy, you may return any selection for full credit and you can cancel your subscription at any time. A TRUE VALUE!